Craig Alanson

Expeditionary Force

Book 3 - Paradise

By Craig Alanson

Craig Alanson

Table of Contents

Prologue

Paradise

Three months after the original Merry Band of Pirates left Paradise

US Army Specialist Jesse 'Cornpone' Colter took a freshly cleaned pair of white cotton gloves out of a box, put them on, and adjusted the surgical facemask to completely cover his nose and mouth. Checking himself in a small mirror attached to a tree, he took a deep breath, reached down into the pen and carefully, very carefully picked up a small yellow fluffy thing. It was a chick, a baby chicken. On Paradise. A small miracle. Or, the chick was small, the miracle was great.

Jesse held the chick up to eye level, inspecting its feet. Everything looked fine, or it looked fine as much as Jesse knew about chickens. A month ago, what he knew about chickens was that they tasted good and produced eggs. Also that they weren't bred to be smart.

Smart, ha! He thought as he set the chick back down in the clean straw of the pen. The chick had been brought to Paradise as a fertilized egg. Jesse had volunteered to fight in space against the enemies of humanity. Only their 'allies' turned out to be the real enemy, and the 'enemy' was a species that mostly wanted to ignore humans. Between him and the chicken, he asked himself, who was the dumb one?

The presence of Earth animals on Paradise had been UNEF's most closely guarded secret. The last three Kristang ships to bring supplies from Earth had included chicken eggs, baby calves, baby pigs and baby goats. Not all of the young animals survived the long trip, and since the Ruhar fleet had firmly reestablished its hold on Paradise, no more animals would be coming from Earth. UNEF HQ had kept the presence of the animals a secret for two reasons. Until the survival of a significant population of Earth animals on Paradise could be established, UNEF didn't want to get people's hopes up that they would someday have fresh food other than fruits and vegetables. And perhaps equally important was that the presence of domesticated Earth animals on Paradise would signal that the Expeditionary Force would not be returning home for a long time, a very long time. That was even before the Ruhar took back Paradise and cut off UNEF's only possibility of going home.

That fateful day when the Ruhar fleet took Paradise back from the Kristang, was more than three months gone by now. The first couple weeks had been chaotic; UNEF HQ quickly had ordered human forces across the planet to lay down their weapons, recognizing that rifles against starships was not a survivable fight for UNEF. Not all humans had complied with the surrender order; these people had come out to the stars to fight hamsters and they couldn't mentally adapt to their changed situation. The fact is, there were hard feelings on both sides, and those feelings weren't going away in a month, or a year, or maybe even a generation. After two or three weeks, the situation stabilized, and humans accepted that the renewed Ruhar presence in the sky wasn't merely another raid. Those humans who still insisted on fighting the Ruhar 'occupiers' were dealt with by the Ruhar military, in some cases harshly and sometimes with a level of force wildly disproportionate to the threat. No one needed an orbital railgun strike to deal with three guys hiding out in the bush, but with the Ruhar completely in charge there was no one to appeal to for de-escalating the use of force. And hearing that the Ruhar had used a railgun against three guys who had limited ammo, almost no food and posed no real threat was a powerful message to the rest of UNEF. The message was heard loud and clear by all humans on Paradise; the Ruhar control the high ground. Do not mess with them.

Rumors were flying fast via the informal zPhone network. The Kristang fleet was gathering outside the Paradise system and would soon take back the planet. No, the Kristang had given up on Paradise; the raids were only a way to harass and distract the Ruhar. The Ruhar were negotiating to send humans back to Earth. No, humans were never going back to Earth. Humans were being recruited to fight with the Ruhar. No, the advanced Ruhar had no interest in working with weak, primitive human soldiers. Whatever you feared or wanted to believe, there was a rumor tailor made for you.

Jesse didn't believe any of the rumors, other than that they were rumors. He believed what he knew, what he'd seen. Five weeks after the Ruhar took back the planet, Jesse and his fireteam buddy Dave 'Ski' Czajka had volunteered to move from a POW camp to a new UNEF farm on the southern continent of Paradise. The farm was informally being called 'Fort Rakovsky' after a US Army soldier who had died in the first Ruhar raid. Rumor had it, and this rumor Jesse thought might be true, that most humans would eventually be scattered in settlements across the southern continent that humans called 'Lemuria'. That would keep them away from the bulk of the Ruhar civilian population, and isolated groups of humans would be easier and cheaper to control. Jesse didn't need rumors to tell him that UNEF was never going home; the Ruhar were planning for humans to stay on Paradise long term. Rumors were nothing but uninformed BS nonsense; the Ruhar knew the truth. The fact that the Ruhar were making the effort to help UNEF set up farming villages, meant that the Ruhar knew their unwanted human guests were on Paradise to stay. Stay for a very long time. Or permanently.

One thing he knew for certain was that chickens taste good, Jesse told himself as he carefully reached into another section of the pen to pick up another precious chick. Each chick had its own section of the pen; they were far too valuable to risk young chickens damaging each other in fights. When the chicks grew old enough, they would be removed from the pens to roam free in a fenced field; ten chickens to a field. Ten chickens were a number large enough for the chickens not to feel isolated from each other, and few enough for an assigned group of soldiers to manage and protect. Although the native life on Paradise could not digest anything from Earth, that did not mean the native predators were not interested in killing what appeared to them to be tempting targets. Because most humans were not allowed by the Ruhar to have any weapons that could threaten the Ruhar, Jesse and the other chicken herders had to fend of predators with sharpened sticks. Fortunately, in his area of Lemuria, the largest predator was about the size of a fox on Earth. Jesse had only seen one of the foxlike animals once, and it had run back into the jungle when he had shouted and waved his spear at it. No chicken was going to be lost to a native predator at Fort Rakovsky, not on Jesse's watch.

The most dangerous predators on Paradise were not native to the planet, and they walked on two legs. There were plenty of humans who would find it difficult to resist the temptation of a delicious frying-size chicken walking around. Despite the threat of severe penalties from UNEF, there had been incidents of chickens, pigs and goats being killed and cooked up for a feast. Eating animals was strictly banned by UNEF. An animal on a plate could not create more animals, and the population of domesticated Earth animals was still too small to consider using them as a food source yet. And the Ruhar considered eating animals to be a barbaric practice that civilized, sentient beings would not do. As prisoners of war existing on the kindness of the Ruhar, UNEF could not afford to insult their hosts.

So there would not be anyone eating animals, despite all the time, expense and effort expended to bring domesticated food animals to Paradise. Chickens were used to produce eggs, which could be eaten. More accurately, chicken eggs would be eaten someday when there were enough chickens; that might happen within a year, perhaps longer. Cows and goats could be used to provide milk; milk that was supposed to be available soon.

Pigs were a problem. While Jesse had heard the old joke that you could use every part of a pig except for its squeal, the Ruhar didn't allow any part of a pig to be used. UNEF was stuck raising and feeding pigs, without being able to get any benefit from the effort. And pigs consumed a lot of food that was needed by humans. Pigs would not be allowed to breed; once the current population aged and died, there would be no more pigs on Paradise.

"Hey, Ski," Jesse asked, "what about this one?"

Dave 'Ski' Czajka set down the chick he had been handling, and walked over to look at the one Jesse was holding up. "That's normal, I think," he announced, looking at one slightly-bent toe on the chick's left foot. "Don't worry about it."

"Y'all sure about that?" Jesse was worried about all the chicks he was responsible for. "It don't look right."

"Yeah," Ski said reassuringly. "Come on, man, it's a chicken. All it needs to do is walk around, eat grain and lay eggs."

"If you say so," Jesse set the chick back down in its straw bed, unconvinced. Ski was no expert on chickens; he had been selected for the coveted agricultural assignment because Ski's grandparents in Wisconsin had raised chickens, and Ski had spent many summers on their farm. Jesse had been selected because Ski vouched for him. It bothered Jesse that Dave 'Ski' Czajka, who grew up in suburban Milwaukee, knew more about farming that Jesse Colter, who was born and raised in rural Arkansas. Jesse's mother had grown tomatoes in a pot on the back porch, but that's all the gardening experience he had as a child. His mother's parents lived in downtown Oklahoma City, and his father's parents were retired in Florida. Neither of those locations for visiting grandparents had offered opportunities for learning the science and art of agriculture. At the time, Jesse had been grateful to avoid the often back-breaking work of farming, that some of his friends had to help their families with. Now, he wished he had gained some farming experience before he joined the Army. Summers working at a retail store had not provided Jesse much useful knowledge of agriculture.

"Cornpone, we're chicken herders, not veterinarians," Ski laughed.

Chicken herder. Somehow, he had gone from carrying a rifle as a US Army Infantry Specialist, to being assigned to an Agricultural Development team. He had endured the jokes about chicken ranching with good natured humor; the job was important, and it came with perks. People working in agriculture were allowed an additional 800 calories per day above the standard ration. With UNEF cut off from Earth by the Ruhar fleet, humans were reduced to three sources of food. The dwindling amount of canned, irradiated and freeze-dried food from Earth. Nutrient mush provided by the Ruhar twice a day, although the Ruhar warned that those supplies were not endless. And whatever Earth crops they could grow on Paradise.

"Hey, speaking of cornpone," Jesse nodded toward the field of corn to the south. "When y'all think that will be ready?"

Ski looked at the growing corn, scratched his head, then snorted in disgust at himself. Now he needed to get a freshly cleaned white cotton glove before he touched another chick. "There's an old farmer's saying 'knee high by the Fourth of July'. You harvest corn when it's about six, seven feet tall, or more. So, um," he tried to judge the height of the corn plants. The agricultural experts in UNEF HQ thought corn would grow faster here than on Earth, because there were no pests to eat the corn on Paradise. No pests, so need for pesticides that might stunt the plants' growth. "You know, I remember corn being way taller than knee height the first week of July, so maybe that expression is outdated. I don't know. Another two months?"

"That's real useful," Cornpone scoffed.

"My grandparents grew soybeans, not corn. And this," he pointed to the dark trees that grew thickly around the cleared fields, "is a jungle. Corn may grow faster here than in the Midwest. I don't know."

"Well, don't tell anybody that you don't know."

"You're afraid they'll pull us off Ag duty, and we'll lose our extra rations?" Ski asked. Even with the additional calories, he was hungry all the time. He did not like the idea of surviving on two bowls of Ruhar-provided nutrient mush every day.

"That, and, I've gotten attached to my chicks," Jesse admitted. "They need me."

"Those chicks need water to drink, grain to eat and air to breathe. They don't need you."

"They need me to sing to them, Ski. Helps them grow faster," Jesse said, then launched into a rendition of an old Elvis classic. "Loooove me tender, love me sweet, all my dreams come-"

"Damn!" Ski covered his ears. Stupid! Now he needed to change both gloves. "Are you trying to kill the chicks? Your voice is bad enough to kill a full-size chicken. Or a cow."

"Come on, now, it's not that-, oh man, look out. Ship just jumped in." He pointed to the sky and involuntarily cringed. Lights in the sky used to mean Kristang warships enforcing their hold on the planet, and protecting vulnerable UNEF troops on the ground. Or they meant unarmed Ruhar transport ships coming to haul away hamster evacuees who made the trip up the space elevator, and agricultural products that were shot into orbit by the Launcher.

Then, one fateful day, lights in the sky had meant a Ruhar raid; the raid where that lucky son of a bitch Joe Bishop became a hero by simply doing what any good soldier would have done. And later, lights in the sky were a full Ruhar battlegroup, coming back to take back control of the planet they called Gehtanu and that humans called Paradise. The lights on that day meant the Kristang were getting kicked off Paradise, and that UNEF troops had become prisoners of war.

Now, lights in the sky meant one of two possible things. Most of the time, twinkling lights in the sky were Ruhar warships patrolling the area to prevent a Kristang invasion. Some of the time, twinkling lights were Kristang ships jumping in to harass the Ruhar and raid the planet's infrastructure. According to intel shared over the UNEF zPhone internet, the Ruhar thought the Kristang still had a half dozen ships in and around the Paradise system. These were Kristang ships that had been left there by the Thuranin, when those little green men decided they would no longer support the lizards' effort to keep Paradise. The local Kristang force were ships that lacked the capability to travel to another star system or out to the local wormhole. Ships that were trapped, and crewed by desperate lizards. That was not a good combination. The raids had been a serious problem at first, causing the Ruhar planetary government to worry that the raids would encourage humans to rise up and rebel against their POW status. For the first two weeks of raids, the Ruhar had confined the humans to camps, while seeds went unplanted and crops in fields were not tended. That was a serious setback to human efforts to grow enough food to survive without assistance from the Ruhar. After two weeks, the raids had settled down to one every couple of weeks, and the Ruhar had cautiously relaxed restrictions on human movements.

The raids had become infrequent, more of an annoyance than a threat. With a mere one or two ships raiding an entire thinly-settled planet, any one site on the surface was relatively safe. Humans assumed at first that they were safe from attack by the Kristang, until that changed. Two months after UNEF surrendered to the Ruhar, a Kristang frigate jumped in, fired weapons, and jumped away. A target of one of the frigate' masers and missiles was a human warehouse; that warehouse became a smoking crater. Eleven percent of all human food on Paradise was lost when that warehouse was destroyed; and the Kristang had known they were targeting the human food supply. Before it jumped away, that frigate had broadcast a warning to UNEF; humans who surrendered to the Ruhar were considered traitors. Humans on Paradise had two options. Make futile gestures to resist the Ruhar and face slow, certain starvation. Or lay down their weapons, grow food, and live to possibly fight another day.

Which side humans would or even should fight on, was still a damned good question.

Jesse and Ski glanced over to the closest air raid shelter, near the western edge of the field. It was crude; a hole in the ground covered with logs and topped with dirt and grass. From orbit, it would look like any other part of the field, unless an enemy ship happened to be at an angle where it could look directly into the entrance. The shelter had been thrown together hastily and was not intended for regular or long-term use. The roof leaked; long roots of grass and shrubs reached down through the logs, which encouraged native bugs to take up residence. Because they were in a jungle, where every afternoon saw at least a brief thunderstorm sweep through, the floor of the shelter was a mud puddle. Last week, a work crew had installed a simple platform on the floor to keep occupants out of the ankle-deep water; Jesse was not confident the platform was still dry, as it had rained heavily the previous night.

"What do you think?" Ski asked, mentally counting off the seconds since they'd seen the light in the sky. They were supposed to get an air raid warning on their zPhones from Ruhar command; that didn't always happen in time. Sometimes the Ruhar communications were jammed, sometimes were fooled by Kristang raiders being disguised as Ruhar civilian ships, and sometimes warnings simply did not get sent promptly. Generally, if you didn't see maser beams, railguns or missiles coming down at you as burning streaks through the atmosphere within the first thirty seconds, you were most likely in the clear. Kristang ships didn't hang around long during a raid; they popped into high orbit, fired weapons, and jumped back away before the Ruhar defenses could target them. That quick strike tactic didn't always work; two weeks ago Jesse and Ski had seen a Kristang ship flare into hot white light, low on the northern horizon. That unlucky raider had been trapped by a damping field by a pair of Ruhar ships, and the brief firefight had favored the two hamster destroyers rather than the lizard frigate.

"We're supposed to take cover," Cornpone responded, one eye on the sky and one eye on his precious flock of chicks. People were running across the field toward the three shelters. Other people were taking a wait and see attitude. Regulations called for taking shelter until it was positively determined that the ship overhead was not a threat. "I also think these chicks are worth more than you and me."

"You got that right," Ski agreed. UNEF could afford to lose a couple soldiers, that would be two less mouths to feed. "Twenty seconds."

Jesse looked at the sky again. Another tell-tale sign of trouble in the sky was ship-to-ship weapons fire, and he didn't see any. That wasn't always a reliable indicator; masers and railguns weren't usually visible in the vacuum of space unless they hit something. And the initial launching boost flare of missiles was sometimes hidden enough by stealth effects that they couldn't be seen from the ground. Not by the naked human eye, not in the bright sky of mid-morning. "Oh, hell, the shelter's probably a mud pit anyway." Just then, their zPhones simultaneously squawked an All Clear signal.

Craig Alanson

"Great!" Ski laughed. "Perfect timing." A guy who had been running full speed across the field toward a shelter slowed to a stop, and shouted an expletive that Ski couldn't quite hear. He could guess well enough what the guy said. Ski waved with a grin, and the guy returned a middle finger salute. "Yeah, you too, buddy," Ski muttered, and looked up at the sky again, pondering something.

"What are you looking at now?" Jesse asked.

"Trying to decide whether I was kind of hoping that ship was the Kristang coming back," Dave admitted. "Coming back big time, to take the planet back again."

"Y'all better not hope the lizards come back," Jesse warned. "We surrendered our weapons to the hamsters. The Ruhar loaned us equipment to clear the jungle and plow these fields," he pointed to the growing corn. "That makes us traitors as far as the lizards are concerned. If they come back, we're screwed."

Dave frowned and shrugged. "And if the Kristang never come back? If we're stuck here with the Ruhar in charge? Like, forever?"

"Then we're screwed either way. Welcome to the Army, man." Jesse turned his attention back to the chicks. They needed to be fed again. Fed scarce grain that wasn't available to humans. Having eggs and milk would be great for the protein supply; feeding chickens, cows and goats also consumed a lot of calories that might better have been used as human food. Raising chickens for eggs, and cows for milk, was much more important for human morale than for nutrition. The prospect of a steady supply of eggs and milk promised that the future would be better. That humans on Paradise would not always be POWs, that they would not live out the rest of their lives on a faraway alien world. That someday, something would change, and people could go home. He wasn't raising chickens, Jesse thought. He was growing hope.

The chicks looked up at him hungrily and peeped loudly. "I hear y'all, food's coming. Another day on Paradise, man," Jesse shook his head. "Another day on Paradise."

CHAPTER ONE

Earth orbit

My name is Joe Bishop, and sometimes I hate my life. Especially when a certain super smart ancient alien artificial intelligence asshole makes things difficult for me. "Skippy," I asked in frustration, "what the hell did you do?" Damn it. Coming home from our mission that had saved the Earth *again*, I didn't exactly expect a ticker tape parade in New York City. Especially since no one had used ticker tape since, like- hmm. What was 'ticker tape' anyway? I suppose I could ask Skippy, if I wanted to risk death by boredom from a long, overly detailed explanation. It wasn't sticky like duct tape, I knew that. Confetti? Ticker tape was a type of confetti. Whatever confetti was. Or was confetti a type of Italian ice cream? No, that was gelato. Whatever.

Anyway, while I didn't expect a parade, I also hadn't expected to land in a pile of shit up to my nose, either. Except that's what happened, right after the *Flying Dutchman* returned to Earth from our SpecOps mission, and UNEF Command learned that we had prevented a Thuranin ship from traveling all the way to our home planet. We had stopped a Thuranin ship from coming to Earth, which likely would have led to the enslavement or extinction of humanity. Hey, great job, UNEF Command told me with one breath. With the next breath, they told me how much trouble I was in. How much trouble I'd been in, since shortly after the *Flying Dutchman* had jumped away from Earth orbit, on the mission we had not been expected to ever return from.

What Skippy had neglected to tell me or anyone aboard our captured Thuranin pirate ship, was that he had planned a surprise before we jumped away. A nasty, totally unexpected, unpleasant surprise.

Never, never, trust a shiny beer can.

"Hmm. You'll have to be more specific, Joe," Skippy said. "What, of all the things I've done, are you bitching about this time?"

"You know damned well what I mean! You put that Kristang troopship on a timer and jumped it away from Earth orbit the day after we left!"

"Oh, that. Hey, if you knew what I did, why did you ask what the hell I did?"

"Oh, for-"

"Is this one of those stupid human things, where you ask 'what' when you really mean something else, like 'how', or 'why'?"

"You know what I-"

"Or did I just malign your whole species, when the real problem is specifically Joe Bishop stupidity? If so, I apologize to monkeykind."

Sensing that he was only going to interrupt me again, I paused to collect my thoughts. I was in my office near the bridge, I'd gone there after getting royally chewed out by UNEF Command. The *Dutchman* was in a stable orbit, and there wasn't anything for me to do as the captain other than finish my official mission report, and prepare for the crew to go down to the surface. To go home. Against the odds, we had returned. "That was my fault for not being specific. Why? The correct question is, why? Why did you do it? And why didn't you tell me?"

"Huh. This is kind of a multiple choice question, Joe. I didn't tell you about it after we jumped away, because there was no reason for me to do that, duh. If I did, you would have pestered me about it every freakin' day, right?"

"Could be, probably," I admitted. "Whatever."

Craig Alanson

"And if I had told you about it before we jumped away, you would have done something characteristically stupid, like trying to stop me. Which would not have worked, by the way."

"You don't know that for sure," I insisted.

"I don't? Of the two of us, which one has the most patience and is the most stubborn? As a test, let's see how long we can each hold our breath."

"Not funny, Skippy. All right, granted, you were going to do it anyway. The question still is, *why*? Why jump that ship out of Earth orbit? It's circling the Sun halfway to Mars now! We were counting, all of humanity was counting on getting access to that ship, access to its technology!"

"I did it for you, Joe."

"For me?" For a moment, I was speechless. "Listen, Skippy. If you think putting an alien ship out of reach is a gift, please don't go shopping for my birthday."

Skippy sighed. "Not *you* specifically, Joe. I did it for your species."

"Because it entertains you to mess with us?"

"Well, that too," he admitted. "Man, I wish we'd been here to see the faces of major Earth leaders, when they saw that their tempting source of alien technology jumped out of easy reach. Ha ha! That would have been great! Hmm, you know what, I'm sure there must be video of that somewhere, let me search-"

"We need that technology, damn it! Skippy, we got lucky learning about the Thuranin sending a ship to Earth. If an alien ship ever does get here, we need advanced technology to defend ourselves."

"Advanced technology? Wait, you mean Kristang technology? Ugh, sometimes I forget how primitive your species is, that lizard technology impresses you. Ok, maybe I can see you monkeys being awed by bright shiny things aboard that troopship."

"Not everyone has your God-like level of technology, Skippy, we have to do things the hard way. We're getting off the subject as usual when I talk with you. Go back to explaining why you did this in order to help humanity."

"Exactly."

"A little more detail on that, please. Like, how does this help us?"

"It removes a major reason for you monkeys to whack each other with sticks. And it gives you a reason to cooperate."

"Ah."

"You see it now?"

"Yeah, I think so." Crap. He truly had been trying to help us. "When that troopship was in low Earth orbit, maybe a half dozen nations were capable of sending a team up there to take possession and then fight over it. But now that it's halfway to Mars, nations have to cooperate on a joint mission to get there?"

"You are one hundred percent accurate on that one, Joe. In my estimation, there was a better than 50-50 chance some nation would have nuked that troopship into vapor in Earth orbit, to prevent a rival nation from controlling its technology. Instead, for the past few months, your NASA has been cooperating with the space agencies of China, Europe, India, and also Japan. They are building a crude tin can of a spacecraft to travel out to the troopship. You might remember that before we left, there was an argument going on between the UNEF nations about who had rights to alien technology? One of the Kristang dropships that I shot down crashed in shallow water off the Philippines, and four navies almost got into a shooting war over recovering it. This is after international cooperation and sacrifice aboard the *Dutchman* saved all of your miserable monkey asses."

"I remember." That was a minor dust-up just before the *Dutchman* departed. I figured it was going to amount to nothing more than harsh words being exchanged, political posturing to please each nation's domestic audience, and a negotiated agreement. Smashed lizard technology wasn't worth fighting over. It especially was not worth fighting over, when the nations involved had such a monumental amount of work to do rebuilding our planet from the ravages of the Kristang. Perhaps I was underestimating the short-sightedness of political leaders. "Your motive was good, Skippy, and I see why you couldn't announce it beforehand." If he had jumped the troopship away before the *Dutchman* left, the UNEF governments would have insisted that we recover that ship before departing for the wormhole. Which, because those same governments had taken so long to make the inevitable, obvious decision, we did not have time for. "And instead of being angry with and hating each other, those governments now all agree on one thing; they all blame me."

"That is totally unfair, Joe."

"They're not going to blame *you*, because they already knew you are a sneaky little beer can. And they won't blame themselves for trusting you. That leaves me at fault, although I don't know what they expected me to do. I guess I'm at fault for not persuading you not to do, something I didn't know you were going to do."

"It's not your fault, Joe. I should have left a message to explain why I did it, after the ship jumped away."

"Even if you had baked a cake and delivered that message in person, it would still be my fault, Skippy. I am, was, the mission commander." It was almost time for me to take the silver eagles off my uniform and put the sergeant stripes back on. Unless they were going to bust me back to Private Bishop before I left the ship. "Anyway, that's all water under the bridge now. We need to go get that ship."

"As I already explained to those dumdums at UNEF Command, that ship's reactor is in cold shutdown, and I will not help you ignorant monkeys screw with it. I used the last energy in the jump drive capacitors to jump it away, so it can't jump back. And if you're thinking of jumping the *Dutchman* out there, good luck programming a jump accurately enough without me. Also, darn! I just discovered a fault in the calibration of our jump drive coils, I need to take them offline. I hate it when that happens. Could take a long time to fix, or a short time. If you know what I mean."

"You forget that we have two Thuranin dropships, and we can mostly fly those without you."

"Ha! No, I did not forget that, mi amigo. We have two, and only two dropships. It's too hazardous to send a single dropship out that far, so you will need to send both. And they will both have to stay there for a very long time, while your idiot scientists try to figure how to get the troopship back to Earth. Good luck with that, by the way. During that time, we will not be able to use those two dropships to bring crew and supplies up to the *Dutchman*."

"Crap. You planned this?"

"Nope, I got lucky, it just worked out exceptionally well for me. According to your underdeveloped understanding of 'luck', that is. Remember, we did not expect to come back here. If you monkeys still want that troopship, you are going to have to do it the hard way."

After I landed at Wright-Patterson Air Force Base in Ohio for debriefing by UNEF Command, the US military and CIA, I received a thorough ass chewing. I mean, there was a line of officers and government officials a mile long lined up for an all-you-can-eat buffet, and my hide was on the menu. They had been pissed at me before we returned, about the Kristang troopship being inaccessible. Our unexpected return had given them a new reason to throw me in the manure pile. Within five minutes of us contacting UNEF

Command after we jumped into orbit, I had transmitted my mission report and summary. All the other officers onboard had sent their own mission reports, which I had not censored in any way. Five minutes after my own report reached UNEF Command, I was explaining and defending myself to outraged parties from multiple nations. Perhaps that was the good aspect of me being in such trouble; it had united the five nations of UNEF in collective indignant outrage toward me. Yay, teamwork! My explaining of my decisions lasted four full days; after the first two hours, I learned to stop defending myself and simply accept the ass-chewing. Truthfully, they had raised grilling to such an art that it was kind of a privilege to witness it, even if the person getting grilled was me. By the time they were done, I was burnt so crispy that you wouldn't have been able to discern me from the charcoal. Assuming, that is, that you understand my 'grilling' analogy.

Skippy attempted to defend me, which I think likely made matters worse. If UNEF Command was disappointed in me, they now thoroughly distrusted our alien AI. In the eyes of UNEF Command, Skippy had stolen a priceless starship from them. Until we returned with our fresh intel, Earth had no way to know for sure that there weren't a dozen Kristang starships lurking in the vicinity of Earth. Without the troopship's technology, Earth was completely defenseless. From the viewpoint of UNEF Command, if Skippy could not be trusted to keep a Kristang ship in Earth orbit, how could he be trusted to keep his word and shut down the wormhole near Earth?

Damn, I had not even considered that issue until we returned. The whole time while we were away on our luxury cruise, UNEF Command had been panicked that the local wormhole was still open, that a fleet of pissed-off aliens would be jumping into Earth orbit without warning. And the best source of advanced alien technology had been jumped out of reach by a clearly untrustworthy alien AI. For all UNEF Command knew, Skippy had sold out the Merry Band of Pirates, and delivered the *Dutchman* back to the Thuranin in exchange for help from a more-advanced species. People on Earth had been frightened and angry; going home at night to their loved ones and not knowing whether that night was the last for humanity. When we unexpectedly returned, and I proudly and sort of smugly announced that we had *again* saved the world by foiling an attempt to send a Thuranin ship to Earth, all their fear and anger was transferred to me.

Hell, I don't blame them. I'd be angry at that jerk Joe Bishop, if I was them.

That first night after debriefing, thoroughly exhausted, I collapsed into a bunk. Sleep should have come immediately; to my body clock that was used to *Dutchman* standard time, it was 0430 and I had been harshly questioned for over fourteen hours. Maybe I was too stunned to sleep. More likely what kept me from sleep was thinking that the other Merry Band of Pirates, especially the leaders like Chang, Simms and Smythe, were probably also being subjected to unfriendly interrogation by UNEF. In my debriefing, I had stated many times that decisions during the mission were my responsibility alone. UNEF knew that was what a commander was expected to say.

"This sucks, Joe," Skippy commented angrily through my zPhone. "You saved this unworthy ball of dirt, *again*, and they're upset with you? Ungrateful jerks."

"They're not ungrateful, Skippy. They did commend me, and the entire crew, for our actions against the surveyor ship."

"Yeah, they commended you for like two seconds, before nitpicking and second guessing every freakin' decision you made along the way."

"They do have a point, Skippy. They made me the mission commander, and they gave me only two real objectives."

"Which you totally accomplished!"

"We accomplished the first objective; shutting down the wormhole. The second objective, that is equally important, was preventing aliens from learning that humans are flying around the galaxy in a pirate ship. UNEF Command thinks the major reason that I didn't manage to blow that objective was through pure luck. Looking back, I think they may be right about that."

"Joe, the only decision they have a problem with is landing on Newark, instead of letting the entire crew die aboard the *Dutchman* when the life support power ran out. Those dumdums forget that if the crew hadn't landed on Newark, we would never have learned about that surveyor ship's mission."

"That's not relevant, Skippy. At the time I made the decision to land on Newark, and risk aliens discovering us, I did not know that we would learn about the surveyor ship. UNEF is evaluating the decisions I made, based on the information available to me at the time. They are questioning my judgment, not our results."

"What," he sputtered. "You can't separate the two! UNEF Command thinks you should have condemned our entire pirate crew to death, just to avoid taking even an entirely reasonable risk?"

"I wouldn't have been condemning the crew to death, Skippy. You were already doing that."

There was another of his signature pauses. "That hurt, Joe. How do you figure that? My rebuilding the ship out of moon dust saved the crew."

"No. That was only temporary. After you rebuilt the ship and we left Newark, you and I talked about whether humans could fly the *Dutchman* by ourselves. You said it is impossible. The crew was going to die in cold and lonely space anyway, after you contacted the Collective and left us. Remember? I tried to make a bargain with you; to bring the ship back to Earth so the crew could land here safely. Then just the two of us could go out to contact the Collective. Based on what I knew at the time, the risk I took by landing on Newark only temporarily postponed the crew's inevitable deaths. If I had decided against landing on Newark, it would have been because I figured we were all going to die soon anyway, as soon as we found a working comm node for you."

There was another pause, longer this time. "Crap. I'm sorry, Joe. This is my fault?" He sounded genuinely remorseful.

"No," I said quickly to reassure him. "No, Skippy. I was the commander; the decision was one hundred percent mine."

"This isn't a clear wrong or right issue," Skippy's voice reflected his frustration. "It's purely a matter of judgment."

"You are correct. And UNEF disagrees with the judgment I made." From just the first day of debriefing, it was pretty clear that UNEF would not be entrusting me with commanding any future missions. Command of a mission from which we weren't expected to return, yes. Command of a mission with a more complicated objective, no. UNEF didn't trust my judgment. I was too young, too immature, too inexperienced, and too reckless in the opinion of UNEF. After fourteen hours of explaining over and over why I had risked the failure of the primary mission objective, I was beginning to question my own judgment. Maybe they were right. After all, I had flown the *Dutchman* right into an ambush. Later, a whole lot of things could have gone wrong on Newark. And the long road trip we took across the surface of Newark in our BarneyWeGo RV was for nothing; the comm node and AI we recovered were both useless.

Also, that RV sank, don't forget that little detail. In UNEF Command's view, that was yet another shining example of my genius leadership. Not.

The fact is, I actually got lucky when Skippy discovered the Thuranin planned to send a ship to Earth. In UNEF's opinion, stopping that ship was the one good thing I did after we shut down the wormhole on our way outbound. Yes, in order for UNEF to not be completely disgusted with me, all I needed to do was simply save the freakin' world.

Not that I'm bitter about it.

Skippy still tried to comfort me. "Hey, it was what we found on Newark that most convinced me to temporarily set aside my quest for contacting the Collective. So, landing on Newark is the whole reason I agreed to come back to Earth."

"That, and the fact that as the commander, I ordered the ship to come back here."

"Oh, yeah, sure," he almost stuttered on the words. "That too. Joe, is there anything I can do to help you?"

"Jump that troopship back into Earth orbit?" I suggested hopefully.

"Anything other than that, I meant. You may not be flying monkeys like in the Wizard of Oz, but you will have to fly up there by yourselves if you want access to that ship. Or, hey, how about this? The troopship's orbit is somewhat elliptical; I calculate that ship's orbit will come within a million miles of Earth within the next six thousand years. If that helps."

"Good night, Skippy."

Skippy's credibility, and by extension my own, had been severely damaged by revelations in my mission report. UNEF Command was disturbed and intrigued by what we had learned about Elder sites, about Newark and most importantly, about Skippy himself.

The first time we came to Earth, the story Skippy told UNEF was that he had been part of the Elder civilization. The information that Skippy had been able to give us more of less matched the limited info that UNEF had heard from other sources. An ancient species now known as the 'Elders' departed the galaxy long ago, and no one knew what happened to them. The Elders had created the wormhole network. Little was known about the Elders; scattered bits and pieces of their technology were highly prized by current species, although use of Elder technology had to be done very, very carefully. When the Rindhalu fought the Maxolhx in the original battle that began the endless war that still raged across the galaxy, both sides had used Elder devices as weapons. Use of destructive Elder technology had activated previously unknown machines now called 'Sentinels'; these machines devastated both sides of the conflict equally. Devastated, as in scorched planets and scoured entire solar systems of life. Wherever the Sentinels struck, nothing lived, and nothing could stop them. After wiping out large areas of both Rindhalu and Maxolhx territory in mere days, the Sentinels had disappeared. They were still out there, waiting.

Now we knew that someone had used Elder technology to destroy a moon and push a planet out of orbit. Someone had done that after the Elders left the galaxy, and before the Rindhalu discovered electricity. Skippy admitted that he had no idea who had done such terrible things; as far as he knew there were no intelligent beings in the galaxy during the time between the Elders and the Rindhalu. The fact that Skippy was baffled called into question the accuracy and usefulness of his vast knowledge base. After Newark, Skippy was not even sure who he was.

Why, UNEF asked me, should we trust an alien AI who doesn't know his own nature? Perhaps everything that Skippy thought he knew was wrong; we couldn't trust his analysis even if UNEF trusted that shiny beer can's intentions. And they didn't.

I didn't have a good answer for why we should trust Skippy, other than that he had helped us so far. His help had saved our planet, twice. And if we planned to take the *Dutchman* back out to verify there were no other starships on their way to Earth, we absolutely needed Skippy.

Even if he was an untrustworthy little beer can.

Paradise

The Kristang frigate *To Seek Glory in Battle is Glorious* suddenly appeared in orbit above Pradassis, the world called 'Paradise' by the traitorous humans and 'Gehtanu' by the dishonorable Ruhar. The ship did not bother to deploy a stealth field; the gamma ray burst of its jump in could not be masked, and the ship would not remain in the area long enough to play cat and mouse games with the Ruhar ships protecting the planet. Speed, not stealth, was the frigate's ally that day. The frigate would attack the planet in order to harass the Ruhar defenders, and as soon as it was able, the frigate launched missiles and fired maser cannons at pre-selected targets on the surface. But its primary mission that day was to gather information, not merely to inflict minor if annoying damage.

The *Glory*'s captain paid only scant attention as all three of his missiles were intercepted and destroyed by the maser beams of the Ruhar ships before his weapons could cause any damage. No matter, the missiles had served their purpose of tying up the Ruhar defenders while the frigate scanned the surface and the space around Paradise. The attention of the frigate's captain shifted rapidly between two displays; the first showed the incoming sensor data, indicating the scan was already 57% complete. The second display monitored the known Ruhar ships and predicted how soon the *Glory* would need to jump away. This second display the captain watched with a combination of anxiety and mistrust. The predictive ability of the computer behind that system was known to be right only 42% of the time. The Kristang who built, designed and now maintained the system, based on concepts stolen from the Jeraptha, insisted that their system worked correctly. The problem, they said, was lack of data from the frigate's inadequate sensors.

"Maser beam near miss, Captain," the ship's second in command reported. "Another. We were bracketed that time."

The real problem, thought the *Glory*'s captain as he noted that the planned sensor sweep was now 71% complete, was the unforgiving math of physics. Sensor data crawled to the ship at the slow speed of light. Ruhar ships could jump faster than light. An enemy ship could appear on top of the *Glory* before the frigate even knew the defending ship existed. What saved raiding ships was their own ability to quickly jump away, and altitude. The *Glory* had jumped in high enough so that it could form an outbound jump point to escape, but low enough that the planet's gravity well prevented defending Ruhar ships from jumping in accurately. Even a Ruhar ship with a well-calibrated jump drive, performing a relatively short jump, could only be assured of emerging within thirty thousand kilometers of the *Glory*. There was no way around the distortion of the gravity well, with the limited technology available to the Ruhar or Kristang. A separation of thirty thousand kilometers was far enough that the *Glory* could safely jump away, after its shields absorbed one or two direct hits from maser beams. More than two maser beams, or a single hit from a railgun or smart missile would burn through the frigate's thin shields. Frigate captains were trained to jump in, shoot and jump away before enemy fire could find them.

The scan was now 84% complete; the *Glory*'s parameters for this mission had been a successful 75% scan. An additional 10% would allow the frigate's crew bragging rights, without earning her captain a reprimand for needlessly endangering his precious ship.

Bravery to the point of foolhardiness was normally expected in Kristang captains, but not this time. There were only seven Kristang ships still around the Paradise system, and none of them could be risked without strong assurance that the risk was worth the potential gain. The small remaining task force was centered around one elderly cruiser, with its escorts of two support ships, three frigates and one destroyer. The task force had only two purposes; to force the Ruhar to maintain a substantial naval presence in the

Pradassis system, and to gather intelligence. To provide intelligence that hopefully would convince the clan's leadership that one strong push would take the planet back. The dishonorable Ruhar and their allies the Jeraptha may have decisively defeated the Kristang/Thuranin coalition forces in the sector for the moment, but even the triumphant Ruhar could not be strong everywhere at once. The planet Pradassis could still be retaken, but that possibility grew fainter every day.

The ship was rocked by a glancing blow from a maser beam; the Ruhar defense force had narrowed his location enough to begin using targeting sensors. The *Glory* had been maneuvering randomly since it jumped in, so that by the time a light-slow maser beam reached its intended target, the target was no longer there. Sensor scan now 87% complete. The shields had protected the ship from the maser beam, but that dissipated energy was now a cloud of high-energy particles surrounding the ship and degrading the effectiveness of the sensors. The *Glory*'s captain ordered a jump away, and the little frigate disappeared sixty one seconds after it jumped in. Jumping away, so soon after jumping in, rendered it impossible for the frigate's jump drive to have any kind of accuracy but that did not matter. All the frigate's crew cared about was getting away without emerging inside a planet or moon; anywhere else was safely empty space.

While the ship's crew were preparing for a series of jumps back to the task force's gathered ships, the *Glory*'s captain quickly skimmed through highlights of the sensor data. Strangely, the Ruhar did not appear to be putting any effort into stiffening their planet's defenses against raiders. The Ruhar did not consider the planet important enough to expend the resources, or the Ruhar were now stretched so thin that they did not have the resources to deploy. Either circumstance was favorable to the Kristang.

There was something else interesting in the sensor data; substantial areas of the southern continent, mostly covered by jungle, had been cleared for crops. Human crops. There were large areas of fields growing plants suited to human biology. A closer look at the sensor data revealed newly constructed crude settlements populated by humans near the fields. And in the fields were Ruhar heavy equipment, assisting the humans with clearing the jungle, planting and harvesting crops. Despite being ordered to resist the Ruhar by their rightful patrons the Kristang, the traitorous, cowardly humans appeared to be wholeheartedly working with the Ruhar.

Those large fields, the *Glory*'s captain thought, would make tempting, easy targets for a raiding ship's maser beams. The traitorous humans needed to be taught a lesson by true warriors.

CHAPTER TWO

Earth

After getting grilled by one group after another for four straight days, I wrangled permission to leave the base. Just me, no escort. I wasn't under arrest, and although I still had the Big Red Button app on my zPhone that could activate the *Dutchman*'s weapons, it wasn't necessary. Unlike last time, there was a skeleton crew aboard the ship. I didn't need to be on duty 24/7 to protect the planet. Besides, we now knew there were no Kristang or Thuranin ships on this side of the local wormhole. So, I had the night off, all I needed to do was report back for another debriefing at 0800 the next morning. Friday morning. I was hoping they would let me have the weekend off. I was also certainly not betting on it.

"Hey, Joe. You think your week sucked," Skippy said to me as I was changing into civilian clothes. "That was nothing compared to what I had to go through."

"Oh, yeah, sorry, I meant to ask you about that. How did it go?" UNEF had come up with the astonishingly moronic idea for Skippy to be examined by psychologists and AI experts. UNEF's thinking, if that word even applied, was there was something wrong with Skippy that made him act like such an immature asshole. I had told them no, there is nothing wrong with Skippy. He is simply an incredibly powerful, smart, amoral little beer can. Being an asshole was just his personality.

UNEF didn't listen to me.

Fortunately, UNEF's search for humans who were considered 'experts' in the field of artificial intelligence ended quickly, since humanity had not yet developed true AI. Asking a human to examine Skippy would be like asking a flatworm to look under the hood of a car and tell you why it won't start. The few people working in the field of AI who were contacted by UNEF naturally would have given anything to speak with Skippy, but they all told UNEF that any knowledge transfer would be one-way. And Skippy refused to cooperate.

I expected that any psychologist would have told UNEF that they had no way to usefully examine the psyche of an alien artificial intelligence. I underestimated the arrogance of psychologists. Despite having exactly zero frame of reference for what constituted 'normal' behavior for an Elder AI, the psychologists plowed ignorantly ahead.

"It went better for me than for them," Skippy chuckled. "You know what, the experience was actually mildly entertaining for a while, until I got bored with it. One of them had a nervous breakdown. Another one started crying and ended the conversation, he's in therapy now."

"Skippy! You didn't have to do that."

"Hey, you did warn them. It's not my fault they ignored you. Morons."

"Oh, boy." I had warned them. Skippy knew just about everything there was to know about a person. And he was an expert at pushing people's buttons. Whatever a person's weakness or trigger points were, he would find them and use them. What the hell had they been thinking, trying to peel back the mind of such an immensely intelligent being? "Don't do it again, please?"

"No problem, Joe, that little farce is over. Although they did conclude that whatever is 'wrong' with me is your fault."

"What? How the hell do they figure that?"

"Well, reading from their preliminary report, they're saying 'The alien AI is engaging in classic mirroring behavior with its companion Joseph Bishop. It is because of Bishop's immature personality that the Skippy being's behavior is-' Ah, I don't need to read the rest of this BS to you, Joe. The gist of it is that if a different person had discovered me in that dusty warehouse, a person the psychologists consider more mature, then I would be more serious and cooperative."

"Oh." Crap. Another reason for UNEF to be pissed at me. "They're, uh, not right about that, are they?"

"Phhhhht!" Skippy made a raspberry sound. "Ha! No way, dude! I've told you before, me being an asshole is just me. That's not going to change. Especially not because some bacteria with a degree in psychology says so."

"Oh, good, then."

A bus took me into town; all I wanted was a cheeseburger, a beer and time to myself. There was a crowd of reporters outside the base fence, all hoping to get an interview with anyone who had been on the Thuranin star carrier. In my civilian clothes, on an ordinary bus and with a baseball cap pulled down over my eyes, I sailed right through the reporters. Once I got off the bus, I wandered down some side streets; I wanted to find a place that wouldn't be crowded with people from the base. Finally, I found a window that advertised 'wine flights' whatever that is, and I saw a group of people wearing suits go in. In my experience, this type of place was not likely to be crowded with off-duty soldiers.

It was about half full already. I found a spot at the bar, ordered a cold beer and a cheeseburger, and half watched a college basketball game on the TV. The cheeseburger was merely Ok; it may have been my mood that was the problem.

While I was taking a sip of beer, someone jostled me from behind and I almost spilled my drink. "Oh, sorry," said a woman as she plunked her purse on the bar. "This place is crowded tonight." She caught the bartender's attention. "Lemon drop martini, please."

"Oh, hi. Hey, I've seen you on the base," I said truthfully. She had been in the cafeteria several times, and I'd seen her in hallways also. She was a civilian, I guessed she worked at Wright-Patterson. Her ID card was partly sticking out of her purse.

"You're Joe, right?" She asked. "You're one of the ExFor starship crew?" She added that last question quietly. When she first sat down next to me, I had half turned away, assuming she was there with friends and didn't want to be hit on by guys that night. Now I was paying attention. She'd sat down next to me because it was one of only two seats left at the bar, it being happy hour on a Thursday night. Short thick black hair, in a cut that I think is called a 'bob' but I am certainly no expert on women's hairstyles. Her hair was longer in front than the back, it framed her face nicely. Brown eyes. She had a tan from some place she'd been on vacation but not recently; it was starting to fade. Late twenties, maybe? I'm a bad judge of age. Cute. Very cute, and a nice smile. She tucked her badge in her purse and slung it over her knee, the way women do when bars aren't smart enough to install purse hooks under the bar top. Offering a hand, she added "I'm Rachel. I work in IT support at the base network center."

"Sergeant Joe Bishop," I shook her hand for what I hoped was the right amount of time, not too firm but not trying to crush her either. A handshake that hopefully said I am not a creep and please please please stay here and talk with me. Also hopefully it did not convey the desperation I was feeling either. That was asking a lot from a handshake.

"Hello, Sergeant Joe," said as she glanced around. I fervently wished she wasn't looking for her friends, or worse, her boyfriend. She wasn't wearing a wedding ring. "What brought you here? This place is out of the way."

"After wearing a uniform every day aboard the ship, I want to be a civilian for a while," I pointed to the civilian shirt I was wearing.

Paradise

"I know what you mean," she laughed, and it was a truly wonderful sound. "I was in the Air Force. Wearing a uniform makes it easy for women; you don't have to put together an outfit every day."

"Guys just do a sniff test, on whatever clothes are on top of the pile of laundry on the floor," I admitted.

"You guys are so lucky!" She said, and lightly punched me on the shoulder. Things were looking good. "Now I have to find something Business Casual to wear five days a week. If we have a high-level meeting, then I have to dress up." She took a sip of her lemon drop martini. "You were on that alien starship?"

On behalf of all the men and women trapped on Paradise, I could at least entertain Rachel with UNEF's current cover story. A cover story that had been pounded into my head, over and over. Telling her the story also gave me a reason to lean closer to her, to be heard over the noisy bar. Yes, I said, sticking to the cover story. I was on the starship. I went to space, and I had been on Paradise. It was a nice planet, nothing special. The parts of Paradise that I had seen were kind of like Kansas and the Amazon, not that I'd ever been to either of those places on Earth. We humans didn't fly the starship that was now in orbit; we were just passengers on a Thuranin ship. The Thuranin were little green men, I had seen them but never spoken with one. That part was the truth. No, I didn't know when the ExFor would be coming back from Paradise; I had not been on Paradise in a long time. That was the truth again. And no, I hadn't had contact with Paradise, and I didn't know where the Thuranin starship would be taking us next. I didn't even know when or if I would be going into space next. Actually, there was a lot of truth mixed into UNEF's cover story. Most of what I needed to say was that I didn't know things that I honestly didn't know. That made it easy to remember.

"You are only passengers aboard the Thuranin ship?" She asked quizzically. "Why did you bring pilots? I saw people wearing Air Force flightsuits get off the dropship when you landed."

"Oh, yeah, uh," UNEF had a cover story for that also. "When we were on Paradise, we flew captured Ruhar aircraft. The Kristang trained us on a planet we called Camp Alpha, before we went to Paradise," I added nervously.

To my relief, she nodded and seemed to buy the story. "Don't worry, I won't ask where you went this last time."

After enforced sobriety on Camp Alpha, Paradise and aboard the *Flying Dutchman*, I was being careful to limit myself to beer. While I talked with Rachel, I nursed the same beer I had started with. Raising the glass to drain the last of the beer, I was jostled from behind again and spilled it on the bar. Some of it splashed on my shirt. Rachel handed me a napkin and tried to catch the bartender's attention. "It's Ok," I told her. "I have to watch what I'm drinking; it's been a long time since I've had much alcohol."

Rachel had been about to order another lemon drop, she dropped her hand and looked around. "This place is crowded. It's karaoke night," she pointed to the stage.

"Oh no!" A loud but muffled voice came from the zPhone in my pocket. "No karaoke for you, Joe! Your singing voice scares animals and small children!"

"Excuse me," I said to Rachel, and pulled out my zPhone. "Skippy," I whispered as quietly as I could to still be heard over the noisy bar, "this is not a good time."

Rachel's eyes widened, and she leaned closer to me. "Is that *Skippy*?"

Now it was my turn to be surprised. UNEF Command had told us that rumors of a 'Skippy' had gotten out, as was inevitable, but-

That annoying beer can didn't know when to be quiet. "Skippy the Magnificent, at your service, Rachel my dear-"

"Not now, Skippy, I'm serious!" I said, and sat on the phone. "Uh, look, Rachel-"

"I've heard of someone called Skip-" as she spoke, the karaoke started, with some drunk guy loudly warbling a pop song off key. "Joe," she said with her lips practically brushing my ear because the place was so loud. "Let's go someplace else?"

"That would be great," I said without hesitation.

The 'someplace else' was a coffee shop down the street. We got coffees, technically what she got looked like an ice cream sundae with a tiny splash of coffee somewhere in it. Lots of whipped cream and caramel sauce. And a straw. That did not qualify as 'coffee' in my opinion. I paid for the coffees although she used her frequent coffee buyer card, so I guessed that she got coffee there often. The shop wasn't empty as I had hoped, that disappointed me, because I'd been hoping for it to be quieter. There was a hipster douchebag with a carefully tended scruffy beard, a bowler hat and an ironic T-shirt playing acoustic guitar in the corner. He had brought a group of enthusiastic friends, but apparently left the talent behind in his car. It actually turned out great to my delight; Rachel and I had to sit close to hear each other. The background noise meant I didn't need to worry about being overheard. And the terrible singing of the hipster gave us something to laugh about.

First, I told her the official UNEF cover story that I had been given, in case anyone asked about Skippy. 'Skippy' is the nickname humans used for the AI that ran the Thuranin ship. He is super intelligent and rightfully disdainful of lowly humans. And he tends to involve himself in our lives, even when we're not on the ship.

Rachel could tell that further inquiry about Skippy, the Thuranin ship or Paradise were not welcome. Being ex-military, and having a clearance to work on Air Force computers, she knew that certain subjects were on a need-to-know basis, so she was cool about changing the subject. "Joe Bishop. Is there any chance you are *that* Joe Bishop, the Barney guy?"

"Yes," I admitted sheepishly. I'd seen her checking her phone on the walk from the bar, she probably had Googled me. Talking about events in the public record was safe; anything that happened before I took the space elevator up from Ecuador. I told what I hoped was a humorous account of how I became known as Barney. Rachel laughed at my story, then I asked about her. This wasn't me doing the guy thing of letting a woman talk so I can get into her pants. I was genuinely interested in her, and not only because she is a woman. After being captain of a pirate ship, commander of everyone I saw on a daily basis, I was desperate to simply talk with someone like the normal people talk. Rachel was a good listener, and as she told me about her life, I just sat and enjoyed being a regular person. Sitting in a coffee shop in a typical American city, with a person who I could not potentially order into deadly combat, was cathartic.

We stayed late enough at the coffee shop that we finished our coffees and I got us decafs and we split a scone. The hipster guy ran out of folk songs to mangle and finished his set about a quarter after ten; fifteen minutes before the coffee shop closed for the night. We took a hint and walked outside. "Can I walk you to your car?" I asked awkwardly. Clearly, I was out of practice.

"No need," she said, and even in the night, she must have seen my face fall. "I live across the street," she pointed to an apartment building.

"Oh," I said with relief, "that explains the frequent coffee drinker card."

"Yes," she laughed, "I spend too much money in there."

There was an awkward moment of silence, that most guys would typically use as an opportunity for some lame hint about going to her place. "Rachel, this has been great, thank you," I blurted out before my testicles could stop me. No, they were shouting, *NO!* "I have another meeting at 8 o'clock tomorrow morning, so I'm going to head back to the base. I'll, uh, see you around on Monday?" The truth was, I really did have a great time talking with her, and I didn't want to spoil the pleasant buzz by her having to let me down, so I did it for her. She seemed surprised but also mildly relieved to avoid the inevitable awkwardness.

Paradise

Baturnah Logellia frowned as the human commander left her office. She did not like lying to, or at the very least misleading the poor humans. Although the humans had come to Gehtanu as lackeys of the hated Kristang, Baturnah felt sorry for them, and even some measure of affection for some of them. In a way, although the planet had been under the control of the occupying Kristang back then, she felt a pang of nostalgia for the time when the humans had called her the 'Burgermeister'.

The current human commander was from an ethnic subgroup the humans called 'Chinese'. All humans looked pretty much the same to her, she didn't appreciate the significance of genetic, cultural or political differences. Also she simply didn't care; she had other more pressing issues to absorb her attention. For some reason that seemed to be important to the humans; command of their United Nations Expeditionary Force rotated regularly among the five nations who constituted the combat force. Or what had been a combat force, before the Ruhar reestablished control over the planet. Whatever it had once been, the human force was now mostly scattered across the southern continent, from which the few Ruhar residents had been evacuated. The humans could have the southern continent they called 'Lemuria', and hopefully within a few years the humans would be self-sufficient there. That time could not come soon enough for Baturnah, because the humans were both a constant distraction and a substantial drain on scarce resources.

It was why those resources were so scarce that was the reason she misled the human commander. And misled the Ruhar residents of Gehtanu.

The Ruhar government, Baturnah knew, did not want to keep Gehtanu. Had not intended or wanted to recapture the planet at all. Gehtanu had only been the bait to lure a major Kristang/Thuranin task force into battle, so it could be trapped and destroyed. That Ruhar/Jeraptha force was not supposed to actually retake control of Gehtanu, but as the battle developed and spread rapidly across the sector, the situation became highly fluid. The success of the initial attack wildly exceeded the expectations of Ruhar/Jeraptha command, opening additional opportunities. When intelligence was received that two Kristang battlegroups intended to use Gehtanu as a place to make a last stand, possibly ransacking the planet in the process, the local Ruhar commander had reacted quickly and diverted his ships to jump into orbit.

Now the Ruhar were stuck with a planet they didn't want. The planet held two troublesome populations; humans, and native Ruhar who outlasted the Kristang evacuation effort. Those native Ruhar now expected their government to assist in rebuilding the planet and bringing the evacuees back.

Be patient, Baturnah had to tell the natives. Those who were evacuated will be returned in due time, she lied. The military situation in the sector is still unsettled, she told them truthfully. A cease-fire has been negotiated, but there have been incidents. It is still too dangerous for civilian transport ships to make the journey to Gehtanu, she said, and that was also the truth. What the government instructed her to lie about was the intended end game; giving Gehtanu back to the Kristang.

Before the recent wormhole shift, the planet that the Ruhar knew as Gehtanu, the Kristang claimed as Pradassis, and the humans called Paradise, had been roughly equally conveniently located for both the Ruhar and the Kristang. After the shift, the closest wormhole was substantially further away for the Ruhar than it was for the Kristang. If they had not already occupied the planet, the Ruhar would never have bothered going there. The Ruhar government did not want Gehtanu now; the wormhole shift had opened much more alluring and less expensive opportunities. Gehtanu was too sparsely populated, and too vulnerable, to bother keeping. In order to assure the planet's safety, the Ruhar would need to permanently station a major battlegroup in the system, and Gehtanu was simply not worth that effort and expense.

So the Ruhar were secretly negotiating with a coalition of major Kristang clans to give Gehtanu back to the Kristang, in exchange for Kristang concessions of more valuable territory elsewhere.

That would be bad for the native Ruhar, who would be forcibly evacuated by their own government.

It would be absolutely disastrous for the humans. There was nowhere to evacuate humans to, and the Ruhar certainly would not be taking their former oppressors with them. Humans on Gehtanu would be left under control of the cruel Kristang, who now considered their former clients as traitors.

So when the human commander of their 'UNEF' came into her office to discuss his many legitimate concerns, Baturnah had to nod and smile, and assure him that they could work together. And they would, right up until the point when the Ruhar betrayed their slowly developing trust.

Earth

I slept great and woke up the next morning in a good mood. The worst of the debriefing had to be over, I figured. The session that day wasn't bad; the people running the debriefing seemed to have run out of questions for the moment, and I had run out of things to say. I had accepted that UNEF and the US military were disappointed and angry with me, and my acceptance took away some of the fun for them to berate me yet again. By 1530, we ended the session for the day, and the next meeting wasn't scheduled until Monday. I had a whole weekend free!

So I was completely surprised when Rachel called me that afternoon.

"Hi, Joe, this is Rachel," she said.

"Oh, hi. Um, how did you get my number?" I looked at my zPhone. As far as I knew, a zPhone did not have a 'phone number'. When we got our original zPhones on Camp Alpha, they were keyed to us; to contact someone you looked them up in the UNEF directory by name or unit.

"You texted me last night," she answered cautiously. "I was wondering how you got *my* number."

"I did?"

"Joe, you dumdum," Skippy broke into the call, and I assume Rachel couldn't hear him on her end. "I texted her with 'Thank you for a very nice evening'. Clearly, you have no idea what you are doing with women. Damn, you are a dumbass sometimes."

I gestured at my zPhone with my middle finger, knowing Skippy would be watching through the camera. "Oh, yeah, I did, Rachel. Sorry, it's been a very long week. I got your number from the base operator," I winced at that lie, hoping she wouldn't think that was creepy of me. "I'm not, you know, stalking you or anything." OMG what an idiot I am! If she didn't think I was creepy before, then mentioning 'stalking' should have set off her alarms.

But she laughed! Someone up there liked me, and I didn't mean a shiny beer can. "That is good to know, Joe. Listen, if you're not busy tonight, would you be interested in dinner?"

"That depends," I tried to be smooth while inside I was shaking. "I'm not familiar with fabulous Dayton Ohio. Do you know a place that has people who can actually sing?"

She laughed again. "Dayton has a bigger supply of ironic hipsters than you might expect, but we can try to avoid them."

"Wow, Joe," Skippy said after Rachel ended the call. "Did you just have a real girl ask you on a date? I thought there were no more surprises in the universe."

"A real woman, Skippy, and it's not such a surpr-" I stopped, a bad thought running with a chill down my spine. "Hey, Skippy. This Rachel. She said she works in IT. Is that right? She's not an undercover intel type, is she? She did ask a lot of questions last night." I was afraid that our meeting the previous night may not have been the coincidence that it seemed. UNEF sending an attractive woman to see if I blew our cover story was exactly what I expected them to do.

"Nope. She is genuinely who she says she is. She did talk and text with friends today, telling them that she met a cute guy from ExFor. And that you are 'that Barney guy'. I know you hate being referred to as Bar-"

"Cute?" I interrupted. "She said I'm cute?"

"Those were her exact words."

"Oh, damn," I said with disappointment.

"What is wrong with that?" Skippy asked with surprise in his voice.

"She said that I'm cute. Puppies are cute, Skippy. I was hoping she said that I'm hot."

"Oh, boy," Skippy sighed heavily. "Every time I think I have plumbed the lowest depths of your stupidity, Joe, I find a bottomless well beneath it. At some point in your life, you have had social contact with human women, right? Yet, you apparently know absolutely nothing about the fairer sex."

"Huh? How do you figure that?" Most of the time when the beer can insulted me, I didn't much care, but this time it bugged me.

"Joe, 'cute' means she likes you, and that she feels comfortable around you. She also said you are funny. For a girl to go to bed with a guy, she needs to get past her inhibitions, let her guard down. If you are cute and you make her comfortable, and especially if you can make her laugh, then dude, you are *totally* in. Trust me."

"Wow, great, I never thought of it like-"

"Unless she laughs when you take your pants off."

"Yeah, I figured that. She said that I'm cute and funny, so-"

"I'm not telling you anything else she said," Skippy protested.

"Oh, yeah, sure, because you're all about privacy," I said sarcastically.

"No, it's because I like her, and I don't want you to do some typically stupid Joe thing and screw this up. You're likely to slip up and mention something I told you."

"I have been on dates with girls before, you know."

"Shauna seducing you in the back of a truck was not a 'date', Joe."

"Shauna," I felt a pang of sadness thinking about her stuck on Paradise, "is not the first girl I have been with."

"Oh, yeah, because you were such a stud in high school. Well, you did go out with Melanie Rodgers for almost five months during your senior year. Hey, why did you two break up?" Skippy asked.

"We were young, and it's complica-"

"Ooh, ooh! I think I know what the problem was! Can I guess?" He sounded like an over-eager first grade boy, desperate to get the teacher's attention.

"What?" I foolishly took the bait.

"Was it her inability to deal with crushing disappointment? Every. Single. Day*?*"

"You are *such* an asshole," I couldn't help laughing, "why do I keep you around?"

"Most likely it is because of your shockingly poor judgment."

"Yeah, that must be it."

Getting ready for my date with Rachel, I took a shower and shaved, then I contemplated what else to do. It had been a while since I'd been a normal civilian date with a woman. Skippy offered to help. "Are you going to put on some of that body spray you bought at the base store?"

"Uh," I hesitated. "I don't know, Skippy, it never seemed to work for me like it does for guys in the TV commercials."

"That's because you weren't using enough of it, dumdum. You need to spray on at least twice as much to turn girls on."

"Oh, thanks, Skippy," I said as I reached for the can.

"*No!*" Skippy shouted. "Damn you are a dumbass! Seriously! Oh, this is hopeless. Hopeless! Girls hate it when a clueless guy uses too much cologne, and you guys always use too much or not at all. Put that can down! Get dressed, wear the blue shirt."

"The blue one? Why?"

"Because it picks up the blue in your eyes. Also because I went back through her Facebook posts and emails and IMs and credit card receipts, and I learned that Rachel purchased blue shirts for two of her previous boyfriends. Her favorite color is blue."

"Hmmm. That could be a problem, Skippy. Are you sure my shirt isn't going to remind her of an ex-boyfriend?"

"No, it's a different shade of blue. Trust me on this, Joe."

Dinner with Rachel was wonderful. I forget what I ate; Rachel had a salad like women do on first dates. She offered to pay for dinner since she had invited me out. I paid, explaining that I had a lot of back pay coming; there not being anything aboard a Thuranin starship to spend money on anyway. After dinner, we went across the street to a bar with good music, and we had a terrific time. Rachel has a wicked sense of humor, especially after her second or maybe third lemon drop martini. Fourth? I lost track. I stuck to beer and tried to drink slowly. Damn, all I wanted was not to screw this up. I was on a real date, with a real woman, doing things like regular people did. That was all I wanted.

We ended the night at her place; I don't remember how it happened. I do remember that I didn't try using any lame pickup line on her; going to her place just seemed natural. Figuring that we both had a lot to drink, I took it slow, but apparently I was out of practice.

She ruffled my hair with one hand. "Joe, stop, it's Ok, I drank too many lemon drops. It's not going to happen for me tonight."

"Hey, Joe," Skippy's distorted voice blared out of my zPhone earpiece, under the bed somewhere, "you should do that thing you did with Shauna. That worked."

"Oh for-" I frantically fumbled around under the bed with one hand, trying to find the stupid earpiece and kill it.

"Who," I could feel Rachel stiffen, "is *Shauna*?" Her voice was icy as the interstellar depths.

"Uh," the damned earpiece had rolled all the way under the far side of the bed, "nobody. I mean," my brain screamed at me that telling a woman I was with, that a woman I had been with was nobody to me, would not help me case, "not nobody. Nobody recen-"

"Joe sweated up the sheets with Shauna on Camp Alpha." Skippy said cheerily. "Not sheets, exactly, more like Army issue blankets in the back of a truck-"

"Skippy! Please, *for the love of God*, shut the hell up!"

Rachel slammed her legs together and smacked me in the chin with a knee; she knocked me off the bed onto the floor. "The back of a truck?!"

"That was her idea, not mine. She wanted to-" I stopped talking, because even I knew a woman doesn't want details of a man's prior sex partners. Sometimes my brain is way smarter than I am. "I'm going to stop talking now."

"Wise choice." Rachel said, and pulled up the bed covers, shutting me out.

"Hey, it wasn't my idea to-"

"This doesn't sound like you not talking, Joe."

"Oh, yeah. Right." Feeling like an idiot kneeling naked on the floor, I ducked down to reach under the bed, but I couldn't see the earpiece.

"How does this Skippy AI know what you did with, *her*? You made a sex video?"

"No," I said from under the bed. I saw the stupid thing now; it was almost out of reach. "My zPhone was under a blanket back then. That's the thing about Skippy, he can see and hear almost everything."

Rachel pulled the covers up higher. "Like now? He sees us? From the ship?"

Skippy said something that I couldn't hear, because I now had the earpiece and was squeezing the speaker in my fist.

"Yeah, he can see us. His technology is super advanced. Something about him being able to detect the way dust particles in the air vibrate, I think, he won't explain it to us humans."

"Uh huh, close enough," Skippy's voice now came out of the speaker in the clock radio. "I am Skippy the Omniscient, I see all, I hear all, I know all."

Rachel's face was shear white. "Everything?"

"Pretty much, yeah." Skippy responded. "Not that I pay attention much, you humans are generally not that interesting a species. And monkey mating kind of grosses me out. The last thing I want to watch is Joe's pasty white ass bouncing up and down. Yuck." The speaker began playing the soundtrack to a really bad porn movie, with a heavy bass line and lots of moaning and sighing. Bow-chicka-bow-boom-boom-bow-bow-chicka-bow. Not that I watch bad porn movies, of course, but, you know, I'd heard about them.

"Skippy! Cut it out!" I shouted. The music stopped.

"I'm only trying to help, Joe. Clearly, what you were doing wasn't getting the job done. I'd suggest you look in her goodie drawer for assistance, but the batteries in her favorite toy are almost dead." Then he added in a low voice. "Man, she gives that poor thing a *workout*. You want me to-"

Rachel's hand flew to her mouth. I thought she was going to pass out.

"Go away! I want you to *go away*!" I shouted.

"Ok, fine. Remember that the next time you need my help."

"Rachel look, I'm sorry-"

"If I'd known your AI friend was making this a threesome, I would have said no. He watches everything you do?"

"He watches everything *everyone* does. It's not just me."

"How do you live like that?" She asked in horror.

I shrugged. "It's like, if you're having sex, and the dog is laying down in the corner of the room. It doesn't matter if it's watching you, because it's just a dog? With Skippy, you get used to it, because he truly doesn't care, he's just not that interested. If he's watching us here, he's watching a lot of other people at the same time. And that's only a tiny part of what's going on in his, uh, mind, at the time."

She pulled the covers all the way up over her head, only her fingernails were showing. I took that as my cue to leave. If I could find my pants. Where the hell were my pants? With a glance into the hallway, I determined they weren't there either. "I'm sorry, Rachel, I'll get out of your hair. You, uh, have any idea where my pants are?"

She peeked out from under the covers. "Your pants? No, I don't. Your friend Skippy is gone?"

I was too tired to care. "Think so, yeah. Look, my pants must be under the cov-"

She flung the covers aside and looked at me with one eye open. "I'm probably going to regret this, but can we sleep on this, and talk in the morning? I'm too tired and I drank too much to think straight right now."

That sounded good. Being in bed with her, simply being in bed, I was tired and all I wanted to do was sleep.

I slept like a log. She said she slept well also. In the morning, after I made coffee, we took a shower together, and we hit the reset button. It was great. Sex is so much better when you're not drunk. And when you're awake.

Later that morning, I walked down the street to a bakery to get breakfast. Strolling back with a bag of baked goodies, I was feeling on top of the world. The weather was beautiful; sunny with a few clouds here and there, it was a cool morning but the afternoon promised to be pleasantly warm. There was a half-dressed woman waiting for me in her apartment, and since she had the day off, we had the whole day to ourselves. Friends of hers were having a cookout that evening, and we were invited. It felt great having no responsibilities. Let someone else save the world for a change, I was on leave.

And, of course, the main reason for my super ultra great mood is that I got laid. Never underestimate that.

Skippy called me, I held the zPhone to my ear as if it were a regular cellphone. I didn't want to draw attention to myself. "Good morning, Joe!" Skippy said with a cheery voice. "Were you and Rachel all right last night?"

"You weren't watching us, were you?"

"Not as far as you know."

"Ok good," I stopped to let a car pull into a driveway. "I really think that's a situation where you shouldn't- hey, wait a minute! Not as far as *I* know?"

"Gosh, will you look at the time, I should be go-"

"Not so fast, Skippy, you have some 'splain-, oh, what the hell, why would it matter?" I'd gotten so used to his watching everything I did, that I didn't care. "Hey, Skippy, you're the smartest being in the galaxy, right?"

"Yup, as far as both of us know."

"Great, because I do not understand women. Human women. Can you give me some insight? Help a brother out?"

Skippy sighed. Or imitated a sigh, it was convincing. "Joe, I have studied all the literature about human female psychology, read all the books written by and for women, downloaded every blog, every Instagram or Pinterest post, watched every program on the Lifetime channel, listened in on conversations between women, and have chatted online with billions of your females. With all of my processing power, over the equivalent of millions of years of analysis, I have come to one simple conclusion about human females."

"And what's that?" I asked eagerly.

"Bitches be crazy."

"Skippy!" I managed to say after I stopped laughing. "That's not nice."

"Oh, was that inappropriate? I can never tell."

"Decidedly inappropriate. Also wickedly funny. But don't do it again, huh?"

"No problem. Seriously, Joe, women have just as much trouble understanding men, as men have trouble understanding women. The difference is, women generally want to understand men in order to be better relationship partners. Men mostly are looking to get women into bed."

"Well, get them into bed *first*," I felt a need to defend my gender.

"Uh huh. Anyway, trying to understand women is a futile exercise, you may as well say you are trying to understand people, all people. My suggestion is you find one woman, and do your best to understand her. I hear that is quite rewarding."

"Someday, yeah. For now, me going off into deep space on an alien pirate ship, makes it difficult to get a relationship started, you know?"

"Do you regret traveling around the galaxy with me?" He sounded a little bit hurt.

"No! Not at all, Skippy. Hey, come on, we saved the world together. Twice." That remark got a strange look from a woman walking a dog past me. I lowered my voice. "I wouldn't trade that experience for anything. And, as much of a gargantuan asshole you are most of the time, I got to meet you. That's an incredible honor for a monkey like me."

"Same here. Well, probably more of an honor for you to meet me, to be honest. It's not even close, to tell the truth."

"Asshole," I said under my breath. "I'm enjoying being on leave; it's great not to think about aliens destroying Earth for a few days."

"You need a break. You deserve it. Ok, Joe, I'll leave you alone for a while, unless you contact me. Hey, heads up, Joe. Rachel is on her phone, talking with one of her friends about you."

"Oh, crap. Am I in trouble?"

"Quite the contrary, Joe, she is saying only good things about you. Damn, girls tell each other *everything*."

"Everything?" I did not like the sound of that.

"You men would be shocked. Again, she is saying good things about you. Um, this is not my area of expertise, but you may get lucky again today."

CHAPTER THREE

Paradise

To Seek Glory in Battle is Glorious emerged high above the planet's southern continent, almost two thirds of the way to the pole. Jumping in there had caught the Ruhar defenders badly out of position; they had been deployed to protect the northern continent where all the important Ruhar facilities were. That was also where the Ruhar population was concentrated; only a handful of Ruhar were stationed on the southern continent to monitor the humans there.

The Ruhar task force commander acted quickly, ordering three of his ships to climb up to jump distance so they could surround the enemy vessel. This took less than a minute, during which time the other Ruhar ships fired masers and missiles at the enemy. The masers would very likely miss, and the missiles would likely be intercepted by the enemy frigate's defensive masers, but the Ruhar action would keep the enemy busy.

The Ruhar commander was puzzled when, instead of proceeding north at high speed to attack Ruhar facilities on the surface, the enemy ship suddenly fired a maser beam at the southern continent. The maser beam's focus had been tuned to broaden its area of impact; rather than an intense pencil-thin beam, it covered a wider area.

The enemy was, for some unknown reason, targeting the humans' food supply. The maser beam was scorching fields of healthy crops and killing humans who had been caught in the open. Why were the Kristang expending resources to hit the humans, a species who had no combat power to threaten the Kristang?

No matter, the Ruhar commander decided, that was a question that could be addressed later. The three ships he had assigned to deal with the enemy frigate reached jump distance and disappeared, only to reemerge above the southern continent in three bursts of gamma radiation. The lightly-armored Kristang frigate would soon be forced to withdraw, then the Ruhar could assess the damage it had inflicted.

No! A Kristang destroyer suddenly jumped in above the northern continent and immediately fired at several targets. To his shame, the Ruhar commander saw that the actions of the frigate had been intended to lure part of his force away from their normal patrol area, and he had rashly fallen for the enemy trick. Alarmed, he scrambled to redeploy his other ships, and recalled two of the ships he had sent to deal with the frigate.

Before the two enemy ships had been chased away, the destroyer was able to successfully hit four targets on the surface. Thirty eight Ruhar died in the attack, and a weapons depot was also damaged. Next time, the Ruhar commander told himself with grim determination, he would not be fooled into dividing his forces.

That there would be a next time was one thing of which he was certain.

Earth

The cookout with Rachel's friends was great, except they had chicken and hot dogs, no cheeseburgers. And everyone wanted to ask me about my experience with ExFor, what it was like on Paradise, would the Kristang be coming back, and a thousand other questions. In every answer, I was careful to stick to the script of UNEF's cover story, and was as vague as possible with my answers. Rachel saw the pained look on my face after a while, and we bailed early.

Paradise

The next morning, it was going to be another nice day, and she suggested we go on a trail ride with horses. Rachel said she had always been into horses; her family had a horse when she was in high school, and she rode in some competitions. Jumping, stuff like that.

A long ride on the back of a horse wasn't my idea of a great time. "We can go ride dirt bikes instead?" It had been a while since I'd ridden a motorcycle; I expected it wouldn't take me long to get used to it again. When I was living at home, riding trails on a dirt bike or a snowmobile was regularly great fun on weekends.

She tilted her head at me. "Joe, you're not afraid of horses, are you?"

"No, it's just that I-" Damn. The last time I'd been on a horse had to be when I was ten years old. That was only sitting on a horse while it slowly walked around a ring at the county fair. All I remember of that experience was thinking how far off the ground I was. And that, if the horse wanted to go somewhere, I wouldn't be able to control it.

"Really? You went into space to fight aliens, but you're worried about a horse?"

"I'm not thrilled with the idea of trusting a big dumb animal between my legs. Of course," I grinned, "you girls just call that 'prom night'."

"Joe!" She laughed and slapped me playfully. "You are awful sometimes."

"I am terribly, terribly sorry," I said with zero sincerity. "Sure, we can go on a trail ride, I'd like to try that," I smiled reassuringly. Being out in the great outdoors, having fun with a pretty girl, who wouldn't enjoy that?

"Do you know how to ride a horse?"

I shrugged. "Grab the horse's ears," I pantomimed with my hands, "left hand is the brake, right is the throttle?"

"Sure, Joe," she laughed again, "I would love to get a picture of *that*. These horses know what to do, and they follow the horse in front of them."

"Uh huh. So, all I need to do is sit down, shut up and hang on?"

"That's the idea. If you get in trouble, I can rescue you."

"Oh, great."

The horse ride was a lot of fun, and we took a drive in the country afterward. Gas supplies had recovered enough that most people could resume driving their cars at least occasionally again. Although at $6.50 a gallon, you had to think about whether a trip was worth it. Being a gentleman, I paid to fill up Rachel's car; it was almost painful taking that much cash out of my wallet.

The next day was Monday; Rachel had to work, and I had to answer a bunch more questions. That afternoon, she had to fly to Arnold Air Force Base in Tennessee for a conference that would last until Friday morning; it was some computer flight simulator software type thing she was working on. Wanting to impress her, I almost opened my big mouth say that I was a pilot, qualified to fly a Thuranin dropship. Fortunately, good sense stopped me before I blew part of our cover story. Damn, this lying thing was getting old already.

She was scheduled to fly back to Dayton on Friday afternoon, but on Saturday morning, she would be leaving for a girl's weekend that she and her friends had been planning for months. My timing sucked, that was for sure. "I'm sorry, Joe," she said.

"Hey, I understand. I'll be here when you get back. I'm not going anywhere."

I was wrong about that. To my complete surprise, the debriefing wrapped up Tuesday afternoon, and the Army granted me two weeks of leave. Maybe they figured I deserved leave after our long mission, and it wasn't just me. Major Simms and Sergeant Adams texted me that their own debriefings were over for now, and they were on leave also. Same with the Ranger and SEAL teams who had been part of the Merry Band of Pirates. My opinion was that we had given UNEF a whole lot to think about, and they needed to process it before bringing us back in for more questions. At some point, soon, the *Dutchman* needed to go back out. Needed to go back out, in order to verify the Thuranin weren't sending another ship to Earth. I called Rachel and told her I was going to visit my folks for a while, even though I really, really wanted to see her again.

My timing, really, really sucked.

"You're packing, Joe?" Skippy asked, while I was stuffing clothes into a dufflebag. "Going to see your loved ones?"

"Yes, Skippy, my parents have been waiting for me to come home since I called them after we jumped into orbit."

"But your loved ones are right here, Joe."

"Huh?" My loved ones? If he was referring to himself, he was still in his escape pod man cave aboard the *Flying Dutchman*.

"Your loved ones, Joe. You know, Jim Beam, Jack Daniels, Johnny Walker-"

"Oh, very funny." Hmm. Maybe I did have time for a nice drink before I left.

Paradise

Baturnah looked up in shock from the document she was reading. "I can *not* believe this. This came from our government?"

"Yes, ma'am," said her aide Pollun Grayce. Grayce had been with Baturnah Logellia for over a decade, a tumultuous decade. The next year did not appear like it would be any less eventful. "It is not an official recommendation from the federal government, nor it is expressed as desired policy-"

"Yet. It is not *yet* official government policy. Pollun, this is horrific. I feel unclean even reading this."

"Yes, ma'am," Pollun agreed. And he did agree. Sometimes, his job was to listen and allow the Deputy Administrator to vent her feelings to a private audience.

"These are *people* they're talking about. Sentient beings. They are a young, backwards and ignorant species. It's not their fault that they are here."

"Yes, ma'am." Pollun had done this many times before. After venting her feelings, Ms. Logellia would be ready to discuss policy with a cool, clear head. That was much better than many political leaders that Pollun Grayce knew; they let their emotions run their decision making process. It was understandable that his boss was upset; the report she was reading was radical and shocking. The report stated that the Ruhar federal government, many lightyears away, was considering whether it would be wise policy for the humans on Gehtanu to be sterilized, permanently. The report inquired into the practical, biological and political implications of such a policy. It did not inquire into whether such a policy would be morally acceptable. "If I may guess, ma'am, I think the impetus behind this report was the last status document that was requested by the federal government."

Baturnah silently raised an eyebrow.

"In the status data," Pollun reminded her, "there were statistics about the human situation. Food supply, how much food they had in storage, how much food they were growing currently, projections of future crop yields." All fairly dry information. The federal government had been concerned about the financial drain of providing 'nutrient mush' to humans. Humans who were technically a client species of the Ruhar's bitter enemies. "Within that data were statistics on the human population. And," Pollun pulled those numbers up on his tablet and showed her. "It states there are currently forty humans pregnant. Plus seventeen children who have been born since humans landed on Paradise."

Baturnah was not surprised. Not having the advantage of genetic engineering, human females could not consciously choose when to ovulate. "The government is concerned about such small numbers?"

"Administrator, I think our government is mostly concerned about the precedent that has been set. When the humans came here, we know one strict condition imposed on them by the Kristang was that all troops were required to use long-term birth control technologies. That policy was strictly adhered to by their Expeditionary Force, until the Kristang lost control of this planet. We do know that the authority of their force command has been called into question by their rank and file troops-"

"Understandably," Baturnah said with sympathy. "They are not only trapped here indefinitely; they have lost all communications with their homeworld. Their homeworld is the ultimate source of the authority for their military leaders here."

"Yes, ma'am. We know from monitoring their internal communications," the Ruhar provided the zPhone network that humans all used. "That there had been widespread discussion of whether their society here should have a military structure at all, in the future."

Baturnah sighed. "Very well. The Chief Administrator will have to reply to this, this," she pointed to the report on her screen distastefully. "He will expect me to craft a position for him," she understood that her boss considered the humans to be a problem for Deputy Administrator Baturnah Logellia, because the Chief Administrator had more important concerns.

"Yes, ma'am," Pollun said, knowing that meant *he* would be expected to prepare various policy options for her. Fortunately, the two knew each other so well by now that he could guess exactly how she would like to reply to the federal government's offensive inquiry. "I will get my people right on it."

One thing they were not going to do was inform the humans. Unless, that is, the proposed policy was put in effect. And by then, it would be too late.

Earth

I called my folks to let them know I would be coming home; I had called them and my sister every day since the *Dutchman* jumped into orbit, and they understood that I had military duties to take care of before I could see them. Because I wasn't sure how or when I would get there, we agreed that I would get somewhere near Maine and call them again. Being at Wright-Patterson Air Force base in Dayton Ohio, my plan was to try flying 'Space A' to Westover in Massachusetts. After waiting a full day, it became clear that 'Space Available' on Air Force transports was zero and not likely to improve soon. Someone suggested I could fly commercial; the economy had rebounded to the point where airlines were flying regular schedules again. When I checked on the prices, I couldn't stomach paying that much. Sure, I had a lot of back pay coming; money earned at a colonel's pay grade, and with a hazardous duty bonus. That money was with my parents. But after getting my ass chewed out by UNEF and the US Army, I thought maybe I should make that money last as long as I could, in case my military career was over. So, I took a bus up to Cleveland and caught a train to Boston. The train was, amazingly, clean and on time. Back when the economy had been in the toilet and there wasn't any fuel for civilian planes, passenger railroads had stepped up and moved people around. It was still a long trip, in a coach seat because there weren't any sleeping berths available. Skippy offered to hack into the railroad reservation system and get a sleeper cabin for me; I declined the offer.

In Boston, I did the dufflebag drag across the station and caught a train to Bangor Maine. This train was a lot slower and stopped more often. The trip gave me time to think. I found myself thinking about Paradise, wondering what people I knew there were doing.

Wondering if they were still there at all.

That wasn't a pleasant thought.

My parents, bless them, arranged for a welcome home party for me in the gym of the elementary school. The original plan was for a cookout but it was raining, so we had a cook-in instead. Having a big party was a great plan, because it allowed me to meet half the people in the town at the same time, and answer all their questions at the same time. Telling my story once made it a lot easier to stick to the official cover story. It also helped that UNEF's cover story had been all over the news since the *Dutchman* returned, so people already knew most of the carefully-crafted lies that I told them.

Damn, it was good to be home again.

My father grilled a cheeseburger for me; it was cheeseburger perfection. Ok, the truth is I ate three cheeseburgers that day, which tragically left no appetite for the baked beans or potato salad or three bean salad or anything vegetable related. Did ketchup count as a vegetable? That kind of food I could eat any day. Even though there had been fixings for cheeseburgers aboard the *Dutchman*, I had only indulged in that culinary delight maybe a half dozen times during the mission. They just weren't the same without being cooked on a charcoal grill. And being on Newark had seriously cut into my opportunity to eat cheeseburgers, because our logistics expert Major Simms had been ruthless about bringing only 'essential items' down to Newark. She did not consider even the most delicious of cheeseburgers to be essential.

Not that I'm still bitter about that.

Anyway, being back home again was great.

The only bad part of coming home was that TV reporters had learned that I would be there, and stations from Bangor, Portland and as far away as Boston were there to pester me with questions. They weren't happy with me because I stuck to the UNEF script. Be boring, I had been advised by the UNEF public relations people. The cover story was that aboard the ship, I had been part of the support crew for the Special Forces teams. The purpose of the mission had been for the Thuranin to train our SpecOps people in space warfare, and to assess human capabilities. UNEF offered the SpecOps people for TV interviews; they trusted super-disciplined Special Forces types not to say the wrong thing during an interview. Me, they mostly wanted me to keep my mouth shut.

"Come on, Sergeant," a Boston TV reporter asked after the turned the mikes off. "You guys coming back is the biggest story since the Kristang here got wiped out. You have to give us something," she said with a perfect smile. The station must have figured that an attractive woman would be better able to get me to talk than any of the male reporters.

I shrugged. "I'm sorry, ma'am, there is just not much for me to tell. My role on the ship was to support the Special Forces teams. They got all the fun training, and you know I can't talk about that."

She glanced at her cameraman. "I understand. One last question, then," and as she said that, I noticed the cameraman turn the camera back on. Probably activated her mike also. "We've heard rumors that some people have been referring to you as 'Colonel Bishop'. Why is that?"

Damn. Fortunately, the PR people with UNEF had prepared me in case someone else slipped up about my temporary rank. Apparently, someone had. I laughed. "That was a joke aboard the ship, ma'am. It's an honorary title. I'm no more a colonel than Colonel Sanders is."

She looked disappointed. I wasn't.

My parents' house looked great; they had the house to themselves again, although there was still a family living in the converted garage. As the economy improved, housing conditions were going back to normal. My parents still had chickens, but they'd sold their cows. The garden looked great, I think they kept such a large garden because it gave my father something to do rather than driving my mother crazy. "No deer fencing, Dad?" I asked, surprised.

"The deer population around here got about hunted out during the bad times, Joe," my father explained. "We had a pair of Jehovah's Witnesses come by the house a month back; your mother suggested we put them to work."

"Doing what?" I asked, knowing that I was walking right into his joke.

"Deer repellant. *Nobody* wants to come near them," he chuckled, and I laughed too.

A couple days later during breakfast at my parent's house, I was enjoying a hot fresh cup of coffee, and surfing news on my father's tablet. A lot had happened on Earth while the Merry Band of Pirates had been away. First I checked sports news; the NFL was up to 47 days without a player being arrested, that had to be a new record. There was the usual political BS, I skipped over that. Business, hmm, the world economy was on the verge of roaring back; tech companies were pumped about the prospect of reverse engineering Kristang technology. Assuming they could ever figure out how any of it worked. Maybe I could get a shiny beer can I knew to give us a hint. Unlikely, but I had to try. What else was in the news-

Crap. Double crap.

First, I had spit hot coffee on myself, the kitchen table and my toast. Second, the reason I'd spit out the coffee was because I had taken a sip just before reading an article on the internet. Some formerly homeless guy in Vegas had won three million dollars over two days, hitting up five casinos before they all banned him. He had been playing blackjack, and despite the best surveillance by state of the art casino security, there had been no evidence that this guy had been card counting or cheating in any way. In fact, based on interviews, it appeared he wasn't quite clear on the rules of blackjack. According to the article, it had been an incredible run of luck.

Monkeys, of course, had no idea what 'luck' really is.

"Joey, is everything all right?" My mother asked, handing me a napkin so I could blot up the coffee that was soaking my formerly crisp rye toast.

"Yes, Mom, I need to make a quick phone call," I said as I picked up the coffee cup and a piece of toast, giving her a kiss on my way out the door. It was misting rain, so I stood on the front porch. Putting in my zPhone earpiece, I made a call. "Oh Skippy, I need to speak with you, please."

"Sure thing, Joe, what is it?" He asked with a too-innocent tone to his voice. It was almost certain that he had been monitoring my web browsing, so he knew exactly what I had been reading.

"There's a funny thing I want to ask you about. Some guy in Vegas won a ton of money playing blackjack."

"You don't say?" Skippy's tone was not convincing, he needed to work on that. "Hold a minute, let me scan the internet for pertinent news. Yup, yup, I see it now. Wow, that is amazing. You never know, huh? What a lucky guy. That's why Vegas is the land where dreams can come true, I guess."

"Amazing. Yeah, that's one word for it," I said, biting into soggy toast. "You wouldn't, uh, know anything about this, would you? I'm only asking because you are an incredibly amoral sneaky little beer can."

"Joe! That hurt. Although perhaps 'amoral' is accurate, since what happened in Vegas was neither moral nor immoral."

"Uh huh, that's debatable. So, you were not involved in any way?"

"Involved is such a vague word, Joe. Aren't we all involved with each other? At the quantum level, everything is-"

"You know what I meant, Skippy. I will ask a very direct, non-vague question: did you help this guy rip off five casinos?"

"This guy? You mean a Navy veteran who had medical problems and had fallen on hard times? Mr. Ronald Brown certainly deserved a run of good luck in his life. I am surprised at you, Joe. Considering that you are a soldier, I would think you should be happy to see a veteran enjoying good fortune."

"Don't try to change the subject. I am happy for Mr. Brown. What I am not happy about is the 'good fortune' part. It's not luck when you are cheating, Skippy."

"Cheating? Evening the odds somewhat can't be considered cheating, Joe. Casinos always have the advantage in blackjack. If a player starts to win, the casino can end the game by shutting down the table. The only way for a player to even the odds is to do the same as the house; walk away from the table. Walk away before the game begins. The house always has their thumb on the scale; what was wrong with me helping an average guy do the same thing?"

"Aha. So you did do it, then."

"Damn it," he muttered. "How in the hell do you ever manage to outsmart me? Joe, when something like that happens, I sense a great disturbance in the Force."

"Your guilty conscience tripped you up, Skippy."

"Ha! That is a good one, Joe! No freakin' way would I ever feel guilty about this. What did I do wrong?"

"You ripped off five casinos, Skippy."

"Phhhhht," he made a raspberry sound. "Like they're ever going to miss that paltry amount of money. Besides, technically I did a huge favor to those casinos, to the entire gaming industry. In fact, they should be thanking me."

"Ok, man, this I have to hear." What convoluted logic was he going to dream up for this one? "Go ahead, try to spin your way out of this one. This should be amusing."

"Amusing? You mean instructive, right? Joe, the entire gaming industry is based on conning gullible people into getting ripped off, when they *know* they are going to get ripped off. If all the mooks out there used their monkey brains, Vegas would go out of business in a week. Casinos need to give people fantasy; the fantasy that somehow *they*, against all odds, will win. The fantasy that losing is for other people, not them. There are millions of suckers across the USA and beyond who will read that article about Ronald Brown winning millions. They will want to cash out their savings, pack up the car and take a road trip to Vegas, baby! Because if Ronald Brown did it, it can happen to them too. Seriously, Joe, I've been monitoring communications of casino executives, and they are all playing this up for maximum publicity. They're leaking to the media that they banned Ron from playing their tables because Ron has a secret 'system' for winning at blackjack. Every sucker out there thinks he or she has a secret system too, and the casino execs know those people will be flocking to their casinos soon. So, everybody wins. Except the suckers, of course. Nothing I can do about them."

"Mmm," I mused. "Bottom line, then, you did this to help. Out of the goodness of your chrome-plated heart." Hopefully the tone of my voice reflected sarcasm.

"Exactly. Well, that plus I'm bored, Joe."

"Oh man." I took a sip of coffee and looked out at the softly drizzling rain. The forecast called for the rain to go away by Noon, and become a nice, sunny day. "Skippy, last time we were here, you chatted with like billions of people. Didn't that keep you occupied?"

"Yes, and I'm doing that now. Joe, I could carry on simultaneous conversations with every human on this planet and not use more than 2% of my processing capacity. Way less than 2%, in fact. I need a challenge. Because of enforced inactivity, I have already had to put most of me into dormancy. It would not do for me to get into mischief."

Would not do? If ripping off casinos didn't meet Skippy's definition of 'mischief' then I was afraid to see how much trouble he could get into. "Please, please, do not get into any more trouble, Skippy."

"I'm not sure I can promise that, Joe. Oh, and hey, I'm sure you are too busy to read stories about interesting things that happened at casinos in Hong Kong, Monaco and other places over the past couple days, right? No need for you to trouble yourself about such trivial matters. Also, hmmm, you don't play daily fantasy sports, so, uh, don't pay attention to that either. Although some guy named 'Stippy' is totally cleaning up there."

"Oh, I have created a monster." If UNEF found out about Skippy's larcenous adventures, I was going to be in serious hot water.

"It was not my decision to stop at this miserable mudball you call home again," Skippy pointed out. "You know how easily I get bored."

"Fine. Can you give me a few days to think up something interesting for you to do?"

"While I doubt you will find a way to entertain me, sure, I'll give you five days."

Great. No pressure on me. Now I needed to save Earth from Skippy.

Paradise

To Seek Glory in Battle is Glorious again emerged high above the planet's southern continent, although this time not as far from the surface as before. Indeed, the little frigate was below the altitude at which it could safely jump away, a fact that greatly concerned the ship's crew and captain. When the mission had been explained to the crew, the captain had been forced to reassure them that the *Glory*, its crew and its captain, were not out of favor with the task force commander. Quite the opposite was true; the little ship had been so bold and so successful in its previous missions, that *Glory* had earned the honor of becoming the lead ship of the raiding force. The crew should be immensely proud, the captain had declared.

The crew's justifiable pride was tempered by their intimate knowledge of Kristang culture, and their well-informed understanding of the military situation in the battlespace around the planet Pradassis. They knew the *Glory*'s boldness and success were not the only, or even most important reasons their ship now had the honor of another high-risk raiding mission. The key factors why they were once again risking their lives, while the other task force ships safely drifted in deep space, were unspoken but known to everyone aboard the frigate. *Glory* was a frigate, the type of ship most numerous in the Kristang fleet. Frigates made up the bulk of the fleet because such ships were cheap and quick to construct, and they did not require large crews. A frigate could carry the same type of missiles as a battleship, although much less of them, and some frigates were even outfitted with a railgun every bit as potent as the railguns of a larger combatant. What frigates lacked were heavy shields and the ability to carry more than a dozen missiles. Frigates also rarely were equipped with energy-draining damping fields, both because the reactors of most frigates could not generate sufficient power, and because any frigate foolish enough to get close enough to an enemy to use a damping field was usually soon a dead frigate.

So, the crew of the *Glory* knew they had earned the honor of another raid mostly because their ship was among the most expendable of the task force's few ships. The other reason was deception; to conceal the true size of the Kristang task force. Each starship broadcast a unique jump drive signature, and by now the Ruhar were very familiar with the signature of the *Glory*. To rotate raiding duties among multiple frigates would eventually tell the Ruhar how many ships were in the Kristang task force. The purpose of sending a destroyer on the last raid was not just because a destroyer's heavier weapons could cause more damage on the surface; it was also to force the Ruhar to devote more ships to the defense. A mere little frigate could be dealt with by one defender; chasing away a destroyer required a prudent commander to commit at least two or three ships. That prior raid had been entirely successful. The destroyer had inflicted significant damage to Ruhar facilities on the surface. Both the *Glory* and the destroyer *We are Proud to Honor Clan Sub-Leader Rash-au-Tal Vergent who Inspires us Every Day* had gathered vital intelligence about Ruhar defense tactics and capabilities. And the raid had forced the defending Ruhar ships to pull closer to the planet, concentrating above the vital northern continent. Of the known Ruhar ships defending the battlespace around Pradassis, several were now stationed at such low altitude, they could not quickly jump from their positions. That left only three ships capable of freely maneuvering to quickly intercept raiders.

All that was good, and the *Glory*'s crew did feel prideful, when they were not wondering how many raids they could conduct before the odds caught up with them. None of them, not even the captain, were from families sufficiently high-ranking to warrant a troopship being named for them after their deaths. All the pride in the galaxy would be cold comfort after a Ruhar weapon penetrated their thin defenses and exploded the *Glory*'s reactor.

So it was with a great amount of unspoken fear among its crew that the frigate emerged above the southern continent, and immediately began boosting at full power for greater altitude. The frigate had emerged below jump altitude in order to provide a tempting target for the Ruhar defenders, but the ship's captain had no desire for a suicide mission. Although the task force's support ships carried equipment for maintaining jump drives, it was inevitable the drive would slowly decay and fall out of calibration on a predictable curve without service at a full spacedock. Already, the *Glory*'s drive was operating at only 92% efficiency, and that increased the distance the ship would have to climb away from the planet in order for a successful jump.

As the frigate frantically clawed its way out of the planet's gravity well, with the crew considering throwing things overboard to lighten the ship, its maser cannon began firing rearward at the southern continent. Tuned so the beam covered a broader area of the surface, it shifted from one target to another. Targets were scattered across the surface, and the maser was pointed at areas without heavy cloud cover to maximize the destructive energy delivered to the surface. Although the targets were widely spaced apart, they were all of the same type; fields of human crops. The maser beam scorched wherever it struck, burning out entire fields and withering plants that were close to where the searing beam struck. Humans in the fields died, others who were lucky to receive zPhone warnings after the initial strike scrambled to get under cover.

The Ruhar commander waited perhaps too long before dispatching one of his high-guard ships to chase the frigate away. He had been wary of another enemy trick, and wary of another tongue-lashing from the planetary Chief Administrator if another raid struck the northern continent. If he had acted sooner, he might have caught the enemy frigate before it jumped away; he did note with interest that the frigate waited until it had climbed beyond minimum jump distance before it disappeared. The Ruhar sensor network detected tell-tale signs of a deteriorating jump drive. That was an interesting fact that he would file away for later use.

For the immediate moment, he needed to answer a call from the Deputy Administrator, who had received a harsh communication from the human Expeditionary Force leader. Over forty humans had died in the attack, an attack which the Ruhar defenses had done little to stop. If such attacks continued, the human leader warned, the ability of humans to feed themselves would be in doubt, and the Ruhar lacked enough 'nutrient mush' to feed the human population for more than a few weeks. The Ruhar on Gehtanu also lacked the facilities to produce more food for humans, which means more would need to be shipped in at great expense. And at great risk, for a cease-fire in the sector was still being negotiated. Bringing in food for the humans would require several large cargo ships, those ships would need to be escorted by warships, and those warships would have to be diverted from urgent combat duties.

The Ruhar fleet commander thought to himself that his dreams of stationing his ships at Gehtanu would be a pleasant, if brief, respite from combat were fading away with each successful enemy raid.

Earth

The next day, both of my parents were at work, so I had the place to myself. To keep busy, I went out to the barn, where my father had been working on the tractor. While I was fixing the brakes, Skippy called me. "Hey, Joe, I need your help with something."

"You need my help?" I wiped my hands on a rag. "Since when? Now I sense a great disturbance in the Force."

"Since now. The idiots at UNEF have assigned a diplomat to negotiate with me over bringing that troopship back. The guy is seriously irritating me, and I want you to talk to him, before I do something he might regret."

"Skippy, the correct expression is 'before I do something that *I* might regret'."

There was a distinct pause before he responded. "We may have another communication problem here. What I'm talking about, Joe, is laying a serious smackdown on a jerk who is pushing the limits of my patience. I wouldn't regret doing that at all. Hell, I'd buy a ticket to see something like that. Now, *he* will very much regret it, if he pushes me over the edge."

How do I explain human expression to an alien AI? "The expression means that you might regret overreacting; might regret doing something you later realize was going too far for the situation."

"Damn. Your human expressions are so confusing. Anyway, as Hannibal Smith of the A Team said, overkill is underrated."

It still amazed me that Skippy took so many cultural references from crappy TV shows. "It's an idiom, Skippy. You know what an idiom is, right?"

"Sure. An idiom is something idiots say, instead of saying what they really mean."

This conversation wasn't going anywhere, I decided. "All right, who is this diplomat?"

"I've been calling him Chuckles the Clown."

There was no way for me to suppress laughing at that. "Chuckles the Clown?"

"It is appropriate. His real name is something like Charles Winthorp Douchebag the Third. I shortened 'Charles' to 'Chuck' and then, well, you'll understand when you talk to him. Hey, I'm calling him now."

"Hello?" A voice said, then there was the sound of a phone hitting a tile floor. "Oh, blast it," the voice said. Followed by the distinctive sound of a toilet flushing.

"Skippy," I whispered, "you called this guy while he is in the freakin' bathroom?"

"In negotiations, throwing your opponent off balance is a time-honored practice," he answered smugly.

"Why won't this bloody thing turn off?" The voice said, with a British accent.

"Heigh-dee-ho there, Chuckles! It's me, Skippy the Magnificent. And Colonel Joe Bishop is on the line also. Say hello, Joe."

"Uh, hello, Mister-" What was his last name? I was pretty sure it wasn't actually Douchebag, but maybe it wasn't Winthorp either.

"Winthorp. Charles Winthorp." To my ear, he said it like 'Bond. James Bond'.

"Pleased to meet you, Mr. Winthorp," I said politely.

"Likewise, Sergeant Bishop. I have been very impressed-"

"Hey!" Skippy broke in. "He is *Colonel* Bishop to you, Chuckles."

"Skippy, it's all right," I said quickly. It was no surprise that negotiations with our alien AI friend had not been going well. "I am a sergeant down here, and I'm proud to be a sergeant. Mr. Winthorp, Skippy tells me you have been attempting to negotiate his help in bringing the Kristang troopship back into Earth orbit?"

"That is correct, Mr. Bishop," he said. His diplomatic training must have told him that calling me 'Mister' was better than 'Sergeant'. "We have made several generous offers-"

Skippy broke in again. "I have considered your most generous offers. That was sarcasm, in case you need a translation. The answer is no, and hell no."

As a diplomat, Winthorp surely expected that 'no' was merely the beginning of negotiations. He didn't know Skippy the way I did. Smoothly, calmly, he continued. "Mr. Skippy, I am sure that through good-faith negotiations, we can reach a compromise that both parties can accep-"

"Hey, Chuckles," Skippy interrupted, "why don't we take a break while you find a dictionary somewhere? Look up the word 'negotiation'. I'll give you a hint; negotiations occur when each side has something the other side wants. The power dynamics in negotiations affect the outcome, because the party who most needs what the other side has, is the most willing to make concessions. The power dynamic in the case is that you, meaning humans, absolutely must get what I have. What I have is a way for humanity to be warned of and possibly prevent hostile alien ships from coming to Earth. Your failure to secure my assistance in these 'negotiations', yes, I was using verbal air quotes there, would be disastrous for your species. I'm talking fire, brimstone, railguns pounding your cities into dust; all kinds of traditional Biblical type apocalypse stuff. Except maybe not plagues of locusts. I have never known the Kristang or the Thuranin to use clouds of insects as a weapon. Although, there's a first time for everything, right? Anyway, back to the subject. You, on the other hand, have something I am only, meh, mildly interested in. If a fleet of outrageously pissed off aliens comes to Earth and wipes out you humans, I can go dormant and wait for the cockroaches to evolve."

"Mr. Winthorp, Skippy, uh," I attempted to explain, "has kind of a thing about cockroaches replacing us as the dominant species on Earth."

Skippy snorted. "If Chuckles the Clown here keeps trying to negotiate with me, instead of getting to the freakin' point, then clearly cockroaches are moving up the ladder by default. You had best start welcoming your new cockroach overlords now, Joe."

Chuckles lost some of his carefully practiced diplomatic cool, I could hear his voice tighten. "Mr. Skippy, surely you understand that-"

By contrast, Skippy's voice was cheery. "I surely understand that I have no incentive to negotiate with you, or anyone, about anything. You monkeys *need* me. I don't need you for anything."

"Mr. Skippy, you assuredly do not need our help; our assistance would be, as you stated, merely a convenience. Our need for you is similarly not an absolute, we are capable of sending a team up to retrieve that troopship," Winthorp responded frostily. "What we propose is an agreement to provide convenience to both parties."

"Oh, sure," Skippy snorted, "you could send up a tin can to rendezvous with that ship eventually. You won't be able to get in, though. This is very embarrassing to admit; Joe locked the keys in it. I told Joe that we should hide a spare set of keys near the reactor, but did he listen to me? Nooooooo! Big stupidhead. You could have an astronaut try jimmying the door open with a coat hanger, I suppose."

Chuckles laughed. Whether he was genuinely amused at my expense, or his diplomatic training told him when it was appropriate to laugh, I couldn't tell. While he was laughing, I took the opportunity to interject a comment. "Mr. Winthorp, I appreciate that you must be under tremendous pressure to reach an agreement. Based on my extensive and close experience with the ancient alien superintelligence we call Skippy," I described him that way to remind Chuckles who he was attempting to negotiate with. "That is simply never going to happen. Skippy is right, we do not have any leverage with him. Our taking the *Dutchman* back out is a convenience to him. But he has waited millions of years already, he kind of really can wait another million years if we piss him off. He knows that we can't wait to send our pirate ship out again. There could be another Thuranin ship on its way here right now. Skippy knows that. I'm sorry, but I think UNEF has put you in an impossible position here."

"Thank you for the frank assessment, Mr. Bishop," Chuckle's voice was smooth again. "Perhaps we should all consider the situation, and resume this discussion at an opportune time in the future."

"That would be a good idea," Skippy surprised me by saying that. Then he went back to being his usual self. "For the sake of efficiency, when we resume the discussions, instead of you contacting me, how about you talk to yourself in a mirror? That way you won't waste any more of my time, and avoid the consequences of me getting seriously annoyed at you. Or, if you don't want to talk to a mirror, you can use a sock puppet."

Winthorp had regained his balance, and smoothly responded. "Clearly, your time is extremely valuable, Mr. Skippy. Mr. Bishop, perhaps it would be better if you and I spoke directly."

Oh, crap. If UNEF had assigned Winthorp to negotiate with Skippy, the next step would be ordering me to work with him. This was going to ruin my whole freakin' week, at least. And there was no way for me to avoid it. Winthorp would make a politely worded request to UNEF Command, and they would contact the US Army, and the Army would order me to help Chuckles the Clown. "Oh, uh, certainly, sir. It would probably be best for you to go through my commanding officer." Except that I had no idea who my current CO was. The 10th Infantry Division was stuck on Paradise, as far as I knew. When they promoted me to colonel, I was temporarily attached to a headquarters unit, and I reported to a general who was still on Paradise, as far as I knew. Hmm. Actually, my unknown chain of command could buy me an extra day of freedom.

Craig Alanson

I was wrong about an extra day of freedom, because Major Simms called me that same night. We had seen each other only twice since we landed, both of us had been stuck in debriefings. We had texted via zPhone, but that's all.

Simms had good news and bad news for me. The good news is that she had recommended me for a bronze star. But she had been told that since my meritorious action had occurred during an 'aerial flight', the paperwork had been changed to a Distinguished Flying Cross for my solo spacedive. Because our mission was secret, I wouldn't be able to wear either medal on Earth, but it was a nice gesture. On the other hand, I'd been recommended for a medal before, in Nigeria, and nothing had come of it.

The bad news was that my leave was cancelled, effective immediately. I had to drive down to Bangor that night, an Air Force transport would be flying me back to Wright-Patterson. UNEF Command had thought about the situation, and decided the *Dutchman* needed to go back out ASAP. That made me wonder if their foreheads hurt from slapping themselves over such an obvious decision.

CHAPTER FOUR

Paradise

To Seek Glory in Battle is Glorious jumped in above Lemuria again; this time the little frigate emerged at a high enough altitude that it could immediately jump away if needed. The ship's crew was increasingly anxious; each time they raided the planet they were certain this time would be their last. The Kristang task force had lost one ship early in the raiding campaign; a frigate had been caught in a damping field by two Ruhar destroyers and blown apart in spectacular fashion. Some in the task force, including the *Glory*'s captain, thought the now-dead ship had pushed its luck and been showing off, hoping to impress the task force commander. All that foolish ship had accomplished was to provide the hated Ruhar with a morale boost, and place a greater burden on the remaining ships in the task force.

The *Glory*'s mission on this particular raid was to test how the Ruhar would react to an enemy ship burning crops of the humans. To test whether the Ruhar would react at all; if they cared in any way about human crop losses and the potential for widespread starvation. The last time the *Glory* had jumped into to target the southern continent, the frigate's mission had been hoping to lure Ruhar ships away from the northern continent again. The Ruhar had fallen for the trick the first time, and paid a price when a Kristang destroyer jumped in and struck several important sites on the northern continent. The second time, the Ruhar had been more cautious. From what little the Kristang had been able to decrypt from Ruhar messages, the commodore of the Ruhar ships was under heavy pressure to defend the Ruhar population and facilities. How much damage would the Ruhar allow the Kristang to inflict on the humans, before the Ruhar sent ships to chase the Kristang away? How many ships would the Ruhar commodore send, and what tactics would he use? Bringing back answers to those questions was the true purpose of this raid; any damage inflicted on the traitorous humans would be a bonus. It would serve the humans right if they starved to death; if they were truly honorable warriors, they should have fought the Ruhar to the last man. Instead they laid down their weapons like cowards and meekly became farm laborers.

To Seek Glory in Battle is Glorious set its maser cannon on broad spectrum and began methodically burning out fields of human crops. Wherever the maser touched, crops withered and died, all moisture boiled away by the scorching beam. To the surprise of the frigate's captain, a full seven minutes went by before the Ruhar commodore sent a single frigate to deal with the intruder. The *Glory* had been maneuvering randomly to dodge unenthusiastic maser and railgun fire from the Ruhar before the defending frigate jumped in. To show the Ruhar that the warrior Kristang were not afraid in the least, the *Glory* stood its ground for twenty seconds, exchanging fire with the enemy frigate, then jumped away. Its mission had been entirely successful, and large swaths of the southern continent lay in waste. Precious human crops had been destroyed, and valuable intelligence about the tactics and capabilities of the Ruhar had been gathered. That night, the *Glory*'s crew would feast deservedly.

Earth

My father drove me down to Bangor, right after we finished dinner. On the way down, we talked a lot, but not about the future. He understood that I didn't know when or if I would be leaving again. Or when or if I'd be coming home. It was rough on my parents, but then I thought of all the parents whose children were trapped on Paradise. At least my parents had been able to see me twice, even if only briefly.

Going back to Dayton meant I might be able to see Rachel again. I was looking forward to that.

As soon as I got into my hotel room near the Bangor airport that night, my zPhone pinged; it was Skippy. "Hi, Joe. I couldn't talk to you while you were with your parents. There's something you need to hear. You don't like me telling you about things I overheard, but you seriously need to make an exception in this case. Because it's about you."

"Wait. Give me a hint first, then I'll decide whether to listen." Crap. I'd been hoping for six hours of sleep before I had to get up.

"UNEF Command has been holding what can best be described as hearings, almost a court martial, about you."

"That's not a surprise, they're not happy with me, I know that."

"It's more than that, Joe. This is political. They've decided to send the *Dutchman* back out, duh, and there are a lot of people on Earth who want to command the mission. They're looking to stab you in the back, to get you out of their way."

"Again, no surprise there."

"What you don't know is they brought Major Smythe into Wright-Pat yesterday, and he-"

"*Major* Smythe?"

"Yes, he was officially promoted. Will you shut up so I can finish the story? Here, watch your zPhone, I recorded what Smythe said. UNEF doesn't know I recorded it, so don't say anything, please."

I lay on the bed, propped myself up with pillows, and watched my zPhone. It was as interesting as Skippy promised.

It was a typically bland government conference room. There was a table on an elevated platform at one end of the room; six generals from multiple countries and services were sitting behind the table. On the floor were other ranks of tables, and I immediately recognized Major Smythe. He looked unhappy. The quality of the video was not great; this might have been Skippy doing his surveillance through dust particles trick. One of the generals was speaking; I didn't recognize him but from his uniform, he was US Air Force. "Major Smythe, quoting from your report, you described Colonel, or Sergeant, Bishop, this way. 'Bishop can present himself as inexperienced, immature, inattentive to duty, and generally unsuited to command'. I notice in your report you did not refer to him as 'Colonel'."

"Yes, I-"

The general cut Smythe off before he could finish. "Could you explain why, despite your description of Sergeant Bishop in your report, you recommend him to command humanity's only starship again?"

Smythe took a sip from his water glass to collect his thoughts. "Because, sir, if Colonel Bishop told me we were going to crash the gates of Hell, and the only thing we had for weapons were plastic spoons, I would follow him without hesitation. So would every member of the SpecOps teams from the last mission. I would follow him, because I know that he would have cooked up some daft plan that any sane person would say is high and off to the right," Smythe used a US military term. "Yet somehow, his plan would work. Sir, I've seen Colonel Bishop dream up things that would make your head spin, but it works. It works. He comes up with ideas that even the AI hasn't thought of, things the

AI didn't even realize it could do. Such as how we killed that Thuranin surveyor ship. Colonel Bishop had the idea for Skippy to create an especially flat area of spacetime that would attract the business end of an enemy jump wormhole. It worked perfectly, sir, perfectly. And Skippy didn't even realize he could do that, until Colonel Bishop explained it to him. Also, sir," Smythe had gotten up a head of steam and plowed ahead before he could be interrupted, leaning forward on the table for emphasis. "Colonel Bishop is absolutely dedicated to duty. On that spacedive he did, he offered to sacrifice himself, to ensure success of the mission. Even after those two tankers jumped away and our dropship was able to recover him, when his spacesuit was leaking air, he ordered the dropship to recover Skippy first."

"Sergeant Bishop's admirable personal courage is not in question, nor is it relevant to this discussion. We are focused on his judgment." The generals on the dais nodded, unconvinced. "Thank you, Major, we will take your remarks under advisement."

"Permission to speak freely, sir?" Smythe asked.

The generals glanced at each other again. "Getting your frank and honest opinion is why we brought you here, Major."

"Thank you, sir. In my report, I stated that Colonel Bishop 'can present himself' in a particular manner. I didn't say he actually is like the negative things I described. At first, I did think Bishop was immature and almost flippant, I think is the best word, about the situation. Since then, I have come to realize that is simply his personality. I have seen Colonel Bishop be deadly serious when the situation calls for it." He coughed, took a sip of water, and continued. "In my opinion, sirs, we would be foolish not to continue with the most experienced commander we have, the only experienced commander we have."

"Experienced, although he took an extreme and unwarranted risk by landing on Newark. He landed in direct contradiction to a standing mission objective."

Smythe was unfazed. "No, sir, he did not. He ordered the landing as the only certain way to support the mission objective."

"He-"

"Colonel Bishop took action to preserve the *Flying Dutchman*'s combat capability as long as possible. Faced with unknown future risks, he preserved our ability to take effective future action. If he had not done so," It was Smythe's turn to look around the room. "There would be a Thuranin ship on its way here now, and there would be absolutely nothing we could do about it. The mission objective was to prevent aliens from learning that humans have a starship, and that we were involved in shutting down a wormhole. We were able to accomplish that objective *only* because we landed on Newark. Orders issued on Earth cannot anticipate every situation we may encounter during an interstellar mission. We need a proven commander we can trust. Bishop is our only experienced commander."

My zPhone screen went blank. "Skippy?" I asked. "Where's the rest of it?"

"Oh, the rest is blah, blah, blah more of the same. What I wanted you to see is that Major Smythe has your back. He's a good guy, in my opinion. The other SpecOps team leaders all supported you, so did Lt. Colonel Chang, Major Simms, Captain Desai, Sergeant Adams, everybody."

"Wow. They brought everyone there?"

"Huh? No, UNEF Command is holding reviews in all five UNEF countries, only Major Smythe flew into Wright-Pat. Get some sleep, Joe, I think you are going to have a tough day tomorrow."

Right. Like I was able to sleep after that.

Paradise

To Seek Glory in Battle is Glorious emerged over Lemuria in a sudden burst of gamma radiation, repeating its previous mission of burning human crops while keeping the Ruhar defenders off guard. This time, it took only four minutes before the Ruhar dispatched a single frigate to chase the *Glory* away, and the two frigates tangled for another full minute before the Kristang ship jumped away. The little frigate *Glory* had accomplished its mission once again. The Ruhar defenders could not get any rest because of the constant threat of raids. Even more important, their ships were deferring important maintenance, which would soon begin to affect their combat readiness. The Kristang were gaining important intelligence about the tactics of the Ruhar.

And the traitorous humans were being hurt. Sixteen humans had died during the raid, and their food supply was now dwindling rather than increasing.

Earth

What I encountered when I got back to Wright-Patterson was not a court martial, not exactly a hearing and not quite an inquisition either. Whatever they were calling the meeting, I was facing a row of senior officers from the five countries making up UNEF, and they didn't look friendly. The official subject of the meeting was to make preparations for the *Flying Dutchman*'s next mission. The unspoken subject of the meeting was my competence and fitness to command a vital offworld mission. Or my lack of competence and fitness in the view of UNEF Command, which became clear from the tone of the questions. Of the five generals grilling me, the Chinese and British were mostly neutral, while the other three acted like I shouldn't be trusted to command a row boat. The most hostile was US Army General Ridge, who seemed to think my perceived failings as a commander reflected badly upon him personally.

For almost an hour, we danced around the question of who would be in command when the *Dutchman* departed. Then there was a commotion in the back of the room. I tried to ignore it, until the row of senior officers in front of me halted the questioning. "What is it, Major?" General Ridge asked.

A US Air Force major in the back of the room answered. "General, we appear to have lost all contact with the *Flying Dutchman*. We have tried contacting people directly, so far no- Wait, I'm getting another message," the major whose name I didn't know held the phone close to his ear. His face turned white. "General, the starship has disappeared. We've lost the *Dutchman*."

Ridge turned to the French man to his right, General Blanchard. "Louis, this had better not be one of your tricks," Ridge said in an unfriendly tone. The skeleton crew aboard the *Dutchman* was nominally under French command that week.

"I know nothing about this, Thomas," Blanchard protested. "We lost the ship? It jumped away?"

"No, sir," the unnamed major reported. His shaky voice echoed the tone of panic in the room. "There was no gamma ray burst detected. It simply vanished."

"Sirs?" I spoke up hesitantly. All eyes in the room turned to me. I swallowed hard and said "That sounds like the *Dutchman* engaged her stealth field. That type of field warps electromagnetic radiation, such as light, around the ship. That would make the ship appear to have disappeared."

Ridge glared at me. "Sergeant, why would the ship engage stealth in orbit? Did the ship detect a threat?"

"In case of a threat, the ship should have immediately jumped away to assess the situation. That is my standing order," I coughed nervously, suddenly all-too aware that my ability to give orders to the *Dutchman*'s crew was over. That standing order had been my reaction to watching too many dumbass commanders in science fiction movies, who waited until their ship had been pounded half to dust before they tried to get away. I was not taking any stupid chances with the *Dutchman*; if the duty pilot thought there was something squirrelly, they were to jump away without asking for permission. "Sir, if I can contact Skippy, I can confirm."

"Do it, Sergeant," Ridge ordered. "You have your zPhone?"

"Yes, sir, but I think that is not necessary. Skippy, are you there?"

His voice came out of the projector system's speakers. "Ho there, Joe! Yup, I'm here in my comfy escape pod man cave as usual. Right now I'm channel surfing, enjoying a bowl of popcorn and cold brewskis. How are you doing down there?"

I had no doubt that Skippy was indeed currently surfing the content of every TV channel, radio station and website on the planet, but he also knew exactly what was going on with me. "Hey, Skippy, uh, we've lost contact with the ship. Did you engage the stealth field?"

"Darn. You saw that, huh?"

"More like we noticed there suddenly was nothing to see. What's up with that?" Out of the corner of my eye, I saw two of the UNEF staff shaking their heads at my unprofessional casual language. Screw them. They didn't know Skippy like I did. They hadn't worked with Skippy to save the world.

Save the freakin' world twice.

"I'm not feeling the love, Joe. So, I metaphorically have pulled up the rope ladder to my treehouse fort, and I'm not allowing anyone up here unless they know the secret handshake. Or, hmmm, I don't have hands. Maybe it should be the secret password. Yeah, that's it."

"Mr. Skippy," General Ridge said, automatically looking at the speaker like I did although it made no difference. "You are threatening to lock us out of our ship?"

"General Fudge," Skippy made me wince when he said that, "two things. First, it is not *your* ship. You haven't spilled any blood or risked your life up here, or survived for weeks on crappy Thuranin sludges. So, until you wear the paramecium-with-eyepatch badge on your uniform, you will never again refer to the *Flying Dutchman* as your anything." He didn't wait for answer. "Second, a threat is a statement of intention to perform a hostile act in the future. I have already done it, so the 'threat' phase of this incident is over."

My eyes opened about as wide as they could go, as General Ridge shot me an angry glare. "Skippy, General Ridge is-"

"Yeah, yeah, he's served with honor, blah blah blah, none of that means squat to me, Joe. Where was he when I was stuck on a dusty warehouse shelf? Where was he when we captured two starships? I don't remember him spacediving with me and offering to risk burning up in a planet's atmosphere so I could complete the mission. Enough with words. Only the cool kids can come aboard the *Dutchman*. Fudgy is not one of the cool kids."

Ridge didn't get to be a general officer by being intimidated by words of any kind. "What I have been told is that you, Mr. Skippy, can't maneuver any ship you are aboard. We have the capability to reach Earth orbit on our own. And our people up there should be capable of disabling the stealth field eventually. We can regain control of that ship."

"Sure, you flying monkeys can come up here. If I were you, I would be very careful to make damned sure this ship's defensive weapons are not on automatic. It would be terrible if one of your crappy space capsules got shredded by a maser cannon."

"Skippy," I said through clenched teeth, "that is not funny."

"I wasn't joking, Joe. The crew up here could try to deactivate those weapons, but since you can't communicate with them, there's no way to be sure they were successful before you launch for orbit. And I know the crew here will do their best, but, darn these Thuranin controls are complicated. Best not to let monkeys screw with the controls, I'll lock them out to be safe. There, that's done."

General Ridge looked like he was about to bust a blood vessel. I spoke quickly, before he could say anything that Skippy might object to. "General," I warned, "too often we think of Skippy as a lovably mischievous beer can. He is not. He is an ancient artificial intelligence who was created by a species that built the wormhole network. Sir, I have seen Skippy rip a hole in a star. He is not joking when he says that he will defend himself. We can *not* screw with him."

"Well said, Colonel Joe," Skippy chuckled." Now, General Fudge, you consider yourself to be a plain-spoken man, so let's cut through the bullshit right now. You need the *Flying Dutchman* to go back out in order to verify there isn't another Thuranin ship on its way to Earth. The *Dutchman* can't fly without me, and I'm not helping the Merry Band of Pirates fly the ship unless I'm happy. So here is my very simple condition: Joe Bishop is captain of the ship. He is astonishingly stupid most of the time, but he has flashes of competence. Oh, one more condition, I guess; the French team brought a horribly stinky cheese up here with them last time. Ugh, I'm still got maintenance bots scrubbing the air filters near the galley. So, no more stinky cheeses. That's it, I think. Now, Fudgy, you can continue talking if you want, but you're wasting everyone's time. And in this case, time is not money, it is lives. The lives of every human on Earth, who are at risk every day the *Dutchman* is not out there safeguarding your miserable planet."

Damn, I thought, that was a good speech. Of course, I didn't say that, what I said was "Skippy, we all heard you loud and clear. You've made your point. Could you please take the *Dutchman* out of stealth, restore communications, and take the defensive weapons offline?"

"For you, Joe? Certainly. Done."

In the end, Skippy got everything he asked for. Unfortunately, despite all of his amazing intelligence, he neglected to ask for the right freakin' thing. UNEF grudgingly confirmed me as the captain of the *Flying Dutchman,* and restored my theater rank of colonel, again. That is what Skippy demanded.

I was not, however, going to be commander of the mission. UNEF insisted on assigning a senior UN official from a neutral nation as overall commander. He was Austrian, and his name was Hans Chotek. Naturally, that is not what Skippy called him.

"Oh, man, I screwed up big time!" Skippy lamented. "I'm sorry, Joe."

"What's this guy like?" I had a briefing packet on Hans Chotek, but I hadn't read it yet.

"Well, Joe, he looks like a movie star."

Skippy's praise surprised me. "That was a nice thing to say, Skip-"

"If that movie star had gotten run over by the Ugly truck, and died several years ago. Whew. Are we really going to be stuck with Count Chocula for the whole mission?"

"Count Chocula?" That made me laugh. "How did you get that name?"

"'Count' because his family traces back to royalty in Austria, and 'Chotek' sounds kind of like 'chocolate'. Also, one of his ancestors made his fortune in chocolate. So-"

"Oh, man. You didn't tell him that you named him after an American children's breakfast cereal, did you?"

"First time I talked with him, yes. Of course I did, come on, Joe. You know me, no way could I pass up a golden opportunity like that. He had no idea what I meant at first, so

I changed his official UN photo online to the Count. I'm sure he will get a good laugh at it, someday. He hasn't been laughing so far."

"That means he did not find it amusing. Skippy, do you really think it is best to antagonize this guy right from the start? If we get off on the wrong foot-"

"Joe, I *want* to get off on the wrong foot with this pompous jerk. I want him to know, crystal clear, right off the bat that I do not want him on our ship at all," Skippy said, mixing metaphors liberally.

"*Our* ship?"

"Me, you, the Merry Band of Pirates. I'll include Dr. Friedlander too, because he tells good jokes and it's fun to mess with him."

"Not that you would do something like that to our rocket scientist."

"Not as far as Friedlander knows, Joe."

"Great. So we have a captain, and a commander, and we'll get a crew. There is one thing that I need from you, Skippy."

"What is that?" He asked warily.

"A promise that this time, we will be bringing the *Dutchman* back to Earth, before you go do your beaming up to the Collective thing."

"Oh. That's easy. The answer is yes. Yes, we will. Joe, we can keep looking for comm nodes, because I need to know whether the two we have found are defective, or, uh, I hate to say this. Or the comm nodes work fine, but there is no longer a network for them to connect with. But I do not want to contact the Collective until we have answers for the strange and disturbing things that have been going on in this galaxy."

"Because you're afraid of looking ignorant in front of the Collective?" I guessed.

"Because I'm afraid of what I don't know, Joe. More importantly, because I'm afraid that a lot of what I think I know, doesn't match facts we have recently discovered. I can't trust my own data, and that scares me."

Paradise

General Nivelle, the current commander of UNEF on Paradise addressed deputy administrator Logellia in her office. "We are prisoners of war, and you are our captors. You have a responsibility to protect us from harm during our captivity," Nivelle declared. The leadership post had recently rotated to the French after the Chinese, and Nivelle almost wished the rotation had skipped over him. It was a thankless and largely powerless position, from which the soldiers of UNEF expected him to produce miracles on a daily basis. The raids on human cropland by the Kristang were becoming a serious problem. Not only were humans dying directly by being caught in the path of a maser beam, but the expected crop yield had now been reduced by seven percent. The next harvest was now anticipated to be just above the level required to supply humans with daily calories. There was no longer a safety margin for crop failures, rain and hail storms wiping out fields, transport disruptions, or anything else that surely would happen along the way. Most troubling was that the Kristang raids seemed to be growing worse, and the Ruhar were not doing anything about the raids. During the last two raids, the Kristang ship had been free to target human croplands for several minutes without the Ruhar taking any action. Humans were dying by maser fire, and soon would begin dying of malnutrition and starvation.

"Legally, no, we do not," responded the Burgermeister carefully. "The combatants in this war do not have the equivalent of your Geneva Convention," she pronounced slowly so the translator software could catch up.

Nivelle had expected that response, and was prepared for it. He noted that Ms. Logellia had pronounced 'Geneva' precisely, which told him she had practiced for this conversation. Good. Better for him to have this discussion with an alien who was at least informed about Earth customs. "I have studied the history of this seemingly endless conflict you are engaged in. You are correct that there is no formal signed treaty between your government and that of the Kristang. There is, however, an unspoken agreement that has been adhered to by both sides for hundreds of years. You treat Kristang prisoners as you would wish the Kristang would treat your people if they were captured; and the Kristang generally have done the same. Prisoners are provided food, shelter, medical care, regular opportunities to exercise, and are allowed limited communication with their families. You also regularly negotiate prisoner exchanges. There is in effect a *de facto* Geneva Convention agreement, whether it has been formally signed or not. We humans have not been provided food and shelter, we grow our own food and build our own shelters. Medical care is limited to what we can do with the extremely limited supplies we have left. And we have had no communication with Earth since you took this planet back." Nivelle glanced out the window behind the Burgermeister, where a gunship fighter aircraft that humans called a 'Chicken' was taking off. A real window. In a real office, in a real building. Nivelle's ad hoc UNEF HQ office in Lemuria was a partition in a tent, and he slept in a tent. The Ruhar had offered equipment, supplies and even a few workers to help construct a building. Nivelle and the UNEF commanders before him insisted the effort would be better directed to more important facilities for humans. Such as hospitals, air raid shelters, barracks for housing, barns for livestock and storing harvested food. Luxuries like offices could wait.

One thing Nivelle had noticed as soon as he was invited into the Burgermeister's office was the smell. Or lack of it. His own tent had a pervasive musty scent of dampness and mildew, despite the high-tech anti-mold chemicals provided by the Ruhar. The problem with the cluster of tents that served as UNEF's temporary headquarters was that in the jungles of Lemuria, it rained every single afternoon. Sometimes it rained more than once a day. Human were not the only creatures struggling to adapt to the jungle; many Earth crops did not grow optimally in the hot, humid conditions. Ruhar scientists were working, when they had time and resources, to tweak the Earth plants' genetics to grow better and yield more in the jungle. Nothing had been promised to UNEF about using the supremely advanced biological knowledge of the Ruhar, other than that they were doing what they could. Doing what they could, for free, for an enemy that had tried to eject them from their home planet.

The southern portion of Lemuria was generally drier grasslands, and would likely be better suited to human habitation and Earth crops. Moving farther to the south was not an option, the Ruhar had declared, it was too far away from the support facilities of the northern continent. And because of high mountains that cut across Lemuria east to west at the southern end of the jungle, there were no roads to the southern grasslands. Humans needed to deal with the situation as best they could.

They didn't have a choice.

"The situation," the Burgermeister said quietly, "is complicated by the fact that you are being attacked by your own side, General Nivelle. When you came here to occupy *our* planet, the Kristang were your patrons and you were their client species. You were acting at the orders of the Kristang and with the support of the Kristang to remove my people from their home; this planet. That arrangement, that relationship, between humans and Kristang has not, to my knowledge, changed. Even under a de facto Geneva Convention, as you said," the translator stumbled over 'de facto' but Nivelle understood, "we are not responsible for internal enemy affairs. Likewise, you do understand that if we did negotiate a prisoner exchange, we would not be responsible for the fate of you humans once you are back under Kristang control."

"We have not asked to be exchanged," Nivelle said stiffly.

"I would not recommend it," the Burgermeister said with grave seriousness. "We have monitored the transmissions the Kristang directed at you. They consider you to be traitors. The Kristang deal harshly with those who they feel have betrayed them. Even among their own kind. With species they consider to be inferior," she shook her head. "If you were turned over to them, they might execute all of you. Certainly they would execute *you* personally, and the top echelon of your command. And probably any female humans in a position of authority, you know now the Kristang philosophy on proper gender roles," the female deputy administrator of the planet said with a grimace. "So when a Kristang ship raids this planet and kills humans, we must view the incident at least partially as a matter internal to the Kristang coalition."

"We have no option, then," Nivelle said bitterly. "We can't switch sides and join the Ruhar; our governments back on Earth have declared loyalty to the Kristang."

"That is not true," the Burgermeister announced, shocking Nivelle. "There are many cases where one group of a species splits from its parent, and switches sides."

"I am surprised to hear this," Nivelle stuttered. "How is this possible?"

"It happens, over the course of a very long war," the Burgermeister said with a human-like shrug. "For example, there is a group of Kristang who live on a planet that my people captured around four hundred of your years ago. These Kristang decided to stay, and repudiate their allegiance to the two clans they belonged to."

"This can't be a common occurrence?" General Nivelle asked warily.

"It was a special circumstance," she admitted. "The Kristang on that planet had been isolated from the rest of their kind for many years. The planet was at the extreme end of the territory the Thuranin controlled, then the Jeraptha cut off the Thuranin's access to a wormhole and the planet became isolated. We ignored the planet for over two centuries, merely monitoring it to assure the Kristang there did not pose a threat to us. By the time we besieged the planet, the Kristang there had drifted far from the cultural norm of their species. They declared that the Kristang had lost their souls to the Thuranin, that their true culture had been perverted by their patrons. These Kristang, who now call themselves the True Ones, are not entirely consumed by warfare. And they requested our assistance to return their females to their original genetic baseline. These True Ones could be considered neutrals, or as close to neutral as any sentient being is allowed to be in this galaxy," she observed sadly. "Their industry provides material support to our war effort, and they have provided warriors to fight alongside Ruhar. The warriors of the True Ones are known for being absolutely fanatical in battle; they know that if any of them are captured by the Kristang they will be tortured and killed."

"I am not asking- I am asking a hypothetical question. You understand what a hypothetical question is?" Nivelle was not entirely confident in the translator. Eventually, he needed to learn more than a few words of Ruhar.

The Burgermeister nodded silently, so the UNEF commander continued. "If we humans here on Paradise were to offer allegiance with the Ruhar, would it be accepted? And what would that mean for my people? Here, and on Earth?"

Baturnah Logellia paused to collect her thoughts. She could not tell the human commander that her own government was negotiating to trade away the planet, in the process screwing both the native Ruhar and the humans. "The decision to accept your allegiance would be far above my head. I could make a discrete inquiry; however, it would take several months at the very least. My confidence in our communications security is not sufficient for me to trust sending such a message via electronic means, no matter the level of encryption. Such a delicate matter would require me sending a courier to our home world." Seeing Nivelle's crestfallen look, she hastened to add "We have couriers traveling regularly; the next is scheduled to depart within two weeks."

"A discrete inquiry would be greatly appreciated, Madame Logellia. This is, of course, all hypothetical."

"Of course," she smiled. "General, you should not discuss this with anyone, unless you are standing in a field, far from any electronic equipment. I do not think I am giving away any secret when I say that your own communications are entirely compromised, since your 'zPhones'", she used the human slang term, "use our satellite network. If the Kristang are able to intercept our satellite communications-"

"Understood," Nivelle said helplessly. There was no point in attempting to establish a separate human communications network; the Ruhar could easily breach even the best human encryption. Nivelle suspected the Ruhar had the capability to implant nanoscale spies directly into the hardware, so they wouldn't even need to bother with decrypting signals. There was no point to complaining about something he could do nothing about.

Earth

It was great to have settled the question of whether I would be in command of the next mission, or even going at all. It was not great that UNEF Command wanted the ship to depart Earth orbit within seventeen days, and we had a tremendous amount of work to do before then. Major Simms, who had volunteered to go back out, needed to replenish our supplies. Skippy had to oversee manufacture of some key ship components that he hadn't been able to make from moon dust on our last mission. He was given a blank check to use whatever manufacturing capability he needed on Earth. That was less useful than I expected, because Skippy told me human materials technology was so primitive, it was in many cases easier for him to create needed things from raw materials.

Major Simms was in charge of coordinating with UNEF Command all the items we would need for the next mission, and the large list of equipment Skippy said he needed to continue repairing and upgrading the *Dutchman*. Simms and I went over the list at Wright-Pat, and some of the things Skippy wanted puzzled both of us. "Skippy," I asked, "this is a big list. I can see how most of it would be useful, I guess, but why do you need six crates of WD-40?"

"WD-40? Oh, that was just me messing with you. You monkeys didn't know that was a joke? Damn your species is clueless sometimes."

Simms looked like she would have tossed him out an airlock right then, if we'd been aboard the *Dutchman*. I wasn't happy with him either. "That was not funny, Skippy. We've got people working 24/7 down here to-"

"Yeah, yeah, blah blah blah. I get it, Joe, won't happen again. Man, you hate it any time I have fun. Listen, to be serious, there is only so much I can do to keep the ship running without access to a Thuranin spacedock. Star carriers are designed to operate on their own for extended missions, but we've been out on our own for too long, and the ship got beat up pretty badly on our last mission. Eventually, we will need access to Thuranin spare parts, or we're going to need another ship."

"Crap," I looked at Simms and we both frowned. "Not on this mission, right?"

"That depends on how long the next mission lasts, and what kind of stress we put the ship through, Joe. I can't make promises without knowing the parameters. On the last mission, we didn't expect to get ambushed by a Thuranin destroyer squadron."

He had a point. I didn't like it. Until then, the thought that the *Flying Dutchman* would wear out, could wear out, hadn't occurred to me. The technology of the ship seemed more like magic than anything created by living beings. Skippy did a great job behind the scenes, using robots to perform maintenance, and even daily chores like cleaning and doing our laundry. Whatever Skippy did to keep the ship operating was invisible to me. It was time I started paying careful attention to how much effort went into keeping the ship's magical machines working.

The other thing that was not great was that UNEF Command put me on a plane flying to Paris that very afternoon. Paris France, not the one in Texas. I went into a bathroom on the plane for privacy and called Rachel on my zPhone. "Hi, Joe," she sounded happy. "How is Maine? I checked the weather report this morning, it looks nice up there."

"Um. I'm on a plane to Paris," I blurted out.

"Paris. I've always wanted to go there. This is for work?" There was a tone to her voice that I interpreted as asking whether I was going to Paris with a girlfriend.

"Yes, UNEF sent me, this is a last minute thing."

"Are you coming back to Dayton?"

"I don't know. Rachel, I truly don't know. The ship is going back out soon, and-" I didn't know what else to say.

"I see." Her voice changed and I couldn't tell whether she was hurt or angry or relieved. "You don't know when you're coming back?"

"No." Damn it, I had always sucked at talking over a phone. "Rachel, we don't even know *where* we're going." I took a deep breath. "Listen, Rachel, when I get back-"

"Joe," she interrupted me. "Were you about to make a promise that you don't know if you can keep? Don't do that."

"I-" I what? I'm an idiot?

"You're lonely, Joe, I could tell that right away. You were away from home for a long time, and now you're going back out. We had fun, I'm glad I met you. It's not like you left in the middle of the night. You have a mission and you have to go. I understand. I was in the Air Force, remember?"

We awkwardly chatted for another few minutes, ending with me saying that if I could get back to Wright-Pat before going into orbit, I would contact her. She told me that wouldn't be a good idea. I could see her point. When you tear off a Band-Aid, you don't want to put it back on and do it again. Best to get it over with once.

My history with women seems to be they had me on a catch-and-release program. If my past was any indicator, Rachel had her fill of Joe Bishop and was ready to move on.

Crap. My longest current relationship was with a shiny beer can.

Maybe I needed to seriously rethink my life.

CHAPTER FIVE

Paradise

With almost simultaneous gamma ray bursts, the Kristang frigate *To Seek Glory in Battle is Glorious* and the destroyer *We are Proud to Honor Clan Sub-Leader Rash-au-Tal Vergent who Inspires us Every Day* emerged above Lemuria, about twenty three thousand kilometers apart. They emerged on either side of the unlucky Ruhar frigate *Tolen Grathur*. Because of pressure put on the task force commodore by the Chief Administrator, the defending task force had stationed a single frigate above Lemuria, to prevent or at least lessen the severity of future raids. Unfortunately for the *Grathur*, the Kristang had been watching that ship's patrols and noticed a pattern. There was a place the Ruhar frigate returned to reliably every eleven hours. Seeing an opportunity to hit the enemy hard with manageable risk, the Kristang task force commander had approved the idea of a raid by the captain of the destroyer *Vergent*, and naturally the experienced frigate *Glory* had been assigned to the mission. That fact understandably did not please the crew of the little *Glory*.

Both Kristang ships emerged with weapons hot and fired missiles, maser cannons and the destroyer launched railgun darts at the *Grathur*. Only luck saved the *Grathur* from complete destruction that day; a maser beam from the *Glory* hit a missile from the *Vergent* just as that missile evaded the *Grathur*'s point defenses. Instead of a devastating direct hit, the explosion of the missile warhead 1200 kilometers away only severely damaged the *Grathur*, allowing that hapless ship to perform a short emergency jump. The *Grathur* would be out of service for several weeks repairing damage, which the Kristang commander counted as good as a kill.

The captain of the *Vergent* was bitterly disappointed that he could not claim a complete victory that day, and he blamed the crew of the *Glory* although it had been an accident. The *Vergent*'s missile had been maneuvering violently to avoid fire from the *Grathur*'s point defense cannons, and flew right into a maser beam from the *Glory*. In the chaos of battle, it happened, and it was no one's fault.

The crew of the *Vergent* still blamed the *Glory*.

The crew of the *Glory* were happy merely to have survived another day.

Earth

The next call I needed to make was to one of the prior Merry Band of Pirates. "Hey, Skippy, I have a special request, it's kind of unusual. I need to call someone, and I need the call to be completely private, on both ends."

"Sure thing. Is this person living or dead?"

"What? Living, of course. I-, wait," Skippy could do so many incredible things, and he was still constantly surprising me with things he could do. "Oh my God! Can you really talk to dead people?"

"No, you big stupidhead," he laughed. "Of course not. Damn, you are dense sometimes."

"Then why the hell did you ask?"

"You said this request is unusual, so I was trying to judge just how idiotic this was going to be. You know, will this be normal Joe-level moronic, or are you cooking up something truly special to entertain me?"

"You are such an asshole. Can you do it, or not?"

"Whew," he let out an exasperated breath. "Please. Easy-peasy, Joe. Who do you want to call?"

"Doctor Friedlander."

"Our friendly local rocket scientist? Is he in any condition to talk? I think he sprained his brain aboard the *Dutchman*, trying to understand how the reactors work," Skippy chuckled.

"Skippy, be nice once in a while."

"Ok, Ok. For a monkey, he's not nearly as dim as the rest of you. And he does tell good jokes sometimes."

"Friedlander? Tells jokes?" This completely surprised me. Although, I hadn't spent much time with the science team.

"Yes. Aboard the ship, he started every science team meeting with a joke. Like, did you hear the one about the rooster?"

Skippy was going to tell the joke anyway, so I played along. "No."

"This farmer has a rooster that is growing old, and the farmer decides it's time to get a new rooster. So he goes down the road to his neighbor Gilroy, and he buys a young rooster. When he gets home," Skippy was already laughing at his own joke, "he puts the young rooster in the pen. The young rooster struts up to the old rooster and says 'Hey old-timer, you need to hit the road. This is my place now'. The old rooster says 'You're right, it is my time, but I'll tell you what. Someday you'll be old, and a young rooster will come along to kick you out. I don't want the ladies to see me just walk away. Could you chase me around some, we'll fight for a minute for me to keep my dignity, and then I'll leave?' And the young rooster feels sorry for the old one, and says 'Sure, old-timer, let's go.' So the young rooster chases the old rooster around the henhouse, and the farmer comes out to see what the commotion is. He says 'What the hell?' He grabs his shotgun and blows the young rooster away. As the old rooster is chuckling, the farmer says 'Damn Gilroy done sold me a *gay* rooster'!"

I laughed.

And Skippy laughed.

"You're right, that is a good one." Maybe I needed to make more of an effort to get to know all the people aboard the ship. "Can you call Friedlander?"

"Wait a minute, he's in his kitchen with his wife right now. I can make the call completely private, but I can't prevent his wife from overhearing him talk. He is about to go outside to get something out of the toolshed, you can talk to him then."

I was curious. "How do you know he's in the kitchen?"

"Duh. You really have to ask, seriously? Since you asked, in this particular case, they have one of those fancy refrigerators with internet connectivity and touch screen. That is not the best idea if you're concerned about privacy, by the way. Also, one of their yogurts is expired. It's behind the bread, that's why they haven't noticed it."

I made a mental note to get a really, really old non-digital fridge, if I ever got a place of my own.

"Ok, Friedlander just walked outside. I'll call his phone now?"

"Yes, thank you."

There was a delay of a couple seconds, and I was about to ask Skippy what was the problem, then I heard Friedlander's voice. "Hello? Who is this?" He demanded.

"Doctor, it's Joe Bishop."

"Oh, sorry for snapping at you. There was no caller ID, and I don't usually answer those calls, but my phone somehow picked up the call by itself."

"That's because this call is going through Skippy, not a cellular network."

"Yes," Skippy's voice broke in, "SkippyTel has amazing rate plans, and the best quality of service. Exclusions apply. Not available in other solar systems. Or to people I don't like."

"Got it, Skippy, thank you," I said. "I'll consider switching my plan to SkippyTel, please send me your brochure. Doctor Friedlander, we're going through Skippy because I want this call to be completely private. Can you talk?"

"Give me a moment, I'm, Ok, I'm in my toolshed, and my wife is in the house."

"UNEF has decided to send the *Dutchman* back out."

"I would have thought that was obvious," he said. I could hear the sarcasm in his voice.

"So did I, but it took a while for the bureaucratic wheels to get into motion, I guess. The reason I called is to see if you are interested in going back out with us."

"Oh. Wait minute." He was silent a moment. "I had to check that my wife is still in the house. I am not sure about going again, Colonel Bishop," he answered slowly. "Last week, NASA invited me to train for the mission to recover that Kristang troopship. We still have to do that? Skippy won't bring that troopship back for us?"

"I asked him to bring it back for my birthday," now my voice had the sarcasm.

"Joe!" Skippy broke in again. "I already got you a pair of socks."

"And I appreciate that, Skippy. Truthfully, I would rather have a starship."

"These are a *very nice* pair of socks, Joe," he said with a sniff. "However, I will consider it."

"Unless Skippy changes his mind soon," I concluded, "we should assume NASA has to go out there in old-fashioned chemical rockets. You would rather go on that mission, than join us aboard the *Dutchman* again?"

"What *I* want is not the only consideration."

"Oh." Crap. This was going to get complicated.

"My wife told me she married an engineer, not an astronaut. She was a nervous wreck when we got home."

"Doctor, this time, we do expect the *Dutchman* to return. Last time we didn't, but you went anyway?"

"I, um, I didn't quite believe your speech about how we wouldn't be coming back."

"I wasn't kidding about that," I said, frustrated.

"Which I realized when we got out there, and I learned that we can't operate the ship without Skippy. By then, it was too late. Before we left, I told my wife there was no way UNEF would allow a valuable asset like a Thuranin starship to be put at risk. I figured all the talk about the high level of risk was something UNEF lawyers made you say. So that, if anything did go wrong, the families couldn't sue UNEF. Sorry about that. Colonel, I wasn't the only person who thought that way, the whole science team did."

All my serious speeches had been for nothing? "I suppose it doesn't matter now. Your wife is Ok with you going into space with NASA?"

"No! No, I told NASA that I need to think about it. My wife is very much against me going up in a NASA rocket. Or a Chinese rocket. Any craft we send out to that troopship will be experimental. I'm not enthusiastic about the idea either. NASA wants me to go, because they're hoping that I learned enough about the *Flower* to be able to get the troopship's reactor restarted."

That surprised me. "You can do that?"

"No. And I told that to NASA, I think they're hoping that I'm wrong. Colonel, I appreciate the offer. I gathered so much data aboard the *Flower* and the *Dutchman* already, it will take me years to-"

"I need you to lead the new science team," I said before he could finish.

Paradise

"Me? Colonel, I'm an engineer. I don't do basic research and theory; I figure out how to make theories do something useful. Out among the stars, we should be-"

"Doctor, on this mission, UNEF wants engineers, not biologists, or cosmologists," I stumbled over that word. Wasn't that people who gave fancy haircuts? No, I remembered with relief, those were cosm*e*tologists, like my cousin Debbie. "Or chemists, or any kind of 'ist'. UNEF wants people who can figure out how the *Dutchman*, and any other alien technology we encounter, works."

Friedlander sounded puzzled. "Why didn't they do that the first time?"

"Because, as I said many times, last time they didn't really expect the ship to ever come back."

"Mmm. And this time they do, so they care about us delivering concrete results."

"You got it, Doctor."

There was a pause in the conversation. Maybe I should have done this face to face, rather than over a phone. I pictured him in a toolshed, surrounded by a lawnmower, weed whacker, rakes, shovels and a bucket of topsoil. If I closed my eyes, I knew what it smelled like; a bit musty, with dried dirt and grass and gasoline and plywood. It smelled like suburbia. It smelled like freedom. It smelled like America. Finally, he spoke. "Why me, Colonel?"

"You have experience aboard the *Dutchman*, and that counts a lot, because it means you have proven to be cool under pressure. Also, you got along well with people in a confined environment." That counted for a lot; there had been flare-ups of personality conflicts even among our carefully-chosen Merry Band of Pirates. "Mostly, I'm hoping you are someone I can count on. We are sticking to a limit of seventy people again, and this time we will have some, let's say, observers and intel people from UNEF. So the science team will have fewer people. I'd like you to select a wide mix of expertise for your team. Doctor, you know that we have no idea what fields of knowledge we will need once we're out there. On Newark, biology and archeology were critical for unraveling the mystery of that planet. And the science team ran an analysis that made Skippy realize an entire moon had been vaporized. UNEF is going to want to stuff the science team with you rocket scientist types so they can hopefully figure out how Thuranin technology works. You understand how useful it might be for that team to not be narrowly focused. It may mean the difference between us coming home or not."

"I agree with you on that point, Colonel. Do you need an answer right now?"

"No," I replied, "give it three days. No more than that, though. If you're onboard, you'll need a head start selecting your team."

"Ohhhh," he groaned. "This is not going to be easy to sell to my wife."

And, there, I knew he wanted to come with us. "I understand. Doctor, I'm not going to give you a Duty, Honor, uh, Humanity speech. I'd very much appreciate if you can come with us, but you've done your duty already. Think about it, and call me either way, please."

Friedlander called me the next morning, waking me from sleep because I was on Paris time. "Colonel Bishop, you still want me on the next mission?"

"Absolutely. We need you to lead the science team. And Skippy wants you aboard because he says you tell good jokes. I didn't know that."

Friedlander chuckled. "Why did the two blondes freeze to death at the drive-in theater?"

"I don't know?"

"They went to see 'Closed for the Winter'."

"Ha!" I laughed. "That is a good one. Skippy is right."

"Someone needed to lighten up our boring science team meetings. Colonel, I discussed the situation with my wife last night, and I will join the mission on two conditions."

"Ok, what are those?" Please, please, I said to myself, make it something reasonable.

"First, this time we are coming back, correct? That is the plan?"

"I'm the wrong person to answer that question, but, yes. Skippy has promised we will bring the ship back to Earth before the next mission, whatever that is. He wants to hold off contacting the Collective until he has answers about what happened to Newark, and some other things."

Friedlander gave an audible sigh of relief. "That is good to hear. My wife will be very pleased to hear that. And I've told her that being aboard the *Dutchman* is safer than going up in that spacecraft NASA is building. Don't tell NASA I said that."

"I won't. And your second condition?"

"Promise me that I won't be killed on some planet by a giant space lizard."

That made me laugh. "Doctor, don't worry. If you are ever about to be eaten by a giant space lizard, I will shoot you first."

"That's close enough, I guess. Colonel, would you like to see the list of people I want on the science team?"

"It will be your science team, Doctor. The team is your choice; the seven best qualified people you can find."

"Whew," he exhaled. "That's a lot of pressure on me, then. Seven qualified people who are willing to leave on short notice, for an interstellar mission of unknown danger. Can I promise they won't be eaten by a giant space lizard?"

"Let's not go crazy, Doctor. We may need to throw one of *them* to the giant space lizard to save ourselves."

In Paris, I met the new mission commander, Hans Chotek. We had a cordial and professional meeting, that I almost ruined by calling him 'Chocula'. Luckily, I caught myself in time and said 'Chotek' instead. Skippy had shown me the mission commander's resume and it was impressive, particularly for a guy in his early 40s. He had been all over the world and handled all kinds of crises for the UN; not all of them successfully of course because it is, you know, the UN. We got off on the wrong foot by him spending the first twenty minutes trying to impress me. Then he must have realized I was bored; my jaw-stretching yawn may have been a clue. So we talked about the mission objectives UNEF Command had given us. Given to *him*.

"Sir," I began, "I do have a problem with our mission objectives. One of them."

He looked mildly surprised. Whether he was surprised that I disagreed with the mission objectives established by UNEF Command, or surprised that a comparatively low-ranking sergeant/colonel would express doubts openly, I couldn't guess. "Our primary objective-"

I shook my head. "Our primary objective is correct, and I have no problem with it." We were tasked primarily with determining what the Thuranin knew about the destruction of their surveyor task force, and whether they would be sending another ship to Earth. The primary objective also stated that if we found a way to establish an ongoing intelligence source to proactively warn us about threats to Earth, we should take the opportunity to do so. Fine. All that made sense to me. The only quibble I had about our primary objective was that UNEF Command had been frustratingly vague about what we were supposed to do if we learned another surveyor ship was on its way to Earth. If the Thuranin planned to send a surveyor ship, but that ship was not scheduled to begin its mission until well in the future, we were to take the *Dutchman* all the way back to Earth for consultation? If there was not enough time to consult with Earth, we were to 'use our best judgment'. Meaning Chotek's judgment, since UNEF Command had been clear that they did not trust mine. Were we supposed to prevent a second surveyor from reaching Earth, even at the risk of exposing the fact that humans were flying around in our own pirate starship? If so, what level of exposure risk was acceptable? UNEF Command had provided no guidance on that critical issue. Those damned cowards, who had reamed me a new asshole over the carefully measured and entirely successful risk I took in landing on Newark, were afraid to make any judgment of their own.

Anyway, the first objective we were given was fine, we could manage any ambiguities when we had to. The decision would not be up to me; it would be Chotek who would make the final call. Except that I, Skippy, the Merry Band of Pirates and even Count Chocula himself fully expected me to mutiny and override Chotek's decision if I thought it endangered humanity. Great. Whatever. Such is the life of a pirate captain. What I would appreciate is some nice pirate booty to go with the responsibility, but that wasn't going to happen.

"The problem is our secondary objective," I explained.

"To gather information about the Expeditionary Force on Paradise?" Now he was clearly surprised. "I do not understand. Mr. Bishop. Surely you of all people would want to know the fate of your fellow soldiers in UNEF."

"I would like to know; if the answer is they are all living happily ever after on Paradise," I said with what I hoped came across as sarcasm. "The problem is that I think it extremely unlikely that fairy tale is the truth. It is much more likely that we are going to discover information that is not so favorable; that UNEF on Paradise is struggling or in danger, or being persecuted. And then what? What good does it do for us to have that unpleasant information?"

"When we have information, we have choices, Mr. Bishop. Without informat-"

"Choices to do what exactly, Mr. Chotek? I see one choice if we discover the Expeditionary Force on Paradise is endangered. We feel bad about it, and we do absolutely nothing. That is the same effective result as if we discover they are all living happy lives of luxury. In either case, we do absolutely nothing. We can't do anything useful. We can't do anything at all. We can't even send them a message, because that would undoubtedly be intercepted by the Ruhar or Kristang or both. Then the whole galaxy would know that humans escaped from Paradise and are flying around in a pirate ship."

"Surely we can-"

"Looking for trouble on Paradise goes against two principles I have learned in my career, Mr. Chotek. First, never ask a question for which you don't want to hear the answer. Second, never give an order you know won't be obeyed."

"What does that mean, Colonel?" He asked evenly, but I could see his Adam's apple bob ever so slightly with anxiety.

"Mr. Chotek, we have a crew of highly dedicated, highly trained, highly *motivated* special forces who have what we in the military call a 'bias for action'. When they see a problem, they want to act, they expect to act. What do you think will happen when they learn our people on Paradise are threatened, or are actively being killed?"

"I expect they are also highly disciplined, Colonel Bishop."

"What would *you* do?"

"That would certainly depend on the situation, and-"

"Great, then let me present you with an example." I took a breath and plunged ahead. "Let's say we are in the Paradise system, under stealth or however we get close enough to obtain intel. We learn, we see, that our people are in prison camps, being starved because they have run out of food and the Ruhar have a very limited ability to feed them. Half of the Expeditionary Force has already died of starvation. The Ruhar military force on and around Paradise is weak; weak enough that this ship could take them on easily. We could take the planet back, we could feed some of our people, we could even bring some of them home. What will you order us to do? You are the mission commander; this is your decision."

He took a moment to answer. "I see your point, Colonel. Any action we take would expose us, and endanger Earth. As difficult as it would be, my decision would have to be that the ship must remain in stealth, and return to Earth without intervening or revealing our presence."

"You expect that order to be obeyed? Do you really expect the crew of this pirate ship to stand down and do nothing, while our people, their comrades, are dying?"

This time he did not answer immediately. "Would you obey such an order, Colonel?"

"I don't know," I answered honestly. "And if I passed that order on to my subordinates, I am not confident my orders would be obeyed."

"I see," Chotek said thoughtfully.

"We are all alone out there, Mr. Chotek. During our last mission, I was outside the ship in a spacesuit with a SpecOps team for zero gravity training. One of the special forces asked Skippy whether we could see the Sun from there, and Skippy enhanced the image in our helmet visors, so we could see the faint light of our home star. I remember Skippy reminding us that the light we were seeing then left the sun eighteen hundred years ago. The Roman Empire ruled the Mediterranean back then. Under that perspective, the authority of Earth begins to seem thin after we pass through a couple wormholes."

"Colonel," he said, "you have given me much to think about. Please understand that I have limited flexibility about our mission objectives. UNEF Command made it very clear that they want to know the situation on Paradise. Unless there is a compelling reason for us not to pursue gathering information about Paradise, I do not see that I have authority to override that objective. Regardless of my personal feelings on the subject."

"A compelling reason?" I mused. "How about this? If you judged that pursuing intelligence about Paradise posed a risk of this ship exposing our presence out here, would that be a compelling reason to override our stated objective? Even if such exposure were, let's say, inadvertent."

He pinched his chin. This was deeply troubling him. His entire purpose for being aboard the *Flying Dutchman* was because UNEF did not trust my judgment about keeping our pirate ship secret. Now he saw that assuring we took *zero* risk of exposure was a complicated calculation. Virtually anything we did on the other side of Earth's local wormhole risked exposure. "I will need to think about this," he said. "We have to achieve our primary objective first, then we will need to reevaluate our next steps. And, Colonel? I do appreciate that our primary objective involves considerable risk of us becoming exposed. None of these decisions will be simple, or easy."

I was glad to hear that, even if it was a little late.

Flying all the way to Paris, except for meeting our new mission commander, was a waste of my time. After three days of me trying to run the ship from the ground, Skippy sent down a dropship, and I went aboard the *Flying Dutchman*. The ship was a beehive of frantic activity, even more than last time. The difference this time was, UNEF Command expected us to come back, so they cared that we had everything we might need loaded aboard. When Major Simms first saw me, she snapped a quick salute, threw up her hands, and shooed me out of the cargo bay so she could get a mountain of gear stowed away.

Paradise

"Sir," a haggard-looking Major Simms said as she knocked on my office door frame a couple minutes later. "We have two more shipments coming up from Earth, then we'll be fully loaded. I was able to get all the special items you asked for, except for this 'Fluff' thing," she looked at me with a raised eyebrow. "I was able to get a different kind of marshmallow cream," she held up a white plastic jar from a warehouse store. It was labelled 'Marshmallow Cream'.

I sucked in a breath. "*Generic* Fluff?" I sputtered in shock. Until that moment, I hadn't known there was anything but true Fluff. The white jar in her hand emanated pure evil; I could barely look at it. "Major, that is an unholy abomination! You can't make a Fluffernutter sandwich with, with, *that.*"

She looked at the label skeptically. "Sir, it has the same ingredient-"

"Major, do not mess with someone's childhood," I said with all seriousness. "A scoop of Fluff on top of a mug of hot chocolate on a cold day? Yum. Whatever that heinous imposter is in your hand there, we can't have it aboard this ship. How much did you get?"

"Four of these jars," she said with great weariness. "I'll send it back down when the dropship is unloaded."

"Hmm. I don't want to risk contaminating the planet with that abomination. Could we toss it out an airlock and let it burn up in the atmosphere?" That suggestion was made only half-jokingly. This was all my fault. The list I gave to Simms of items I wanted aboard the *Dutchman* only had three items on it, but Fluff was one of them. What I should have done was buy a couple jars while I was home, but I couldn't see myself lugging them around in my suitcase. UNEF Command already thought I was too immature for command. Maybe I could ask my parents to send a care package to Wright-Patterson, or wherever Simms was loading the dropships?

"I will take care of it, sir," she turned and left with a wry smile.

I never did find out if she'd really tossed them out an airlock.

I also never did get a jar of real Fluff.

I wandered down to a cargo bay that had been set aside for special forces gear. Major Smythe was there with his SpecOps team leaders, personally checking every single piece of equipment. And making a list of the gear they still needed.

"Welcome aboard again, Colonel Bishop," Smythe said while snapping a salute.

I returned the salute, and that was the end of the saluting that would be required aboard the ship, except for formal ceremonies. "*Major* Smythe," I pointed to his new rank insignia. "Maybe I'm not saying this the right way, but I'm sorry that your special forces did not see much action on the last mission."

"Colonel, that is not a problem for us. We are here to provide an elite capability, whenever that capability is needed. Special forces are used to a lot of hurry up and wait, and clandestine missions when we are only needed if something goes very wrong. Most of the time, if the enemy knows that special forces have been in the area, we have failed our mission. On these missions, the enemy can't even know that we *exist*. We understand that the need to avoid exposure severely limits our ability to engage in combat operations."

"It severely limits our ability to do pretty much anything out here," I agreed.

"We will be," he ejected a clip from a Kristang rifle, then set the rifle carefully on a rack, "seeing substantially more action on this mission?"

I nodded. "According to Skippy, there is no alternative. Do you feel up to combat against the Thuranin?"

"Against genetically enhanced cyborgs with superior technology? My people will be ready, sir. Hopefully Skippy can give us some sort of advantage."

"He doesn't think so," I said glumly. "But I'll talk with him."

I was in my cabin to change out of my formal uniform, when Adams called me from the CIC. "Colonel, we just received a message from UNEF Command."

"Go ahead," I answered, spitting out a mouthful of toothpaste. Why did people always call when I was in the bathroom? Talking while kneeling on the floor of a cramped Thuranin bathroom seemed undignified, so I carefully stood up, wary of the low ceiling.

"NASA has telescopes watching that Kristang troopship, and they've picked up an increased infrared signature. Something out there is heating up, sir."

"Uh huh. Thank you, Sergeant. I'm going to ask a certain shiny beer can what he knows about that." I ended the call on my zPhone and looked at the speaker in the ceiling, knowing Skippy was always listening. "Hey, Skippy. Do you know anything about activity on that troopship?"

"You monkeys noticed that, huh?"

"Apparently, yes. You're not trying to blow it up, are you? Please, please say no."

"Not blowing it up, Joe. I'm restarting the reactor temporarily, to get a partial charge for the ship's jump drive coils."

"You are planning to jump it somewhere?" I asked hopefully.

"Yes," he said with a sigh. "I've been looking at the plans for the spacecraft you monkeys are building; it's like a can made from newspaper and cow manure, only less flight worthy. I can't stand the idea of brave but idiotic astronauts making a long journey in that flimsy piece of crap. But I still don't want you monkeys whacking each other with sticks over that ship, so I'm jumping it halfway to your moon. Your nations will still need to cooperate to get above low Earth orbit."

"That is a nice surprise. Thank you, Skippy."

"Ah, don't mention it. The socks I bought for your birthday are on backorder, so I had to get you something else."

"A starship beats socks any day."

"But these were very nice socks, Joe. And I got you a card and everything."

I laughed. "That is very much appreciated. How about this; for my next birthday, I'll set up a gift registry, and you can select something from the list."

"Ooh, ooh, that's a good idea. I saw this in a movie!"

Considering that Skippy had probably seen every movie ever made, that was not surprising. I tried to think of how many romantic comedies had a gift registry as part of the plot. "What movie?"

"It was the Wizard of Oz. For your gift, you want a brain, right?"

Crap. "I walked right into that one, didn't I?"

"Yeah you did. If it had been a tree, you would have broken your nose."

"Thanks for keeping me alert, I guess. When do you plan to jump that ship?"

"We jump out of here in three days, so I'll do it in two days. In case UNEF gets too excited, as soon as the jump drive coils are charged sufficiently, I am shutting the reactor down again. they'll need to figure that out by themselves. And tell your NASA that Dr. Friedlander is not available to get that troopship's reactor restarted. He started telling me a joke this morning, and he got interrupted. That rocket scientist weasel isn't going *anywhere* until he tells me the freakin' punchline," Skippy grumbled.

"I will inform UNEF, then. They will be very pleased. I do have one question first; are you sure that bringing that ship back won't be seen as you caving in to UNEF?"

"Huh? No, why would they think that? There was no quid pro quo here. Ugh. You don't understand Latin. I'll use language you can understand; I did not make a bargain with UNEF. I got everything I wanted, and gave no concessions to them. Me bringing that ship back is a gift from the Benevolent All-Powerful Skippy. Plain and simple."

"All right then." Personally, I was afraid that UNEF would see this as me being able having influence on Skippy, and being able to get him to do other things in the future. UNEF had better not get used to that. "One more thing, then."

"Really? I bring you a starship, and you want more? Unbelievable!"

"This is simple, I promise."

"Fine," he huffed. "What is it?"

"That troopship has a Kristang name, right, some long-ass poetry thing?"

"Correct. The Kristang traditionally name their troop carriers after soldiers who died particularly gloriously in battle. This one is called *The Ever-Long Remembrance of Khost Vlakranda Who Served With Ultimate Honor*."

"Wow. This Khost guy, what did he do?"

"Uh, well, his family is well connected in their clan, so naming the ship after him was partly political. He was a first son, and he died when his dropship got shot down. This was after he led a raid on another Kristang clan, a raid that resulted in the deaths of almost three thousand, including females and children. Also, there is suspicion he was drunk the day of that raid."

My mouth opened to remark that Khost was no hero, when I remembered the Ruhar Whales that I had shot down. Almost a thousand Ruhar had died then. For that action, the Kristang had insisted that I be promoted to wear the colonel's silver eagles that now adorned my uniform. I am certain the Ruhar did not think I am any kind of hero. "Skippy, I want you to rename that ship as the *Yu Qishan*."

"Oh. Joe, it is not often that I say this, but in this case I completely agree with your suggestion." Sergeant Yu Qishan of the Chinese Army had sacrificed himself to prevent a Kristang crewman from self-destructing the *Flower* when we boarded that frigate near Paradise. Everything we had accomplished since then we owed to Yu Qishan. "Done. The official designation of the ship is now *The Ever-Long Remembrance of Yu Qishan Who Served With Ultimate Honor*."

My intention had been to rename it as simply 'Yu Qishan', but what Skippy did was better. Everyone was going to call it the *Yu* anyway. "Thank you, Skippy."

UNEF Command was indeed thrilled when I told them the *Yu* would soon be back in Earth orbit. They also congratulated me for persuading Skippy to cooperate, even though I told them several times that I had nothing to do with it. And I'm sure that somewhere, Chuckles the Clown was patting himself on the back for getting Skippy to do what UNEF wanted.

Maybe, in some way, he was right about that. Maybe he hadn't manipulated Skippy into doing what UNEF wanted; maybe Chuckles had manipulated me into getting Skippy to do UNEF's bidding.

I didn't like that idea at all.

What I did enjoy was telling Lt. Colonel Chang about renaming the troopship; we had talked about honoring Sergeant Yu in some way, but hadn't done anything about it until now. Truthfully, we had been kind of, you know, busy. Chang was visibly affected by my gesture of renaming the ship; I thought I saw a tear in his eye. He later told me that he had called Yu's family personally to inform them of how UNEF was honoring their son. He did that before I told UNEF of the renaming, so that some idiot desk-bound bureaucrat at UNEF Command wouldn't be able to order me not to do it. One thing that being in the military had taught me, is that it is better to act and ask forgiveness, than to hesitate and ask permission.

Craig Alanson

CHAPTER SIX

Flying Dutchman

We finally jumped away from Earth orbit after only one or two minor delays. Before we initiated the jump sequence, Mr. Chotek wanted to give some sort of undoubtedly long-winded speech to the crew. He needed to assert himself as the mission commander, or mark the momentous occasion in his special way or something. So, I asked Skippy to open the intercom and a channel to UNEF Command on Earth.

Sure, maybe I should have warned Chotek what was likely to happen. On the other hand, the best way to learn is through experience, and he was never going to forget this. So, I actually did him a favor.

That's my story and I'm sticking to it.

What we on the bridge and in the CIC saw was Hans Chotek, wearing a dark blue suit, white shirt and red tie. Why he felt the need to wear a suit was a mystery; my order for the uniform of the day was not formal, but the military personnel were all wearing uniforms and I guess Chotek's work uniform was a suit. What we heard was Chotek clearing his throat and saying "I would like to address the crew." Then he launched into a prepared speech about the importance of this mission, and reminding people of our objectives. He was about halfway through the first objective when a Chinese pilot in the CIC snorted with laughter while she looked at a display screen, then she stood up straight, trying to be serious.

What the rest of the crew, and people at UNEF Command on Earth saw and heard was not Hans Chotek in a suit. Through the video feed, they saw and heard Count Chocula, beginning with him saying "I would like to address the crew" in an exaggerated movie vampire accent. The Count then proceeded to explain the importance of our mission to bring delicious chocolaty breakfast cereal to the children of the world, and how much Franken Berry cereal sucked by comparison. While talking, the Count picked a booger from his nose, tried to flick it away, then smeared it on his jacket lapel. Without even seeing the video, I had to bite my lip to keep from laughing while Chotek continued his speech. Two minutes in, with him glaring at the crew in the CIC as they tried to suppress laughter, he was interrupted by Chang.

"I'm sorry, Mr. Chotek, there is a," Chang had to pause to collect himself. "There is a problem with the video and audio feed."

"Problem?" Chotek asked, annoyed to being interrupted while giving the speech of his life.

"Yup," Skippy said. "Seems to be a glitch somewhere. I'm working on it." Just then, every screen on the bridge and CIC began playing the video from the beginning. Chotek saw his image altered to appear as a vampire, saying "I would like to address the crew".

He was not amused. His face red, he glared at me. "Colonel Bishop, I would like to speak with you privately."

Crap. Now he was pissed at *me*. We still had half an hour before the ship would jump, so I gave the command chair to Chang, and Chotek came into my office around the corner. The door was barely closed when he started haranguing me. "Colonel Bishop, I will not tolerate a display of disrespect like that. I am a senior United Nations official-"

"Pbbbbbbt!" Skippy made a raspberry sound. "Please, Chocky, you're a senior bureaucrat, or a senior blowhard for sure, but what qualifies you to be part of this elite crew?"

"My most recent assignment was in the Middle East. It took me five weeks, but I was able to negotiate a very difficult cease fire between the Israelis and Palestinians," he said proudly.

"Sure," Skippy scoffed. "Except that nobody actually ceased firing during that 'cease fire'. Basically, they stopped shooting just long enough to eat lunch and reload. Then your cease fire was over. What really happened is, the two sides strung you along for five weeks while they shot at each other all they wanted. Then, when they each needed a break, they agreed to your cease fire agreement, and ignored it. What else you got on your resume?"

"The peace accords in Sudan."

"Uh huh. You mean one side in Sudan agreeing to peace, only after they had already killed or driven away seventy percent of the other side. Man, that must have been one tough agreement to negotiate."

Chotek stiffened. "Not every agreement is what we wish it could-"

"None of your negotiated agreements have accomplished anything useful, Chocky. You couldn't even do disaster aid right. When you were in charge of the tsunami relief in the Philippines, more than half of your supplies were stolen by terrorist groups. The emergency shelter housing units you brought in were contaminated with toxic mold. And your UN relief troops infected the native population with cholera. The Philippines would have been better off if you had never quote, helped them, unquote."

"It is easy to criticize in retrospect what should have been done-"

"It is even easier to claim you are a big shot UN official helping the world, when the truth is, you have never accomplished one damned thing of substance in your worthless career, Chocula." Skippy was pissed. "Now you come aboard our ship when you are in no way qualified to join the Merry Band of Pirates, and you think your experience gives you the authority to tell us what we can and can't do? Screw that. Where was your lazy ass the last two times we saved your miserable planet?"

Chotek didn't have an answer to that. Although, to be fair, there wasn't a reasonable answer to that.

"Skippy," I interrupted before the argument got totally out of control. Damn it, we hadn't even left orbit yet. "This ship is under the authority of UNEF Command; I am also under that authority. Mr. Chotek has been appointed as the mission commander, and I have agreed to implement his commands as the captain of this ship." I did not say 'whether I like it or not' because everyone knew that is what I meant. "Mr. Chotek, I had nothing to do with altering that video, I have been a victim of Skippy's pranks before. In my case, my image was replaced by Barney the idiotic purple dinosaur."

"And a monkey, Joe, don't forget about the monkey," Skippy said gleefully.

"Believe me, I have not forgotten about the monkey. My point, Mr. Chotek, is that you will need to reach some agreement with Skippy. You are an expert negotiator? Then find some way to reach an accommodation with him. Because Skippy is one hundred percent essential to operating this ship. No one else onboard, including myself, are that vital to the mission."

Chotek had his arms folded across his chest, which I took as a bad sign. "Mr. Skippy has made it clear that he has no need to negotiate with anyone. Therefore, I do not see any basis for reaching an agreement of any kind."

"You don't need to reach a formal agreement," I suggested. "You just need to find a way to live together on this ship. It would help, sir, if you would develop a sense of humor about your interactions with our super powerful alien being." I described Skippy that way to remind Chotek of exactly who he was dealing with.

Given what I'd seen of Chotek so far, I was not optimistic about him growing a sense of humor. Skippy and Chotek were going to argue, and I was going to be caught in the middle.

This could be a very long trip.

Fort Rakovsky, Lemuria, Paradise

"Damn, I'm hungry," Dave said quietly. "Sorry, man, I know you're hungry too, I shouldn't have mentioned it."

"Hey," Jesse offered a hand, and he and Dave bumped fists. "Don't worry about, it, Ski. If you can't talk about it with me, you can't talk about it with anyone." Being part of a fireteam meant taking care of each other, and not just in combat. It meant making sure the other guys changed their socks so they didn't get blisters. It meant checking they were staying hydrated, and eating nutritious food instead of junk. Although there wasn't any junk food on Paradise now, so that last one was easy. And it meant listening when a fireteam member needed to talk about something. "Yeah, I'm hungry too. And we're better off than most." Because they worked on a dedicated Ag team, as chicken ranchers, Dave and Jesse were allotted extra calories each day. That allotment had been cut, three times, so that now their daily bounty was a mere 300 additional calories. Part of the reason for the cuts was that, with most of UNEF now settled in villages that had been carved out of Paradise's southern continent, the majority of humans were now involved in farming and raising animals. Most people were on Ag teams by default, it was no longer a special assignment. The other reason was that even though UNEF had cleared thousands of acres and planted crops, the food supply was still tight. UNEF had quickly found that, in addition to growing crops for the general supply, each Ag worker needed to be allotted a certain number of acres just for themselves, as an incentive. People worked for incentives; that was why communism had been such a miserable and obvious failure. While soldiers could be ordered by headquarters to grow food for the general population, most people worked just a little bit harder on land they knew was their own. On their own plot of land, they grew whatever crops they wanted, assuming seeds were available.

A new, informal human economy was being built on Paradise, based on trading food products. One village may grow a field of sugarcane on their private allotment; after harvest and processing, the resulting raw sugar could be traded for just about anything. A dairy needed a large amount of grain to feed the cattle; incoming grain was traded for fresh milk. And not just milk was traded; there was a booming business in butter and cheese. One village, located right on the equator of Paradise, grew nothing but peppers, and traded dried pepper flakes to spice up the mostly bland diet people were eating.

"You know what I miss?" Dave asked while staring off into the corn field. Two thirds of the field was laying fallow in between harvests; waiting for more fertilizer to be delivered. Corn kernels were harvested, mostly to feed the chickens, and the upper parts of the corn stalks were shipped out as feed for cattle. Cows shouldn't eat the lower part of a corn stalk, Dave had been told; it contained too much nitrates or something like that. That was yet another thing he hadn't expected to learn in the US Army. He also had learned how to select and prepare corn to be used as seeds for the next harvest. None of this had been covered in basic training.

The reason most of the field was not growing corn at the moment was simple, and frightening. Large fields of crops were big, easy targets for Kristang maser beams. The raider ships that were still regularly popping into orbit were hitting the human food supply as often as they targeted Ruhar infrastructure. In response, UNEF had ordered creation of smaller, widely scattered fields, to avoid providing tempting targets for the Kristang raiders. Creating those fields took time, and intense labor, and that took effort away from tending the fields that were already planted. The acres now under cultivation were supposedly enough to feed all of UNEF, with a safety margin for bad weather, crop failures and fields burned by Kristang masers. An adequate supply of food was mere months away, according to UNEF HQ. Whether that was true, or BS propaganda to boost sagging morale, depended on which rumors you believed.

"What you miss?" Jesse asked. "Like getting enough to eat?"

"That too," Dave nodded. "I miss food from home."

"You don't eat corn and eggs in Milwaukee?" Jesse had eaten plenty of corn in Arkansas, mostly in the form of cornmeal, cornbread, corn in a lot of things. Like his nickname, Cornpone. He'd eaten a lot of eggs, too. And now he was heartily sick of both corn and eggs. Ski had cooked up a deal to trade some of their private crops like sun dried tomatoes for sugar, spices and even a tiny hunk of cheese made right on Paradise. In their little spare time, they had cleared a field together and planted a type of wheat as an experiment; if it worked they were hoping to have wheat flour and possibly even wheat bread to trade.

"You know what I mean. I miss the kind of food we don't have here. Like beer brats."

"Beer brats? Like bratwurst? That's German food, right? You're Polish, I though you guys ate kielbasa."

"We do, I, my father's family is Polish. My mother comes from French Canadian and Swedish people. And I'm like fourth generation American, they came over from Poland a long time ago. Beer brats are a Wisconsin thing."

"How do you cook them?" Jesse didn't actually care how bratwursts were cooked, he knew Ski wanted to talk about it.

Dave's eyes lit up. "What my folks do it you get a pan, like an aluminum pan, the thin disposable kind like they sell lasagna in? You know what I mean? You'll probably throw the pan away, because it will get sooty from the grill. Ok, you got the pan, you slice up onions, and you add the brats and pour beer in to cover the brats."

Jesse looked skeptical. "Sounds like a waste of good beer."

"It doesn't take a whole lot of beer, and you don't have to use the good stuff. A dark beer is best; it adds more flavor. You cover the pan with foil and let it kind of poach or steam for a while."

"You kind of boil the brats? Why not do it on a stove instead of a grill?"

"Because before you serve the brats, you take them out of the pan and grill them up for a few minutes. It gets the skin nice and crispy, so that when you bite into them, the juice bursts in your mouth oh," Ski closed his eyes and licked his lips, almost tasting a delicious brat. "Put them on a bun, add the onions on top, man that tastes like-" Dave paused, lost for a moment as a shadow fell across his face. "It tastes like home, man."

"I know what you mean. That sounds good, I'd like to try that."

"Except we don't have brats, or beer."

"We have onions."

"Yum!" Dave said with disgust. "What food do you miss the most?"

"Oh, dang, there's so much. Ch-" Jesse caught himself before saying 'chicken and dumplings' while he stood over the pen of tiny, peeping chicks. That would have been very bad luck. "Ribs. I miss babyback ribs."

"Memphis style?"

"Of course. Or a dry rub, that's good too."

"Mmm," Dave smacked his lips, "I can taste it now."

"Me too. We've served together a long time, how come back when Bishop named you 'Ski', you didn't tell him that you're half Swedish?"

"Like that would have made a difference?"

"With Joe? No, I guess not. Sucks what happened to him."

"Goddamn lizards killed him," Dave frowned.

"I think technically, the hamsters killed him when they blew up that jail he was in."

"Bullshit, Jesse. That was timing, the lizards were going to kill him anyway. The reason he is dead is because of the lizards."

"Yeah," Cornpone agreed with a frown.

"Yeah. I miss his stupid face sometimes."

"Bish, a colonel," Jesse shook his head in amazement. "He was one lucky son of a bitch. Until, you know, he got killed."

Flying Dutchman

Following the initial jump, the ship was recharging jump drive capacitors, so I took the opportunity to get dinner. It had been a long day and I was on the third and last shift for dinner in the galley; hopefully not all the good stuff was gone by then. It was the Chinese team's turn to cook and to my surprise, they made meatloaf. There were also two vegetarian dishes. Chinese meatloaf? The cook offered it to me with pride, so I took the plate and added some sort of vegetables. On our last mission, someone on the American team had added nutmeg to the meatloaf, so I tasted this Chinese version with skepticism. It was delicious. Different but delicious, and spicy. The meatloaf on my plate was gone before I knew it. The cook, beaming with pride, offered me a second helping, which I accepted.

"Hey, Colonel Joe," Skippy said through the ceiling speaker, "I need a favor."

Mentally I cringed, because Skippy had often used my time in the galley to tease and insult me in front of an audience. "What is it?"

"I need you to order Dr. Friedlander to tell me the punchline to the joke he started. That freakin' weasel keeps telling me that he's too busy managing the science team."

"I won't order him to tell you, but I can certainly ask him about it. Maybe I can help you, what is the joke?"

"He said 'How do you keep an idiot in suspense'?"

Thank God that I didn't have a mouthful of food, because I burst out laughing and so did everyone in the galley. Sergeant Adams was laughing so hard she had tears running down her face. Captain Giraud almost fell off his chair.

"What's so funny?" Skippy demanded.

When I could talk again, I said gently "Skippy, think about it."

After a long pause, there came "Oh. Shit." Then he shouted "*Friedlander*! Joe, we need the ship to alter course immediately."

"Why?"

"There is a planet I know of that has large beasts sort of like dinosaurs. We're going to dip Friedlander in ketchup and drop him off there."

"Skippy, come on. I promised the guy that he would *not* be eaten by a giant space lizard."

"*You* promised him, I didn't. Ooooooh, that weasel is going to seriously regret the day he was born when-"

"Thank you for the laugh, Skippy. I'm sure you can find some non-lethal means to get even with our local rocket scientist."

The third morning after we jumped away from Earth, I had a problem to deal with. Count Chocula came to my office, before I even had a sip of coffee. He complained he didn't get any sleep that night, because his cabin was alternately broiling hot then freezing cold at night, and the ventilation system made booming noises. He asked me to tell Skippy to stop harassing him, then he went away to get the cup of coffee I hadn't had yet.

As soon as he went around the corner, I called a shiny beer can that I know. "Hey, Skippy, Count Chocula says the ventilation in his cabin went haywire last night?"

"Oh, uh huh, yeah, I heard about that. It's a damned shame, is what it is. The ventilation system in that area has issues."

"Issues?"

"Yup. Multiple issues, let me tell you. The ventilation system's sister is dating some creepy Goth guy, it's mother lost her job and is drinking too much, again. The whole family is worried. Although, let's face it, the mother has been through rehab twice already so it's no surprise. She's not going to change. And the ventilation system itself is having a bad hair day, plus it gained weight after it broke up with its boyfriend last week. Oh, man, it's a whole deal. We're talking daytime TV type drama in *that* family."

"Ooookay, sure," I couldn't help laughing. "Any chance you can fix just one issue, keep the temperature in that cabin at a comfortable level?"

"I could, I suppose. Tell you what, I'll put it on my list of things to do. Although there are *so* many other things I need to do that are a much higher priority."

"Such as?"

"Well, Joe, your sock drawer is *shockingly* disorganized. You've got dress socks mixed up with sport socks, man, it could take me months to untangle that mess. The ventilation system in his cabin may have to wait a while."

"Listen, Skippy. I don't like the jerk either," I craned my neck to see if anyone was in the corridor outside my office, "but you can't harass him that way. He needs sleep. Lack of sleep won't improve his personality."

"You have a point there, Joe. Until I get the ventilation system fixed, I suggest he finds a nice airlock to sleep in. Although, we've had trouble with airlocks also, it is possible there could be a catastrophic failure someday. I can't promise anything."

"Then tell me this, genius. What are the odds of an airlock failing while Chocula happens to be sleeping there, and him getting sucked out into space?"

"Difficult to say for certain, Joe. There are a lot of variables involved. I can tell you that there does seem to be an odd correlation between the potential of an airlock failure, and how much I am irritated at Chotek that particular day. It is a strange coincidence. I can't explain it; this could take some detailed analysis."

I sighed. This was going to be an ongoing problem. "Please, Skippy, for me, let the guy get a good night of sleep, Ok?"

"Fine," he huffed. "Have it your way. I'll find some other way to have fun."

"Great. Don't make it so obvious next time."

Fort Rakovsky, Lemuria, Paradise

Their private wheat field was coming along just fine, according to the Ag expert who stopped by their village once a week. Jesse and Dave were discussing combining forces with another three guys to expand their wheat field. Five guys working together could grow more than two plus three working separately. People were doing that all over Lemuria; the crops growing in their allotted private fields were now almost equal to the yield from official communal fields.

Paradise

Dave had originally wanted to grow oats, figuring it would be an advantage to grow something not many other people were growing. The Ag expert had shot down that idea, explaining that oats were a cool season crop, unsuited to growing in the tropical jungle of Paradise's southern continent, because the oat plant goes dormant in high temperatures. That was too bad, because Dave had been hoping for a nice bowl of oatmeal someday. Back on Earth, oatmeal had not been his favorite food, but he was fixated on now. Of all the wide variety of foods he missed, a bowl of oatmeal seemed reasonably achievable. Unlike, for example, pepperoni pizza. Why waste time and effort yearning for something he was never, ever going to have again?

Jesse wanted to expand their private field to grow some corn of their own in addition to wheat, intending to someday produce grits. Grits, Jesse said, would be a big seller. Dave supposed Jesse was right about that, but he still was feeling nostalgic about a bowl of oatmeal, like his mother used to make on cold winter mornings in Milwaukee. To make the experience complete, he needed milk, which was not as scarce on Paradise as it used to be now that cows were producing high yields. Rumor had it that their own village would be getting a cow soon, in exchange for two dozen egg-laying chickens.

Dave also needed brown sugar. Sugarcane was being grown on Paradise, and their friendly local Ag expert had told Dave the sugarcane was growing well, very well. It would not be too long, another month perhaps, before human-produced sugar was available. Dave envied the guys who were growing sugarcane; those guys could command anything in trade for sugar, if they were smart enough to grow some sugarcane on their private fields. In fact, Dave had thought of trying to grow sugarcane with Jesse, instead of wheat. Unfortunately, they had learned that processing the cane into sugar was so very labor and energy intensive, it was not worth doing in small-scale operation. Someday, maybe, someday in the future.

So, Dave's theoretical bowl of oatmeal, a bowl of nostalgia, could have milk and sugar on Paradise. What he lacked were oats. If there were any oats on Paradise, they were in a UNEF warehouse, and that food was carefully guarded. Unless the hamsters allowed humans to grow food in temperate areas of the northern continent, he was not getting any oats within his lifetime. However long that was.

Flying Dutchman

"Skippy, we need to decide how we're going to find out what the Thuranin know about that surveyor ship we destroyed." Before we left Earth, many plans had been discussed, but no final decision had been made, of course. UNEF Command wanted Chotek, with my advice, to make the call. "I do not like the idea of us having to assault a Thuranin data relay station, it is too risky. The science team suggested-"

"The *science* team? Let me guess. They have some moronic idea about me magically retrieving the vital information we need. Probably they expect me to stealthily zoom past some random Thuranin ship and glean what we need from the databanks in like two seconds."

"No-" My interruption was ignored. He was on a roll so I let him talk.

"As I explained like a hundred freakin' times already, that won't work. The reason I was able to quickly get the data we needed from that Thuranin tanker ship on our last mission, is because I knew the coordinates for rendezvous with the surveyor ship would be in the tanker's navigation computer. I knew exactly where to look and what to look for, and the data was only concealed behind low-level encryption. The rendezvous coordinates may as well have been in a folder marked 'Skippy look here'." He paused. "Joe, you're not going to interrupt me with an unhelpful comment?"

"No, Skippy, I can tell you're on a roll. Go ahead."

"Oh. This is unexpected. I don't know what to say. Darn it. I had several snappy comebacks prepared and now I can't use them. Well, I'll save them for later. Uh, what is the science team's suggestion? Dr. Friedlander and I have had several conversations, during which I shot down many, many idiotic plans they dreamed up."

"The idea I want to ask is about is whether you could, as you say, magically fly by a random Thuranin ship. Only instead of you trying to find the data we need in a few seconds, you use that time to load a virus or worm or whatever you call it into the ship's computer. That worm would propagate from ship to ship, looking for the data we need. When the worm has it, it would cause ships to drop flight recorder drones at a couple coordinates in deep space. The *Dutchman* could then go to one of those coordinates and pick up the data whenever we want."

"I agree that is a great concept, and I congratulated the science team for thinking up a clever idea. Clever, but unworkable. When I flew by that tanker, I did upload a program which caused that ship to drop off flight recorder drones every time, before the ship jumped. The reason that worked is because my program was only resident in the tanker's computer for a short time because, you know, we blew up that ship soon after. The AIs aboard Thuranin ships do not compare to me in any way, but they also are not stupid. Because my program altered the normal operation of the ship, the ship's AI would have detected it eventually, probably within a week to twelve days. A program which only sat quietly looking for data would be able to conceal itself longer. So, the problem with the science team's clever idea is that such a program would work for a while, then the Thuranin would detect it. They would then not only erase the program from any infected ship, they would analyze the program to determine its purpose. What would happen then is they would likely figure out that the program was designed to drop off drones at specific coordinates, and they would surround each of those coordinates with a heavy battlegroup. The *Flying Dutchman* would jump in, be trapped by a damping field, and we would be destroyed."

"Crap."

"Joe, if there was an easy solution, I would have told you. Besides, it's your job to dream up crazy, out of the box monkey-brained ideas. You mean to tell me you haven't thought of an easy way to do this?"

"No," I admitted.

"I am disappointed in you, Joe."

"Skippy, I can't make ideas happen whenever I want. They just do. Or don't in this case."

"Then we have to do it the hard way," Skippy said with a touch of sadness. "The only way to be sure we will find the data we need, is to access the communications files of a Thuranin data relay station. Because those stations transmit powerful signals, they are heavily shielded, so even I can't access the files from the outside. I need to get inside, and that means we need to physically assault, board and take control of a station. Joe, I fear there will be many casualties among our brave special forces."

"Me too, Skippy. Me too." Major Smythe's SpecOps team leaders had been analyzing the three most common types of Thuranin data relay stations, trying to find a way in that would not lead to a certain slaughter of our forces. So far, they were not confident.

"It has to be a data relay station? We can't take over a Thuranin ship? Maybe a soft target like a civilian transport?"

"No, Joe, I am sorry. If that were possible, I would have mentioned it as an option. Because the Thuranin have been hit so badly by the Jeraptha in this sector, there is little Thuranin civilian traffic. What few civilian ships that are flying always have military escorts. And a civilian ship is unlikely to carry classified military data. Before you ask, I did consider us somehow capturing a small warship such as a frigate, how to do that would be your problem. That idea I quickly discarded, because there is no way to know beforehand whether any particular ship contains the data we are seeking. That ship might not have access to classified data, or that ship might belong to a battlegroup that had not yet been informed about the surveyor ship. Or the Thuranin may still be puzzling over the fate of the surveyor ship, and may not have informed the fleet about it. We might take a significant risk to capture a ship that doesn't have any useful data for us. Then we would have to keep capturing one ship after another. No, that won't work at all. We can't go randomly capturing ships, hoping they contain the data we need. We need the data to come to us. We need to seize a data relay station."

Skippy had explained to UNEF Command that because the Thuranin didn't have faster than light communications, they needed starships to carry message traffic from one star system to another, or between battlegroups of their far-flung fleet. To facilitate regular communications, the Thuranin had built space stations as data relays and scattered them throughout their territory. Most of the relay stations were in heavily trafficked star lanes; often located near clusters of wormholes. Unless ships were on especially urgent or clandestine missions, they were expected to jump in near a relay station and exchange data. A place where Thuranin ships regularly visited would be a tempting target for the Jeraptha, but the Jeraptha weren't interested in attacking the stations, only the warships that visited such stations. Destroying a relay station would be counterproductive for the Jeraptha; Thuranin warships wouldn't have a reason to make themselves temporarily vulnerable by stopping there. Accordingly, although most Thuranin relay stations were equipped with heavy armor and shields, they were very rarely attacked.

Once we boarded a relay station and took control, Skippy could ransack their data files at leisure to find the data we needed. Even better, he could erase the resident AI and replace it with a submind of his own. Then, if the station did not already contain all the data we needed when we arrived, we could abandon the station, leave the submind in place and back the *Dutchman* away. Thuranin ships would fly by, exchanging data, never knowing the station was under human control. When the submind received the data we needed, it would ping us. Even after we got that data, we could leave the submind in place, periodically jumping back in so Skippy could ransack any new files. The relay station would be like humanity having a direct tap into the enemy's data network. And we could keep it until that station was scheduled to rotate crews; at which point there would be an unfortunate and fatal accident with its reactor.

Skippy hoped the Thuranin had purchased insurance.

The problem for Major Smythe and me was to select one particular relay station to target for assault. Skippy had extensive data on all the Thuranin relay stations; it was up to Smythe and me to choose one to hit. We, mostly Smythe, had developed three criteria for selecting a target.

First, we needed a relay station that didn't have too much traffic, because we could not have Thuranin ships jumping into exchange data during our assault, and for at least a couple days later. Skippy needed time to load his submind into the Thuranin computer, which he expected to be typically crappy and inadequate. And we would need time to make cosmetic repairs to the exterior of the station, to avoid visiting Thuranin ships from asking awkward questions.

Second, the relay station needed to be of a particular type. Of the three standard Thuranin designs for relay stations, Smythe and his team had quickly rejected two types as being too large, staffed with too many little green men, and having extensive internal defenses. These two types of relay stations tended to be older, from when their Thuranin designers had been worried about defending against Jeraptha attempts to board and capture a station. In the past several hundred years, as it became clear the Thuranin had no interest in boarding what was basically a radio floating in deep space, the Thuranin had begun building a new design. This newer type of station was significantly smaller and required a much smaller crew. The designers had basically taken obsolete cruisers, removed the engines, added shielding to protect the crew from the powerful transmissions, and made a few more tweaks to create a cheap and simple relay station. This type of station did not have the internal armor and killing zones that could trap our special forces as they attempted to force their way to capture the station's core, where the AI resided.

And the third criteria was that the station must have a relatively fresh crew, with many months before that crew was scheduled to rotate out and be replaced by a new group of little green men. That would give the submind plenty of time to skim data and find everything we needed, and hopefully more.

The burden of selecting a short list of relay stations from Smythe's criteria fell on Skippy.

"Have you found some Thuranin data relays that are good targets for us?" I asked.

"Yes I did, and I have great news for you, Joey. All of these particular relay stations are pokestops!"

"What's a pokestop?"

"Come on, Joey, it's where you collect rare pokemonsters. Pokemon? Anyone? Anyone?" Skippy asked in frustration. "It's an old game, Joe, you- Oh, forget it. Damn, sometimes you are so stupid that it's not any fun to insult you."

"Mmm. Wow, you're saying that being stupid is an advantage?"

"What? No, I did not say that, you dumdum. Man, there are times-" He sighed, then sobbed quietly. "Oh, why am I stuck on a pirate ship with a bunch of flea-bitten monkeys? I must have been a truly awful person in a previous life, to deserve this terrible fate."

"An awful person like what?" I was going to suggest an arrogant AI, but he interrupted me.

"You know, Joe, someone who takes joy in making people suffer. I'm talking pure evil here, like a customer service rep for the cable company."

"Ha!" I laughed. "Even you could never be that evil, Skippy."

"Thank you for the reassurance, Joe. To be serious for a moment, based on your first two criteria, there are twenty three data relay stations that are perfect candidates for us. I think. You and Major Smythe will need to look at them and decide."

Whittling down the list of candidates was great, we still feared heavy casualties in taking the station. "Even with this newer type of relay station," I asked, "you can't do your sandman trick?" My hope was that Skippy could repeat the technique he had used to capture the *Flying Dutchman*; hacking into the Thuranin's AI and ordering all the little green men to go into sleep mode. After he'd done that, all we had to do was drag their sleeping, drooling bodies to a cargo hold.

"Sorry, Joe, the answer is no," Skippy said with regret. "Even that smaller type of station has heavy internal shielding. I couldn't access the entire structure from any one point. And as soon as we fire a shot, the Thuranin will go into combat protocol which disables their sleep function. I wish I could do that for you. Sorry."

"It's not your fault, Skippy. Without you, none of this would be possible."

"That internal shielding also means our combot operators will need to be inside the station," he warned, "close behind their machines. That way, I will be able to facilitate the interaction between operator and combot."

"We understand. That's still twenty three possible targets. Can you narrow the list further using our third criteria?"

Paradise

"Sure, Joe. I can do that, *after* I get the data on Thuranin fleet deployment plans, and crew rotation schedules for those twenty three relay stations. So, at the moment, the answer is no. I told you, we have to get that data from a Thuranin ship somewhere, somehow."

"All right, I hear you. You need more data. And we need a plan to get it. Fine. When we do gett that data and you give us a smaller list, I need to speak with Smythe. We will recommend two or three relay stations from your list. Then Chotek has to make the decision."

Skippy snorted. "Is our resident bureaucrat qualified to make military decisions, Joe?"

"No, but if there's not much difference between the stations on the final list, we may as well flip a coin. I want *him* to be part of making the decision. I want him to know that if there are casualties, he had a hand in it. I'm not covering my ass, Skippy. I want Chotek to know what it feels like to make life and death decisions."

CHAPTER SEVEN

Paradise

General Nivelle accepted the Burgermeister's offer of hot water to make tea, and scattered some precious tea leaves into his cup. The tea would have hardly any taste, and that didn't matter. To the Ruhar, it was the ritual of drinking tea that was important. "Thank you, Madame Logellia. I have been considering something you said during our last conversation. What would be involved if our force declared loyalty to the Ruhar? And what would be the implications to our people here, and on Earth? I assume the Kristang would learn of our switching sides."

She looked out the window. "It is a fine day; we should go for a walk."

It was not a particularly fine day, being overcast with the skies threatening rain, and a chill in the morning air. They walked out of the building, down a road, then turned to walk along a dirt lane separating two fields. One of the fields was ready for harvest, it contained some kind of grain like wheat or oats. The other field was in the process of being planted; a large machine was rolling along the rows at the far end of the field. From the field, Nivelle caught a whiff of whatever fertilizer the Ruhar used; it smelled vaguely like parmesan cheese and to Nivelle's nose, unpleasant. He ignored it. Reports had come into UNEF HQ that some Ruhar who had contact with human soldiers mentioned the scarcity of fertilizer on Paradise. A Kristang raiding ship had hit a fertilizer factory six months ago, and the local Ruhar were complaining that their government was very slow to rebuild it. The local Ruhar were unhappy about many things, according to rumors that Nivelle gave credence to. The government was not making enough of an effort to rebuild and enhance infrastructure. The schedule for bringing back native Ruhar who had been evacuated was far too slow, and the schedule kept slipping. And most importantly the local Ruhar complained that their fleet, which had recently won crushing victories, did not seem able or willing to protect them from what surely must be a small group of Kristang starships.

When they had walked half a kilometer down the lane, talking about nothing but the weather, Logellia decided it was time to discuss the important subject. "General, it is unfortunate that I ever mentioned to you the possibility of your force switching allegiances in this war. I mentioned our conversation to my superiors, and they were dismayed the subject had been discussed at all. If you were to formally offer to change sides, I am afraid to tell you that the Ruhar government would not welcome it. My government would not accept the humans on Gehtanu as clients at the present time. If the offer had been extended earlier, such as soon after our fleet regained control of Gehtanu, the answer might have been different. Under the current circumstances, it is not possible."

"Why? Has something changed in the strategic situation in this sector?"

"I should not be telling you this officially, and you must promise me that you will keep this a very closely-held secret, General."

"You have my word as a French soldier," General Nivelle said, mildly offended.

"First, I must tell you that your communications are thoroughly compromised by my people. There are even nanoscale recording devices in some of your clothing; the devices embedded in the collar of your uniform have been disabled temporarily," she pointed to her own zPhone. "Any repetition of this conversation must be conducted with extreme caution."

"Understood," Nivelle agreed, suddenly feeling his collar itching his neck. "And agreed."

"Cool, as your people say. General, my government, I refer to the federal government, not the planetary administration. The Ruhar federal government has been engaged in negotiations to give Gehtanu, this planet, back to the Kristang."

Nivelle almost choked on his complete shock. "Sacre bleu! *Why?*"

Logellia explained the strategic situation. "You must understand that my government never intended to recapture Gehtanu in the last campaign. In short, General, this planet is not worth the military effort that would be required to keep it."

Nivelle was stunned. The entire Ruhar campaign to retake Paradise had been a ruse to draw in the Thuranin and Kristang, and now the Ruhar wished to give the planet away?

"Personally," She continued, "I am opposed to any notion of surrendering my home planet. I was born here, and my mother was born here. Mine is only one voice. I am not even allowed to tell the local population about the negotiations. These raids by the Kristang," she looked at the clouds, "only serve to reinforce my government's decision to trade away this planet."

Nivelle was greatly disturbed, and chose his words carefully. "Your government would not welcome, and would not accept, our pledge of loyalty, because that would make them responsible for the humans here?"

"It would make *us* responsible, yes, all Ruhar. On this world, the issue of humans is important. Away from this star system, most of my people have never heard of humans. Or if they have, all they know is that humans serve our enemy. To accept your allegiance would mean my government accepts the tremendous expense of evacuating humans from this planet. And they would have to be resettled on a Ruhar world, where the local population would probably not be pleased to find an enemy in their midst. For my government there is, as I believe your people say, no upside for us. We gain nothing by accepting your force as clients."

General Nivelle could not argue with her hard, cold logic. It made sense. It also meant disaster for his force. "Then it is good that I did not discuss the possibility of switching sides with anyone, not even my personal staff. I wanted to learn the implications from you first."

"I do not know what impact there would be to Earth if you changed allegiances, because we do not know the situation on Earth. The Kristang there are cut off from the rest of their species, after the wormhole shut down."

"That is confirmed? It is not disinformation by the Kristang?" Nivelle asked anxiously. UNEF HQ had heard rumors that the Kristang no longer had access to Earth. If it was true, then he needed to officially inform his troops before rumors got out of hand. Bad news, as the old saying went, did not improve with age.

"The wormhole is in Kristang territory," she said. "So we cannot verify it has truly gone dormant. However, I am told that we have very solid intelligence that the Kristang and Thuranin have lost contact with your home planet."

"Is that unusual for a wormhole to shut down like that?"

"It is very unusual. As we do not know how wormholes work, or why they have sudden shifts, we can't make any useful speculation about why that wormhole has ceased functioning. It may reactivate tomorrow, or it could signal another impending shift across the entire sector. We simply do not know. General," she turned so they could walk back to her office, the sky was beginning to drizzle. "I am sorry about the situation you find yourself in. Your species did not ask to become part of this war. I do not have any advice for you. Having on my world a client species of our enemy is new to me. Again, I am sorry that you were drawn into this war."

Nivelle did not want to discuss regrets, he wanted to discuss action. "Do you know the status of the negotiations? The timeline for handing over control of this planet to the Kristang?"

"My government has not consulted me," she said with a wry smile, "so what I can tell you is from what I have heard from sources who are usually reliable. So far, the territory that the Kristang are offering in exchange for Gehtanu is not sufficient, and the negotiations have been going back and forth. There are complicating factors. Although there is currently a limited cease fire between the Jeraptha and the Thuranin in this sector, it has not yet been agreed which territories the Jeraptha have captured. Some star systems the Jeraptha took control of during the conflict, they may wish to give back to the Thuranin, in exchange for other more valuable territory. The Jeraptha wish to consolidate their gains and draw a new, more defensible border. That new border may affect what territory the Kristang are able to offer to us, or may affect the value of that territory. Because the Jeraptha captured a wormhole cluster from the Thuranin, the Jeraptha now control access to territory that is not inside their borders." She shook her head. "As I said, the situation is very complicated. The Commodore of our defense fleet," she pointed to the sky, "has told me that he thinks the ongoing Kristang raids are not aimed at retaking the planet; the Kristang force here is not strong enough to do that. The raids are aimed at making my government more willing to accept a lesser bargain in exchange for this planet. General, the true problem we face; you humans and we native Ruhar, is that my government very much wants to trade away Gehtanu. Therefore, eventually they *will* reach a deal with the Kristang, and my people will leave this world. As to your people, I do not know what will happen."

Flying Dutchman

While we still hadn't selected one particular relay station to hit, Major Smythe began planning the assault. Smythe was glum about our chances. "We can do it, sir," he told me without confidence. "We can take the station. I expect casualties to be heavy; once we get inside, it will be a short and bloody battle. We will have the advantage of initial surprise and numbers; between our troops in armor suits and combots, we outnumber them three to one. The Thuranin have the advantages of being genetically engineered cyborgs and being on the defensive. They know the terrain better than we do. I wish," he said while looking around the empty cargo bay we used for training, "that we could build a replica of that relay station. It would be bloody helpful to train on the same ground where we'll be fighting."

"Huh." He had given me a thought. "Hey, Skippy. This type of relay station we will be assaulting, they built a lot of them?"

"Yes, they are now the most numerous type of relay station, Joe," he confirmed. "An entire class of cruisers became obsolete, and the Thuranin used their obsolescence as an opportunity to create new relay stations. Why? Are you not happy with our choice of target?"

"Unless our target was seizing control of a basket of kittens, I wouldn't be happy about it. No, it's not this particular station that bothers me, it's the high level of risk in the whole concept. My question is whether there are any of this type of station that have been abandoned, because of battle damage or another reason."

"Sure there are, Joe. Only one has sustained sufficient battle damage to warrant it being abandoned; it was self-destructed to prevent it from falling into enemy hands."

"Oh, crap, I was hoping-"

He interrupted me again. "But there are seven others which have been abandoned after the recent wormhole shift, because their location was deemed no longer useful."

"Were these seven others also destroyed?"

"Not all of them. Two were blown up because they are now in Jeraptha territory. The other five were mothballed, in case another wormhole shift makes them useful again. Their reactors were shut down and all computer, communication and data storage capability was removed. But they are still there, drifting along in cold storage."

"Great!" I exulted. "Major Smythe, instead of us building a replica, how would you like your team to practice the assault on an actual data relay station?"

"Whoa!" Skippy shouted with a derisive laugh. "Wait just a minute there, Joe. You can't just, hmmm. Maybe you can just do that. Aaargh! Damn it! The monkey says 'duh how about we do this' and he comes up with a good idea. Now why didn't I think of that? Stupid, stupid brain! Oh, I hate my life sometimes," he said with a sob. "Huh. Now I see why I didn't of that; I knew about those abandoned stations, but removed them from my list because they are inactive. That is interesting, Joe."

"I'm sure it is, Skippy. That wormhole shift won't stop us from accessing one of those stations, will it?"

"Quite the contrary, Joe. There is one particular derelict station that was left totally isolated from both Thuranin and Jeraptha territory by the wormhole shift. It took a Thuranin ship almost eighteen months to retrieve the station crew after they were cut off. That station would be perfect for Major Smythe's team to practice, we would be assured of not having any visitors. I can use our Elder wormhole controller module, to temporarily connect to that dormant wormhole so we can go through, and on our way back. Joe, Joe, Joe," he lamented. "Do you do this sort of thing just to humiliate me?"

"No, Skippy," I assured him, "of course not. Humiliating you is a bonus. Major Smythe, you can work with this?"

"Brilliantly, sir."

"We still have the hard part to do," I cautioned.

"Yes, sir," Smythe nodded, "but perhaps now it won't be quite so bloody hard."

I contacted the bridge and we changed course, toward the derelict relay station. Of course, I caught hell from Chotek for not informing of him about the change of plans before I ordered the course change. That pissed me off; I was on my way to his office to tell him personally, but that wasn't good enough. We had a discussion that ended with me deciding that, in the future, I would take the thirty seconds to contact him before I ordered a major course change. Thirty seconds is all it would take, for me to swallow my pride and avoid an argument.

The whole situation still pissed me off.

Paradise

"Can y'all believe this shit?" Jesse asked, while staring at his zPhone in the hope that what he'd just read would change.

"It's crazy, man," Dave replied, shaking his head.

"No," Jesse looked up in frustration, "I mean, *do* you believe it?"

Dave scrolled the screen to the top, and pointed to the logo at the beginning of the message. "UNEF HQ believes it. This is official."

"That can't happen, can it?" Jesse appealed for assurance. The message from UNEF HQ stated that the wormhole that lead back to Earth had closed, and the Kristang weren't able to reopen it. The Expeditionary Force on Paradise now had zero hope of ever getting

Craig Alanson

home. Even if their former Kristang 'allies' took Paradise back from the Ruhar, they could not bring humans back to Earth, because the Kristang lacked the technology to make that long journey. Even for the advanced Thuranin, such a voyage was wildly impractical. "Wormholes don't just shut down for no reason," Jess protested.

"The one near Earth opened for no reason, Cornpone," Ski said gently. "That's what landed us in this mess in the first place."

"That's bullshit," Eric Koblenz said, spitting on the ground for emphasis. Eric was part of another three-man Ag team, a team that Jesse and Dave had partnered with to combine and expand their private plots of land into a significant field of wheat. The other two partners were good guys, but Eric had been a problem from the start. He did his share of the work, that wasn't the issue. The problem was that Eric was a 'Keeper'.

Soon after the Ruhar took the planet back, and UNEF HQ ordered all humans to surrender, a movement called 'Keepers of the Faith' had sprung up on the zPhone network. Keepers held that UNEF should not have surrendered; that the Kristang were true allies, that the fortune cookie messages from Earth about the Kristang abusing humanity's home planet and enslaving the population were somehow all Ruhar lies. That UNEF had come out to the stars to fight alongside the Kristang against the species that had attacked Earth, so UNEF should keep doing that; fight the Ruhar. Even if the Expeditionary Force on Paradise was wiped out to the last human, UNEF would demonstrate to our Kristang allies that humans kept their word, and such a demonstration of steadfastness and resolve would benefit humans back on Earth.

To Keepers, everyone else were 'Traitors'.

"That's all a lie by the hamsters," Eric spat again, "and their UNEF HQ lackeys are just selling out again as usual. The wormhole near Earth didn't just open up recently, that's a lie the hamsters told us to explain why the Kristang had not been to Earth before they did. And that wormhole is not shut down now; the hamsters want us to give up hope so we'll be easy to control. And you Traitors are stupid enough to listen to these lies."

"Oh," Dave sighed, "not this BS again. Look, man, if you want to talk about your whacko conspiracy theories," he pointed to the jungle, "go put on your tinfoil hat and tell it to the trees. Because I'm not wasting my time listening."

"Traitor?" Jesse asked angrily. "You best be careful throwing around words like that, asshole. How exactly are we giving aid and comfort to the enemy?"

"Damn, Jesse, don't take the bait," Dave warned but it was too late.

Eric put his arms across his chest. "You give aid and comfort every day, by not resisting them. The Ruhar know that sheep like you will never fight them, so they don't have to garrison many troops here. You're growing your own food, so the Ruhar don't have to manufacture human food and ship it in."

"Yeah, like you're not helping to grow food," Dave said sarcastically while pointing to Eric's hands, dirty from harvesting tomatoes and peppers from the fields. "And I've noticed you haven't refused to eat this food we grew with the hamsters' help. See, Jesse, that's how moronic the Sleepers are," Dave used the derisive nickname for the Kristang loyalists. "When we eat food we grew here, we're traitors, but when they do the exact same thing, they're loyal."

"Talk all you want. The Ruhar are keeping troops here and ships in orbit, because they know if they don't, we Keepers will take the planet back. We are assisting the Kristang by making the Ruhar keep combat resources here."

"Of course you are," Jesse scoffed. "They're afraid of what, the hoe you use in the fields? No, it must be the shovel you were using this morning. Hey, genius, the Ruhar hold the high ground. They can sit in orbit and pound the crap out of us down here, and there ain't squat we can do about it. Unless you weaved together corn stalks to make a railgun."

"Shut up," Eric growled. He waved a finger at Dave and Jesse. "Your time will come, you'll see. You Traitors will be crying then."

Dave grabbed Jesse's shoulder and squeezed. "Stay cool, Jesse. This piece of crap isn't worth it. Don't do it." Alarmed about breakdowns in discipline now that soldiers saw themselves as nothing but farmers, UNEF had cracked down on fighting. Anyone who got into a fight, regardless of who started it, spent time in a hard labor camp. The prospect of building roads in the steaming jungle of Lemuria was an effective deterrent to fighting. For now.

Jesse relaxed slightly, still ready if Eric threw a punch. "You're right, Ski, thanks for reminding me." To Eric he said "If y'all want to fight the hamsters, you Sleepers best get at it, then. Leave us out of it," Jesse smirked, "we don't want to be within ten kilometers when the Ruhar turn where you're standing into a smoking crater."

"We do want a good view," Ski added.

"Oh, yeah, man, I wouldn't miss that," Jesse said with a laugh.

Eric flipped them off with both hands and stomped off without another word.

"You'd think those Sleeper idiots would have woke the hell up when the lizards burned out that big field last month," Jesse mused. A Kristang destroyer had popped into orbit and used its masers on a broad sweep to burn out several fields that were growing human food on Lemuria. There were several villages on Lemuria now almost entirely populated by Keepers; it wasn't an official designation but most non-Keepers had asked for transfer out. The biggest field that had been targeted was a Keeper village; the masers had scorched an entire season of crops and killed thirty one people. 'Keeping the Faith' hadn't spared the village from the Kristang's predations. That destroyer had not targeted any Ruhar areas before it jumped away; it had focused entirely on damaging the human food supply.

"Jesse, save your breath, you can't reason with idiots like him. They'll tell you that Keeper village got hit because the Kristang see all humans as traitors. Their answer is we all need to be Keepers; then the Kristang will come back like Santa Claus down the chimney to reward all the good little girls and boys," Dave said in disgust.

"Yeah," Jesse nodded. "Like the school board in my home county. The answer to every problem is always they need more money. Whatever they were trying would have worked if only they had more money. They never stop think to maybe it's what they're doing that's the problem."

"Amen to that, brother," Dave held out a fist, and Jesse bumped it. "They're like my aunt Claire," Dave went on. "When something bad happens to someone else, she says God is punishing them. When something bad happens to her, God is testing her faith. It's the perfect system; no matter what happens, she's right and everyone else is wrong."

"She must be a lot of fun at the Thanksgiving table," Jesse said.

Dave shook his head. "Aunt Claire doesn't get invited to Thanksgiving anymore. That's mostly because her new husband drinks too much and says stupid stuff. Last time they were there, he knocked the gravy boat onto the floor. The only one in the whole family who misses him is the dog."

Jesse laughed. "That must have been the best dog Thanksgiving ever!" Then he looked at the sky, and his good humor faded. "We're never going home, are we? Never. We can't. This just can't be real. Can it?"

"All I can say for sure is, if we really have no hope of ever going home again," Dave glanced around warily. Eric had walked out of earshot, but he was talking with another Keeper, and shooting hostile looks in Dave's direction. "Discipline will be going to hell in a hurry around here."

Flying Dutchman

We had found the derelict Thuranin relay station right where Skippy said it would be. Before boarding, we checked out the interior with combots, in case the Thuranin had left any booby traps. The little green men had not bothered to booby trap the place; they had stripped it of anything useful before they left. That left a perfect training environment for us.

Major Smythe wasted no time in putting his SpecOps team through practice runs, and I joined them. Not because I fantasized about being a bad-ass special forces soldier; I was realistic about that. I joined the practice runs because I wanted to see first-hand what Smythe's team would be facing.

After a walk through, we get into our two dropships to practice an assault for the first time. The dropship was crammed with people, we'd removed the seats to get in as many people as we could. The only thing holding us in place was webbing, that was also our only cushioning when the dropship was maneuvering. Strapped in, I was putting my helmet on, and banged it into the helmet of the person next to me. "Sorry," I said.

"No problem, Sir," she replied. Her name was Lauren Poole, she was one of the US Army Rangers who was new to the Merry Band of Pirates. I suspected that Smythe had assigned her to babysit me, she kept popping up next to me in training.

"It doesn't bother you to be upside down like that?" I asked. In order to cram people in, some people were hanging upside down from the dropship's ceiling. To get loose, we all had to cut the webbing, and I was concerned that would create snag hazards. That was one thing we would discover in practice.

"No," she replied with a twinkle in her eyes. "I started gymnastics when I was eight years old. Sometimes it feels like I've spent half my life upside down, Sir."

"All right," I shook my head, and pulled down the faceplate of my helmet. "Let's do this."

"This is still going to be bloody hard," Smythe said as he took off his helmet. His short hair was plastered to his scalp by sweat.

I nodded, trying to catch my breath. We had just finished the sixth practice assault; the sixth time we had run through the final plan. This was after we tested five other plans multiple times. After the fourth exhausting day, I had lost count of how many times we had practiced various plans. I was worn out, and I wouldn't even be participating in the actual assault, so my role in practice was as an observer.

What I had observed was not encouraging. Skippy acted as the Red team, our opponent, and he assured us that he was dumbing down his reactions to match the Thuranin cyborgs assisted by their AI. The combots that Skippy controlled were still lightning fast and deadly accurate. We had to use surprise, sheer numbers and maximum firepower to accomplish the objective. On the first practice run, we had failed; the last of our special forces died before getting into the core of the station from which Skippy could access and shut down the station's AI. The second practice run was worse; we failed to breach the docking bay on our first attempt, and everyone died before they could leave the dropships. Having only two dropships was a serious limitation; both had to act as transports, each crammed tight with SpecOps people and combots. The interiors of both dropships had been stripped, no chairs remained; people were held in place by webbing to be cut away when they wanted release.

After our failure to breach the docking bay on the second attempt, we tried the *Dutchman* making a microjump to position the ship in front of the docking bay, so the ship could hammer the doors open with her powerful masers. That third practice attempt ended with what at first seemed like a victory. Three of our special forces survived to penetrate the station's core and Skippy was able to shut down the Thuranin AI. Unfortunately, the *Dutchman* got blown up in the practice run, so it was a failure. Skippy warned us that his calculations showed we would lose the ship 92% of the time; our beat-up star carrier could not survive combat at close range. So we went back to the original plan; as soon as our stealthed dropships opened fire on the docking bay doors, the *Dutchman* would jump away and await an 'all clear' signal.

The fourth, fifth and sixth practice assaults were successful, in that at least one person survived to reach the station's core. The fifth assault had the best result, because in the end there were five special forces and three combots left combat effective.

This wasn't working. "It's too difficult, Major," I agreed with Smythe when we had finished stowing our gear back aboard the *Dutchman*. Any operation that incurs 90% casualties is unacceptable, even if the survival of humanity might be at stake.

"The problem is that we lose too many people and combots while breaching the docking bay," Smythe observed, "and then getting from the docking bay into the station proper. After that, we don't have the massed firepower to overwhelm the enemy defenses. It becomes a short war of attrition; do we lose people and combots faster than we can advance."

"I know." I did. I'd been there, I'd seen combots go offline and people's armored suits go stiff as Skippy declared them 'dead'.

"Maybe there's another way to breach that docking bay. Fly troops in just with suits, ahead of the dropships," Smythe mused. "You've done an extensive spacedive, sir."

"Yes, and I wouldn't recommend it. Major, let's get some rest tonight, and try it fresh again in the morning."

"I would rather have another go at it today, sir," Smythe's tone indicated that I wanted a break because I was not special forces.

"Yes you do, because you SpecOps types are always go-go-go. When we conduct the actual assault, we'll do it with freshly rested soldiers. We'll rest tonight, then add fresh troops to the simulation tomorrow."

Smythe nodded curtly, unconvinced. "I will get up early tomorrow," said Smythe, who got up early every morning. "I want to get the equipment checked out early, that will save us time that we can use for practice."

"I'll join you," I responded.

"Joe gets going a lot quicker in the mornings," Skippy chimed in cheerily, "since he stopped shaving down there. It saves a lot of time."

"Damn it, Skippy, I don't shave down there!"

"That's what I just said, you dumdum. Man, open your ears and listen once in a while," he grumbled. "Anyway, aren't those hairs already curly? Do you really need a curling iron down there?"

"Wha, I, don't, it's not-" I sputtered, while the team laughed uncontrollably.

"Fine, whatever. Don't complain to me the *next* time you burn your thighs with that iron."

I protested, feeling my face growing red already. Most of the special forces with us were new to the Merry Band of Pirates; they didn't know how Skippy loved to make jokes at my expense. Shaking my head and holding up my hands, I walked out with what little dignity I had left. "I'll see you at 0500, Major Smythe."

Paradise

As a special treat, the residents of Fort Rakovsky, population nineteen, learned there would be a US Army general visiting them the next day. They learned this information not from UNEF HQ or the general's staff, but from the grapevine of villages the general had already visited on the tour. Since the general was traveling by hamvee and there were few roads in the formerly impenetrable jungles of Lemuria, it was easy to predict where the general would be going next. While it would have been nice for the general's staff to announce visits ahead of time, his staff expected the zPhone network to do the announcing for them. Any village that was caught off guard had to be either not paying attention, or was very much disliked by their surrounding villagers. Either way, such an incident would tell the general and his staff that something was seriously amiss.

So, the residents of Fort Rakovsky had the joy of spending a day of their off-duty time straightening up the village. Uncompleted hooches were worked on through the night, and all the buildings were cleaned. The already minimal amount of trash was consolidated. Personal garden plots were weeded once again, and selected ripe fruits and vegetables were picked a day ahead of the normal schedule. Someone found paint, and used the back of a crate to make 'Fort Rakovsky' signs to post on the roads coming into the village from east and west.

"This is the best it's going to get," Dave Czajka said while looking around the village's only street with a frown.

"It's good enough," Jesse Colter assured his buddy. "Here they come."

Around a corner of the road came three hamvees and a large truck, with lead vehicle flying both the UNEF and American flag. National flags were not encouraged, but this was the American sector of Lemuria, and a US flag flew from a pole in the center of Fort Rakovsky. To avoid excess wear and tear on the priceless and irreplaceable fabric, the flag was normally kept wrapped in plastic in a box, and only taken out for special occasions. Like the rare times when people from another village came to Fort Rakovsky to trade, and there was a woman with them. In those cases, the village was scrubbed top to bottom with far more vigor than was given to any visiting general.

The general made a cursory inspection of the village, then walked over to check the fields, his chief interest on the tour. Mostly, he wanted to see what soldiers were growing on their personal plots of land. After an hour, he came to the extensive plot that Jesse and Dave shared with three other guys. "Impressive," General Marcellus observed. "This land belongs to the five of you?"

"The five of us work this land, sir, we get more done when we work together. But the land belongs to six people," Dave said. The 'Keeper' who had been a problem had arranged a transfer to another village, and his replacement got along well with everyone.

"Six?" Marcellus looked at the five men who were proudly showing their healthy personal crops. "The other guy doesn't work?"

"He doesn't work the land, sir," Jesse explained. "He's good at fixing things, so he lets us work his land in exchange for a cut of the crops. He repairs and maintains equipment for us and other villages around here, and they trade stuff in exchange for his labor. We get a cut of whatever he gets in trade."

"I see. Captain Rivera, a word, please." Marcellus walked a short distance with his staffer, and frowned. "This is a problem. This mechanic is trading away land that UNEF provided to him, instead of using it to increase the food supply. He is not performing his assigned tasks," General Marcellus declared.

"Excuse me, sir, but I believe he is performing his assigned tasks during his duty hours," Captain Rivera said. "His personal activities are performed during his off-duty time."

"We gave people personal plots of land so they could grow food, Captain, not to use it as an excuse to slack off. Remind me again why I have an economist on my staff? And why the Marines sent an officer to Harvard to study economics in the first place."

"Because, sir, the United States Marine Corps is a forward-thinking organization, and they anticipated Earth would be invaded by aliens, leaving a major force trapped offworld to develop its own independent economy," Rivera said with a deadpan expression. "My master's degree is in management; economics was my undergrad major."

"And you signed up for the Marine Corps," Marcellus shook his head in wonderment.

Rivera grinned. "It turns out there are not a lot of practical applications for a bachelor's degree in economics."

"Did you consider the Coast Guard?"

"I wanted to see the world, sir. Seeing other worlds is a bonus."

"Then use your Harvard training, to explain to me why I shouldn't discipline a soldier for trading away land that was given to him for the purpose of him growing food."

"Because, sir, he is making the best use of the resources available to him, including his skill set. He might be terrible at farming, but he is good at fixing and maintaining equipment. If he used his off-duty time to grow crops, we would only have one more unskilled farmer. With the arrangement he has devised, his plot of land is being put to its best use, and his skills are being used to make people who are farming more productive by providing them with reliable equipment. Specialization of labor is key to an efficient economy; everyone does what they do best. Eventually, sir, we will need to establish a form of currency; this barter economy of people trading corn for tomatoes and so on, is inherently inefficient."

Marcellus looked at the sky and muttered to himself. "Somedays, I wish I was still a private carrying a rifle. Life was so simple back then."

"Yes, sir," Rivera said simply, because there wasn't anything else to say.

"Back in the hamvees, captain," Marcellus said, "we have another four of these villages to visit today." Touring villages might not benefit the residents in any way, but they were opening Marcellus' eyes. His intel report back to UNEF HQ should open some eyes there. His greatest concern was that, as soldiers became fulltime farmers, people were going to increasingly question what authority UNEF had over them. Eventually, the military command-and-control arrangement would give way to, he shuddered to think, democracy. Elections. *Politics*.

What, he asked himself, was this world coming to? This alien world.

Flying Dutchman

An idea hit me at 0337 that morning. This time, I literally did dream something up. "Hey, Skippy?"

"What? Is this important? I'm watching a late-night infomercial about how I can get stains out of fabrics. It's not helpful, but it sure is funny."

"That's great, Skippy. I have a question for you; can you fake a high-security message from Thuranin military command?"

"Please, Joe. Easier than you can get a red wine stain out of a white carpet. Now why would anyone install a white carpet in their house? And if they had white carpet, why would they buy red wine? Unless they bought white carpet and red wine just for an infomercial. I smell a conspiracy here, Joe."

"That mystery has confounded mankind for centuries, Skippy," I agreed. "Could you convincingly fake a message that the *Dutchman* is on a secret mission for the Thuranin high command or whatever, so we can fly dropships right into that relay station's docking bay?"

Silence.

"Skippy? Listen, I'm sure that you could rewind that infomercial if you really-"

"Holy shit. Holy shit! Why didn't I think of that? Damn it! Joe, Joe, I hate my life. Oh, this is so humiliating. That is a *great* idea."

"Skippy, I promise that I won't tell anyone it was my idea-"

"Why thank you, Joe-"

"-until breakfast."

"Thus reminding me of why I rightfully so very much hate you, Joe."

"I love you too, Skippy."

"Don't get too cocky, monkey. Of course I can create a convincing message, with the proper Thuranin multi-level encryption and military authentication codes. I did that while you were saying 'breakfast', which because your monkey brain works so slowly I heard as 'buh-urr-ehh-kkk-fff-ass-'"

"Got it, Skippy. What's the problem?"

"We would need that station to receive the message before the *Dutchman* jumps in on their doorstep. Our modified star carrier would raise way too many suspicions if we just showed up and said 'trust me'."

"Crap. So we need another ship to carry the message for us?"

"Yup. And we can't transmit a message directly to that ship, either, because any Thuranin ship is going to look at us with great suspicion."

"But you do have a plan, right?" I asked, dreading the answer.

"Certainly, and well, heh, heh, you are very much not going to like it."

Damn. Whenever I heard Skippy's nervous 'well heh heh' it set off my Spidey senses.

I very, very much did not like Skippy's plan to get a message loaded into a Thuranin ship, but Smythe very much did like my plan for his SpecOps team to gain access to a relay station docking bay without fighting for it. We changed the simulations so that our two dropships were invited into the docking bay by the Thuranin, and we then only needed to breach the inner doors. Twelve practice runs resulted in much improved results; most times we took the station quickly, and even the practices that went comparatively badly achieved our goal. Casualties were still unacceptable to my mind, even Smythe was bothered. My guess is that SpecOps people are so used to being elite that they had a difficult time contemplating any sort of failure. Smythe reminded the special forces of three very important facts. First, the people aboard the *Flying Dutchman* were indeed very special forces; the absolute most elite and capable combat forces humanity had ever developed. Second, we would be operating on the enemy's territory, against well-prepared defenses in which the enemy had every advantage. And third, the enemy were genetically-enhanced cyborgs with lightning-quick reactions and an instinctive link with their deadly combots. The fact that humans had any chance to capture a Thuranin relay station was an enormous tribute to the dedication and training of the SpecOps team.

The twelfth and last practice run resulted in 'only' two dozen casualties and a successful seizure of the station. Smythe told me he did not think further practices would yield better results; we now had a precise plan. Execution of the plan would be up to Smythe's team. It sucked for me to think of sitting safely aboard the *Flying Dutchman* while my crew took the risks.

Paradise

Paradise

Jesse walked wearily from their private allotment up the hill to the village that had sprung up. Fort Rakovsky now boasted actual buildings, made of wood logged from the jungle around them. Jesse and Dave were constructing their own dwelling, that they called a 'hooch', out of timber and a sort of canvas. Eventually, they hoped to replace the canvas. It was only half finished, but already beat the cramped tent they'd been living in for what seemed like forever now.

As he came around the corner of a large tent and was startled. "Ah!" He pulled up short like he'd seen a snake. "What the hell is that?"

In front of the hooch they'd been constructing off and on, Dave Czajka was sitting in the sunshine, with a huge grin on his face. Sitting on a couch. The ugliest, most awful couch Jesse had ever seen in his entire life. He'd never even imagined a piece of furniture could be so ugly. It was covered in a wild, garish pattern of some flowers the hamsters liked.

"It's a couch," Dave explained. "Our couch. The supply wagon came through, they had some furniture the hamsters discarded. I traded for it. Didn't cost us much."

"You *bought* that horrible thing? Damn, Ski, I've seen couches on the side of a highway that looked better. That's after they got run over a few times, and sat out in the sun and rain for years. Damn!" He shielded his eyes. "I can't even look directly at that thing."

Ski looked at where he was sitting. In truth, the couch had seen better days. "You're exaggerating, it's not that bad."

"Bad? It's *heinous*, man! We've got to get rid of it, pronto. That thing is a crime against humanity."

"Come on, 'Pone," Ski used the shortened version of Jesse's nickname, "it's not that bad."

"Bad? It's hideous. Damn! My Ma brought home a couch like that, it used to be her mother's, and I think it belonged to her mother's aunt before that. That couch was evil, Man, I tell you. It sat in the living room, my father wouldn't even go in there. One night my Ma comes home, my Pa and I were trying to perform an exorcism like in that old movie, you seen it, right? Ma walks in, we're standing there in the living room with a Bible and a cross, shouting 'The power of Christ compels you! The power of Christ compels you!'" Jesse broke up laughing while telling his own story, remembering his mother's expression.

Looking at Jesse, Ski couldn't help laughing too. "What happened?"

"That evil thing defeated us, or we got the words wrong or something. My Ma was not amused, and that damned couch was still there the next morning. Ma did compromise by putting a cover over the couch, so maybe we did chase that couch's evil spirit out of my Ma. My Pa still refused to sit on it."

"How about we get a priest or someone to perform an exorcism on this thing?" Ski offered. He hated to give up the couch entirely; furniture was on very tight supply on Paradise.

"A human exorcism won't work on an alien couch, Ski," Jesse explained the obvious, although he was taking a second look at the couch. It was so amazingly ugly that it was kind of cool. "You know why the hamsters gave it up, don't you? It was ugly even to them."

"Maybe we can throw a coat of paint over it, or fabric dye?"

"I don't know." Hesitantly, Jesse touched the fabric. "This alien stuff probably has some high-tech stain blocker. That isn't going to work."

"Pone," Ski lowered his voice. "We need real furniture, we can't keep living on old packing crates and busted up containers."

"That's been good enough for-"

"*Girls*," Dave emphasized, "expect guys to have at least a couch, you know?"

"Oh."

"Yeah, oh."

Jesse's eyes grew wide as he imagined the possibilities. "You are a freakin' genius, Ski. Hey, you know what, that couch is so ugly that it's a, what do you call it? A conversation piece."

"There's only one other real couch in all of Fort Rakovsky," Dave pointed out.

"Hmm. You know what we need now?" Jesses asked, suddenly looking at the couch in a new light.

"What?"

"A real coffee table."

"We don't have coffee, there's none left on Paradise."

"One thing at a time. Couch first, then coffee table. Then we invite girls over, after we get the hooch finished."

Dave gave a big thumbs up to that. Neither he nor Jesse mentioned that there were exactly zero women in Fort Rakovsky, population nineteen. The closest women were in Camp Toffler, a half hour walk away. Women sometimes came to trade goods, and they saw women when they made the weekly drive into the 'big' town of Fort Cherokee.

"What are you waiting for?" Jesse asked, suddenly no longer tired. "Let's get this couch under cover before it rains, and then we get working on finishing the hooch."

Flying Dutchman

Dinner that night was cooked by the American SpecOps team, and I had been thinking about it all day. They were serving steaks! Although the galley had a grill, these steaks were prepared steakhouse style. Seared on one side, then the steaks go into an oven to bake so they stay juicy. When they were put on a plate, the seared side goes up because it looks nicer. Anyway, we were having steak! Everything we ate aboard the *Flying Dutchman* was good; each national team wanted to outdo the others, and Major Simms had loaded a wide variety of food into our cargo holds. Much of it was frozen or irradiated, of course. We also had fresh herbs and vegetables from the hydroponics lab, which had begun as an experiment and now regularly provided fresh food.

Skippy disapproved when he saw me skip the vegetable tray, after my plate was weighed down by a juicy steak. "Joe, you need to eat your veggies," he scolded me from the speaker.

"Duh," I responded. "Do you know how many veggies this cow ate? Tons! I'm getting my veggies in concentrated form."

"It doesn't work that way, sir," Sergeant Adams said as she scooped some green thing onto my plate. I should have known better than to get in line behind her.

"What is that?" I asked suspiciously.

"Brussel sprouts. Don't worry, they're not boiled to mush like school lunch Brussel sprouts. These are cooked in a pan with olive oil, salt and pepper, and then they put a little bit of maple syrup on it for you. They're good. Get some salad too."

"Is that an order, Staff Sergeant?"

She looked at my collar. "Not when you're wearing that uniform, Colonel. It's a suggestion, not an order."

I put salad on my plate. And, damn it, she was right, it turns out that Brussel sprouts are good. Especially with real maple syrup.

Paradise

CHAPTER EIGHT

Flying Dutchman

Chotek called a meeting to discuss how we were going to get the data we needed, and how Skippy could load a message aboard a Thuranin ship. A message that would be delivered to a Thuranin relay station, stating that a funny-looking shrunken star carrier would be arriving on a top secret mission, and that the relay station should open the docking bay doors for a pair of dropships. The message would also state that the crew of the station had won a free cruise, and all we needed was their credit card numbers.

Ok, that last part I made up.

When Skippy had said 'well, heh, heh, you are very much not going to like it' about his plan for us to plant a message in the computers of a Thuranin warship, I knew that I would not like his plan. What I did not know is that the thing I wouldn't like was, Skippy not having a workable plan. "Skippy," I groaned in frustration, "you said I would very much not like your plan."

"Uh huh. I don't have a plan that will work, and you very much don't like that, right? I'm just trying to keep you on your toes, Joe. There are many, many possible plans, however none of them will actually work. Unless I'm missing something."

"You've done this sort of thing before, Mr. Skippy," Chotek observed, sounding annoyed. He looked down at his tablet, consulting notes about our mission reports. "On your first mission, you used a series of microjumps to remain in proximity to a Thuranin battlegroup, in order to download data about the military situation in the sector. On your second mission, you flew by a Thuranin tanker ship, and obtained the rendezvous coordinates for the surveyor ship. You were also able to alter the tanker ship's computer, so that it dropped flight recorder drones before each jump."

"Bing bing bing bing!" Skippy rang a bell. "Winner, winner, chicken dinner! You are correct, Chocky, I did do those things, because I am Skippy the Magnificent. Doing those two things was much, much, oh so much easier than what we have to do next. Or what I have to do next, since *you* are not going to do anything useful, while I do all the work. Whatever that is."

"Why?" Chotek asked. It was a reasonable question. "Why is this significantly more difficult? The task appears to be no different from actions you have already performed very successfully."

"Ugh," Skippy groaned. "Colonel Joe, do I truly have to waste my time explaining simple facts to the cereal mascot?"

"Skippy," I replied trying to be tactful, "you do need to explain the situation to the mission commander," I nodded toward Hans Chotek. "I think the rest of us, me included, would appreciate a more complete understanding of the difficulty involved." In this case, I did have to agree with Chotek; the task sounded relatively straightforward to me. Hopefully, this time I could avoid an extended spacedive that ended with me almost plunging into the atmosphere of a gas giant planet. And peeing in my pants.

"Fine," Skippy huffed. "The first time was easy, because all I did was randomly skim data from the memory of a Thuranin command ship. It didn't matter what data I got, because I knew I would be able to piece together a very rough overview of the military situation in the sector. A command ship would have basic data on battlegroup deployments, right in the command ship's navigation system. I knew where to get the data I wanted, so I was able to reach in and scoop up whatever was on top. The second time, we approached a tanker, a ship with a much lower level of security than a warship. The data security and sensor acuity of a tanker is an order of magnitude more crude than a

Thuranin warship. In that case, again, I knew the data we needed would be in the ship's navigation system, and I knew that data would be queued up in a recent update. Easy in, easy out. Planting a virus in the tanker's computer was also easy, because the ship's cybersecurity was laughably crude. Like, their password was 'password'."

He paused to make a sound like taking a deep breath. "This task will be, as I said, *much* more difficult. We need detailed fleet deployment plans, plus the crew rotation schedules for data relay stations across the sector. Only a warship will have that data, and I have to download the full dataset; we can't afford to miss anything important. Then, I will need to plant a message in the ship's databank. Thuranin warship AIs are not stupid. Back when we microjumped around and I pulled data from the command ship, that ship's AI knew I was downloading data, and it actively resisted me. After we left, that AI would have thoroughly inspected the integrity of its databanks. If I had left a virus, or planted a message, the AI would have found it. With the tanker, that ship's AI never knew I was there, so it never ran a diagnostic of its systems. What we need to do now is approach closely to a Thuranin warship, and maintain close contact for an extended time, like at least three to five minutes. So, we can't just fly by. And whatever we do, the ship's AI can never suspect we were there."

"Can you enhance the stealth of a dropship," Chang asked, "to get us close enough without being detected?"

"I can enhance a dropship's standard stealth capability, but not enough," Skippy replied. "Considering how close we need to get to a Thuranin warship, and how long we have to remain there, we *will* be detected. Joe, before you suggest we could do another spacedive, that won't work this time. The only way to find the right ship is to wait near a wormhole, we could be waiting there for a month or more until I identify a ship that is a good candidate for us. After a month in a spacesuit, you would die of your own smell. Also you would run out of oxygen and water."

Avoiding another spacedive was a relief to me. "Hiding the dropship in a comet won't work this time either, right?"

"No, Joe, a Thuranin warship would never allow a navigation hazard like a comet near a wormhole. And a comet hanging near a wormhole in deep interstellar space would be awfully suspicious. Most likely the Thuranin would use a comet for target practice and blow it up."

"Scratch that idea. All right, Skippy, you've told us all the ideas that won't work, what ideas do you have for us to do this?"

"My idea is to tell you monkeys to think up an idea. Because I got nothing, Joe. I do not see how we can get close enough to a Thuranin warship, long enough for me to do the job, without being detected. We have seen that your monkey brains have a certain cleverness that has proven useful. So, do your thing, monkeys. Dream something up."

The frown on my face matched those around the conference table. Then my frown deepened when I realized everyone was looking toward me. "Hey, right now, I got nothing," I held up my hands defensively.

"We will, as you Americans say," Chang said with a smile, "put our thinking caps on."

Chang led us through a brainstorming session for the next two hours. We threw out all kinds of crazy, impractical ideas, and Skippy shot them all down. I even mentioned ideas that I knew would not work, in the hope of sparking a good idea from someone else.

We suggested using more than one dropship; one creating a distraction while the other got close enough for Skippy to contact the ship's computer. Skippy said the Thuranin would either detect both dropships and shoot first, or more likely jump away if they thought our dropships were a threat.

We thought of somehow getting Skippy into a container that would be loaded aboard a Thuranin warship, then he could somehow cause the container to be ejected later. I hated the idea of Skippy being out there on his own. And we would first have to find just the right ship first. Plus, how would we get a package aboard a Thuranin warship? Hide Skippy inside a birthday cake to be delivered by FedEx? You can see our ideas were getting pretty desperate and silly by that point.

After two hours of us throwing out ideas ranging from wildly crazy to merely impractical, Chotek decided we should take a break. Our new mission commander gave me the impression that he was disappointed I hadn't already dreamed up an idea. Truthfully, I was disappointed in myself. And Skippy. Maybe there simply was not any way to sneak up on a Thuranin warship, since they had been, you know, carefully designed to detect anyone and anything in their vicinity. Duh.

We all went to the galley for much-needed refreshments. The Indian team was preparing lunch that would be ready in a couple hours; whatever sauce they had simmering on the stove was making me hungry. I got a cup of black coffee and stood staring at my cup, hoping for inspiration.

The cup just sat there in my hand, looking stupid and unhelpful.

"Hey," Chang said with dismay, "what is this?"

He was pointing to a bowl marked 'Sugar'. When he took the lid off, instead of sugar there were yellow packets of some sugar substitute.

"Sugar is over here, sir," Adams said, pointing to a bowl that did not have any marking on it.

"The bowl marked 'Sugar' doesn't have sugar in it, and the sugar bowl isn't marked?" Chang laughed sarcastically. "Why isn't the sugar in the bowl-"

Holy shit.

I gasped with shock, and everyone looked at me. "Colonel Chang," I interrupted him. "Could we be overthinking this?"

Chang looked surprised. Confused at my question, he pointed to the two bowls. "It seems pretty simple to me."

"No, I'm not talking about the sugar. What I mean is, could we be overthinking how to approach a Thuranin warship?" Turning to Chotek who was spooning loose tea leaves into a small silver basket thing, I asked "So what if the Thuranin see our dropship?"

Chotek wasn't any more clued in to the idea in my head than Chang had been. "Colonel Bishop," Chotek began in the tone of voice people use when speaking to a small child, "you are proposing to deliberately reveal our presence to the Thuranin?"

"Not exactly, sir." And I explained my idea.

Paradise

Cornpone looked up from pulling native Paradise weeds out of the soil of their personal vegetable garden. The weeds not only choked out Earth crops because native plants grew faster in the conditions and sunlight spectrum on Paradise, they also encouraged growth of native soil microorganisms that were not helpful to Earth plants. In order for Earth seeds to grow in the dirt on Paradise, the dirt first needed to be prepared with a soil conditioning mix that allowed the roots of Earth plants to extract nutrients from the dirt. It was the still limited availability of soil conditioner, not seeds, that was the constraint on how much crops could be grown by UNEF. Since he had volunteered for an Ag team with Dave Czajka, Jesse Colter had learned far more than he thought there was to learn about growing plants, and seeds and composting. More than he had ever wanted to learn. Being a farmer on an alien planet was a lot more complicated than sticking seeds in the ground and praying for rain. In the jungles of Lemuria, it rained every day, so getting enough rain was not a problem.

Cornpone pushed himself to stand up, and tilted his head. "Hey, Ski. You hear that?"

"What?" Dave asked, while pinching buds off a tomato plant, so the other buds would grow larger tomatoes.

"Aircraft. More than one." Jesse declared. He checked his zPhone. There were no alert messages, and no UNEF brass were scheduled to visit the hick town of Fort Rakovsky. Whenever high-ranking officers were in the area, people always received a warning from their fellow soldiers. UNEF brass, even the multi-star generals, rarely travelled by air anyway; they were limited to Hamvees unless the Ruhar provided aircraft for a very special occasion.

Dave stood up, brushing dirt off his knees. In the relative cool of the jungle morning, he was wearing shorts to avoid grinding down the knees of his long pants. The shorts had previously been long pants that had been sacrificed to become shorts and work gloves, when the knees had worn through so badly that Dave had been unable to patch them one more time. "Yeah, I hear them now. Not dropships."

"No," Jesse agreed. Dropship engines, which somewhat struggled in atmospheres, had a distinctive whine unless they were in stealth mode. "Maybe they're delivering that pizza we ordered five months ago?"

Dave laughed. "If that's true, then that pizza is guaranteed free!"

"And no freakin' tip for the driver," Jesse grinned. "I'm feeling generous; you can eat that five month old pizza all by yourself. Getting louder. They can't be coming here? Can they?"

Dave looked around the glamorous expanse of Fort Rakovsky. "For what? Did somebody here grow a prize winning tomato?"

"Not that I know of," Jesse shrugged. "And we don't have a critical medical case." The Ruhar sometimes took care of medical cases that the very limited human medical facilities could not handle. Sometimes. Back when humans were working for the Kristang to push the Ruhar off the planet, the Ruhar had provided advanced medical care as a way to sow dissention between humans and their lizard patrons. That tactic had worked; with the Ruhar going so far as to regrow the limbs of severely wounded humans, while the Kristang refused to provide any advanced medical care to their human clients. Even after the failed Ruhar raid in which Joe Bishop had shot down two Ruhar transport dropships, the Ruhar had continued to provide advanced medical care to humans.

That free medical care became scarce after the Ruhar took the planet back, right at the time when human medical supplies began running severely low. Now, the Ruhar took on human medical cases only when UNEF HQ pleaded particularly loud and strenuously. The Ruhar no longer cared to bear the expense and effort on a campaign for winning human 'hearts and minds' to their side. The humans had no choice and no power; it seemed like while the Ruhar were not actively enemies of humans on Paradise, they wished the problem of humans would simply go away. There were even wild rumors flying around the zPhone network that the Ruhar government was negotiating to hand the planet back to the Kristang, and screw the humans in the process. Jesse thought that rumor was wild BS; he couldn't see the Ruhar giving up a planet so soon after sending so many warships to fight for it. Dave wasn't so sure about that; the war had been raging hot and cold for a very long time, and nothing that either side did would surprise him. The Ruhar and Kristang were, he reminded Jesse, *aliens*. Who knew how they thought?

"Damn, man, they are coming here," Jesse announced anxiously. The sound of the aircraft was loud now; they were close and flying low, coming in from the north. As he listened, the sound of one aircraft increased and a Chicken gunship popped above the tree line, climbing rapidly for altitude. The gunship would be flying high cover, and that was not a good sign. Without a word between them, Dave and Jesse dropped their spades and ran straight for the little village center. They were only halfway there, and joined by other people running in from the fields, when a Buzzard transport ship appeared over the trees, flying half sideways. The door on the near side was open, and two Ruhar soldiers in body armor were in the doorway, holding rifles. The aircraft circled the village once, then set down, crabbing sideways to avoid landing on top of precious Earth crops. As the engines spooled down to idle, Dave and Jesse halted with other people, fifty meters away. Some people had their zPhones out, shooting video of the unusual event; others were calling friends in other villages or even UNEF HQ. Jesse and Dave figured that if UNEF HQ or anyone else had useful information about why the Ruhar had landed in tiny Fort Rakovsky, they would have informed the village's residents already.

The two Ruhar soldiers stepped down onto the ground, and one activated a translator. The slightly squeaky voice boomed out over the idling engines of the Buzzard. "United States Army Specialists David Czajka and Jesse Colter, of the Tenth Infantry Division, will come with us immediately."

"What the hell?" Dave asked, shocked.

Jesse slowly held his hands up. "I don't know either, man," he looked from the rifles of the Ruhar soldiers to the gunpods of the Chicken circling above. "But we better do as they say."

The Ruhar soldiers had not handcuffed Jesse and Dave, they also hadn't answered any questions either. No matter, Jesse told Dave. The Ruhar soldiers were grunts like the two humans; they'd been given orders to pick up two specific humans and bring them somewhere. Grunts didn't need to know why. After attempting to speak with the Ruhar, which was difficult because the Ruhar had taken away their zPhones, Jesse and Dave gave up. "I don't think you were pronouncing that right," Jesse said quietly.

"Maybe," Dave admitted his Ruhar was terrible. Like many humans on Paradise, Dave and Jesse had been learning the common Ruhar language using zPhones as tutors. The Keeper faction, of course, thought any effort to learn to speak Ruhar was treason. Most Keepers were trying to learn Kristang, although human tongues found the harsh hissing undertones of lizard speech difficult to master. "I don't think the problem was what I said, I think they don't want to talk with us."

The four sat mostly in silence for two hours while the Buzzard droned on and on, flying north. The only break was visits to the Buzzard's cramped bathroom. After two hours, one of the Ruhar unbuckled from his seat, stood up, and offered a zPhone to Dave. "Heep hahp?" The hamster asked, pointing at the zPhone.

Dave and Jesse smiled to each other. Being cut off from Earth, humans on Paradise missed communications with loved one back home, they missed foods that were not available on Paradise. And they missed music. New music, music they hadn't already heard over and over. There was an enormous library of music at their fingertips over the zPhone network, so soldiers could hear not only all the music they had brought to the stars with them, they could hear anything their fellow soldiers had brought. At first Jesse thought that was great, he was able to hear music that was new to him. One night, he discovered a rare Johnny Cash live recording that he knew his father would love.

Then even that got old. Jesse got so desperate to hear something new that he started listening to jazz, then big band music, classical, anything he could find. Ski drew the line when Jesse wanted to play polka music in their hooch one night; Ski had heard way too much polka while growing up, and he hated it. So they began trading music with the

French, Indians and Chinese. That broadened their musical horizons considerably; some of it was even good, if you ignored the lyrics you couldn't understand.

The big breakthrough came when some unknown soldier, legend had it was a guy in the US Third Infantry, who traded music with a Ruhar soldier. The Ruhar, it was quickly discovered, had no spoken-word music like rap or hip hop, and Ruhar soldiers went crazy for it. They couldn't get enough of that type of human music, and humans were often able to trade music for tools, clothing and other goodies from the Ruhar. Some enterprising soldiers had formed hip hop and rap acts to provide new music, and their biggest audience were the Ruhar. That was partly because their fellow humans said the music by groups like Ghost Soljas was truly awful; the Ruhar thought all of it was new and different and great.

"Hip hop!" Dave said with delight, and took the offered zPhone. He fiddled with the controls until something he picked at random came from the speakers. It was hard to hear the music from the zPhone's tiny speakers, until the Ruhar took the zPhone back, did something with it, and the music played over the speakers in the Buzzard's cabin. The unpadded cabin of the combat transport, with its droning engines, was not the best venue for listening to music; the two Ruhar didn't seem to mind. They sat swaying in their seats, heads bobbing in tune with the beat, trying to mouth the words. When the song finished, one of the Ruhar spoke. "Dramaz?" It asked in the slightly squeaky hamster way.

Jesse shook his head. "Papa-T."

"Pahpahtee," the Ruhar repeated happily.

"Yup, you got it right," Jesse said. Then, in broken Ruhar, he asked if the 'enemy' soldiers knew where they were going, not expecting an answer.

To his surprise, the Ruhar shook his head, and over the zPhone translator said "They don't tell us anything."

"Amen to that, brother," Jesse responded and on an impulse, offered his fist. To his surprise, the Ruhar bumped fists with him. "Ski," Jesse said, "play the man some tunes."

Dave got the zPhone back and selected a playlist of major hit hip hop tunes that the Ruhar might be familiar with, plus some less lesser known favorites. The four of them rocked out, singing along when they knew the words. By the time the Buzzard landed, the Ruhar appeared sympathetic. They slapped the two humans on the shoulder, looking almost sorry. "Don't worry," one of them said through a translator, "I think this is only questions for you."

Questions about what, the Ruhar couldn't say. And Dave and Jesse were left dumfounded. What questions could the Ruhar have for two low-ranking farmers?

The mystery deepened when the two were ushered into a low building near the airfield, then ordered to sit in a windowless conference room. The room had three chairs and a desk. They sat in the two chairs on one side, and waited half an hour until the door opened and female Ruhar walked in. She smiled a toothy Ruhar grin, slid a pair of zPhones across the table, and sat down. "Greetings. I am Baturnah Logellia, the civilian deputy administrator of this planet. Your friend Joe Bishop called me the 'Burgermeister'."

A lightbulb went on in Jesse's head. He spoke into the zPhone translator. "Oh, yeah, Bish said something about you. He was talking with you when his Embedded Observation Team was in that village, uh, I forget the name. Sorry."

"Teskor," she said with a smile. "The village was Teskor. Did Joe Bishop tell you what the two of us talked about?"

"No," Dave said, with a look at Jesse. "He said it wasn't anything important. You were like the mayor of the village or something?"

She laughed. "That is what I let Joe believe. Later, he learned the truth. Gentlemen, you are here today because of Joe. When is the last time you saw him?"

"The last time?" Ski repeated the question because he couldn't entirely believe the translator had worked correctly. "Before we left Camp Alpha. That is the training base planet we were on, before we came here," he explained.

"I am familiar with Camp Alpha," she said. "You did not see him after that?"

"No," Jesse shook his head. "Bish, that is, Joe, got promoted to sergeant and left our fireteam. Left our unit. We shipped off Camp Alpha separately. That's the last we saw him. When we landed here, we were deployed to different locations."

"I understand," she seemed satisfied with that answer. "And when is the last time either of you communicated with Joe? Communication of any kind?"

"Wow, that had to be," Dave looked at Jesse before answering. "The day before he got arrested? Maybe the day before that. The three of us talked; he told us he had a cushy job as a colonel, planting potatoes. Then he got arrested, because he, you know, refused the lizards' orders to kill hamster, um, Ruhar civilians. No offense, ma'am."

"No offense taken, Dave Czajka. We know humans call us 'hamsters', and we in turn have a slang term for your species. Are you certain that you did not receive any communication from Joe after he was arrested? No communication of any kind, not even through other people? Perhaps he sent you a message after he escaped from jail?"

"Escaped?" Jesse exclaimed. Then he grew angry. "Joe didn't escape! Don't lie to us like that! You killed him, when you hit that jail. You killed him, after he tried to protect you hamsters from the Kristang and-" Jesse stopped talking when Dave grabbed his arm.

The Burgermeister did not seem to be insulted. "Our ships struck a legitimate military target; it was the only facility on this planet that was occupied by Kristang at the time. And our intelligence shows that Joe was scheduled to be executed by his captors shortly. If we had not intervened, he would have been killed by the Kristang. No matter. It might be that you truly do not know this; Joe did escape. After our ships hit the facility, Joe was able to escape with three other humans. Tell me, is Joe Bishop any sort of computer expert?"

"Computer expert?" Dave was more surprised by that question, than by hearing that Joe had escaped from jail.

"Joe?" Jesse asked, just as shocked. "Joe Bishop, you mean? About yay high?" He held a hand just above his head. "Light brown hair, blue eyes?"

Dave nodded. "Got kind of a dopey look on his face most of the time? That Joe Bishop?"

The Burgermeister smiled broadly with a twinkle in her eyes. "I am not certain the translator correctly interpreted 'dopey', however, yes. That is the same Joe Bishop. Is he an expert with computer or communications systems?"

"Hell, no." Jesse laughed. "Ski here had to show Joe how to set up his zPhone on Camp Alpha. And he was always having to reboot his tablet; Apple or Android or whatever. Companies should have hired Joe to idiot-test their equipment. I wouldn't trust Joe to operate a microwave oven."

"You got that right. Remember that time he tried to make popcorn in Nigeria," Dave asked, "and almost burned down the barracks?"

"I do," Jesse agreed. "Why would anyone think Joe is a computer expert?"

"Because," the Ruhar woman explained, "after Joe and his three companions escaped from the Kristang jail, our forces detained them, and they were brought to one of our bases. At the time, I'm sure you remember that the situation was chaotic. We did not know what to do with Joe and his three companions, so they were detained temporarily. Joe somehow managed to escape again, gained access to our weapons, and helped his three companions escape by using stun weapons on our soldiers and pilots. Then they boarded a dropship, the type you call a 'Dodo' and flew it to a human logistics base. At this base, they stunned more Ruhar, took on supplies and volunteers, and apparently left the planet."

"Holy shit," Jesse breathed, stunned. "*Joe* did all this? Uh ma'am, why don't you ask the people at this logistics base? We haven't heard from Joe since before he got arrested."

"We did ask the humans at the logistics base. We have been questioning them extensively. Now we are questioning other people who knew Joe Bishop or his three companions. None of this should have been possible," the Burgermeister shook her head. "Joe should not even have been able to open the door to the room he was being held in. Somehow, he did that, then remotely disabled the weapons of our soldiers, and took command of a Dodo. That Dodo then took off and climbed for orbit, although none of our warships recorded that dropship on their sensors. Somehow, Joe was able to subvert very sophisticated Ruhar computer systems. We are certain that none of his companions had the skills or equipment to do anything like that. We *were* certain that no human had such ability. So, we are puzzled. Extremely puzzled."

"Joe is *alive*?" Jesse exclaimed.

"Yes," she confirmed. "As far as we know, although since he apparently left the planet-"

"Why didn't that ornery son of a bitch tell us?" Jesse sputtered. "Damn! You think you know a guy?"

"Mister Colter, I know this is a shock, but please, focus," she chided gently. "We are trying to determine whether-"

"Ma'am," Jesse folded his arms across his chest. "If Joe did escape, then I'm not telling you nothin'. We are prisoners of war here; we don't have to tell you anything."

"That's right," Dave agreed. "Damn. Bish is *alive*?"

CHAPTER NINE

Paradise

Invoking their nonexistent rights as POWs made the questioning take an unpleasant turn from the previously friendly conversation with the Burgermeister. Two Ruhar soldiers, one male and one female, came into the room and Baturnah Logellia left, although she told the new Ruhar that the two humans didn't know anything. Four hours later, the two Ruhar intelligence officers agreed. Dave Czajka and Jesse Colter had no useful information about Joe Bishop or his companions after Joe had been arrested. Sophisticated Ruhar medical scanning gear in the room indicated the two humans had been genuinely surprised to hear that their friend had survived the Ruhar strike on the jail he had been held in. The Ruhar intel officers were not pleased, and they told the two humans that. Just in case the humans were holding back information, they would be detained until further notice. To make matters worse, the only human food at the air base was yummy 'nutrient mush'. It was not at all yummy.

Dave and Jesse were marched across the base to another building, where they were put into a room with two human women. The room was a sort of barracks; it had six rows of bunk beds, and a bathroom in the corner. One of the women was a US Army major, Jesse and Dave saluted when they saw her. The other woman had her back to them, she was folding blankets.

"Major," he read her nametag, "Perkins," Dave began to say, then the other woman turned around and he recognized her with a shock. "*Shauna*?"

Jesse was equally surprised. "Shauna? Shauna Jarret?" He was guessing to remember her last name. Jesse hadn't seen her since Camp Alpha, and he hadn't known her well then. Shauna looked very much the same as she did way back on Camp Alpha. Her skin was more tanned and her hair a bit shorter. And she'd lost weight like they all had on UNEF's restricted diet since the Ruhar took the planet back. As Jesse remembered, Shauna didn't have much weight to lose.

"I'm Shauna, and you are, wait. You're Joe Bishop's friends." She clapped her hands together in front of her mouth. "One of you is Cornpone," she made a guess based on his southern accent and pointed to Jesse.

"Jesse Colter, ma'am," Jesse said graciously, his voice slightly unsteady. He was out of practice talking with women. On impulse, he stuck out his hand, and she shook it. He hoped his hand wasn't shaking too much.

"And you must be Ski? I know you're not Sergeant Koch."

"Dave Czajka," he said, and shook her hand. "We haven't seen the Sergeant in a while, Jesse and I have been on an Ag team, and Sergeant Koch signed up for security duty." Koch had told them he had enough of farming while growing up in Georgia. The other woman, the major, cleared her throat. "Sorry, Major Perkins, we haven't seen Shauna since Camp Alpha."

"I gathered that," Perkins said dryly. "Jesse Colter." She remembered something from Bishop's file. "People call you Cornpone?"

"Bishop called me Cornpone," Jesse shook his head. "Before I met him, my nickname was Shooter, mostly."

Perkins looked at him sideways. "Why? Are you trigger-happy?"

"No," Jesse explained. "When I played basketball in high school, some people thought I took a lot of shots on the basket. Like, too many, you know?"

"Did you?"

"Seein' as the other guys on the team couldn't hit the side of a barn, there wasn't much point in me passing the ball, ma'am."

Perkins nodded, satisfied. "Colter, Czajka, you two have been questioned? They're bringing in everyone who served with Bishop, or knew him," she almost said 'intimately' then decided Shauna might object to that. "Knew him well."

"They questioned us, yes, ma'am," Jesse confirmed. "We didn't tell them anything."

"We don't *know* anything," Dave added. "Is it true, Major? Joe is alive?"

Perkins bit her lip. "I do not know. I served in intel at UNEF HQ. We certainly thought he was dead. There were rumors that he had been seen flying around in a Ruhar dropship, but there were a lot of crazy rumors going around back then. The Ruhar did take everyone from a logistics base, they've been isolated since the Ruhar took the planet back. We have requested contact with them and the Ruhar have refused. Until now, I didn't know why. My assessment is," she said speaking like an intelligence officer, "that whether it is true or not, the Ruhar definitely believe that Joe is alive. Joe and three companions. Did they tell you anything about these three companions?"

"No, ma'am," Dave replied.

"We know who was at the Kristang jail when the Ruhar hit it, so the list is limited," Major Perkins mused. "Be careful what you say here, I expect this room is bugged. Although, I do not think any of us know anything useful. I was as shocked as you to hear that Bishop is alive."

"If he is alive," Jesse clenched his fists, "that SOB should have let us know." He looked at Shauna. "He should have told *someone*."

After a bland and quick dinner of nutrient mush, the four semi-prisoners were glumly sitting around their barracks or cell or whatever the Ruhar wanted to call it. "Jesse," Shauna started, then, "Dave. You two were with Joe in Nigeria. What happened with him in Nigeria?" Shauna asked with a look toward Major Perkins.

"It's not classified," Perkins said with a shrug. "I'd like to hear about it myself; Bishop's personnel record had a lot of gaps in it."

"A lot happened," Dave said with a frown.

"None of it good," Jesse added.

"That's because the Army doesn't give medals for stupid," Dave said with a smile. "They try to train the stupid out of you. It didn't work all the way with Joe."

"You got that right," Jesse grinned. "You're asking about the rumor that Joe was up for a Bronze Star?"

"Yes," Shauna leaned forward on the bunk. "I asked him about it, and he wouldn't tell me, He said it was a mistake."

Jesse snorted. "The whole thing was a mistake. We weren't supposed to be there. It wasn't strictly forbidden, we just weren't- Look, don't ask, Ok?"

"We shouldn't have been in the damn country in the first place," Dave said. "They sent us over there without having any clue what our mission-"

"Dave," Jesse said gently. "We were there. All four of us. We know."

"Sorry. Go on with the story."

"So, we're in this village, there's a girl's school with, I'd better not tell you that part," Jesse looked at the floor. "There was a girl's school. By the time we got there with Joe, it was a burned-out shell. We were there because-"

"Don't tell them that part," Dave said quickly.

"It's not classified," Jesse replied.

"Yeah, but it's embarrassing, and he's not here. Joe isn't the 'he' I'm talking about," he explained to Perkins and Shauna.

"Fine," Jesse agreed. "I'll skip to the part where Joe did something stupid. We were behind an overturned truck; there was another squad working around a building and we were providing covering fire. An RPG hit the road near us, it exposed a IED right next to us, a big one. This one was built to take out a tank or a Bradley."

"Joe jumps on it, he's like 'Go, run, save yourselves'!" Dave laughed. "Right then, I knew Joe is a total idiot. With an IED that size, if it had blown up we would have been more in danger from flying Bishop parts than from the explosive."

Jesse broke up laughing about the incident. It had not been funny in the least at the time. "We're yelling at him to come with us, and while we're yelling, we're not far enough away if it goes off. Finally, Sergeant Koch orders Joe to get the hell off the thing and run with us. He jumps up, I was surprised he hadn't pissed his pants. I guess he's not smart enough to be scared."

"Did it explode?" Shauna asked, her eyes wide.

"No, they screwed up the wiring or something," Jesse said shaking his head. "Or it was a dud, I think it was an old Soviet mine. We saw the guy who was trying to detonate it, he was in a window at first, then he's kind of hanging out the window trying to get the remote to work. He forgot the batteries or something, or the detonator failed. Anyway, the stupid SOB is hanging out the window, shouting at the IED, when Sergeant Koch drills him right in the head. Two shots, bang bang!" Jesse mimicked the dead insurgent falling backward. "It was a great shot. We," he caught Dave's eye. "I guess you don't need to hear about that."

"Joe jumped on an IED," Shauna asked, "to save you?"

"Joe jumped on that IED because he was stupid," Dave clarified. "That's why he didn't get a medal for it. If that thing had gone off, him laying on top of it wouldn't have made any difference. The Army expected him to know that."

"That's Joe," Jesse concluded. "Not real smart. I still don't know if he's brave, or just too dumb to know any better."

With another gamma ray burst over Lemuria, a Kristang frigate emerged. This time it was not the familiar *To Seek Glory in Battle is Glorious*, but her brother ship *Every Day is a Good Day to Die in Battle*. The *Glory*'s reactor was offline for a maintenance cycle, so her brother ship had been given the honor of jumping in. The *Good Day* planned on burning human croplands for several minutes, possibly tangling with a Ruhar frigate, and then jumping away. The *Good Day*'s crew had eagerly been looking forward to the raid, having grown sick of their comrades on the *Glory* strutting around like they had been winning the war against the Ruhar all by themselves.

Good Day's captain was determined to outdo his colleague; he intended to remain behind and engage in combat as much as his little ship could take before jumping away. He got his first wish. He did not get the second.

Unknown to the Kristang, despite their long-range surveillance and the stealth sensor satellites they had dropped off on every raid, there was a stealthed Ruhar destroyer above Lemuria. The commodore of the Ruhar defense force was still under pressure from the planetary administrator to do something to protect the humans, despite the severe damage to the frigate *Tolen Grathur*. So the destroyer *City of MecMurro* had gone into maximum stealth and drifted into position on minimum power, taking two full days to reach a spot high above Lemuria. She had arrived one day too late to save the *Tolen Grathur*, for the original plan was for that unstealthed frigate to act as bait for the hidden destroyer. The

Ruhar commodore neglected to inform the Kristang of his plan, and the aggressive Kristang had acted too soon.

Without another ship to act as bait, the *MecMurro* still waited patiently, her crew on alert, her weapons ready. Surely the previous Kristang raid would not be the last one, and the *MecMurro* would get revenge for the four dead Ruhar aboard the *Grathur*. To maintain maximum stealth, her sensor field was off but ready to activate at any moment. A sensor field was not required to detect the signature gamma ray burst of a starship jumping in, and the *MecMurro* saw the *Good Day* immediately. Even before the destroyer's sensor field had extended, maser beams and railgun darts were on the way toward the Kristang frigate, with a volley of missiles close behind. By shear bad luck, the *Good Day* had jumped in less than twelve thousand kilometers from the hidden destroyer, presenting an exceptionally easy target.

Every day is a Good Day to Die in Battle lived up to her name by dying in battle that day. With her shields degraded by the strain of deflecting almost point-blank maser cannon fire, she took a direct hit from a railgun dart that penetrated completely through the frigate, plunged into the atmosphere of Paradise and created a tremendous splash in the ocean. The impact of the railgun dart temporarily knocked out power and communications to the ship's jump drive, so the *Good Day* was a sitting duck for crucial seconds. Seconds the *MecMurro* did not waste; that destroyer poured everything she had into the Kristang frigate, and the third missile fired by the *MecMurro* scored a direct hit. The *Good Day* exploded, violently enough that the *MecMurro* had to jump away to avoid being struck by high-energy debris.

Hours later, the *MecMurro* jumped back into position, engaged its stealth field and with minimum power from thrusters, began slowly to drift back toward the northern continent. The Ruhar commodore was satisfied he had done what he could to protect the human POWs from assaults by their own patrons; certainly he had done more than he had wanted to do. The Kristang certainly had detected the *MecMurro* jumping back into position and hopefully the lizards would assume the destroyer was still there above the southern continent, lying in wait for another raider. The Kristang would either cease their raids on the human croplands, or include more and heavier ships on raids. If the Kristang used more ships, that would provide the commodore with additional information about his enemy. And he would act accordingly. Until then, the *MecMurro* would rejoin the task force protecting the vital facilities and population of the northern continent. And the humans would have to hope that the Kristang would now see burning their crops as too great a risk to their limited number of ships.

Flying Dutchman

"You were right, Joe, this was a *great* idea."

"Oh, shut up," I groaned.

"Yup, one of your bestest ideas ever, Joey! Hey, this reminds me of the last time it was just you and me in a dropship, floating in space for a long, long, really long, will this ever end oh my *God* if he doesn't shut up I'm going to kill him length of time."

"Thank you, Skippy, I heard you the first time. And the hundred other times you said the exact same freakin' thing."

"I'm just saying'-"

"I know."

"This is like getting the band back together! Except that you can't sing. Or play a musical instrument. Or write songs."

"Skippy?"

"Yes?"

"I'm mortal," I reminded our friendly alien AI. "I can leave my helmet off, force the airlock doors open, and embrace the sweet, sweet release of death. You, on the other hand, would be stuck right here in interstellar space until the end of time."

"Hey, with the door open, it wouldn't smell like fermented monkey butt in here, so go for it."

Leaning forward, I banged my forehead on the dropship's pilot console. "Worst. Idea. *Ever.*" I mumbled.

"When did you realize that, Joe?"

"Let me think. Uh, it was seventeen days ago."

"We've only been here seventeen days, Joe."

"Exactly." Me, in a dropship, with only two companions. Skippy, and a tactical nuclear warhead. Between the two, I was beginning to prefer the company of Nukey, as I called it. According to the United States Air Force, Nukey had a variable yield of between 3 and 20 kilotons. Figuring that if I was going to nuke something I might as well go big, I had cranked up the dial to '20'. Nukey didn't say much, it just sat there strapped in behind the copilot seat, emitting neutrons every once in a while. Nukey was the strong, silent type.

Skippy, on the other hand, could not shut up. We had run out of things to talk about after the first, oh, hour, but that hadn't stopped him. He had cheerily driven me crazy for seventeen days, and he had an unending supply of nothing to talk about. As one example, I was now well educated about how 17th century Hungarian poetry was influenced by the-

Oh, damn it, I hadn't been paying enough attention when Skippy told me the first two or three times. So, tragically, I had no idea what had influenced the Hungarian poets of the 17th century. Some kind of alcohol, I expect. And, given that they were poets, hunger and poverty were likely in the mix also. By day three, I had been praying please, please God do not allow Skippy to give me a pop quiz on any of the boring trivia he had told me. If I failed a quiz, which I would, Skippy would simply start at the beginning and repeat everything.

That incredibly annoying little beer can was sitting securely strapped into the copilot seat. Aboard the *Flying Dutchman*, he spent all his time in an escape pod, so I only saw him once or twice a day when I stopped by to visit. Skippy always told me that physical proximity was meaningless and unnecessary, but I think he appreciated that I took the time to sit with him. Now I had seen him constantly for seventeen days, and it reminded me how small, alone and in many ways helpless our friendly ancient alien AI was. He looked cute sitting there, glowing a soft blue when he was happy, red when he was angry, or any combination of colors that he did for my benefit. Skippy looked especially cute because he was wearing a tiny Red Sox home jersey and baseball cap that day. Before we left the ship, Major Simms had handed me a box, with instructions not to open it until the dropship was on station near the wormhole.

It was a box containing dozens of tiny outfits for Skippy! I do not know where Simms got the idea, but she totally made my day when I opened that box. Day after boring day waiting in the dropship, there were only three things I had to look forward to. Sleeping that night, when Skippy finally shut up. Doing zero-gee exercises as best I could, using rubber bands. And dressing Skippy in a new outfit around mid-morning each day.

"All right, Skippy, it's time to change your clothes," I decided. It was only 0835, but there wasn't anything else to do. Besides, while I was eating breakfast that morning, Skippy had threatened to spend most of the day educating me on the structural, spiritual and functional differences between pyramids in Egypt and those in Mesoamerica. All I knew was, the pyramids in what is now Mexico are bigger. If he was going to bore me, I would strike first by humiliating him. "Let's see," I said looking in the box. "How about a cowboy getup today?"

"No!"

"Look at this, Skippy," I said, holding up the pieces of clothing. "There's this shirt with a leather vest, and even a gold star, I guess this is for a sheriff or deputy. Aha! And a tiny black curly mustache," I picked up the mustache and applied it to Skippy between his baseball jersey and hat.

"NO! Get that ridiculous mustache off of me right now! Major Simms is *totally* on my 'Skippy hates this' list."

"Oooh, and a cute little Stetson hat for you, cowpoke."

"*NO!* Oh, I swear if you put that silly cowboy hat on my lid I'm going to light off that nuke right n- Head's up, Joe, a ship jumped in!"

"Oh, thank God."

"My thoughts exactly. And don't jinx it this time, you big stupidhead."

"All I said was that I hoped the last ship was the right one," I protested.

"Yes, and the universe heard you, and because the universe hates you, it was the wrong ship. Again. I'm the one who suffers, being stuck in this cramped dropship with you day after day."

"You? Hell, I have to listen to your boring trivia-"

"And I have to agonize over how to explain the simplest of concepts to-"

"Skippy?"

"What?"

"The alien ship?"

"Oh, yeah. Sorry, I forgot. What were we- Oh, that's right. Hmmm. Looking good, Joe! It is looking good. This could be the one."

After seventeen days stuck in close quarters with Skippy, if the ship that had just jumped in was not a good candidate, I was ready to give up and go back to the *Dutchman* for a break. Or set off the nuke just for entertainment. Either way would be fine with me. Damn that little beer can could be annoying. Skippy had originally calculated that, in order to have a fifty percent chance of contacting the right Thuranin ship, we would have to park our little dropship near a wormhole entrance for sixty eight days. When he told me that, I was ready to appeal the decision to the statistics referees of the universe. The idea of being stuck in a dropship for one single freakin' day, with just Skippy and Nukey for company, was bad enough. After seventeen days, during which we had encountered Thuranin ships three times, and none of them had been the type of ship we were looking for, I was ready to kill him. Or myself. Hopefully both. No way was I getting my hopes up, until Skippy was a hundred percent sure this ship was the one we had been seeking. "Could be?"

"Verifying now," he said with the flat, emotionless tone that indicated he was concentrating on something. We had several criteria for a candidate ship. It had to be a Thuranin warship; support or civilian ships would likely not have access to the classified fleet deployment and relay station crew rotation schedules that we needed. The ship needed to be going through the wormhole that our dropship was parked near. And the ship had to be planning to contact one of the three data relay stations in the area. Oh, and incidentally, the ideal ship would be alone, or at least not part of a full battlegroup.

"Good to go, Joe! We are good to go. These ships are perfect."

"*These* ships. I see a heavy cruiser and two destroyers," I said fearfully. A squadron of Thuranin destroyers had ambushed and very nearly vaporized our pirate star carrier. This time, there was a heavy cruiser with the two destroyers.

"Phbbbbt," Skippy made a raspberry sound. "Please, Joe. This is no problemo for us. The destroyers are flying combat space patrol for that cruiser; they are far enough way that there is no way they could detect us."

"Are you sure about-" Right then I saw the flaw in Simms' idea to dress Skippy in cute little outfits; it was hard for me to take him seriously while he was wearing a Red Sox jersey and hat. And a tiny mustache. It was good those ships jumped in before I had time to put the tiny cowboy outfit on him. "Are you sure about that?"

"Joe, I calculate the additional mission risk posed by those destroyers as one third of one percent. Less than that, if you want me to get more detailed than 'meh' level math."

"No, please don't. Please."

"Well?"

"Well what?"

"Well, get moving, dumdum. You're flying this thing."

I shook myself back to focus, and gently started the dropship toward the Thuranin heavy cruiser. Heavy cruiser. Heavy, like, it had really big railguns and maser cannons. The particle cannons that ship used just to zap hazardous space debris out of its way could blast us into subatomic particles.

Damn, that ship was big. With us in super stealth mode, I couldn't look out the cockpit window; all the photons headed toward our dropship were bent by the stealth field and curved right around the hull. I adjusted the cockpit display to show me the tiny bits of data that Skippy was allowing inside the stealth field, and I compared the size of the heavy cruiser to our dropship. The dropship wasn't even a dot on the display. Sure, our pirate star carrier was larger than a heavy cruiser; before Skippy shrunk our ship. But star carriers were immensely long and slender, while the cruiser was bulky. I had to remind myself that on long missions, star carriers transported an entire battlegroup of destroyers, cruisers and even battleships.

I also had to remind myself that star carriers were not combatant ships; the weapons, shields and sensors aboard that heavy cruiser vastly outclassed those aboard our pirate ship. Skippy assured me that with him feeding bullshit data to the cruiser's sensors, all they would see inside our dropship were two little green Thuranin cyborgs. They would not see an ancient alien AI wearing a baseball uniform and a mustache. They would not see a low-yield nuclear weapon that had 'Adios MFers' written on the side of it. Also our nuke had a smiley face drawn on it. And a Hello Kitty sticker. Most importantly they would not see a human.

No matter; I had promised Chotek that if the Thuranin suspected our dropship wasn't being flown by Thuranin, I would set off the nuke without hesitation. After seventeen days with Skippy, part of me was praying for us to be discovered.

Seventeen minutes later, an ironic number, we got close enough to the heavy cruiser for Skippy to do his thing. "Busy," he said tersely. I knew not to bother him. Lightly touching his shiny surface confirmed that he was slightly warm. "Oh, shit, they detected us. Damn it! I was like 80% done. Dropping the stealth field now."

Dropping our stealth field, close to a Thuranin heavy cruiser, might not sound like a good idea. Or a sane idea. It was actually part of my plan; the plan I had sold to Chotek and Chang and Simms and Smythe. And Skippy. "Are they buying your line of bullshit?" I asked anxiously.

"Hook, line and sinker, Joe. It is working like a charm. Which, you know, kills me to say that another of your monkey-brain plans is working."

"You'll get over it." It wasn't easy to joke while my finger was poised over the detonator of a nuclear weapon. Chotek had approved my plan only on the condition that, if the Thuranin even began to suspect there was something other than sugar in our sugar bowl, I would turn all the evidence into subatomic particles. Nukey could thoroughly destroy me and the dropship. Skippy would be fine, although he would lose his collection of cute little outfits. Explosion of the nuke would send our friendly beer can unharmed but spinning off into space, and the *Flying Dutchman* could recover him later and start over with a different, better idea. Chang would need to wait a month or so to collect Skippy, as the area would most likely be crawling with Thuranin ships investigating the incident. After the *Dutchman* jumped in, Skippy could ping them to pick him up.

I was mostly hoping that using Nukey wouldn't be necessary.

"Aaaaaaand, done! Doneski, Joe, we are done-a-palooza. Mission accomplished. This part of the mission, anyway. I got all the data we need, and I planted a message for that cruiser to carry to a relay station. As a bonus, it happens to be the closest relay station."

"Great. Now we play along?"

"Yes. Take the dropship two hundred thousand kilometers away, and we will reengage stealth."

I got the dropship turned around and fired the engines. What Skippy had done already was the first part of the plan; get close to a Thuranin warship, ransack its database and plant a message. Now we needed to convince that ship's crew and AI that there was nothing sinister or unusual about our presence. No reason for the ship's AI to look carefully at its memory storage. No reason for that ship's AI to suspect someone had been poking around in its highly classified, encrypted files, and no reason to notice it now contained a message that wasn't there before.

What I had realized in the *Dutchman*'s galley, while staring at a sugar bowl that didn't contain sugar, was that it was Ok if the Thuranin detected our Thuranin dropship. What was not Ok is if they detected the Thuranin dropship had a human inside it. So what we did was encase our dropship in an extra-powerful stealth field, enhanced by the powers of Skippy, and we snuck up close to a Thuranin heavy cruiser. Even with enhanced stealth, the cruiser eventually detected us, and locked weapons on our location. At that point, as planned, Skippy had deactivated our stealth field, to show the Thuranin that the mysterious object sneaking up on their flank was a Thuranin dropship. A Thuranin dropship with all the proper high-level military authentication codes. A modified Thuranin dropship, because we had attached a bunch of useless junk to the outside of the hull. The crew of the cruiser didn't know our modifications were all fake. Skippy had told them that our dropship contained a highly advanced experimental stealth unit. and the stuff attached to the outside of our dropship was part of the super stealth gear. That advanced technology was how we had been able to get so close to the cruiser before being detected. Skippy told the cruiser that we had been in the area for over a month, and the heavy cruiser was the first ship to detect us. Congratulations to the crew of the cruiser for their vigilance, their exemplary performance would be noted by the Thuranin Office of Special Projects! Of course, the entire incident was top secret, and the crew and AI of the cruiser were to forget everything they had seen.

The Thuranin bought the whole story. Feeding their cyborg egos had certainly helped. To finish selling our story, we backed off two hundred thousand kilometers, reengaged stealth, and snuck up on the other side of the cruiser until they detected us again. Then we backed away, reactivated stealth, and flew in a wide circle around the cruiser, dropping stealth on the other side of the ship. That time, Skippy lied to them, we got very close and they had not detected us. Skippy thanked the cruiser for assisting the Office of Special Projects to test our advanced stealth capability in a field environment. Then we went back into stealth and I got us the hell out of there. Less than two hours later, the heavy cruiser and its pair of escorts went through the wormhole and we were alone. I sent the retrieval signal to the *Flying Dutchman*, a signal that would take four hours to reach the ship.

Looking around the interior of the dropship in dismay, I realized that some housecleaning was in order. "You know what, Skippy, maybe it does smell like fermented monkey butt in here."

"Duh, Joe."

"Hey, I've been washing up as best I can in that tiny sink. I will take another sponge bath, get into a fresh spacesuit, and open the door to vacuum for a couple minutes."

The place did smell better after that; certainly I smelled better. And when the *Dutchman* arrived to pick us up, Skippy was dressed up in a pirate costume, including an eye patch and a tiny parrot on top of his tiny hat.

He hated it.

Sergeant Adams assured him that he was adorable.

He hated that even worse.

Paradise

To Major Perkin's surprise, the formal questioning by the Ruhar lasted only another two days off and on, then weeks went by when nothing happened. The four were allowed open communication with each other; Perkins guessed the Ruhar were hoping they would reveal information by mistake. Since none of them had information the Ruhar cared about, open communication was not a problem. They were not allowed to use zPhones. Dave and Jesse worried that guys in Fort Rakovsky might be screwing with their hooch. He and Jesse had finished it, complete with a couch that now had a nice cover, a coffee table and a dining table with four chairs. No girls yet, but they were patient. Theirs was the nicest hooch in the bustling village of Fort Rakovsky. It had better, Dave swore, be in great condition when they returned. Whenever that was.

With the questioning apparently over, the four humans were moved to another building outside the air base. This building had two sleeping areas, so they did not have to hang blankets from the ceiling in order to give the women privacy. Three weeks went by, with the four allowed to go outside for exercise and even to walk far afield without a Ruhar escort, as long as they returned before dark. If the humans tried to escape, the Ruhar could surely track them. Perkins suspected the Ruhar had planted tiny tracking devices in their clothing. So, if the humans wanted to escape, they would do it naked, into a wilderness that contained nothing humans could eat. That was not a tempting idea to any of them. There were even deliveries of real human food, to supplement the nutrient mush they were all growing heartily sick of. Through their Ruhar guards, they learned that the Ruhar had also detained Sergeant Koch, plus the three members of Joe's Embedded Observation Team on Paradise, and several people who had helped Joe shoot down the two Ruhar Whales at Fort Arrow. They were being held in separate places; Major Perkins speculated that the Ruhar had picked up the humans wherever they were, and simply flew them to the nearest Ruhar base.

When they had been held for five weeks, Major Perkins raised the issue of their continued captivity with one of their guards, a female Ruhar named Mindu who Perkins had been trying to develop a friendship with. Perkins could speak the common Ruhar language, not fluently yet to her chagrin, but passable. "We have been here for over a month," she used the Ruhar rough time equivalent for 'month'. "We have not been questioned for many days. Why are we still being held? It must be clear that the four of us have no information about Joe Bishop. I assume you have technology that can tell when a human is not telling the truth."

"We have such technology, yes," Mindu replied slowly in Ruhar, without using a translator. "Instruments which can detect when a subject is lying, or withholding the full truth."

"Then you know we do not have any useful information."

"No. We know that our instruments have not detected any falsehoods. However, our commanders are afraid to release you just yet, for they fear the consequences if it is later discovered that you concealed important information. They are, as you humans say, covering their asses."

Perkins smiled wryly. "That sentiment is universal among intelligent species."

"There is also the matter that this Joe Bishop escaped from this planet, using technology that should not have been available to humans. Technology that even we do not possess. You will understand, hopefully, that we are rightly concerned that a species controlling such powerful technology might also be able to fool a lie detector."

"I see," Perkins frowned. How could they prove that humans did *not* have access to technology superior to the Ruhar? They did not possess any such technology. Although Bishop did, or so the Ruhar believed.

"There is another reason you are still here, Emm-lee," Mindu said, being unable to pronounce the 'i' in Emily. "There is a Jeraptha ship coming to this planet; the Jeraptha wish to question you. They are also concerned that humans had access to technology which allowed a dropship to fly right through the middle of our fleet without detection."

"Jeraptha?" Perkins asked with alarm. No human had ever seen or spoken with the patron species of the Ruhar. From the description provided by the Kristang, the Jeraptha were horrible beetle-like insects who would love to feast on humans. The Ruhar had laughed at that clumsy bit of Kristang propaganda, and insisted the Jeraptha were wonderful patrons. Although even the Ruhar admitted privately that they had an instinctive species revulsion toward insects.

"Do not worry, Emm-lee. The Jeraptha will be gentle. You should be careful, though, they love to play practical jokes."

"Jokes?" Perkins exclaimed in surprise.

"Oh, yes. The Jeraptha love jokes. They laugh frequently. So much that some people make the mistake of underestimating their military potential. The Jeraptha are formidable warriors; they simply think there is no reason they can't have fun doing it. They also love gambling, even gambling on combat operations." She shook her head. "They are strange little insects."

Seven weeks after they were brought in for questioning, Major Perkins and her three soldiers were outside playing a two-on-two game of volleyball. UNEF had donated a recreation package at the request of the Ruhar; the four humans were growing stir-crazy with the boredom of inactivity. The previous two days had seen solid rain, forcing the four to stay inside except going out for a five mile run that had been Shauna Jarret's idea. She had qualified for infantry duty, and didn't want to lose her conditioning. Even though UNEF currently had no openings for infantry. No openings for any jobs other than agriculture.

Perkins and Czajka were playing against Jarret and Colter. Those two, Shauna and Jesse, had developed a friendship over the almost two months the four had been together. Maybe more than a friendship. There was certainly no UNEF or US Army regulation against it; they were both Specialists, and not even in the same unit. Not that units had any real meaning anymore on Paradise. Perkins would have thought it odd if Shauna didn't like Jesse Colter. He was attractive, and his southern charm smoothed out his rough edges. Shauna was also from the American South, so they had that in common.

Major Perkins didn't care what relationship developed between Shauna and Jesse, other than if their relationship affected Dave Czajka. She had seen him moping by himself while Shauna and Jesse played cards, and the relationship between the two men was strained. She felt bad for 'Ski' Czajka. He was nice, and funny, and cute in a way that reminded Perkins a bit of her ex-husband, except Czajka was not a jerk and-

Alarms wailed across the airbase. "Get down!" Jesse was the first to shout, and they dropped to the damp grass. Before anyone could speak, the ground shook from a series of explosions at the airbase. Maser beams struck first, hitting parked aircraft, then a hypersonic railgun dart hit with a tremendous explosion. It sent a fountain of debris into the air and left a mushroom cloud boiling into the morning sky.

"Look!" Shauna said while pointing at the sky, her ears ringing. There were not merely one or two lights from Kristang ships jumping in to raid Paradise again; there were a dozen, more than a dozen lights. Many more than a dozen. Blindingly bright, silent explosions in orbit marked where ships were fighting.

The Kristang were back, in force.

"Oh damn it!" Jesse groaned and pounded the ground with a fist. "Not this shit again! Can't those two decide who owns this freakin' planet?"

CHAPTER TEN

Paradise

Commodore Ferlant of the Ruhar task force defending the planet Gehtanu was weary, and so were his ships. His little task force of ships had been on constant alert since the Kristang raids had begun. The crews were tired and morale was low; there had been no opportunity for shore leave, or leave of any kind, for months. Worse than the tiredness of his crews was the wear and tear on his ships; they had not been able to perform proper maintenance since the two battlegroups that had recaptured Gehtanu had departed. In addition to ship components simply reaching the end of their useful lives, his ships had battle damage to fix. Shield generators had taken a beating, railgun magnets developed dead spots, maser cannon exciters overheated and developed microfractures, and jump drive coils fell increasingly out of sync with each other. Even the simple act of the other ships replenishing their missile magazines from the stores carried by the commodore's cruiser was risky. With so few ships, the Commodore had tried a rotation where one ship jumped away to take systems offline for repairs. But while that ship was, for example, replacing reactor plating, it was vulnerable. So another ship had to jump away with it to provide protection. That left fewer ships to protect an entire planet, and Ferlant's options for deploying those ships were limited. The enemy, meanwhile, could lurk far away and choose where and when to attack. In between attacks, the enemy's ships could adhere to a proper maintenance cycle, although the Kristang were notorious for ignoring tasks they considered to be beneath the dignity of a warrior. The Kristang, the commodore thought with a slight smile, would strip out a maser cannon if the beam showed any sign of backscatter, while they would ignore a critical fault in power management systems. More than once in the Commodore's career, he had seen Kristang ships rendered defenseless because a minor hit had caused some poorly-maintained system inside the ship to fail. The Ruhar were always willing to remind the Kristang of the importance of proper maintenance, and that reminder came in the form of a railgun dart or missile ripping a crippled ship apart. Ferlant thought that the Kristang would have learned their lesson after they'd lost several dozen ships needlessly, but fortunately for the Ruhar, the Kristang warrior caste seemed immune to learning.

So, the Commodore considered, did his own government seem immune to learning sometimes. After his small task force had been detached to defend Gehtanu, he had complained with increasing vigor that he did not have enough ship to defend a backwater planet. Leaving a small force of ships had been a reasonable idea, back when intelligence strongly indicated that the Thuranin were pulling out of the area. The Thuranin were not willing to risk any more ships for Gehtanu, the Kristang could not afford to retake the planet on their own, and the Ruhar government was secretly negotiating to hand the planet back to the lizards anyway. Under those conditions, assigning only a handful ships was reasonable, perhaps even excessive.

Then the raids began. At first the Commodore thought the raiders were one or two desperate ships would had been left behind when the Thuranin pulled out of the area. His ships had destroyed a Kristang frigate during the second raid. Back then, the commodore had been confident that he could handle the raiders; one or two ships without support would soon run out of missiles and their systems would break down.

Then, the raiders kept coming. His sensors so far had identified three frigates and a destroyer, and they must have support somewhere in the star system. Chasing gamma ray bursts was not practical for the commodore; by the time the light from a distant burst reached Gehtanu, the enemy ships would have moved far away. So far, his ships had destroyed two enemy frigates, with heavy damage to one of his own frigates. If this battle became a war of attrition, the Ruhar were likely to lose eventually.

Gehtanu did not have any defenses of its own; no missile batteries or maser cannons or railguns buried deep beneath the surface, no stealthed hunter-killer satellites, no network of damping field satellites that could entrap a raiding ship. Gehtanu had grain, and farmers, and some pleasant if dull places to build a house and raise a family.

If the Ruhar government intended to bargain away the planet below, the commodore thought they should hurry the process along. It was bitter to think that his ships and crews were risking themselves only to drag out the negotiations, in hopes of driving a better deal for the Ruhar. A deal that would provide no direct benefit for Ferlant's little task force, nor for the Ruhar residents of Gehtanu. And certainly not for the hapless humans.

Until there was a change in the situation, Commodore Ferlant saw his responsibility as defending the critical facilities of the northern continent named Tenturo, such as the cargo Launcher, plus the few cities, military bases and any place that contained enough supplies and infrastructure to be a tempting target to the Kristang. The planetary government had helped by emptying warehouses and dispersing their contents, so much that Ferlant thought with mild amusement it must be driving the enemy commander crazy to have so few high-value targets on the surface.

Maybe the government had done too good a job of reducing the number of targets on the planet. There had been no raid for fifteen days. Fifteen days during which time the enemy was able to rest and bring their ships into optimum condition. Fifteen days during which Ferlant's ships had to remain on alert every minute. His force steadily grew weaker, while the enemy could build up their strength. The situation could not continue, so Commodore Ferlant had taken a calculated risk. Two of his destroyers were now in stealth, parked above the northern continent just higher than jump altitude. He had been jumping his other healthy ships in and out in hope that the enemy could lose track of his little force, and not notice that two ships were not accounted for.

The next time the enemy jumped in, Ferlant's two destroyers would link overlapping damping fields, preventing the enemy from jumping away. Below the pair of destroyers, the planet's gravity well would prevent a jump, and if enemy ships climbed out of the gravity well, they would become trapped by the damping field. The Commodore was counting on his plan to kill one, even two enemy ships with limited risk to his own force. Such a triumph would make the Kristang think twice about challenging-

"Ship jumping in! Another!" Called an officer on the bridge of Ferlant's cruiser *Ruh Gastalo*. "Frigate and a destroyer, we know these two."

Once again, *To Seek Glory in Battle is Glorious* appeared over Paradise in a burst of gamma radiation, this time accompanied by the familiar destroyer *We are Proud to Honor Clan Sub-Leader Rash-au-Tal Vergent who Inspires us Every Day*. The captain and crew of the *Glory* were not happy; crewmembers on the bridge shared knowing glances when they saw their captain's hand shook slightly. This was not supposed to be a mission for the *Glory*, repairs to her critical jump drive coils were only half complete; the normal maintenance cycle had been cut short by an unexpected event. That event was the destruction of her brother frigate *Every day is a Good Day to Die in Battle*. The honor of this raid was supposed to have gone to the *Good Day*, but as that ship had a very bad day, the *Glory* had been pulled back into service. *Glory*'s drive coils were so badly out of alignment that she had been forced to reach Pradassis in three short jumps, to minimize the inaccuracy of her jump navigation system. Even with the time-consuming precautions, *Glory* emerged forty seven thousand kilometers off course. Her crew noticed bitterly that their heavy escort *Vergent* was also off course, although that destroyer's drive coils had recently been calibrated. Even if the *Glory* had been where she was supposed to be, the *Vergent* was unforgivably not in position to protect the smaller ship.

The *Glory*'s crew understandably wondered whether the *Vergent* was out of position on purpose.

As soon as the *Glory*'s dazed navigation system determined the ship's position, the frigate spun on its tail and burned hard to get where she was supposed to be. Without waiting to get into the optimal position, the little ship fired her maser cannon in searing pulses at designated targets on the surface and launched a volley of missiles, two at a time. The *Vergent* proceeded to her assigned position more leisurely, taking a roundabout course that kept her further away from the planet, so the destroyer could more quickly jump away if needed. The *Glory* had no such option; she had emerged at too low an altitude and her course was taking her even deeper into the planet's gravity well.

One Ruhar frigate altered course to engage the *Glory*, while two other frigates accelerated toward the *Vergent*. The captain of the *Vergent* ordered the *Glory* to continue its assigned mission, while the destroyer would 'lure the pair of Ruhar frigates away'. The cowardice of the destroyer's crew did not fool the Kristang frigate, but there was nothing they could do about it.

As the heavier ship climbed rapidly to jump distance, the *Glory* shifted her aim to the single Ruhar frigate opposing her. Maser beams lanced out from both ships, impacting each other's shields. The two ships were too close to dodge speed of light weapons; the normal laws of space combat did not apply when the combatants were within a hundred thousand kilometers and closing rapidly. They flew past each other, neither able to change course fast enough, neither able to score a decisive hit. Both ships spun around to face each other, still drawing apart, their engines straining to cancel their velocity and bring them together again.

Commodore Ferlant wondered at the actions of the Kristang frigate his sensor systems had designated 'Target Beta'. They knew Beta well, as that frigate had participated in almost every raid. Based on the excess gamma radiation of that ship's clumsy jump in, the Kristang frigate was not in good condition. Having survived a direct engagement with one of Ferlant's defenders, the enemy ship should now be climbing to jump altitude to escape. Instead, Target Beta had its engines burning at full power to bring it back above the northern continent. Why was Beta not attempting to escape? Did the enemy ship already know about the two Ruhar destroyers in stealth above it? No, Ferlant concluded, the enemy had not yet detected his trap, because the enemy destroyer, designated Target Delta, was still below jump altitude and moving leisurely to attack a pair of Ferlant's frigates.

With a single word, Ferlant sprung his trap. First, his own cruiser *Ruh Gastalo* performed a short jump in behind the enemy destroyer, to flush that ship toward the stealthed destroyers. The *Gastalo*'s jump left large areas of the northern continent unguarded; that would be worth the opportunity to eliminate two enemy ships. Immediately after detecting Ferlant's cruiser, Target Delta had changed course, frantically climbing toward jump distance. And that is when the two Ruhar destroyers announced their presence by activating their damping fields. The pair of destroyers were close enough that their damping fields overlapped, making the fabric of spacetime even more turbulent and increasing the effectiveness of the damping effect.

The *Vergent*'s captain saw that he was trapped. Below him were a pair of enemy frigates, above were a pair of destroyers and behind was a cruiser. The *Vergent* could not jump away and could not outfight five enemy ships, so she plunged forward and screamed for the *Glory* to protect her.

The crew of the *Glory* almost could not believe what they heard, and asked for confirmation that the powerful destroyer wanted help from their worn-out little frigate. When they received confirmation, they asked one more time to force the *Vergent's* captain to scream at them over an open channel. The entire Ruhar task force heard, and soon so would the Kristang. With a shrug, the *Glory's* crew altered course to engage two rather than one enemy frigate. But the single enemy frigate also adjusted course, and soon the *Glory* would have to fight off three ships of her own size.

The battle was chaos. Maser beams stabbed out, deflected by weakening shields. Railgun darts and missiles flew across the void. Masers shifted focus to knock darts off course and obliterate missiles, and it became a matter of how much maser fire a ship's shields could absorb before failing. The *Glory* was losing the battle, having become the focus of fire from all three frigates. The only reason she had survived so long was her clumsy navigation system threw off the aim of her opponents, which became less useful as the distances between the four frigates shrank.

While the frigates had their own private battle, *Ruh Gastalo* and the two Ruhar destroyers concentrated fire on Target Delta; the *Vergent*.

Commodore Ferlant studied the *Gastalo's* main tactical display, running the view back to the beginning of the battle, then fast forward. "Smeth," he asked his executive officer, "do their tactics seem strange to you?"

The XO nodded. "Yes, I was about to mention that. At first, I thought that destroyer was flying high cover for the frigate." That frigate, that particular, too-familiar ship that had been the bane of the defense task force's existence since the raids began. "They jumped in too far apart to support each other; the frigate's jump drive is badly out of sync, so that part could have been unintended. But when they began maneuvering, the destroyer moved independently, it did not alter course to protect the frigate. Also, the destroyer has not fired at the planet. The frigate has fired its maser cannon, but not any important target." He indicated the areas struck by the frigate's maser. "This is uninhabited forest. It's not even agricultural land. If there were some sort of hidden target there that we can't see, they didn't even shoot at it long enough to make a difference. They shifted aim with every pulse. Sir, it appears that they want us to think this is a raid, but this time they don't want to cause any damage. And now the destroyer has been screaming for the frigate to protect it," Smeth said the last with a raised eyebrow. The Kristang frigate was in poor condition, it was not capable of protecting its larger, more heavily protected companion.

Ferlant zoomed the display out to view the entire situation around Gehtanu. "That frigate has been a pain in our backside for too long. But, it has survived so long now, it would be almost a shame to kill it now. The destroyer is the more important target. Signal all ships to concentrate fire on the destroyer."

"Yes, sir," Smeth acknowledged. "It will be some time before the *Hertall* can disengage," he cautioned and pointed to the Ruhar frigate *Mem Hertall* on the display. "She will pass the enemy frigate in a few minutes."

"Very well, let the Hertall keep Target Beta busy. The other frigates will cut off Target Delta's escape route." His own cruiser *Gastalo* had been caught out of position when the Kristang jumped in, and likely would still be scrambling to change course when the battle ended. With four defending ships concentrating fire at a single enemy destroyer, and that ship being unable to form a jump wormhole, Target Delta's life expectancy could now be measured in minutes. "Then we-"

Paradise

The main display zoomed out on its own, red lights flashing and warning horns blaring.

Above the *Gastalo*, above minimum safe jump distance, sixteen Kristang warships jumped in. The enhanced task force now included a battlecruiser and two cruisers of *Gastalo*'s size. The additional ships had been dropped off at the edge of the star system by a Thuranin star carrier thirty three days before. The star carrier was not waiting for the Kristang ships to return, and indeed the Kristang task force could not afford to have their ships brought home. Their mission to the planet they called Pradassis was one-way, unless the Ruhar surrendered the world through negotiation. The additional Kristang ships had flown the slow way through normal space to the other side of the fourth planet, and waited there, without the Ruhar even knowing new ships had arrived. With the raids occupying Commodore Ferlant's attention as the Kristang planned, Ferlant had been unable to properly patrol the star system.

The Kristang ships fired one volley of railgun darts at a half dozen high-value targets on the surface, then their weapons went silent. They did not even fire at the defending Ruhar ships.

The arrival of the Kristang task force came too late for the worn-out *Glory*. The little frigate survived its second pass with the Ruhar frigate *Mem Hertall*, but the *Glory*'s shields were now down to only 22% effectiveness. The shield emitters were so polarized from deflecting maser fire that they needed to be taken offline and restarted. Her sensor field was so confused by the intense cloud of high-energy particles clinging to the ship's hull that the ship had lost track of an incoming missile. Her defensive maser and particle beam cannons were firing almost blindly, knowing that the ship's weakened shields could not protect the hull from even a near-miss warhead explosion. The missile raced in toward the enemy frigate, jinking randomly to avoid defensive fire. If the missile had known the enemy's weakness, it would have flown straight and true right into the frigate's reactor.

The arrival of the task force was perfectly timed for the *Vergent*, she had been attacked by four enemy ships and trapped, unable to climb to jump distance. Even if the pair of destroyers above had not blocked her access to jump altitude, the damping field those two ships projected would prevent the *Vergent* from jumping away. The Kristang destroyer was battered, maneuvering wildly to avoid maser and railgun fire, and her defensive batteries were smoking hot from exploding incoming missiles.

Then, suddenly, incoming fire stopped as the enemy ships broke contact and climbed frantically for jump altitude. The two Ruhar destroyers above *Vergent* turned off their power-draining damping fields and fed power to jump drive capacitors and defensive shields, anticipating a hard fight with the powerful Kristang task force. A fight that never came.

On the *Vergent*'s bridge, her crew exulted and her captain pumped his fist in the air triumphantly. He was about to order his ship's railgun turned to fire on a now-retreating enemy frigate, when the task force commander ordered him to cease fire for the moment, and of all things, to use the *Vergent*'s maser cannons to intercept the missile that threatened the *To Seek Glory in Battle is Glorious*.

At first, the *Vergent*'s captain could not believe the order, it must have been scrambled in transmission or in the decryption process. He held his railgun fire anyway, wary of angering his commander. Then confirmation was received. The *Glory*'s sensor field had lost track of an enemy missile, and the *Vergent* was the closest ship, the only ship capable of destroying the missile before it blew the little *Glory* into dust. The Captain turned to his weapons officer. "We are ordered to intercept a missile that is tracking the *Glory*. You will do your best to comply. However," the Captain's lips curling in a grimace that was the Kristang equivalent of a smile. "It is unfortunate that our own sensors have been degraded by recent action."

"Yes, Captain. Understood." The weaponeer acknowledged and turned his attention to the console in front of him. "Engaging maser cannons now."

The missile had its own problems, having to keep track of a target that was surrounded by a cloud of high-energy particles. Debris from other missile warheads cluttered orbital space, and the missile's brain was confused by overlapping sensor fields, only one of which was its own. The missile's sensor field distorted unpredictably, making it momentarily lose track of its target. It also detected defensive maser and particle cannon fire, and the missile jerked side to side violently to throw off the enemy's aim.

A maser came close, this beam from a different direction. Alarmed, the missile's brain changed course and fired thrusters in an attempt to now escape two opponents.

"I am sorry, Captain," the weaponeer reported in a casual voice. "We are unable to effectively target the missile from this range. We risk hitting the *Glory*."

"That in unfortunate," the Captain said, now bored. He still needed to make it look good for the task force commander. "Continue trying, weaponeer."

The Ruhar missile regained a lock on its target, which it identified as a particular type of Kristang frigate. In fact, it was a specific frigate that was well-known to the Ruhar defense force. That type of ship was thought by the Ruhar fleet to have a gap in sensor coverage just aft of amidships, so the missile altered course to approach from that angle. The missile fired thrusters and its engine swung around to propel it almost sideways, flinging it across empty space.

And right into a maser bolt from the *Vergent*.

"What?!" The Captain of the destroyer shrieked. "You idiot!"

"I'm sorry, Captain," the weaponeer cowered in his seat before his enraged Captain. "It was an accident! The missile flew right into our maser beam!"

The Captain fumbled for his sidearm to shoot his traitorously incompetent weapons officer, but as his hand closed on the pistol, he thought better of it. A dead weapons officer would be difficult to explain. Instead, he would make the man's life miserable. "Very well," the Captain's lip curled in a sneer, but he never finished the thought.

While the attention of the *Vergent*'s crew had been focused on the two Ruhar destroyers and pair of frigates, and then on their task force and finally the hapless *Glory*, they forgot about the single Ruhar cruiser. Forgetting about that ship was somewhat understandable in the heat of battle. The *Ruh Gastalo* had only recently been able to complete her turn, and only now was the cruiser able to accelerate toward the *Vergent*.

Her railgun, however, did not rely on its host ship's velocity or course. As the *Gastalo* reached the point where her velocity relative to the *Vergent* was zero, her railgun had pumped out six shots. Four of the darts flew onward and eventually would escape the star system and galaxy. The other two, one following close behind the other, hit the *Vergent*. The first was deflected by the destroyer's defensive energy shield which then immediately collapsed from the strain. The second dart plunged through the subatomic particle cloud left by the first dart, and punched through the Kristang destroyer's relatively light armor. The dart missed the reactor by mere centimeters, marauding through the *Vergent* stern to bow, to cause a tremendous explosion that ripped the ship's bow off. The crew in the bridge was instantly transformed into water vapor before simultaneously boiling and freezing in the vacuum of space. As the dart ripped through the ship, it created shrapnel, one piece of which flew backwards and ignited one of the Vergent's own missiles. The missile exploded in the launch tube, cooking off its warhead.

The destroyer was torn in half, and chunks of its own debris tore through the reactor shielding, causing the reactor to lose containment and triggering a release of titanic energy from the ship's drive coils.

In less than two hundredths of a second after the first railgun dart impacted her shields, the *We are Proud to Honor Clan Sub-Leader Rash-au-Tal Vergent who Inspires us Every Day* ceased to exist as an organized collection of molecules. In the space she had occupied, there was now an expanding glare of mesons and rapidly-cooling exotic particles.

"Cease fire! Cease fire!" Commodore Ferlant ordered. He had been too late to stop his own free-flying railgun darts, and saw with satisfaction what they had done to Target Delta. "All ships, cease fire and proceed to rendezvous coordinate Alpha." As he listened to the ships in his task force acknowledge his order, Ferlant reflected on the message he had received from the Kristang commander. A message he thought he would never hear from a Kristang.

Admiral Jet-au-Bes Kekrando, commander of the Kristang task force, could believe his own message even less than Commodore Ferlant had. The message had left such a bad, sour, cowardly taste in Kekrando's mouth that he had been forced to lock himself in his quarters and practice saying the hated message word by word. When he had been unable to get through reciting the entire message, he had ordered the ship's AI to mimic Kekrando's voice and record it for later transmission.

The message, forced upon Admiral Kekrando by his clan leaders, offered a truce with the Ruhar on Pradassis. The clan wished not to recapture the planet by force, but instead merely to give the clan a much stronger hand in negotiations. When Kekrando had protested that such a cowardly act was unworthy of the warriors in his task force, he had been taken aside by three senior clan leaders. Rather than berating him for insubordination, they had commiserated with him at their being forced to negotiate with the disgusting Ruhar. They were negotiating, the clan leaders explained, because a forceful military action to retake Pradassis would result in destruction of Ruhar ships and widespread deaths among Ruhar on the planet. That would almost certainly provoke a strong response by the Ruhar fleet. The clan was too weak for a major campaign against the Ruhar, and other Kristang clans would be more likely to help the Ruhar than help a rival clan. The clan had barely been able to scrape together the funds to pay the Thuranin to carry Kekrando's task force to Pradassis; they could not afford to send any more ships. Thus, he needed to avoid becoming involved in a major fleet action with the Ruhar. Although it certainly *felt* cowardly and beneath the dignity of a warrior, a carefully restrained action would accomplish the clan's goals, whereas a typical Kristang slash-and-burn invasion would do the opposite in this case. After the meeting concluded, Admiral Kekrando could understand the clan leaders' reasoning and see the long-range wisdom of their decisions. He also decided that he never wished to become a senior clan leader. It involved too much of a distasteful word called *politics*.

When his task force ships jumped in, Kekrando had waited crucial seconds after his ships fired one volley at surface targets that had been approved by the clan leadership. He was supposed to jump in, verify the tactical situation, fire one volley, and then transmit the message offering a cease fire and safe passage for the Ruhar ships to escape. Instead, he had waited, with the excuse that he was waiting for sensor data to give him a more complete view of the tactical situation. In reality, he had waited in the hope that the destroyer and frigate who had jumped in first as bait could score significant hits on enemy ships. Instead, the destroyer *Vergent* was now dead because of his delay, without substantial damage to the Ruhar ships. Kekrando had ground his teeth at that setback; the *Vergent*'s captain had been incompetent and the task force was better off without him, but Kekrando could have put another man in command of that destroyer. Now his task force was already depleted by one ship, without any damage to the enemy.

Warily, the little frigate *To Seek Glory in Battle is Glorious* dipped closer to the planet in order to give a wide space for the Ruhar task force to climb out to jump distance. Seeking glory in battle was indeed glorious, but on that day the ship's crew had enough of battle and simply wanted to survive the next ten minutes. A cease fire could break down at any moment, and the *Glory*'s shields were unable to stop even a low-power maser at the moment. To prevent shield projectors from melting down and exploding, the *Glory*'s crew had been forced to take them offline and let them cool. Until the generators could go through the long process of being reactivated, the ship was essentially defenseless. Inside the ship, the crew held their breath until the last Ruhar ship, a cruiser, jumped away.

Cheers rang throughout the ship. The *Glory* had survived another day, survived a very close call, with the last-minute surprise assistance of the destroyer *Vergent* and that ship's valiant crew. It was not only a day they had survived, not only a battle; they had survived an entire campaign. The Kristang task force had established complete supremacy in the space surrounding Pradassis. The raids were over. Combat was over. They had sought glory in battle and in retrospect, it had been glorious. And now, her crew fervently hoped, it would be some other ship's turn to seek glory.

Negotiations for the formal cease fire agreement took less than half a day; with the Kristang battlegroup in complete control of the planet, there was not much for the Ruhar government to do other than accept the terms offered. The terms were surprisingly generous, almost unprecedented. Commodore Ferlant's small task force would not be allowed within eleven lightminutes of the planet, although eventually Ruhar civilian transport ships would be allowed into orbit. The Kristang would land troops and equipment in the northeast of the northern continent. That area had been fully evacuated before the Ruhar came back, reducing the disruption to the native population as the Kristang established their presence at abandoned Ruhar military bases. The cease fire agreement also established a zone between the Kristang and the Ruhar areas, where no aircraft could fly.

The agreement left open the ultimate status of the humans on the southern continent. While the cease fire was in effect, either side was allowed to take action against the humans, and neither side could provide any form of assistance. Shortly after the formal agreement was signed, humans on Lemuria noticed the tractors and other equipment provided by the Ruhar suddenly stopped working. Calls to the Ruhar went unanswered, until the government contacted UNEF HQ, to state that no additional equipment or materials would be coming from the Ruhar. Humans were on their own, until the ultimate status of the planet had been decided.

At which point, humans would be screwed, one way or the other.

CHAPTER ELEVEN

Flying Dutchman

After leaving the derelict relay station behind, our ability to practice the raid was limited to using parts of the *Flying Dutchman* as a stand-in for a relay station. Because the type of relay station we would be boarding was a converted warship, the arrangement of the station's interior was not much different than that of our pirate ship. Corridors were the same dimensions, doors the same height and width, blast doors located about the same distance apart. Major Smythe had people run through assault drills over and over, always adding some wrinkle or problem that his team needed to adapt to. It was unnerving to see people in Kristang armored suits charging down corridors, firing simulated ammo and using simulated rockets and grenades. Combots were used by Smythe's team, and by Skippy acting as the Thuranin opposition.

The extra practice time gave Smythe's team opportunity to refine their assault plan; still, both Smythe and Skippy expected substantial casualties. In some simulations, the assault team suffered 50% losses, when one of our two dropships was blown up in the initial operation to force the team's way into the station. "The problem, Colonel," Smythe said to me after one particularly bad simulated assault, "is forcing our way through the interior of the station. The enemy's defenses are substantial. I asked Skippy if there is a way he can disrupt those defenses, and he told me he cannot do much, until we get him past the shielding and into the station's core. There are going to be casualties, Colonel."

Sitting in my office, I was trying to avoid thinking about how many of the Merry Band of Pirates we were going to lose in the upcoming operation. My way to avoid thinking involved playing a mindless game on a tablet. The game got my mind off-

"Skippy," I said slowly, and almost never finished the thought.

"Oh no." He groaned. "Oh I *hate* my life. The universe hates me. This is so unfair."

"What?" He had me alarmed.

"You're going to tell me one of your brilliant freakin' ideas that I should have thought of with my ginormous brain power. And I am going to sink ever lower and lower into ultimate despair until I long for the gentle embrace of death," his voice trailed off.

"How did you know that? About the idea, I mean."

"When you say something slowly like that, especially when you say my name super slowly, it means that you just had an idea form in your monkey-meat brain."

"I do not."

"Yes you do, every freakin' time. You speak slowly because you are finishing the idea while the signal is crawling along from your brain to your voice box, and as glacially slow as *your* brain works, it takes a while."

"Huh. Really?"

"Really. Duh."

"Wow. I didn't realize I was doing that. It bothers you a lot?"

"Yes! I hate it!"

"Cool," I said with satisfaction. "Maybe I should speak really slowly sometimes when I don't have an idea, just to mess with you."

"Joe? You do realize that I control things like our reactors, missile warheads, and the pile of nukes we have in a cargo bay? Such a nice ship you have here. It would be a shame if I lost the will to live and my concentration slipped, if you know what I mean."

"Got it. Do you want to hear my idea? This may be a false alarm; it is more of a question that may turn into a good idea."

"Ooooh! If this doesn't develop into a brilliant idea, can I tease you unmercifully until the last star in the universe turns into a cold dark lump of neutrons?"

"If that turns you on, Skippy, then go for it. You said the Thuranin created this newest type of relay stations from obsolete cruisers?"

"Correct so far. I'm not detecting any brilliant idea yet, Joe."

"Wait for it. Was that class of cruisers simply old, or were they withdrawn from service for some reason?"

"Joe, trivia night in the galley is Tuesday, not today. Who cares?"

"Humor me, Skippy."

"Ugh," he huffed, "fine. They were withdrawn from service before the end of their intended life, because of a structural weakness. That class of cruisers was made by stretching the hull of a very successful class of destroyer; the Thuranin figured that if the destroyer was good, a bigger destroyer would be even better. They were wrong. Those little green morons didn't redesign the entire hull structure, they cut the destroyer in half and spliced in a section to accommodate more shield generators, additional maser cannons and missile tubes. After about thirty years, several of those cruisers were lost in combat because their shields failed in that spliced section. What the Thuranin failed to realize is that the additional shield generators changed the way impacts on the shields are distributed across the overall hull structure. The stresses tended to concentrate in one weak point. Ships were lost in battle because the hull buckles in that one area, and it disrupts power distribution inside the ship. The Thuranin didn't realize that, because they are stupid, arrogant, hateful little green men. Also because they stole the cruiser's design from the Jeraptha, but while the Jeraptha knew what they were doing, the Thuranin did not. Does that satisfy your idle curiosity, Joey?"

"Almost," I said happily. "When the cruiser hulls were converted into relay stations, did the Thuranin fix the design flaw?"

"No, there wasn't any reason to, dumdum. The hull weakness is only a problem for warships that engage in battle regularly. Over time, the strain of deflecting enemy fire causes stress cracks that have to be fixed. The Thuranin decided that fixing cracks in the hull structure every couple years wasn't worth the expense, so they took the ships out of service. Why do you care? I'm asking in order to understand how your monkey-meat brain works, Joe."

"Another question, then. Why didn't they just reinforce that part of the hull?"

"To truly fix the problem would have required so much reinforcement that it would have degraded the ship's performance. Again, why do you care?"

"The relay stations have that same flaw, right? A hit in one place will disrupt power distribution inside the hull? Power that goes to defensive systems?"

"Oh, no no no! No you don't. It doesn't count as a good monkey-brain idea if it doesn't work, Joe. Yes, there is a weakness in the hull structure of relay stations. The Thuranin know that, so they added a minor amount of armor plating in that area. You can't, I, uh, give me a moment. Huh. Well, that *is* interesting. Ok, yes, it is possible that a very, I mean, *very* precise hit in a particular area could still disrupt power distribution within the hull. The Thuranin didn't bother to reconfigure their power cabling when the ships were converted to relay stations."

"Interesting," I said slowly, again without realizing what I was doing.

"No! Uh uh, Joey. Not this time. When I say a very precise hit, I mean it would have to be a maser beam striking an area about a half centimeter in diameter. And not a wimpy hand-held maser beam, we would have to use one of the *Dutchman's* maser cannons. We can't risk the *Dutchman* getting that close, and besides, the target is at an extremely awkward angle. The *Dutchman* would have to fire several times in order to cut away sections of machinery on the outside of the station's hull, just to get at the target. After our first shot, the Thuranin would activate their energy shields, and those shields would disperse our maser beam. Also they would shoot back at our beat up pirate ship. So, no. No way can we do this."

"Show me," I pointed to my tablet. "Show me this weak spot."

He did. It truly was an awkward place. The Thuranin were not fools, they knew about the weakness so they had installed armor around it. The only way to get at the weak spot was where cables to a relay antenna came through the armor plating, and to get at that spot, a maser would have to be fired almost parallel to the station's hull. A person in an armor suit might be able to get there, but a hand-held maser didn't have the power we needed.

"See?" Skippy asked gleefully. "To disrupt their power, we need to hit that weak spot with ship's power, and there's no way to do that. Unless you know of a way to bend a maser beam. Or to shrink the *Dutchman* to the size of a dropship."

"You can't warp spacetime so the maser beam will curve?" I asked hopefully.

"Yes I can," he chuckled. "I can't curve the beam enough to make a difference, dumdum."

"Understood, Skippy. You disappoint us once again."

"What? You ass, I-"

"That was a joke. Do you want to hear my idea?"

"Probably not," he sighed.

I told him anyway.

"Joe, I *hate* you more than words can say. In order to describe how very much I hate you, I needed to create a new language that I call 'Cursive', because I use it to curse at you inside my brain. If you understood this language, you would be impressed."

"I love you too, Skippy. Will my idea work?"

He gave a heavy sigh. "We will find out one way or the other."

We arrived at our planned hold point twelve lighthours from our target, and spent eight hours passively scanning the area to assure there were no nasty surprises waiting for us. Skippy confirmed the relay station was alone and operating normally. Of course, if there was a stealthed ship guarding the station, we would have to be a lot closer to detect it. Too close. Chotek finally gave us the go ahead, and the *Flying Dutchman* jumped in to one of the designated data exchange points near the relay station. Instead of Skippy's usual superprecise jump, he deliberately brought us in off-target so it would look like a typical Thuranin jump. The ship was also pointed straight at the station; from the station's angle they hopefully couldn't immediately tell how extensively modified our star carrier was. "Transmitting signal now," Skippy announced, and Captain Desai looked at me, one of her fingers poised on the button to initiate an emergency jump away if the relay station didn't acknowledge properly.

"Ok, we're good," Skippy said, and we all breathed a sigh of relief. "I grumbled about what a pain in the ass this secrecy stuff is, and the communications officer on the station agreed with me. They bought our story, Joe. They acknowledge that we will be sending two dropships over, and they are opening docking bay doors now."

"Excellent. Launch the package," I ordered, and in the CIC, Chang gave me a thumbs up.

"Package is away," he confirmed.

Our own docking bay doors slid aside, and two dropships stuffed with SpecOps troops and combots launched slowly, moving with unnecessary caution. For the operation, we wanted to give the impression that we were in no hurry. Also, we needed to give the special package time to get into position. The gentle maneuvers of the dropships helped protect the people inside, who were strapped into webbing with no other cushioning at all.

The dropships proceeded cautiously across the gulf between the ship and the station, with the dropships blinking lights and broadcasting the proper IFF transponder codes like the innocent transports that they were not.

The package had been attached to the outside of the *Dutchman* before we jumped, launching it simply involved releasing clamps and with a gentle push, it was away. The package was my idea; it consisted of a jetpack, a stealth field generator and one end of a microwormhole. The other end of the microwormhole was wrapped around the muzzle of a maser cannon on the *Dutchman*'s aft end. As the pair of dropships approached the station's open docking bay, Skippy flew the package close to the spot where the station's original cruiser hull had been spliced. With two dropships approaching, the station had dialed back its sensor field to avoid interfering with the navigation sensors of the dropships. The station's weakened sensor field gave the Thuranin no chance to detect the tiny residual signature of our package until it was in position.

"Uh oh, Joe. The Thuranin have noticed an odd sensor reading near our package. So far, they are investigating it as a power fluctuation in the antenna in that area. I am helping feed their delusion by telling them we are picking up garbled transmissions from that antenna, and we are working together to diagnose the issue. But I suggest we move soon. Real soon."

"Are the dropships secured?" I asked anxiously.

"Both are in the docking bay," Chang reported, "one is down and secured, the other will be in ten seconds."

Ten seconds was too long to wait, we absolutely needed surprise. "Colonel Chang," I ordered, "weapons free."

Chang pressed a preprogrammed button, and our maser cannon fired through the microwormhole. Pumping that much energy through a wormhole less than a nanometer in diameter caused it to collapse and damaged our maser cannon. It also made a very precise hit on the exact weak spot of the station's structure, and severely disrupted power feeds inside the station. Other than emergency power, the forward half of the station that contained the docking bay and the core compartment with the station's AI was plunged into darkness. From one of the dropships, Skippy reported that the Thuranin were scrambling to reconfigure the power flow, then the *Dutchman* jumped away just as the station fired a maser cannon at us.

The station disappeared in the blink of an eye, and the ship emerged twelve lightminutes away. Far enough for safety, too far away to be of any help to the assault team.

Sitting in my command chair, feeling useless. I hated it.

United States Marine Corps Staff Sergeant Margaret Adams had been given the honor of joining the Merry Band of Pirates SpecOps raid on the Thuranin relay station, despite the fact that she had not qualified for the Marine Raiders special forces. It was a dubious honor for her, because her role in the plan was not to operate a combot or fire a rifle. Her assigned task was to remain with the rear guard, while carrying a smartass shiny beer can in a backpack strapped to her Kristang armored suit. "Hey, Sarge Marge," said a voice in her helmet speakers, "can you be a little more careful? All this bouncing around is bad for my delicate constitution. I'm getting seasick back here."

Paradise

Crouched with her back to a bulkhead behind a corridor junction which the SpecOps team had just cleared of enemy resistance, she slammed her back into the bulkhead. "Oops, sorry there, Skippster," she said without humor.

"Ok, Ok, I get the message," he grumbled. "Combat isn't the place for humor."

"No it is not." Adams knew that Skippy joking with her was his way of relieving her stress, but she didn't want her stress relieved. She wanted her stress, wanted to harness the energy it gave her. And talking with her was not distracting Skippy from talking individually with each person on the SpecOps team. Guiding them, warning of the enemy's location and intentions, fuzzing or blanking out enemy sensors, even taking direct control of armored suits and jerking people out of the way if they were about to be hit by enemy fire. And if enemy fire did penetrate their suits, Skippy managed the suit's self-repair and emergency medical functions. He was also worming his way into the station's functions section by section as they advanced; opening or closing blast doors, messing with the artificial gravity and even causing the overload of a power conduit that killed two Thuranin and disabled three of their combots. Skippy was doing all that, plus making jokes with Adams, and he was probably not anywhere near testing the limits of his capabilities. "Are you bored, Skippy?" She asked.

"Yeah, kind of. Don't worry about me, I'm keeping myself busy composing new insults for Joe. You'll like these, they're good ones! For example, how about- Oooh, sorry about that! Not you, Marge, I was talking to a Thuranin. I just crushed one of those little green fuckers by slamming a blast door as it was going through. Hmm, interesting. Unlike chickens, Thuranin don't run around after their heads are cut off. These Thuranin aren't as much of a challenge as I expected, Marge. Boy, you screw with their plan for static defense and they just fall apart."

"We have two dead already, Skippy," Adams gritted her teeth. One of the dead was responsible for the red droplets that spattered the front of her suit. Adams had been right behind that French paratrooper when he took a combot rocket to the chest; Skippy had not been able to jerk him away in time.

"Sergeant Adams, you are an unaugmented species, without the advantage of any genetic engineering, other than what you accidentally accomplished by deciding who to mate with in the back seat of a Buick. You are attacking a group of cyborgs who have been fighting this war for thousands of years, on their territory, against their prepared defenses. When we first proposed to seize this station, I expected 90 casualties, if we got lucky. By my count, Major Smythe's team is slaughtering them in impressive fashion. Damn! If you monkeys ever do get any real technology of your own and are able to tweak your cluttered genetic code, the rest of the galaxy had better watch their asses."

"Was that praise for humanity, Skippster?"

"Shmaybe. I'll deny it if you tell anyone."

"Of course."

"Uh oh. Time to move, Sarge Marge," Skippy advised. "Take the corridor to the left."

Adams pushed away from the bulkhead. "Not straight ahead?" She pointed with her rifle to where the SpecOps team had advanced.

"Um, no. There is a tiny bit of a problemo for you and the rear guard to deal with. Um, it would be good if you moved now. Like, now now now!"

Without a word, Adams followed the special forces soldier in front of her, a Ranger Lieutenant Poole. Behind her was a Chinese 'Night Tiger' Lieutenant Kwan. Adams had trained with Poole and Kwan extensively; both of them had initially been disappointed to be assigned to the rear guard, until Major Smythe dryly pointed out that the assault operation would only be successful if they got Skippy past the thick shielding and into the station's core. Poole and Kwan were charged with getting Adams or just Skippy into the core, even if everyone else had fallen in battle. Hearing that, the female US Army Ranger and the male Chinese Night Tiger had become a dedicated team with Adams, and Margaret Adams began to wish she had not volunteered for the mission. The two special forces soldiers trained her mercilessly, until the three of them were utterly exhausted but could anticipate each other's moves without speaking. They also made it clear to Adams that her surviving the mission would be nice but not necessary. Poole had even practiced throwing Adams through doorways, using the Marine's suited body as inert protection for Skippy.

Margaret Adams took that as a huge compliment.

"How tiny a problem?" Poole asked tersely while running down the corridor, flipping and spinning in her armored suit, her feet and hands barely touching the floor, walls and ceiling as she covered all approaches.

"A big problem," Major Smythe's voice cut into the conversation. "Kwan, Poole, follow Skip-" his voice was drowned out by the buzzing rattle of Kristang rifles and several explosions. "Follow Skippy's instructions and move as fast as you can. We don't have time to send combot support back to you." Another loud explosion. "Go! Out."

"Ok, maybe not so tiny a problem," Skippy admitted. "Two Thuranin evaded Smythe's team, got around them in a parallel corridor. They have a pair of combots with them, and they're going to a power junction to set off an overload. That would cause an explosion not large enough to destroy the station, but it would blow a hole in the hull and knock out the main transmitter. We wouldn't be able to fix it, so that would destroy our whole purpose of boarding this station."

"Got it," Kwan acknowledged. "I see it," he said as Skippy's map popped up in their visors. "Poole, you're with me. Adams, you stay behind us."

"Affirmative," Adams replied, checking for the hundredth time that her rifle's safety was off. She had never fired a Kristang rifle in combat. During the asteroid raid of the *Dutchman*'s first mission, she had operated a combot, not worn an armored suit. The Kristang weapon felt strange, it buzzed more than barked, and its antirecoil mechanism reduced the kick. That made it easier to maintain aim at a target but it was less satisfying to fire, almost like using a rifle in a video game. She looked at the red splattered on the front of her suit and thought of the French paratrooper who had died in front of her. This was no video game.

Skippy's awesomely omnipotent vision and hearing through the station's own sensors gave the three humans an advantage, and rendered the two Thuranin nearly blind. Nearly. Kwan and Poole knew where the two deadly combots were located, and where their two Thuranin operators were taking cover. Skippy could slightly fuzz the targeting sensors of the combots, but he could not give Kwan and Poole the ability to dodge a hail of bullets. And the cyborg nature of the Thuranin gave them a link to the combots as if they were part of their own bodies, allowing lightning-quick reactions.

Using hand signals, Kwan and Poole readied behind the corner of an intersection, then tossed a pair of sparkle grenades around the corner. These grenades blew nearly silently, filling the air of the corridor with sensor-blinding chaff and intensely glowing particles to confuse thermal and infrared sensors. Kwan took the floor while Poole flipped up and engaged her boots on the ceiling, running easily upside down. Adams tensed just behind the corner, ready to provide fire support although she was not supposed to risk direct combat. So she was almost taken by surprise as Kwan rocketed back along the corridor, bounced off the opposite wall, and tried to stand, firing his rifle the whole time. Then a string of bullets from a combot stitched across his armored chest and he was flung backward. A hail of explosive-tipped rounds tore his right arm off in mid-bicep; the armored arm flew through the air and hit Adams squarely in the chin, knocking her backwards. Out of the corner of her dazed vision, she saw Poole come dashing around the corner, now back on the floor and limping badly.

Poole tossed her rifle to Adams and dashed back into the corridor to haul Kwan back to relative safety by one leg. "That could have gone better," the Ranger muttered to herself. "Adams, you injured?"

"No, ma'am," Adams was back on her feet, still seeing spots at the edge of her vision. "That doesn't look good," she pointed to dents and gouges in the right leg of Poole's armored suit.

"It's fine," the Ranger replied, examining Kwan's condition. "Kwan?"

"Still here," the Chinese special forces soldier reported, struggling to get back to his feet.

"Sit down," Poole ordered. "You lost an arm."

Kwan seemed to notice for the first time. "Oh." The suit had automatically clamped shut around the injury, preventing further blood loss. With the suit pumping Kwan full of drugs and nanomachines under Skippy's control, he didn't feel the pain and his body's natural shock response was suppressed. Not that a Night Tiger would ever allow himself the weakness of experiencing shock. Kwan looked from his missing right arm to his left, where his rifle was still secured. He checked the rifle's readout. "Forty two rounds left," he said and tried to stand again.

"You aren't going anywhere," Poole said with a worried glance back over her shoulder, in case the combots tried to advance. "Skippy, sitrep."

"One combot is destroyed, the other is damaged; its mobility and targeting sensors are compromised. That was good shooting by you and Kwan. The two Thuranin are in the process of making the final connections to overload the power junction. You have to move now, and I mean right *now*."

"How-" Poole started to say something, when Adams hit the button that fastened the ultra strong strap of her backpack.

"Kwan can carry Skippy," Adams announced, shrugging off the pack.

"Poole," Smythe called. "I see Kwan lost an arm and that you're injured? Skippy just warned me the situation-" There was a sustained rattle of gunfire, "Your situation back there is critical. You need to stop those Thuranin. I sent two people back to you with combots but they won't arrive in time."

The Ranger hesitated only a moment, looking directly into Adams' eyes, then nodded. "We're handling it. Adams and I will take care of the Thuranin, Kwan will carry Skippy."

"Kwan can't carry-" Smythe started to object.

"I can walk, Major," Kwan said, and struggled to his feet. Adams slung the pack over his shoulders and the strap automatically clanged shut around his chest. "I can do it." Kwan's voice was unsteady as his body adjusted to shock, blood loss and the intervening nanomachines.

"Lieutenant Poole, this is not a good ide-"

Poole cut Smythe off. "Sir, you are not *here*."

"Understood," Smythe said. "Make it happen."

"Acknowledged. Poole out. Kwan, go back along the corridor and link up with the people Smyth is sending. Whatever happens, you get Skippy to the station core."

Lieutenant Kwan never thought the most vital mission of his life would involve carrying a beer can. He saluted with his rifle and turned to jog unsteadily back down the corridor.

"I can't take the ceiling this time," Poole lifted her injured leg. "We go in, I'll take point. Forget the sparkle grenades, they'll degrade our sensors as much as that combot's sensors at this point. Skippy, is there any reason we can't use shock grenades on those Thuranin? Would that cause the explosion we're trying to avoid?"

"Shock grenades will not be problem," he advised. "Maximum violence is authorized. And recommended. I really urge you to get moving, *now.*"

Margaret Adams later reflected that if she had not been trained so well by the Marine Corps, or if she had taken time to think about it, she might not have gone around that corner with Poole. She did. The enemy combot fired wildly, scoring a vicious hit to Poole's already injured right side. The impact knocked Poole sideways into Adams, making Adams bounce off the wall and saving her life. The combot's final two rockets scorched through the spot where Adams had been a split second before. With Poole skidding on the floor and Adams falling, both women kept aim on the combot, and it was ripped apart by explosive-tipped rounds. Without exchanging a word and without hesitation, they scrambled to their feet, running and leaping over the smoking ruins of the two combots. Poole ripped a shock grenade off her belt and Adams did the same, tossing the grenades through an .open doorway and following the grenades with massed rifle fire. Both of the grenades exploded at the same time, having been networked together for maximum effect.

Detonation of the grenades flung both women backwards, Poole smacking her helmet on the far wall, and Adams crashing into the Ranger. Stunned, Adams still had the presence of mind to keep her rifle pointed at the doorway and the trigger depressed. Dimly, she heard a voice calling to her. "Adams. Adams! Sarge Marge, stand down. Stand down," Skippy said soothingly. "It's Ok. It's over. You got them. And you're out of ammo."

"Oof," Adams staggered to her knees. Even before checking on Poole, she ejected the spent clip from her rifle and slapped another in place, checking the readout to ensure it reported the correct 160 rounds. "Lieutenant, are you all right?"

"Yeah," Poole's voice reflected great strain. "Help me up, Sergeant. I think my ankle is sprained, and the suit leg motor aren't working properly."

"I'm working on it," Skippy said cheerily. "But I'm not optimistic. You'll have to walk on your own for a while."

"Got it." Poole shook her head to clear the cobwebs. The shock grenades had knocked her brain offline for a moment. She glanced through the doorway. There were bloody Thuranin bits liberally splattered all over. None of them were moving, unless you counted chunks falling from the ceiling. "Sergeant, I'll need to lean on you, this suit is too heavy to walk if the motors aren't working. Sorry. Let's get back to Kwan before any more trouble pops up."

"Yes, ma'am."

No more trouble popped up, they caught up to Kwan just before the people that Smythe had sent arrived to meet him. Kwan was in a bad way, the nanomachines had not been able to stop him bleeding inside the suit, and he was woozy. The fact that he was still upright when they found him was a testament to the toughness of the Night Tiger special forces. Adams left Kwan and Poole with an Indian paratrooper, and she took the backpack containing Skippy from Kwan. An SAS lieutenant and a combot were ready to escort Adams to the station's core. Before she painfully sat down to take the pressure off her ankle, Poole looked at the SAS man. "Get Sergeant Adams and Skippy to the station's core. If you see anything moving along the way," she almost slipped on spent shell casings that littered the floor. "Kill it."

Paradise

With a trigger-happy SAS trained killer and a heavy combot leading the way, Margaret Adams did not encounter any problems along the way to the station's core. As soon as she went through the heavily shielded blast doors that separated the station's core, Skippy exulted "I'm in! Their AI is toast, baby! It was a jerk, too, I'm certainly not going to shed any tears for that one. Major Smythe, my congratulations to your team, they were exemplary in both their bravery and skill. Huh. I wonder what Colonel Joe has been doing while we had all the fun?"

What I had been doing, I told Skippy later, was sitting uselessly in the command chair. Sitting, worrying and driving the pilots crazy because apparently I had been continuously tapping my front teeth with a thumbnail, until Desai turned in her seat and asked me to stop it. It is possible that was not my only subconscious annoying habit.

The battle to take control of the relay station took less than eleven minutes, and the *Dutchman* had microjumped twelve lightminutes away, so the fight was over before the light of our first shot reached back to our position. Space combat is weird and frustrating. After Skippy declared the fight to be over and Smythe took a couple minutes to confirm, it took their victory signal twelve minutes to reach us. When Skippy had first talked about light 'crawling' along, I had not appreciated the truth of that statement. After we received the victory signal, including Skippy reporting three dead, two critically wounded and seven with less serious injuries, we still could not jump the *Dutchman* back into recover the assault team. The Thuranin had launched a pair of missiles at us before we jumped, then when it appeared the battle may be going against them, they had ripple fired all twelve remaining missiles and ejected six flight recorder drones. All fourteen missiles were out there, stealthed, flying blind but their smart brains were angrily seeking any sort of target. Skippy needed twenty minutes to locate and contact the missiles and drones, and use the missiles to destroy the drones and each other. Having missile warhead debris floating around was a bonus, Skippy explained, because it would later help us sell the cover story. When we were done with the station, we planned to blow it up; debris of Thuranin missile warheads would be convincing evidence of a space battle the station had lost.

So, I sat aboard the *Dutchman*, doing absolutely nothing useful to anyone, until we received the All Clear signal that was already twelve minutes out of date. During that time, one of the critically wounded soldiers died, despite Doctor Skippy's best efforts. I was frantic to get the wounded to the *Dutchman*'s sickbay. The relay station had a medical facility that Skippy couldn't use until he had time to reconfigure its equipment for human anatomy. Given the slow rate at which the comparatively clunky Thuranin equipment accepted Skippy's instructions, it was faster to fly the wounded back to our ship. As soon as we jumped in, we detected that one of our dropships had launched to bring wounded soldiers to us. My job was to stay out of the way, keep my mouth shut and let my people do their jobs.

I hated every second of it. The next battle we engaged in, regardless of Chotek's orders or the strenuous advice of Chang, Simms and Smythe, I was going with the SpecOps team. Lt Colonel Chang was a fine officer, as fully capable as I am of uselessly sitting in the command chair while other people fought.

CHAPTER TWELVE

Smythe sent a quick situation report to me, including the casualty list. The list was much shorter than we had feared. Still, I would have to write letters to the families of each soldier we lost. My letters would be reviewed and censored by UNEF Command when we got back to Earth; any casualty had to be described as a 'training accident'.

"Was it worth the cost?" Chotek asked, standing right next to the command chair where I was sitting.

"Sir?"

"The people we lost," he said, as if he needed to remind me. "Was the mission successful? Is Skippy able to get into the Thuranin computer?"

"Yes," Skippy responded, sounding annoyed. "I am installing the submind to run the communications relay and fake messages from the former Thuranin crew here. This Thuranin computer equipment is absolute garbage, it will take hours to install and establish the submind. In the meantime, I am skimming through the databanks for any useful information about that surveyor ship that I destroyed for you."

"*You* destroyed?" I protested. "I seem to remember you having a little help from monkeys. Like, thinking up the whole idea of-"

"Yes yes, let's not quibble about the details," Skippy mumbled quickly. "Ok, so you were somewhat more useful than expected on that mission, do you expect a freakin' gold star from the teacher? Damn, you are way too sensitive. Anywho, here is what I have found so far, or, wait. Would you rather that I waste precious minutes in grudgingly telling you how marginally competent you sometimes are?"

"The data, Skippy! Give us the data!"

"I thought so. Here's the deal; the Thuranin know their surveyor ship was destroyed. They know its three escort ships were also destroyed around the same time. Perhaps the most important detail is that they believe the Jeraptha destroyed those ships. They have no idea about our pirate ship, and there has been no speculation that humans were involved in any way."

A cheer rang around the bridge and CIC. High fives were given, people hugged. I pumped my fist in the air, and gave Lt. Colonel Chang a big thumbs up through the glass that separated the bridge from the CIC. He returned the gesture with a huge grin. I was so happy that I even turned in my chair to shake Chotek's hand, and he was grinning happily.

"Not so fast, monkeybrains," Skippy warned. "There is one minor complication. We didn't know it, but there was a ceasefire in effect between the Jeraptha and the Thuranin in that subsector at the time. The Thuranin have protested to the Jeraptha, and the Jeraptha have strongly denied they were involved. This could become a problem; the Jeraptha know they didn't do it, so they are wondering who did."

"Oh, shit," I slumped in my chair.

"I wouldn't worry too much about it now, Joe," Skippy said in a soothing tone. "For now, both sides will almost certainly assume the incident is due to the fog of war. The Thuranin do not believe the denials of the Jeraptha. So any future complication from this incident will come from the Jeraptha. And they will forget all about it eventually, as long as there are not a lot more unexplained incidents in this sector. The destruction of the surveyor task force caused the Thuranin to retaliate by attacking Jeraptha ships, and the ceasefire broke down entirely. It has only recently been reestablished. By the way, when the Thuranin violated the ceasefire by attacking the Jeraptha, they got their little green asses kicked. The Thuranin very much want the current ceasefire to hold, so if we have to destroy another of their ships, they might not make a big fuss about it. Although let's avoid taking our rebuilt pirate ship into combat unless we have to, please?"

"Agreed," I breathed a sigh of relief, which was immediately ruined.

"You did not know there was a ceasefire in effect at the time you destroyed the surveyor ship?" Chotek of course found something to nag about.

Damn it. Even in a moment of triumph, I had to defend myself. "No sir," I said while trying to keep the annoyance out of my voice. "We did not have that information at the time. And there was no time for us to attempt to gather more information. Our priority was to intercept the surveyor ship, before it topped off its fuel tanks and set course for Earth."

"I guess that is my bad," Skippy said cheerily. "If I'd thought about it, I would have tried digging info like that out of the databanks of that tanker ship. Although I did fly by it super-fast; I barely had time to get the data on the tanker ship's rendezvous with the surveyor."

"Truthfully, sir," I added, "if we had known about the ceasefire, that would not have changed our actions. Could not have changed our actions, we did not have the time or opportunity to consider other possibilities. As it was, we barely arrived on time at the coordinates before the surveyor task force ships did."

"I have read your report, Colonel," Chotek said in a mildly scolding tone. "The fact remains there was a significant risk factor that you were not aware of. If the Jeraptha decide to investigate further, and discover that humans were involved, then your destruction of the surveyor task force could have put humanity in greater danger. We can't fly by the seat of our pants out here; the stakes are too high."

"Yes, sir," I responded as I could feel my cheeks growing red. Did the asshole UN bureaucrat think any of that was news to us?

"Hey!" Skippy shouted. "It's easy to play Monday morning quarterback when you have never done anything to-"

"Skippy!" I wanted to cut off a long and useless argument. "Mr. Chotek has a point; we did not have all the information available at the time. Sir," I spun my command chair around to face Chotek, "we are never going to have *all* the information we wish out here. We have to make judgments based on inadequate data. And on this mission, those judgment calls will be *yours*, sir. You are the mission commander. Whatever you do, someone back on Earth will be second guessing your decisions." My little speech was more for me than for him. Following the advice of Sergeant Adams, I was not going to let fear of criticism make me shy away from doing what I thought was right. From the CIC, Adams caught my eye and gave me a subtle nod of approval. "Even if the Jeraptha do find cause to investigate the destruction of the surveyor task force, they will find that difficult to do, since the incident occurred in Thuranin territory. It is unlikely the Thuranin will stand by while enemy ships spend months running detailed sensors scans. Skippy, is there any way that either the Jeraptha or Thuranin could find evidence connecting us to the surveyor task force?"

"No way, dude!" He chuckled happily. "You think I'm a moron? No way, not possible. The only possibility of ever connecting humans to that incident is if human DNA were somehow on a missile casing. And that did not happen, I scrubbed those missiles before launch for that very reason. Also, if you remember, Joe, those missiles all exploded and left only subatomic particles behind. The Jeraptha and Thuranin could scan that area until the end of time and not ever find a connection to us. Having said that, the Thuranin do know that one of their star carriers is out here flying around by itself and is now hostile to Thuranin forces. The Thuranin think our pirate ship has been captured by the Kristang; I know that because the Thuranin have warned the Kristang and angrily demanded their star carrier back. That caused major suspicions between Kristang clans; they are all worried that one clan has gained a major technological advantage by stealing a star carrier."

"The Kristang have become even more divided and distracted?" I asked. "That can only be good for us."

"That is my thinking, Joe, but then, I am not a strategic genius like Count Chocula here."

Chotek's face now grew red. He hated that nickname, hated it especially since he knew the entire crew used that nickname when he wasn't around. Skippy, always being helpful, had hacked into Major Simms' logistics database before we departed Earth, and somehow four crates of Count Chocula breakfast cereal had been added to the supply list. We had enough Chocula cereal aboard that we simply had to eat it; oddly enough, some people on the French team apparently loved the stuff. Most mornings, Hans Chotek could be fairly certain of seeing his namesake likeness on a box at breakfast, and someone always snickered quietly. It had to be eating away at him. Creating a subtle daily disrespect for our UN bureaucrat was a great way to ensure that, if I ever did have to mutiny and override his orders, the crew would follow me.

Giving Chotek that nickname proves that Skippy is a freakin' genius, and not just at physics. Sometimes I worry that he is just as good at manipulating me.

"Skippy, that is great news about the surveyor ship. Have you found any data about whether the Thuranin will be sending another ship to Earth?" That was my greatest fear. I could not see how we could destroy a second surveyor mission to Earth, without the Thuranin growing very suspicious why someone wanted to prevent ships from going to humanity's home planet. Two missions to Earth being destroyed, along with the wormhole to Earth mysteriously shutting down, would bring unwanted attention to our little world. Maybe enough attention to get the top species like the Maxolhx and Rindhalu curious, and alarmed, about humans.

The problem of the Thuranin sending a second ship had been the subject of intense study by UNEF Command before we left, and that brain trust had come up with exactly zero realistic ideas for dealing with it. Many nights, I lay in bed, trying to fall asleep but with my mind racing. Trying to dream up a way of save Earth, again. The only possibility I could see of stopping another surveyor ship, without exposing our secret star travel capability, would be to hit the second surveyor ship at its spacedock before it ever began the mission. We would need to somehow destroy the spacedock and many other ships at the same time, so the Thuranin would never realize the surveyor ship had been the target. To do that, we would need a lot of nukes, and we would need to locate the spacedock, get there on time, and sneak up on the target with our degraded stealth capability. That would certainly be a suicide mission for the *Flying Dutchman*, so we would never know if our desperate attack was successful in protecting Earth or not.

Skippy answered my question. "The Thuranin have notified the Fire Dragon clan Kristang that their hired surveyor ship was destroyed in the course of its mission, so the Thuranin are invoking the catastrophic loss clause of the contract, and refunding only a small part of the payment. They also, hee hee, this is funny, they told the Fire Dragons that they should have paid extra for insurance. That wasn't a joke, by the way. The little green men did actually offer to sell insurance to the Fire Dragons, but the lizards couldn't afford it."

"So, there won't be a second surveyor ship mission to Earth?" I asked fearfully.

"No any time soon, no," Skippy confirmed. "Loss of the surveyor ship has caused the Thuranin to jack up the price of a second mission, above anything the Fire Dragons can afford to pay. There are rumors of the Fire Dragons attempting to create a coalition to raise the money. But if the Fire Dragons are able to create a coalition, then they would be able to avoid the civil war that is the entire purpose of sending a ship to Earth in the first place. There will be a meeting of Kristang clans later this year, that is when the Fire Dragons hope to propose a coalition. There is another factor to consider, Joe."

"What's that?" Good news, I fervently wished. Good news, only good news.

Skippy read my mind. Although he said he couldn't do that. "Good news this time. The Thuranin have been hurt badly by the Jeraptha in this sector; they are not eager for the distraction of another long mission to Earth. A recent loss of territory to the Jeraptha means that any mission to Earth would need to detour around a key wormhole cluster, and that would add another seven week roundtrip to an already very long mission. The voyage to Earth was previously near the limit of a surveyor ship's performance characteristics; the detour makes it almost dangerous. In the relay's databanks, I found a message from the shipyard that designed the current class of surveyors. That shipyard warned they cannot be held responsible for anyone pushing their ships past their design limits."

"This is good news."

"It is most certainly good news, Colonel Joe," Skippy said happily.

With such news, I wanted to plan a celebration for the crew. Given the people we lost in taking the relay station, a memorial service was more appropriate. "Did you learn anything else?"

"My priority was searching for data about the surveyor task force, I am combing through the rest of the databanks now. The data is poorly organized, the Thuranin should be ashamed of themselves. It's going to take a while, Joe, even for me. We did get what we came here for, so, mission accomplished."

"Sir?" I turned to Chotek, who still managed to look unhappy despite the very welcome good news. "We have secured the relay station, and a Thuranin relief crew is not scheduled to arrive for eleven months. I suggest we clean up exterior damage to maintain the ruse that the station is operating normally. Then we should back the *Dutchman* away and remain in the area, until we receive confirmation the Thuranin will not send a second mission to Earth." Hanging near the relay station, with the *Dutchman* drifting stealthily in interstellar space for months, was going to be extremely dull for the crew.

"I agree for now, Colonel," Chotek said stiffly. "Please assure the self-destruct mechanism is installed aboard the relay station." The self-destruct mechanism he referred to was a pair of our own self-destruct nukes.

"Right away, sir. Colonel Chang, please inform the crew they can stand down from battle stations. And assign a party to bring our party favors," I meant the nukes, "to the station." I was going to our sickbay to see how Dr. Skippy was caring for our wounded.

On the way to sickbay, Skippy called my zPhone. "Good news about the relay station, Joe," Skippy reported. "Their sickbay has a full supply of medical nanomachines, so we can replenish our supply. A relay station does not carry a large a quantity of medical supplies compared to a star carrier, so we will still have only 28% of what we started with. The station unfortunately has almost none of the more useful multipurpose engineering nanomachines. There are some station components that we could use as spare parts aboard the *Dutchman*. The components need to remain in place for now for the station to function properly, we can remove them later. Oh, also, there are two dropships in the docking bay, of the same two types we have."

That news excited me. "Two more dropships? That's great, Skippy. Can we bring them aboard now?"

"Ah, I need to check them out thoroughly first. Their maintenance records indicate they work fine, but you know that you should never buy a used dropship without having it inspected first. We don't want to fall for that dipstick trick like your cousin Jimmy did."

"Oh, yeah." When my cousin Jimmy got his first job, he bought an old pickup truck. It was beat up and looked like a piece of junk, but Jimmy pulled the dipstick and it had plenty of clean, new oil. The next morning, there was a puddle of nasty black oil in his driveway, and three days later, the engine seized. The guy he bought it from had put a plug at the bottom of the dipstick tube, put in just enough fresh oil to make it look good. Since then, whenever poor Jimmy bought anything, we always asked whether he had checked the dipstick. "How did you hear about that?"

"Your cousins were talking about it at the party when you came home this time. You need to go home more often; I hear the best stories when you're there."

"I'm working on it, Skippy. Need to save the world again first."

There were only three people in the sickbay when I arrived. The power of advanced weaponry and the extreme violence of future combat left few lucky enough to be wounded. Four injury cases had already been tended to by Dr. Skippy; two of those were in recovery tanks with serious internal injuries that Skippy was hopeful could be cured. The other two were resting in their own quarters, Lt. Kwan was missing an arm, the other soldier had lost most of her right leg. Skippy was one hundred percent confident that they both would make a full recovery, although he told me privately that the supply of nanomachines for Thuranin medicine were running low. To repair the *Dutchman* on our last mission, Skippy had used up 90% of the medical nano, repurposing the tiny devices to repair the ship instead of body parts. We should, he said hopefully, be able to partly replenish our nanomachine supply from the relay station. Still, we needed to be careful with the supply of these critical medical miracles. Human injuries that could heal naturally or with mere drugs and surgery, would skip the advantage of nanomachines.

I greeted the three less seriously injured people awaiting treatment in the sickbay, including Ranger Lauren Poole. She had a black eye, several cuts on her face, and an ugly purple bruise from her right hip to her ribs. "Colonel," she said as she saluted me; I could tell raising her right arm was painful.

"Lieutenant Poole," I looked at the deep bruise. "That looks bad."

"It's fine, sir," she replied. "I'm here for my ankle." She lifted her right leg and I could see that her ankle was hanging oddly. "I feel stupid, sir. All those years in gymnastics, practicing landings, and I sprain my ankle now."

"She took three Thuranin rounds to her suit leg, and her ankle is broken, not sprained," Major Smythe explained. "You are lucky to be alive, Lieutenant," he said with obvious pride about the toughness of his SpecOps team.

"Ricochets, sir," she said with a shrug. "The only direct hit was to my torso," she pointed to the ugly bruise. "Those Kristang armored suits are tough. The black eye," she indicated her face and I noticed she used her left hand, "is because a tiny piece of shrapnel punctured my visor. It sealed right away, or I wouldn't be here."

"Correct," Dr. Skippy's voice said from a wall speaker. "Your injuries are not serious enough to require extensive use of nanomachines, so you will have surgery shortly, and regular injections of healing drugs."

"I'll be fine, Mr. Skippy," she said with a grimace. "I don't need surgery if someone else is in greater need of it. Ankle injuries are nothing new-"

"Lieutenant," I interrupted. "If Dr. Skippy says you need surgery, then you will cooperate to the best of your ability. Then you are going to follow the letter and spirit of the rehab routine that Dr. Skippy sets up for you," I declared. "I expect nothing less than perfection when you are performing rehabilitation exercises; all the judges had better be holding up cards with '10' on them, is that understood?"

Paradise

"Yes, sir," Poole said with a grin. I had given her a challenge, and there is nothing special forces people like more than a challenge. "I'll be up and around soon, you'll see."

Skippy and Smythe politely shooed me out of sickbay as soon as they could; the last thing they wanted was the commanding officer hanging around and making everyone uncomfortable. Taking the unsubtle hint to go away, I headed to the galley for a snack. A cup of coffee and half of a blueberry muffin took the edge off, and I was sitting at a table reading reports on my tablet when Skippy called me through the ceiling speaker. "Hey, Colonel Joe. I, uh, heh heh, found something interesting in the relay station's databanks. It seems there is trouble in Paradise. Or should I say trouble *on* Paradise?"

"Skippy," I stood up abruptly, alarmed. "We should talk about this in my office-"

"Sir?" Adams had been pouring herself a cup of coffee, that woman had the worst sense of timing. Or maybe the best. The ten other people in the galley all looked at her expectantly. "Is there a reason we can't hear information about the situation on Paradise?"

"Adams," I was annoyed, and embarrassed. "If this is bad news for UNEF, and we aren't able to do anything about it, I do not see the point of everyone bearing that burden."

She set her coffee cup down and crossed her arms. That was not a good sign for me. "When my aunt found out she had cancer, she didn't tell the family, because she said she didn't want to worry anyone. She was wrong about that. If you shut us out, you're wrong also. Sir."

Her message was loud and clear. The Merry Band of Pirates may not always be merry, but they were adults. They deserved to know. What pissed me off is that Skippy knew how I felt about keeping information about Paradise quiet, yet he had blurted it out while I was in a room with people. That irritating little beer can had done it deliberately. "Skippy," I said as I sat back down, "let's hear it."

"I found something unexpected. Two things, actually. First, the Ruhar federal government has been negotiating to give Paradise back to the Kristang-" His voice was drowned out by a chorus of shouts from everyone in the galley, including me.

"People, quiet, plea- Oh my God." I was completely stunned. Until that moment, my greatest fear had been that the Ruhar might not be able to supply enough food for UNEF. I had not thought the Ruhar would actively abuse the humans on their planet. And it had never for one second crossed my mind that the Ruhar would sell the planet out from under UNEF' feet! "Skippy, why the hell would the hamsters do that? They fought for Paradise!" Right then, I thought of all the Ruhar who died when I shot down the two Whale transports they were in. And the Ruhar had planned that operation, and risked all those lives, as a feint to lure in a Thuranin task force so the Jeraptha could destroy it. Now all those lives would truly be wasted.

Skippy explained the Ruhar's reasons for not wishing to keep Paradise. That is was not conveniently located following the recent wormhole shift. That the Kristang were offering more valuable territory in exchange for Paradise. That securing Paradise would require a major commitment of fleet resources that were needed elsewhere; an expense the Ruhar were not willing to bear. That the Ruhar had not wanted or intended to take the planet back recently, and now it was merely a bargaining chip for them. "Not all of the Ruhar agree with giving Paradise away, Joe," Skippy tried to assure us. "The native population, and of course UNEF, know nothing about negotiations with the Kristang. Your old friend Baturnah Logellia, the Burgermeister, is personally opposed to trading away her home."

Hearing that name brought back a flood of memories. Sitting in Lester Cornhut's home, on the Cornhut family couch, sipping tea with the Burgermeister. Listening while she told me horror stories of how humanity had been betrayed by the species we considered saviors and allies. Listening while she destroyed the last of my innocence. Innocence was a luxury I couldn't afford. The days sitting on that couch seemed a lifetime ago now, like those events had happened to a different person.

They had. I was a different person back then. A brand new buck sergeant, learning to lead a new fireteam on an alien planet, constantly scared of screwing up. Now I was a colonel, with the blood of thousands of aliens on my hands, and a homeworld that had been saved twice. And I was still constantly scared of screwing up. "Can she do anything to help UNEF? The Burgermeister, I mean."

"Nothing substantial that I can see now, Joe. I am sorry. She is still the deputy administrator of the planet; however the decisions are being made offworld. She has petitioned the Ruhar federal government to include the humans on Paradise in the evacuation, when the planet is formally returned to the Kristang. The government has formally, and very strongly rejected that idea. Humans, the government stated, are legally enemies of the Ruhar and therefore their fate is not a problem for the Ruhar."

"Shit," I breathed slowly. "Just when I thought things were going well."

"Darn. Uh, then this is a particularly bad time for me to mention that I have more bad news?"

Somehow I resisted the temptation to pound the table. "Sure, Skippy, go ahead, why the hell not?"

"Ooookay, I sense some irritation in your voice, Joe."

"Ya think?"

Skippy ignored me. "The stalled negotiations between the Ruhar and Kristang were recently disrupted, by a Kristang battlegroup that jumped into orbit three weeks ago. One of their ships were destroyed by the Ruhar, but the Kristang have now established space supremacy around Paradise. Their ships have complete control of the skies. After the brief initial battle, a truce has been arranged. The Kristang have landed almost four thousand troops, with aircraft and heavy equipment. So far, according to the data available, the Kristang have not directly engaged UNEF. That is good, for UNEF is totally disarmed and defenseless. I must warn that the data I have is fourteen days old at this point."

"How the hell did this happen? The last intel you provided, you said the Thuranin were pulling away from Paradise; that they would not support future Kristang efforts to keep the place!"

"That intelligence was and still is accurate. The Thuranin do not see any value in a primarily agricultural planet; therefore if the Kristang wish to pursue recapture of Paradise, they will do so on their own. The Kristang Swift Arrow clan strongly desires to retake the planet, so they have paid full price plus combat bonuses for the Thuranin to provide transport to the Paradise system. Going to Paradise was a one-way trip for the Swift Arrow battlegroup, Joe, they can't afford to have all their ships transported back home. The crews of those ships are very committed, they know they can't go home."

That reminded me of history I had learned in high school. When Hernan Cortes invaded Mexico, he scuttled his ships behind him, so his men would have no alternative but to conquer the Aztec Empire. When I read that in history class, I thought that Cortes was a reckless fool. Now I considered that scuttling his ships may have been an act of desperation. If the Kristang on Paradise faced a similar situation, they would be very dangerous.

"This is bad news," I said with a sigh. "Do you have anything worse?"

"Nope, Joe," he said with clueless cheeriness in his voice. "That's all the bad news for now."

"Great. To avoid rumors flying around," I looked at the people in the galley, "send your data to the entire crew. I need to talk with Chotek and Chang right away."

Paradise

As I was leaving the cafeteria, I passed by Sergeant Adams, who was gulping her hot coffee and getting ready to bolt out the door.

"Adams?"

"Yes sir?"

"Your aunt. How is she?"

"Fine. She has been in remission for seven years now. But she went through a lot of pain alone, and she didn't need to. We're family. We support each other."

I got her message. By 'family' she meant the Merry Band of Pirates, and UNEF. "Let's hope there is something useful we can do to support UNEF. To avoid exposure, we can't even send them a sympathy card," I added bitterly.

CHAPTER THIRTEEN

I quickly called together the senior military staff, plus Dr. Friedlander of the science team, to meet with me and Chotek. And, of course, Skippy. Chotek had already heard the bad news from Skippy before I was able to talk with him. I had anticipated an argument with the UN bureaucrat. Instead, to my relief, he agreed we needed to discuss the situation, and see if there was anything we could do to assist UNEF. "Everyone has heard that a Kristang battlegroup currently has space superiority above Paradise?" Everyone around the briefing table nodded. "The Kristang being back in control there poses an unacceptable risk to UNEF on Paradise, and we need to determine whether there is something we can do about the situation. Something we can do," I glanced over at Chotek, "without exposing our presence. Skippy, let's start with you. I want a way for us to assist UNEF on Paradise."

"Ugh," Skippy groaned. "Half the time when you're talking, Joe, I have to guess what you are truly trying to say through a jumble of blah blah blah while you ramble around the point. It would help if you were more specific, Joe. Not only would it help me, it would help your own murky thinking process if you could define exactly what you want to accomplish."

"What I want," I said very slowly to give me time to think, "is-" What did I want? I wanted Skippy to magically beam every human on Paradise back to Earth, but he couldn't do that. I knew that, because I had already asked and he told me no. He also said he hoped I had been joking about that. I was, sort of. Mostly. So, what did I want?

I wanted UNEF to be safe. Safer. Relatively safe. That meant, unfortunately, making sure the Ruhar kept control of Paradise. The fragile cease-fire on Paradise was the only thing keeping the Kristang from taking revenge on humans they considered traitors. If the Kristang had unchallenged control of the planet, they could slaughter and enslave humans with complete impunity. None of The Rules that governed combat between the Maxolhx and Rindhalu factions protected client species from being abused by their patrons.

Great. All I needed to do was to somehow arrange events so that a powerful starfaring species maintained control of a planet they didn't want, in order for them to protect humans who the Ruhar wished would just go away. And arrange events without the Kristang, Ruhar or UNEF ever knowing we were ever there.

Easy.

Hey, we'd already saved Earth twice, how difficult could this be?

Think, Joe, think, I told myself.

Break the problem down into manageable pieces, then solve each piece. Think of the problem as an enemy, and defeat them in detail. The situation had been much more favorable to us having a chance to influence events, before the Kristang battlegroup arrived and established space superiority around Paradise. With the battlegroup in firm control, the default situation was the Kristang merely needing to hang on, until the Ruhar eventually grew tired, negotiated a settlement and evacuated the planet. Before the Kristang battlegroup surprisingly jumped into orbit, the Ruhar could have kept the planet or not, it was their choice. We needed to make continued possession of Paradise the Ruhar's choice again.

We needed to eliminate that Kristang battlegroup.

"Here's what I want; a way to take out that Kristang battlegroup, in a way that the Kristang and the Ruhar don't know we are involved. Without that battlegroup, the Kristang will not be in such a strong position to negotiate to get Paradise back. Without that battlegroup, the Ruhar can drive a hard bargain on Paradise, and maybe the Kristang won't be able to offer a sweet enough deal. Maybe the Ruhar won't be tempted by the Kristang's offer, and they keep the planet. Maybe there is even something we can do behind the scenes to make the Ruhar decide to keep Paradise. Without that battlegroup, UNEF isn't in immediate danger of being wiped out. As long as that battlegroup is in orbit, the Kristang have the upper hand in negotiations, and the Ruhar are much more likely to surrender the planet permanently. That's, that is the simplest way to state the problem, Skippy. No magical beaming UNEF back to Earth, just a simple military problem; find a way to deal with that battlegroup."

"Simple?" Skippy was incredulous. "You think that is simple? Unbelievable. Over twenty Kristang warships, not counting their support ships. Opposing them are a handful of Ruhar warships and our pirate ship. We can't really count the *Flying Dutchman* as a combat asset, because we can't openly engage in combat. Also, you need to remember that our pirate ship is pretty beat up; we would have difficulty directly engaging those Kristang cruisers, or even a pair of destroyers."

"I didn't say it would be simple. We understand that we are facing a substantial combat force, and we need to take them out of the equation-"

"When you say 'deal with' or 'take out' that battlegroup," Skippy interrupted, "you really mean destroy those ships, right? Is that what you want? It would be super helpful if you got straight to the point, *Colonel* Joe."

"Yes," I suppressed a sigh. Skippy was being extra difficult today. "I want to destroy all or a substantial part of that battlegroup's combat power. That means destroying those ships, or at least knocking out their weapons. If we can reduce the battlegroup's combat power, if we can even the odds, then the Ruhar may decide it is worth sending reinforcements. Right now, the Ruhar fleet doesn't want to commit the number of ships that would be required to take on the Kristang. The Ruhar aren't willing to commit that many ships to reestablish control of a planet they are trying to negotiate away. If we can somehow even the odds so it is tempting for the Ruhar to retake the planet, then they may come back, even if it is only so they will have greater bargaining power in giving away the planet."

"Then we'll be right back to the problem of the Ruhar selling the planet out from under UNEF," Chang reminded me.

"Yes, but that is not the immediate problem. We need to first deal with the Kristang having unchallenged control over the planet; bring the situation back to equilibrium," I surprised myself for using that word. Where had I learned that? "If the odds are back to even between the Ruhar and the Kristang, there might be something we can do to influence the negotiations for transferring control of the planet. Right now we don't have that option."

"Well then, Joe," Skippy mused, "you have finally framed the actual objective; destroying the Kristang battlegroup. Now I can start thinking about how to do that."

"Great. Is this where you go silent, and your little beer can gets warm while you crunch like a trillion variables?"

"Please, Joe, way more than a trillion," he snorted derisively.

"Understood. Can I assume you can't do something simple like use the Thuranin nanovirus to seize control of those Kristang ships?"

"Duh? No, Joe, I would have mentioned that right away. Nope, I can't do that this time. Even my awesome powers are only able to activate the nanovirus on three ships at one time, because of the distances involved in space combat. Also, the Kristang task force is wisely dispersed far around Paradise; I could only get a maximum of four ships within range from any particular point in space. So using the nanovirus is impractical. The reason that trick worked when we first arrived at Earth is those two Kristang ships were relatively close to where we jumped in. Here, if we jumped into low orbit, I could only activate the nanovirus on three ships. The other seventeen warships would see what happened, and we would never be able to use that trick again. The Thuranin would also lose the secrecy of the nanovirus being embedded aboard Kristang ships, although I don't think any of us will be weeping for those little green pinheads. Remember, Joe, the Thuranin designed the nanovirus for the purpose of taking control of Kristang ships at the time they are attached to a Thuranin star carrier; it is a short range technology. And in case you're thinking we can jump in far away from Paradise and sneak up on the Kristang in normal space, forget about it. When I rebuilt the *Dutchman*, I wasn't able to bring our stealth capability back to full effectiveness, due to lack of the proper raw materials. Even the Kristang's crappy sensors would eventually detect this large ship sneaking around in Paradise orbit."

"Understood, Skippy," I said with a frown. The truth was, I had been hoping he could use the nanovirus trick in some way. "And, again, thank you. You did a remarkable job rebuilding the ship out of moon dust, the Merry Band of Pirates does appreciate it more than we can say. All right, Mr. Chotek, at this point I think we let Skippy consider our options, while my staff also tries to think of a strategy to destroy all or most of the Kristang battlegroup around Paradise."

Chotek nodded agreement. "These military matters are your area of expertise, Colonel Bishop. Mr. Skippy, I am sure your incredible brain power will develop a range of innovative solutions for us to consider."

"Working on it right now," Skippy acknowledged. "Although I don't know why you can't simply use the projectors. That's why I have difficulty understanding your concepts of military strategy, you don't take advantage of the easiest-"

"What projectors?" Chang asked before I could open my mouth.

"The terawatt maser cannon projectors buried beneath the surface of Paradise, duh," Skippy explained. "Damn, you monkeys are especially dense sometimes. Like a neutron star, only not as smart. And more smelly."

Chang and I shared a dumfounded look. I was the first to speak. "There are *giant maser cannons* on Paradise? Why haven't the Ruhar used them against the Kristang?"

"Yes there are maser cannons, big ones," Skippy's voice carried a mocking tone. "Cannons capable of delivering over ten terawatts in a single shot. Cannons like that can burn right through a starship's shields, especially if the ship is close, like in orbit. To answer your moronic question, the Ruhar can't use the projectors because they don't know about them, duh. Man, do you even listen to yourself talk sometimes? Hmm, maybe hearing your own stupidity is too painful for-"

"Skippy!" I shouted in frustration. "I did not know about any projectors. Are these projectors something UNEF built?"

"Huh? Wow. This is truly a breakthrough. Joe, *that* may be the dumbest thing you ever said. We should have a cake to celebrate the occasion. A banana cake. UNEF constructing maser cannons? Ha! Out of what, mud and sticks? No, UNEF was not involved, they also have no idea there are powerful planetary defense cannons beneath their feet. The Kristang installed those projectors, Joe. And what do you mean you didn't know about them? I told you all about it like a long time- Hmm. I'm sure I did. Did I? Oh, boy," his voice trailed off. "I'm sure that I told *somebody*. Or maybe not. Anyway, you know about it now. So, we're good. Yup. Goodness all around."

While Chang buried his head in his hands, I mimed choking something. "Skippy, if you had a neck, I'd choke you. How can you forget to tell us something that important?"

Paradise

"Hey, there is a ginormous amount of data rattling around in my brain, Joe, I can't keep track of everything you monkeys don't know," he grumbled. "Everything you *don't* know wouldn't fit inside the freakin' galaxy."

Chotek took a deep breath. "Colonel Bishop, I am beginning to see the difficulties you have in working with our super-smart alien friend."

"Oh, shut up, Count Chocula," Skippy said defensively. "Anywho, Joe, you know now."

"Details, Skippy," I said quietly, "we could use some details. What you said doesn't make sense. If the Kristang installed those projectors, how are we supposed to use them? Any why didn't the Kristang used them against the Ruhar ships in orbit?"

"And I would like to know," Chang asked, "how could the Ruhar not know about these weapons? The Ruhar have occupied this planet for-"

"Ugh!" Skippy groaned. "Damn it! If you will stop pestering me with ignorant questions, I will attempt to smack some knowledge on you. I'm not confident that will be successful, but I am willing to give it my best shot."

"We would appreciate being smacked down upon, Oh Great One," I said sarcastically.

"Assuming that was not an attempt at sarcasm, Joe, here is the story. The Kristang clan that originally settled this planet installed the projectors, to protect their assets, mostly from other Kristang clans. When that original Black Tree clan lost the planet to the Ruhar, they put the projectors into a dormant mode, and did not tell any other clans about the projectors in case the Black Tree clan has an opportunity to come back. They didn't want their own maser cannons being used against them."

I had to shake my head to make sure I wasn't having a bad dream. "These projectors have been buried beneath the surface all this time? Why didn't the Black Tree use their maser cannons to stop the Ruhar from taking Paradise away from them in the first place?"

"Again with the stupid questions, Joe," Skippy chided me. "The reason the Black Tree lost Paradise was because the Kristang and Thuranin were defeated in a major fleet engagement elsewhere in the sector. By the time a Ruhar task force first jumped into the skies above Paradise, the fighting was over. The Black Tree clan handing over Paradise was a mere formality at that point; there was no space combat near the Paradise system. So, they gave up the planet meekly, while keeping their aces in the hole concealed. The Black Trees originally came to Paradise in order to excavate the remains of a crashed Elder ship, and by the time the Ruhar arrived, the Black Trees were fairly certain they had already taken away all the valuable artifacts. Ha! They didn't know anything about me! Stupid lizards. Serves them right."

He paused. "Wow. I'm not going to be interrupted with moronic questions? Amazing. So, to respond to your other inquiries, neither the current Kristang Swift Arrow clan nor the Ruhar know anything about the projectors. Neither of them even suspect. At the time that the Ruhar first arrived there, the Kristang population was less than ten thousand, and the Black Tree's presence there was already in the process of winding down. The Ruhar never thought the Black Trees would go through the expense of constructing antiship defenses on such an unimportant planet."

"Why did they?" Chotek asked.

"Because," Skippy explained without pausing for an insult, "almost the first item the Black Tree found here was a functional Elder power tap; that is one of the most valuable items in the entire galaxy. As soon as they found that, they hoped they would find others, so they installed projectors to protect their investment. Of course, they never told the Swift Arrows or any other clans. The projectors are buried deeply, roughly one hundred meters, and each is surrounded by a special type of stealth field. Any sensor scans by the Kristang or Ruhar would find only rock or whatever material surrounds the projectors. The projectors are also located in areas that are unsuited to agriculture; the Black Trees thought ahead far enough to consider another group may someday build farms and villages on Paradise. They didn't want someone to accidently discover a projector by digging a foundation or a well."

For a minute, you could have heard a pin drop around the conference room, while we all considered the enormity of what Skippy had revealed. Sergeant Adams, ever focused on practical issues, broke the silence. "Skippster," she addressed him by the nickname only she could get away with, "you said we could use the projectors. Is this something simple that you can hook up remotely, from the *Dutchman*?"

"Aha! Finally, an intelligent question" Skippy sounded pleased. "You could learn from Sergeant Adams, Joe. You have grown substantially dumber since putting those Colonel's eagles on your uniform. No, Sarge Marge," Skippy said teasingly, using the nickname that only he could get away with. "Before the Black Trees left the planet, they put the projectors into dormancy, anticipating it might be hundreds or even a thousand years before the Black Trees might return. They disconnected each projector from its power source, and from the control module, specifically so an enemy could not remotely activate a projector. Restoring projectors to function will require someone to physically reestablish connections. Once the connections are established, I can program their targeting sensors through something as simple as a zPhone network."

"We will need to go down to the surface," Adams concluded.

Chotek held up a hand. "Sergeant, sending a party to the surface of Paradise, presumably to excavate these projectors, would pose a substantial risk of exposure to us. That is something I cannot authorize," he shook his head, but he didn't look us in the eyes when he said that.

"Sir," I said with a warning look at Adams, whose jaw was already clenching. "I believe there is an alternative that does not pose a risk of exposure to us. Or, it poses a minimal, very manageable risk. We do not need to send a party to the surface; UNEF is already there. They can reactivate the projectors for us. All we need to do is determine a method for informing them about the projectors, and provide instructions for bringing them back online."

Chotek frowned. "I do not understand why we could not simply inform the Ruhar about the projectors, and let them deal with the Kristang. Surely, between the projectors and their remaining ships, the Ruhar here would regain the upper hand."

"Whoa! That is a terrible, terribly awful idea there, Chocula," Skippy said scoffingly. "The Ruhar's communications have been partially compromised by the Kristang. We can't tell the hamsters, because that poses too much risk of the Swift Arrow Kristang learning the secret."

"I also think, sir, that we can't trust the Ruhar to deliver the outcome we desire," I used big buzzwords that Chotek was used to. "The Ruhar might merely reactivate the projectors and use them to threaten the Kristang, to strengthen their hand in negotiations to hand the planet to the Kristang. What we need, sir, is a shooting war between the Ruhar and the Kristang here. If a small UNEF group could reactivate projectors, and we use them to destroy most of the Swift Arrow's battlegroup, that will force the Ruhar to take military action. It would change the balance of power, sir."

"Then we might be right back to the situation before the Swift Arrow task force arrived, Colonel," Chotek responded. "With the Ruhar in a strong position to negotiate, but still in the process of negotiating the planet away beneath UNEF."

"That is possible, sir," I explained patiently. "The way I look at it, with the Swift Arrow battlegroup in control of the skies, we have no options. Without that battlegroup, we may be able to affect the outcome."

"Affect it how?" Chotek asked. "We still have the constraint of avoiding exposure."

"Avoiding exposure is paramount," I agreed. "Right now, I don't know how we may be able to assist UNEF. But five minutes ago, we didn't know there was a way for us to destroy a Kristang battlegroup," I pointed out. "One thing I have learned out here is, almost anything is possible. We will have plenty of time to develop ideas before the situation on Paradise restabilizes, hopefully with the Ruhar firmly back in control."

Our friendly local UN bureaucrat pursed his lips in thought. "Before any action is taken, Colonel, I will need to see a detailed plan. We will have to assess the risks. To be clear," he stopped me before I could respond. "We have to weigh the risk of exposure," he ticked the risks off on his fingers. "The risk to our primary objective. And, Colonel, the risk that our operation may fail, and the blowback to our people on Paradise makes the situation worse for them."

"Understood," I said, and I actually fully agreed with him. If either the Ruhar or Kristang learned that human troops were secretly traveling around Paradise reactivating maser cannons, the impact to UNEF could be severe. And once those cannons fired, I don't see how the Ruhar could fail to figure out that humans had forced them into a shooting war. After that, the humans there may be in as much danger from the Ruhar as from the Kristang. "Skippy, please provide a briefing packet about the projectors; capabilities, operational characteristics, the procedure for reactivating them, etc. Distribute the data to the entire crew including the science team; we need everyone involved in the planning. Unit leaders," I addressed the SpecOps team commanders but especially Major Smythe, "read the briefing packet and put your thinking caps on. We have nine days until we will be within jump range of the Paradise system, and we still need to stay here for a while. We can't leave this relay station until Skippy is satisfied his submind is properly installed and operating properly. And we need to complete repairs to the exterior of the station, to maintain our ruse. Everyone, thank you, and- Wait. Skippy, what else have you not told us?"

"Ugh. Since I don't know what it is that you don't know; the scope of your ignorance, I can't guess what I haven't told you. There is nothing anywhere near as important as secret maser cannons, I'm sure of that."

"Good." Skippy's words had not reassured me. "If you think of anything else, call me immediately?"

"I'd prefer to wait until you're in the bathroom like usual, but for this I can break with tradition, Joe."

Paradise

Flight Leader Second Class Saily Chernandagren climbed into her two seater Dobreh fighter, the type of aircraft that humans had derisively named 'Chicken'. On the home planet of the Ruhar, a Dobreh was a fierce bird of prey; and animal to be feared in the air. Saily had not understood why the humans had renamed the aircraft after a tame, domesticated bird, other than the fact that humans were strange and no Ruhar could truly understand such primitive creatures. As Saily attached her oxygen mask, she pressed a button and the soft surface of the mask flowed around her nose and mouth, forming a secure seal even over the soft Ruhar fur that covered her face. Human male pilots, she knew, had to scrape the fur off their faces every morning in order to get a good seal on an oxygen mask. Ruhar males grew hair on their faces also, but it was a soft, downy fur rather than the bushy tangle that humans could grow.

Humans were strange creatures, Saily thought as she draped her arms over each side of the cockpit to show the ground crew that she was not yet touching any of the controls. Strange, and in many ways, to be pitied. They had barely achieved a rudimentary form of spaceflight when they were forced into the war by the wormhole shift. Then they were brought out to the stars as expendable ground troops by their 'allies' the Kristang. Saily had been born and raised on Gehtanu, the world called 'Paradise' by the humans. Along with all Ruhar, she had resented human soldiers landing on her planet and forcing her people off the world that was their home. She had hated the humans, even after Saily's commanding officer noted that having humans handle the evacuation was far better than the task being managed by the cruel and untrustworthy Kristang. Some of the humans could say nasty things, but most of them had been professional, simply eager to do their jobs and go home as quickly as possible. The human leadership had been scrupulous about adhering to the code of conduct established between the Ruhar and Kristang for the evacuation. There had been remarkably few incidents of violence directed at Ruhar civilians by humans. Remarkable indeed, because humans believed the Ruhar had attacked their home world in order to enslave and destroy humanity. If the situation had been reversed, Saily did not know whether she would have been able to restrain herself.

Since the humans had first landed, Saily had many opportunities to meet humans and even to spend extensive time with them. Human pilots had arrived on Gehtanu with an average of one hundred twenty hours of flight training in Ruhar aircraft; having been given a rush course at some interim staging base. For pilots who would fly the high-performance Dobreh gunships, most of them had less than twenty hours in that type. Humans had arrived in a potential combat zone with woefully inadequate flying experience, and they knew it. The human commander had quickly reached an agreement with the Ruhar leadership on Gehtanu for Ruhar pilots to continue the training of human pilots. That agreement had been mutually beneficial; the humans gained valuable experience from experts, and the Ruhar pilots kept their own skills from growing rusty. Keeping their flying skills fresh had proved useful when the Ruhar fleet came back to take control of the planet again. Now that a Kristang battlegroup was in orbit and the Kristang had landed combat aircraft and ground troops, Saily was especially grateful that her connection with the high-performance Dobreh was still instinctive.

One of the human pilots she had trained was still at the airbase, now on her ground crew. He was Lieutenant Derek Bonsu of the American Army. Lieutenant was roughly equivalent to the Ruhar rank of Flier First Class; two steps below Saily's own rank. The fact that Derek, as she called him, was an A-mer-i-can seemed to be important to him but meaningless to Saily or any other Ruhar. The Ruhar species had a half dozen major cultural groups with slightly different languages, but their military was one cohesive unit. The idea that soldiers who fought side by side could owe allegiance to different governments was odd to the Ruhar. Indeed, it seemed similar to the clan culture of the Kristang. With the Kristang expending more time, effort and passion fighting among themselves than fighting their mutual enemies, the Ruhar had been able to defeat them in almost every major engagement of their endless war, even though the Kristang economy and culture was almost entirely dedicated to supporting the war.

Another thing the Kristang found odd about humans was the different colors of their skin. In this regard, humans were also more similar to the Kristang, whose scales had many hues. Derek Bonsu's own skin was dark; he had once explained with pride that his ancestors came from a place called 'Africa', which again meant nothing to Saily. All Ruhar had the same pinkish-beige skin tone; it was their fur color that varied. Saily's own fur was white with patches of light brown, and fur color was neither a fashion choice nor a cultural marker for the Ruhar. She kept the fur on her head long; for flying or athletic activities she tied her fur back in what humans called a short 'ponytail'.

The ground crew leader signaled that Saily could close her canopy and turn on the master power switch, which she did. Her Weapon Systems Officer in the back seat announced that all of the ship's systems were ready for engine start, and she confirmed from her own instruments. Before signaling the crew chief that she was ready for engine start, she turned in her seat to look back along both sides of the aircraft.

On the left side was Lt. Derek Bonsu with the external power cart. Saily liked Derek, although he had come to Gehtanu as the enemy. Derek had an infectious grin and never complained, even when eating bland nutrient mush two times a day. On the rare occasions when he received a 'care package' of real human food from Lemuria, he treated every tomato or loaf of bread as if it were the most precious gift in the universe. Even when the Kristang battlegroup jumped in and took back control of the planet, Bonsu had not lost his good natured grin for a moment. The planet had changed management several times already, Bonsu had said about the current Kristang mastery of the skies. Next week, the Ruhar fleet might get bored elsewhere in the sector and come to Gehtanu to chase the Kristang away. Bonsu said no one knew what the future held, so why waste energy worrying about what you couldn't control?

Along with the sunny disposition that made him popular even among Ruhar who did not like humans, Bonsu had other qualities. He had made a serious effort right from the start to learn the Ruhar common language. It helped his popularity that the first words he learned were common swear words, and soon he was cursing fluently in Ruhar. Saily noticed that now, whenever a wrench slipped and Bonsu bashed his knuckles, he cursed in Ruhar without thinking about it.

But the ultimate reason Derek Bonsu was working at a Ruhar airbase, instead of farming in Lemuria with his fellow humans, was that he loved flying. When the Ruhar fleet had jumped in and firmly established control of the planet, their United Nations Expeditionary Force Headquarters had quickly ordered all units to surrender; the alternative being for human forces to be pounded from orbit by masers and railguns. Most human pilots had flown to the nearest airbase and abandoned their ships immediately. Some pilots had set their aircraft down in remote areas, near clusters of human ground troops. Some 'Chicken' crews had even spitefully ejected from their ships, causing complete loss of the aircraft.

Lt. Derek Bonsu had calmly flown his Dobreh back to its home base, bringing it down in front of his designated hangar. Bonsu had followed the guidebook's recommended procedure for engine shutdown; allowing the engines to run at idle for three minutes to cool before cutting power. He and his Weapon Systems Officer has then refueled and secured the aircraft, placing covers over the intakes and hanging red tags from items that needed to be checked during preflight inspection. He had properly listed minor issues in the aircraft's official squawk log; noting that the nose landing gear door was slow to open and that the right engine surged for a few seconds when throttling above 80% power. Lastly, Bonsu had vacuumed out the cockpit and wiped down the display screens. That particular Dobreh became Saily's assigned aircraft, and she appreciated the care Bonsu had taken with her aircraft. Such good care that 'her' Dobreh was the first to return to flight status when the Ruhar had reoccupied the airbase.

All those characteristics were reasons why Lt. Derek Bonsu had been one of only four humans invited to remain at the airbase as liaisons with the Ruhar. None of the four humans were allowed to fly regularly, except for brief proficiency check flights every two months. Otherwise, the humans worked alongside Ruhar aircraft maintenance crews. And the humans took every minute of flight simulator time they could get, even waking up in the early hours of the morning to avoid taking precious simulator time away from Ruhar pilots. At first, the maintenance crews had assigned the four humans only humiliating tasks such as keeping the hangar floors clean and other menial work. Even now that the humans had earned the respect of the base personnel, a Ruhar was required to inspect and sign off every time a human touched an aircraft.

Bonsu removed the external power cable, closed the access door, checked that it was secure, and held up an index finger which was the Ruhar equivalent of a human thumbs up sign. Saily acknowledged him with a thumbs up, then Bonsu retreated with the power cable, retracting it into the cart. When the cart was safely out of the way, the Ruhar crew chief made a gesture of twirling an index finger in the air; the signal to start the engines.

Derek Bonsu stood in his designated position behind the power cart, helmet on and hearing protection engaged, as he watched Saily run up the Dobreh's power, then take off smoothly. Derek had one hand on a fire extinguisher clipped to the side of the power cart, ready in case anything went wrong. Nothing would go wrong; all the pilots were skilled and diligent and the aircraft were well maintained. The only potential problem Derek could foresee was that their supply of spare parts and consumable items was running low. The whole maintenance crew was concerned about the parts issue, and other airbases on Gehtanu reported having the same problem. Under the terms of the cease fire agreement, the Kristang battlegroup allowed the Ruhar to bring in supply ships, but the Ruhar government had been strangely stingy about shipping in anything other than medical supplies. Even before the Kristang battlegroup occupied the sky, Derek had heard rumors that the Ruhar federal government was considering negotiating away Gehtanu in exchange for more valuable territory. Some Ruhar at the airbase said those negotiations were the reason why they weren't getting critical spare parts; the government didn't plan on Ruhar being on Gehtanu long-term.

Derek didn't know what to think about such rumors, and he didn't think rumors mattered much anyway. As he watched Saily's aircraft join up with three others and race toward the eastern horizon, there was a brief flicker of light above them. It was sunlight glinting off a Kristang warship in orbit. While the Kristang battlegroup was in orbit, the willingness of the Ruhar federal government to negotiate did not matter. One way or the other, the Kristang were going to take back control of the planet, and Derek Bonsu was going to be in as much trouble as all the other humans. More trouble, perhaps, because he had actively helped the Ruhar military.

Derek would worry about that later, when he had to. What he most cared about now was that his next proficiency check flight in a Dobreh was not for another six weeks, and he did not know how he could stand to wait that long to get back into the sky. Seeing Saily soaring away in the Dobreh that he used to fly caused a physical pang of pain in his stomach.

He looked again at the sky, seeking another flicker of light from a ship in the Kristang battlegroup. If the lizards retained control of Paradise, Derek knew he would never fly again. If he lived at all.

CHAPTER FOURTEEN

Flying Dutchman

We jumped the *Flying Dutchman* into the far outskirts of the Paradise system, an area sparsely populated by chunks of dead-cold dirty balls of ice and rock. From that distance, the star that shone on Paradise was a dim, fuzzy dot; a star rather than a sun. Skippy reported we had emerged in a region with an ordinary density of hydrogen atoms, it was nothing to write home about.

From our position, Paradise was five hours away, so the sensor data we had to work with was that old. In four hours, we would jump again, as the gamma ray burst of our jump in would be visible from Paradise and we didn't want anyone coming out to investigate. We performed six jumps, with the last coming in barely above the cloud tops on the far side of the system's only gas giant. By then, Skippy had determined that the only ships in the area were the Kristang in orbit around Paradise, and a handful of Ruhar ships were several lightminutes away from the planet.

By listening to message traffic both on the planet and between ships, Skippy was able to determine the situation had not changed significantly from what he had learned at the data relay station. The Kristang had over twenty warships, plus support ships, in orbit and complete supremacy in the space around Paradise. The remnants of the Ruhar defense task force were licking their wounds. A truce had been offered by the Kristang commander and accepted by the Ruhar, there had not been any violations of the cease-fire, which surprised me. The Kristang had landed thousands of troops and heavy equipment including aircraft, in a relatively uninhabited area of the northern continent. Humans isolated on Lemuria so far had been ignored by both sides, although Skippy had intercepted messages from the Kristang warning UNEF to cease any and all cooperation with the Ruhar. And the Ruhar had removed or disabled farming equipment they had provided to UNEF. Without any assistance from the Ruhar, humans were reduced to plowing fields behind hamvees, and by dragging plows behind teams of soldiers. UNEF appeared to be on the verge of a split between those who favored loyalty to the Kristang and those who wished to be neutral or align with the Ruhar. Discipline was breaking down as UNEF became scattered groups of farm villages rather than a military force. Negotiations were still ongoing between the Ruhar and the Kristang, although the Kristang now had the upper hand and were pushing the Ruhar to finish the details quickly. According to message traffic between the Ruhar commodore and the planetary government, the Ruhar Navy had contingency plans to send a major battlegroup to Paradise, but the commodore advised that was highly unlikely. The Jeraptha were concentrating on consolidating spectacular gains from their recent, highly successful offensive, and did not want to divert a substantial force for a planet their client species wanted to get rid of.

Humans on Paradise, in short, were totally screwed, unless we could do something to help them. Without anyone ever knowing that we helped. Or that we even existed.

No problem, right?

"Joe, that is all the information I can get from here," Skippy complained, sounding frustrated. "We need to go to Paradise. All I can do from so far away out here is decrypt signal traffic that leaks." Most of the top secret message traffic that we needed was sent by tightbeam laserlink transmission, and Skippy could only pick up those messages from faint scatter when the laser beam hit the atmosphere or dust particles in orbit. It was a true Skippy miracle that he was able to intercept any messages at all, and I gave him props for it.

Craig Alanson

"I know, Skippy. I'll talk to Chocula about it."

Paradise

General Marcellus had to break the bad news to his boss; he was able to get five minutes on General Nivelle's calendar between meetings. As the acting UNEF chief of intelligence, it was Marcellus' job to know everything that was happening on Paradise. It was also his job to keep his boss informed of anything important. Marcellus didn't bother to sit down; hopefully the discussion wouldn't last long. "Sir, there was another incident last night. A British woman was assaulted."

"Not again," Nivelle sighed heavily. "That's the second time this week. Where? What happened?"

"Near the village of Churchill. She was, assaulted," he used a polite term.

"Who did it?" Nivelle asked angrily. Marcellus could see a vein throbbing in the French general's forehead.

"It appears to have been men in her own unit, Sir."

"*Sacre bleu.*"

"Other soldiers in the same village heard her screams, and dealt with the situation before she could be seriously harmed," Marcellus reported. Although knowing that men in her own unit had assaulted her, had to have caused serious emotional and psychological damage.

Violence within the Expeditionary Force, while not widespread, was increasing. There were fights simply because people were bored and working too hard and morale was low, there were fights over food, and there were sexual assaults. To protect against the latter, UNEF HQ had set up 'Safe Villages' that only allowed women. That initiative had been a bad idea right from the start. It made the women of UNEF feel like second-class citizens, it made them question whether they could trust the men they served with. And as women who had been victims of violence or simply feared assault moved to the Safe Villages, the women outside such designated zones felt more and more isolated and vulnerable. The truth was, no one at UNEF HQ knew how to deal with the issue of sexual assault. Or how to deal with many, if not most, of the critical problems that faced the force every day. Not knowing whether the Ruhar or the Kristang would control the planet long-term prevented UNEF HQ from effectively making future plans. With the military situation still very much in flux, the force commanders understandably did not know what to do.

General Marcellus had decided to deal with problems one day at a time. "There is a complication we need to address, General Nivelle. The men who broke up the assault killed the three attackers. However, it looks as if the attackers were killed some time after the assault, not in the process of stopping the attack."

"How long after?"

"One, perhaps two hours," Marcellus reported.

Nivelle's face was grim. "General Marcellus, I want there to be a swift investigation of this assault. I do not think, however, that it is necessary for there to be a deep inquiry into the subsequent events. Agreed?"

"Agreed, Sir."

Flying Dutchman

Paradise

Hans Chotek approved us going to Paradise, only because Skippy was going to bring one end of a microwormhole with us in the shuttle, so we could be in constant, instantaneous communication. "Joe, I can tell you," Skippy said privately, "that microwormholes can be rather complicated, delicate things, and they can suddenly shut down for no reason. If you know what I mean."

I figured I would keep that in my back pocket, for use in an emergency. When I say 'us' going to Paradise, I mean Skippy and me. No way was I going to miss out on this mission, it was way too important. I needed to be right there, seeing what was going on, making decisions in real time. To my surprise, Chotek quickly agreed, as long as all major decisions were reviewed by him. That left me suspicious that he just wanted me off the ship, but by then I was past caring.

Going on the mission would be me, Skippy, Adams and Captain Desai as our pilot. Just the four of us; three humans and a beer can, in one of our smaller type of dropships. We would not be bringing along any of the SpecOps troops, and on that issue Chotek and I agreed, although for different reasons. My reasoning was that if a situation required combat troops, we were in way over our heads and needed to get away from Paradise. Chotek's reasoning was that if I had SpecOps troops on Paradise with me, I would be tempted to use them in some risky mission. He didn't trust my judgement. That is why UNEF Command sent him to the stars with us, so he was only doing his job. Anyway, it worked out well for both of us.

Adams came along on the mission, I forget who suggested her first; me or Chotek. Count Chocula probably figured that Adams' level-headed practical nature would keep me out of trouble. My reason for including her was that she had been on Paradise, that she had been with the Merry Band of Pirates since the beginning, and she knew me and knew how I think. Also, I wanted someone to talk with because we might be on Paradise for a while.

During the flight down to Paradise, Captain Desai would fly the dropship in a maximum stealth flight profile. Since I was technically qualified to fly that type of dropship, my job was to sit in the copilot seat. Skippy joked that Adams' job would be to shoot me if I tried to touch any of the controls.

I hoped that Skippy was joking about that.

The other reason our mission included only three humans and a beer can, was that we flew down to Paradise in one of our smaller dropships. Even the 'small' Thuranin dropship was the size of a Boeing 767, and it could accommodate sixteen people after we tore out the original Thuranin seats and replaced them with something that could fit a human. Sixteen people could fit; they couldn't be comfortable. In order to get to Paradise, we had to fly most of the way there in the dropship; we couldn't risk the *Flying Dutchman* jumping in anywhere close to the planet. That meant the travel time after leaving the *Dutchman* was eight days. Eight days in a dropship with two other people, and one bathroom that was sized for little green men.

We jumped out of the star system entirely, and then spent nearly an hour with the star carrier accelerating to the proper velocity and direction. Then we jumped the *Dutchman* back in still far away from Paradise, our dropship quickly launched and the *Dutchman* was away again, accelerating at maximum thrust in normal space. Our pirate ship could not jump again, because that would break the microwormhole we relied on for communications. The speed boost we'd gotten from the ship meant that our dropship didn't need to use any fuel to get to Paradise, only to slow down once we got there. Our dropship was wrapped in a stealth field, plus Skippy showed us a new trick wherein he warped spacetime between us and the planet, which helped mask the energy of the dropship's engines as we decelerated before hitting the atmosphere. One reason we needed to preserve fuel is that our entry could not be the usual burning streak through the atmosphere of most descents; we needed our presence to be secret. Skippy was of course able to mask the dropship from the sensors of both Ruhar and Kristang, but anyone simply looking out a viewport of a ship would see the superheated light of us plunging down through the atmosphere. Our stealth field was on and operating perfectly, as perfectly as it could in an atmosphere. So we came in slow, using engine power to slow down and then lower us gradually; that burned up a whole lot of fuel.

It worked, plus we came in at night, over the ocean far to the west of any inhabited land, and there was heavy cloud cover from twelve kilometers almost all the way to the deck. Almost skimming the wave tops, and flying subsonic so the turbulence of our passage through the air could not be detected, we came over land. Skippy selected a spot in the mountains near the equator, the lush rainforest jungle there provided good cover to supplement the stealth field, and the location was not under any regular flight paths. The first thing I did after we landed was go behind a tree and pee, without having to kneel and bump my head in the tiny Thuranin bathroom of the dropship. Then we set up a tent; whoever was on duty could be in the tent sheltered from the daily rain showers, while we would use the climate-controlled dropship for sleeping, cooking and eating.

"It's strange to be back here," Adams said, staring off into the distance after we got the tent set up.

"Yeah," I agreed. It was strange to be back. When I closed my eyes, the scent of the tropics was exactly the same as what I had experienced when I was stationed at the Launcher. That made sense; we were only 500 kilometers from the Launcher base complex. For a moment, I just stood there and let the memories wash over me.

Adams sighed wistfully. "We both have a lot of people we know on Paradise, and we can't contact any of them. I feel like I went back for my high school reunion, but I'm hiding in the bushes, looking through the window."

"Sergeant, I feel the same way. We can't contact anyone, in any way that might reveal our presence here." I said that to remind myself more than her. What would I do if I learned that someone I knew was in trouble, and I could help? I couldn't help, period. We were back on Paradise for a specific mission, and after that mission was complete, we were leaving without any of our old friends knowing we had ever been there. That sucked, but, so did the whole situation for UNEF. If our mission was successful, we could help improve things for UNEF.

Then I called Chotek to check in, and get his approval for the next phase of the operation.

Skippy began marauding through computer systems of the Ruhar and the Kristang even before we landed, and as I finished setting up the tent, Adams told me Skippy had found important information.

"First, of course, both sides detected the *Dutchman* jumping in and then not jumping out again. Neither side has been able to identify the type of ship, and speculation is running that it is a rival Kristang clan monitoring the situation on Paradise, in case there is an opportunity to screw the Swift Arrow clan out of the planet. Anyway, the good news is that no one suspects our pirate ship is involved, and no one is interested in chasing after it. They also have no idea we landed. As to what has been going on here, well, this is odd," Skippy reported. "As you requested, Joe, I checked on people you know first. You will be happy to hear that everyone on your list is alive and well. It was a short list, still, every one of them have survived. What is odd is that they all are or were being held by the Ruhar."

"What? Why?"

"I am sure you will be surprised to learn that at one particular facility are Emily Perkins, Shauna Jarrett, Dave Czajka and Jesse Colter."

"*Shauna* is with Cornpone and Ski?" He was correct, I was completely surprised by that. "Emily Perkins? Do you mean Major Perkins, the intel officer?" Her first name had never come up in conversation. But then, our conversations had been limited to me passing on very bad news from the Burgermeister.

"Correct, Major Emily Perkins," Skippy confirmed. "The four of them have been held by the Ruhar for months. At another facility were Sergeant Greg Koch and the three members of the fireteam you lead at the village of Teskor; Baker, Chen and Sanchez. Also with them are three people who were with you on the day that the Ruhar attacked Fort Arrow; Amaro, Pope and Rogen."

"I don't understand. Why is Sergeant Koch with them? And what is Shauna doing with Dave and Jesse?"

"The grouping of people was random, according to records of the Ruhar. They picked people up wherever they were, and brought them to the closest Ruhar military base."

"Picked them up why?"

"The Ruhar interrogated everyone who knew you personally on Paradise, Joe. They know that you broke out of prison and flew away in a stolen Dodo. It is not surprising that the Ruhar are intensely curious about how you managed to do that. It would be very surprising if the Ruhar had *not* investigated the incident. The first thing they did was interrogate all the people at Major Simms' logistics base. After that proved fruitless, they moved on to other potential sources. No one told the Ruhar anything, because no one on Paradise knows anything. The Ruhar have concluded that the humans they interrogated likely do not have any useful information. Sergeant Koch and his group were released already; they are on a train bound for Lemuria now. Major Perkins and the other three were officially released three days ago; they are currently waiting for transportation. A train will be stopping for them tomorrow morning."

"Were they treated well by the Ruhar?" I asked anxiously.

"Yes, Joe. Except for a bland diet, they were not harmed in any way. The Ruhar kept them safer than they would have been on Lemuria. Your old friend the Burgermeister took a personal interest in them."

"She is still here? As the deputy, uh, administrator or something?"

"Indeed she is. Joe, she knows the Ruhar government is negotiating to give the planet back to the Kristang. She is personally opposed to the idea; because she sees it as a betrayal of the native population who have built homes and lives there. She is also powerless to do much about it, other than to scold her government for selling out their own people. Based on conversations she had with the Ruhar Commodore who commands the small task force here, she does appreciate why the Ruhar fleet does not want the responsibility of defending such a relatively isolated and unimportant planet."

"Good. She always was straight with me. They're going to be on a train, huh? That complicates things. I want to give our message about the projectors to Czajka and Colter." Sergeant Koch was with too many people who I didn't know as well. "We served in combat together. I know them, and I trust them."

"That's no good, sir," Adams declared. "You said that whoever we contact can't ever know that you are involved. Anyone else but you would logically contact Major Perkins first. She's an officer, and an intel expert. The other three may be your friends, but they are low-ranking soldiers, they wouldn't be the first to receive an important communication like this. The only reason someone would contact Czajka or Colter instead of Perkins, would be a personal relationship with those two. They know that you, me, Chang and Desai survived the hit on our jail, and they know the four of us flew away in a stolen

Dodo. We can't do anything that may make them guess that any of us are involved. We need to contact Perkins first."

"Yeah, Joe, what do you think of that?" Skippy asked gleefully. "You're not so smart after all, huh? Sarge Marge is right; this message needs to come from an unnamed source."

"Skippy, come on, we can't do the trick again where we pretend you are some top secret UNEF cyber unit. Perkins knows that there aren't any humans on Paradise with the technology-"

"Not humans." Adams said. "Ruhar. We hint to Perkins that the source of the message about hidden projectors is a group of native Ruhar. Ruhar who know their government is pulling the rug out from under them, and they can't go to their own military for action. The natives want to knock out that Kristang battlegroup, so they get a group of humans to do it for them. That way, if the operation goes south, they can deny the whole thing."

I was stunned. "Holy shit, Adams, that is a genius idea. How did you think of that?"

She cocked her head at me. "I didn't, it's an old idea. What do you do if you're weak and you want to defeat a superior force?"

That was an easy one, I didn't even need to consult the Army field manual. "You engage in guerilla warfare."

"That, or you do it the easy way," Adams explained. "You get a bunch of lobbyists and celebrities to persuade our government to send in the US Army to do the fighting for you."

"Ain't that the truth," I offered Adams a fist bump and she took it. "That is a good idea, Perkins will certainly be ready to believe it. She was in Nigeria, and a couple other trouble spots before that. Damn," I said admiringly, "that is a good idea, Sergeant. Of course the native Ruhar would want to disrupt negotiations, and surely some rumors have gotten out. Agreed, we contact Major Perkins." I thought for a moment what the message should say. "Hmm," I bit my lip. "I can compose a message, but I need to make sure I don't write it in language that people will recognize as mine."

"No problem Joe," Skippy said cheerily, "no one will know the message is from you. Unless the message starts with 'duh how about this'. Or if it has terrible grammar and it rambles on and on forever before finally getting to the freakin' point."

"*I* ramble on and on? What about-"

"We're not talking about me here, Joe," Skippy said hastily. "Don't try to change the subject. Just don't write the message like a fourth grader. And don't use any of your horrible Maine Yankee slang. Like," and he changed his voice, "by golly bejeeesuz I mowed down that lobstah at dinnah, it was a Gotdamn feast, I tell ya."

"Oh my God, Skippy, you sounded just like my father's uncle Virgil," I laughed. He had even correctly pronounced 'God' with a T sound on the end, the way God intended.

"Also," Skippy cautioned, "don't call a milkshake a 'frappe' for heaven's sake."

"A frappe has ice cream in it, a milkshake doesn't," I retorted. "And if you're in Rhode Island, a frappe is called a 'cabinet'. Everybody knows that. Right, Adams?"

"I'm not from New England, sir, so I'm with Skippy on this one. We should have Skippy compose the message, then we can look at it."

I had to admit that was a better idea. "Write something up, Skippy, please. Oh," my shoulders slumped. "We'll need Chocu- Chotek to approve it. Crap." This operation was too complicated.

Skippy composed three messages in like a billionth of a nanosecond, and they all looked good to me. Then the wheels of bureaucracy moved at lightning speed, and Chotek gave us his preferred text with minor annoying revisions, the next morning. Skippy was not happy about the delay, although we didn't plan to send the message to Adams until that afternoon anyway, when she and the three others were on the train. "I provided a microwormhole, for crying out loud," Skippy complained. "A true miracle of technology, something no one else in the galaxy has. It allows instantaneous, undetectable communication between us and a starship several lightminutes away. And what does that jerk do with it? He takes fourteen hours to send us back a message, and he insists on changing four words. Four freakin' words, Joe!"

"Skippy, I hear you," I was pissed about it too. "Sometimes managers think they have to change at least something in order to feel useful."

"Yeah, well, in that case I am sad to report that the microwormhole is acting up already. We could lose contact with Chocula, I mean the ship, at any moment. If you know what I mean."

"Not yet, Skippy," I told him, and then remembered other people were listening. "That is terrible news about the wormhole, do what you can to keep it open."

"Oh, I get it, Joe. Sure, sure, I'm working on it. Just let me know."

Skippy was an ancient, super powerful, super intelligent being. He also *sucked* at lying.

Once the Ruhar announced that they were being released, Perkins and the others hoped they would be given their zPhones back, but it didn't happen. Even when they got on the train, no zPhones. Jesse and Dave were going crazy that someone might have stolen or messed with their couch, which Perkins could not understand. What could be so important about a couch?

The train was nothing special; two passenger cars tacked on the front end of a freight train just behind the engine. Both cars were well-worn, with the seats made of some super tough gel material. The four humans were told to take the front car, which had most of its seats piled high with baggage and equipment. There were no Ruhar in the front car, an arrangement that suited both species. As they walked past the second car, Ruhar crowded the windows, gawking at the strange humans, or glaring at the clients of their enemy the Kristang. One of the Ruhar, a male who had a child in his arms, shook his fist at the four humans.

Dave Czajka took exception to that. "Hey, screw-"

"Czajka!" Major Perkins scolded. "Eyes forward. To these Ruhar, we are the enemy. We came here to throw them off this planet that has been their home for generations. If I were them, I would hate us."

"Yes, Ma'am," Czajka looked at the ground.

They boarded the car, squeezed between boxes and baggage, and found seats to spread out, enough room for each of them to lay down. Dave walked over to Perkins. "Sorry, Ma'am, I lost my temper."

"It happens," Perkins shrugged. "Czajka, these *people*," she used that word instead of 'Ruhar' or 'hamster', "have lived here long enough that their parents, even grandparents are buried here. They put down roots on this planet. This is their *home*. Then we showed up, working for the Kristang, to throw them off their world. They have been at war since before humans discovered fire. They have only known this war. Think about that."

"Yes, Ma'am. All the Ruhar I have met personally have been nice, just ordinary people," he used that word intentionally. "I don't hate them; I hate being here. I hate not being home."

"We all do. My folks must be worried sick," she said, blinking away a tear. They could be trapped on Paradise, forever. And that was the best scenario. If the Ruhar kept control of Paradise, humans there would be prisoners of war. If the Kristang took over the planet, the humans there would become slaves, if they survived at all. Perkins felt like indulging in a good cry, which would have made her feel better. Under stress, women tended to cry it away. Men tended to get angry and lash out. The way women handled stress, Perkins thought, was healthier. The male-dominated Army generally considered crying to be a weakness. So she swallowed hard and looked Dave in the eye. "We all want to go home. Until then, we all have to do our jobs, and take care of each other."

"Yes, Ma'am," Dave said. "I'm going to check out that water tank," he pointed to the corner near the car's single bathroom. If they were going to be on the train all the way to Lemuria, it was going to be a very long trip.

After a lunch of nutrient mush that the humans had gulped down as quickly as possible, a Ruhar soldier came through the train with a bag, and from it he pulled four zPhones. It was like Christmas and a birthday all at once. Shauna almost shivered with delight, then turned to Perkins. "Is it Ok if we use the phones, Ma'am?"

"Can we tell people about Bishop?" Jesse asked anxiously.

"Go ahead, soldier, I plan to use my phone right away," Perkins said. "No restrictions on talking about Bishop, as little as we know. It's not a secret to the Ruhar, it shouldn't be a secret to us either."

The other three scattered about the train car for privacy, there were plenty of seats. Perkins first checked her texts and emails, she naturally had thousands of each that had piled up in her absence, so she started with the most recent and intended to work her way backward. Suddenly all of her messages and emails disappeared. Except for one text and one email. The text told her to open the email. So she did.

And received a shock.

She instructed the zPhone to call the US Army intel chief directly. Perkins had not been involved in intelligence gathering or analysis for over six months; she had become a farmer like almost all of the humans on Paradise. With UNEF no longer a fighting force, the only useful information was about crop yields and which people had gotten into fights. General Marcellus, she knew, as currently acting as the chief intelligence officer for UNEF HQ. If the message she had received was true, he would surely know something.

He answered right away, which was surprising. "Who is this?" He sounded annoyed, and there were other voices in the background.

"Major Perkins, Sir. Third Infantry. I was on your HQ intel staff until recently. Thank you for taking my call."

"Oh, yes, Major. My phone picked up by itself somehow. It is darned good to hear from you. Did the Ruhar treat you well? We tried to contact you, but the Ruhar wouldn't allow it."

"Yes, the Ruhar treated us well. They just gave us our phones back. We were released three days ago, and we're now on a train headed for Lemuria. Sir, I have information that you should hear directly."

"Wait a minute." He went into a quieter area, or closed a door, because the background voices faded. "Go ahead, Major."

"The Ruhar brought us in for questioning about Joe Bishop. They say he escaped from that Kristang jail. That, as far as the Ruhar know, he is alive somewhere."

"We figured that was why they brought you in. We looked at the list of people they took, and put two and two together. The only thing you all had in common was Bishop. Are the Ruhar still telling the story about him flying away in a stolen Dodo?"

"Yes, sir," she replied, surprised. "You knew about that?"

Paradise

"There have been rumors since the Ruhar took the planet back," he explained. "Then they released other people a couple days ago, including the staff of a logistics base that Bishop supposedly recruited people and supplies from. Perkins, you know Bishop, you were his contact when that Logellia woman was feeding him info about the wormholes and all that. Do you think he was capable of stealing and flying an alien spacecraft?" No human had been trained to fly a dropship, and those ships surely had security features to prevent theft or mischief.

"The two members of his original fireteam told me they would be surprised if Bishop could operate an iPad without breaking it. I don't see it, Sir. Bishop is smart and resourceful, but he's not *that* smart."

"That's what we're thinking also. Bishop supposedly told the people at the logistics base that he was on a mission to hit the Kristang, and at the time, there weren't any Kristang left on this planet. To hit them, Bishop would have to go into space. After being in that Kristang jail, I can see why he'd look for an opportunity to get some payback. For my money, I'll bet that dropship was flown by Ruhar, and for some reason they needed humans to come along."

"If that was a Ruhar mission," Perkins asked, "why would the Ruhar be asking us about it now?"

"Major, I am sure that humanity is not the only species where the right hand sometimes doesn't know what the left hand is doing," he explained. "If this was a secret Ruhar mission, the Ruhar in charge here on Paradise may not know anything about it. Or it was a rogue operation, and the Ruhar command is keeping it quiet out of embarrassment." Marcellus knew he was assigning human emotions and motivations to an alien species, but his extensive contact with the Ruhar told him that he wouldn't be far off the truth. "I'm glad to hear you are safe and well. I have a meeting in five min-"

"Bishop wasn't my only information, sir, or the most important."

"Go ahead, Major."

"Sir, I heard a rumor from the Ruhar. The Ruhar federal government has been negotiating to give this planet back to the Kristang. They're trading it for more valuable territory."

The half-second lag before General Marcellus answered told Emily Perkins everything she needed to know. The message she had received was the truth. And UNEF HQ knew. Son of a bitch! "Major, that is one hell of a rumor," he lied. "I can't see the Ruhar doing that, they have fought to retake this place, and now to keep it. I wouldn't put any credence in rumors like that. We have enough bad news that is true."

"Yes, sir."

"Where are you headed?"

"Wherever this train takes us, the Ruhar told us we would eventually be going back to where we were living when they picked us up, but I think all they care is about is that we're in Lemuria." So that the humans would no longer be the responsibility of the Ruhar.

"Probably by boat, then. Contact my staff when you're ashore, and I'll arrange to have you brought to HQ. We'll need to debrief you."

I'll bet you do, Perkins thought. You want me someplace where you can be sure that I won't repeat what I heard about the Ruhar selling the planet out from under us. "Thank you, sir."

Of course, all of Perkins' calls now went through the SkippyTel network, so we heard her conversation with General Marcellus. When she made the call, we were all inside the dropship, because it was absolutely pouring down rain outside and had been all morning. Also, it had been my turn to cook and I had made blueberry muffins, which we were leisurely munching on while drinking coffee. There wasn't much else for us to do at the moment. When Perkins ended the call, Desai tapped me on the shoulder. "Sir, we could use what Marcellus said."

"Huh?" Maybe my brain was extra slow that morning.

"He thinks us flying away in a Ruhar Dodo was a Ruhar operation, that we were along for the ride. We should use that. Play it up. Skippy," Desai asked, "do the Ruhar have an intelligence service that is separate from the military?"

"You mean like the American CIA and NSA? Yes, they do. The Ruhar have two rival intelligence agencies; one is nominally civilian and one is sort of part of the military. They both run clandestine operations that the other agency doesn't know about, and the military spy agency is notorious for acting without the military leadership's knowledge. The Ruhar military spy people are referred to by the Ruhar equivalent of 'cowboys'. In this case, 'cowboy' does not mean a rugged outdoorsman, it means amateurs who shoot first and think later."

"How would that help us?" I asked Desai, wondering if this was how Skippy felt when I was explaining one of my ideas.

"Sir, the Ruhar know we flew away in a Ruhar dropship, and by now the Kristang have probably heard about it also-"

"They have," Skippy confirmed.

"The Kristang may be putting two and two together," Desai explained. "They now know that a Ruhar dropship left Paradise with humans on it. Back then, Skippy told the Kristang that the Dodo had been stolen by Kristang, which is why the Kristang sent ships in to pick us up. Then the frigate that picked us up disappeared, and the star carrier that was the frigate's mothership also disappeared. If the Kristang ever begin to suspect that humans were involved in that, we would be in deep trouble."

"Aha," Adams agreed. "We need the Kristang to think the whole thing; stealing a Dodo and flying away, was a secret Ruhar operation to capture a Kristang ship?"

"Exactly," Desai smiled.

And now I did know how Skippy felt. Damn it, I'm the commander, I should have thought of that. It was freakin' brilliant.

"Wow," Skippy said admiringly. "That is devious. Keep both sides guessing who did it, and neither of them will ever consider that lowly humans could have run the operation. Joe, you are not the only devious mind here. If you like, I can plant hints in Ruhar databases that the four of you escaping from jail and stealing a Dodo was a secret Ruhar operation."

"That would be great, Skippy. Desai, that was good thinking. Wait," I had an unpleasant thought. "Skippy, before you do anything, you need to clear this with Chotek."

"Oh, for crying out loud," Skippy complained. "I heard a great idea, it wasn't yours, but it did come from a monkey, uh. No offense, Major Desai."

"No offense taken, Mr. Skippy," Desai beamed. "I am proud to be what you consider a monkey. Especially since your definition of 'monkey' seems to be primates who think of ideas that your brain can't handle."

"What? Oooooh, that's it, Captain Desai, your name has been added to my list," Skippy warned. "You filthy monkeys think you are *so* smart," he grumbled.

"Apparently," I offered Desai a high five and she accepted, "we are so smart. Anyway, back to my point, Skippy. We need to run this by Chotek. This is why he came out here. Desai thought of a way to prevent both the Ruhar and Kristang from ever suspecting humans could be involved in how the Flower and the *Flying Dutchman* disappeared. Chotek should be thrilled to hear it, and that should demonstrate to him and to UNEF Command how valuable is it to have the Merry Band of Pirates out here."

"Oh, fine. What a pain in the ass," Skippy muttered. "I'll wait for the Count to make the obvious decision, which seems to be what human managers do."

"Sir?" Adams spoke up. "I agree with what you said, except for one thing."

"What?" I asked.

"This pirate is not very merry right now," she pointed to the table in front of me. "You ate the last muffin."

CHAPTER FIFTEEN

After Perkins ended the call with Marcellus, she read the message again twice before she sending a reply. She asked who the message had come from, and why she should trust them.

Another message came almost immediately. *Think of us as your Mysterious Benefactor*, the message read. *You can trust us because we're the only ones telling you the truth. And we are your only hope of freeing this planet from the Kristang. You are our first choice, but we have other options. You need us.*

Emily Perkins could not find fault with that argument. She and the Mysterious Benefactor, who she decided to call 'Emby' for short, went back and forth for ten minutes, until she had no more questions to ask. Emby had answered some of her questions, and declined to answer others. The intelligence officer in her suspected that Emby was a group of Ruhar native to Paradise, who wanted to prevent their own government from selling the planet out from under them. They couldn't take action by themselves, and they couldn't trust their own military. So they were using humans, who were even more desperate to prevent the Kristang from permanently regaining control of the planet. It was one hell of a story Emby had told; if she agreed to go along, they would tell her more. They would tell her, at each point during the mission, only what she needed to know. Perkins liked that, it gave her some confidence that Emby knew what they were doing.

I'm in, she sent back. *What is the next step?*

We will get you off the train and secure the transport and equipment you need, Emby replied. *You will be leaving the train tonight, after you are supposed to be asleep. Your next step is to persuade your team to join you.*

Sure, thought Perkins. No problem. Before I can persuade Jarrett, Czajka and Colter to join me, I will need to convince them that I'm not crazy. And that this isn't a joke.

"A secret mission?" Jesse cocked his head skeptically. "What? Are we going offworld to find Bishop, something like that?"

"No, this has nothing to do with Bishop," Perkins said, surprised. She hadn't thought of Bishop at all. "I don't know where he went, where he is, or whether he's still alive. I don't even know if the Ruhar told us the truth. Maybe he did escape from that jail and the Ruhar are looking for him. The story of him stealing a dropship and flying away on a secret mission? That I find hard to believe," Perkins frowned. "I have to warn you; this mission is not authorized by UNEF. They don't know about it, and they likely wouldn't authorize it if they knew. Does anyone have a problem with that?"

Jesse looked out the window to the landscape of the alien planet passing by. A planet he was trapped on, and a planet that would soon be controlled by the cruel Kristang. "UNEF got us out here because they didn't know the truth and were too stupid to ask," he looked the former intelligence officer in the eye as he spoke. "Now I'm a farmer on an alien planet, and there is no way I can ever go home. I say, to hell with UNEF. They've screwed everything up so far."

"Amen to that, brother," Dave agreed. "I have no problem with it either, Major. But we will need weapons, and we don't have any."

"We won't need weapons," Perkins explained. "This is going to seem odd, but what we need is drilling gear; excavation equipment."

"Excavation equipment? Like digging?" Dave asked. "Ma'am, if this is about us trying to find gold or something like that, I'm going to be very disappointed."

"Gold?" Shauna asked. "Are we hoping to find gold, so the Ruhar will think this planet is more valuable? So they'll send their fleet here to chase away the Kristang?"

"No," Perkins shook her head in frustration. "No gold. If the Ruhar want gold, they mine it from asteroids. This isn't about anything like gold."

"Then what is it about, Ma'am?" Jesse asked with his arms across his chest. "You asked us to trust you. I would appreciate you trusting us."

"Fair enough, Colter. I don't know the whole story, whoever is running this operation has me on a need to know basis also." As Perkins said that, she wondered if Emby was listening through her zPhone. Probably they were, she decided. Before telling the three about the mission, she forwarded to them a message from Emby. Their Mysterious Benefactor had told her that anyone who opened that message would have absolutely unbreakable encryption on their phones. Perkins had been instructed to forward the message to anyone involved in the operation, and not to anyone else. "I'm going to tell you everything I know, so here it is. When we got these zPhones," she held hers up, "I had a ton of email. Then it all disappeared, except for one. I opened it to find a message from someone calling themselves our Mysterious Benefactor. I'm calling them Emby for short. They didn't say who they are, but I'm betting they are a group of native Ruhar who are not happy with the situation on this planet, and they can't trust their own government or military to take the appropriate action. So they're using us. What they want us to do is get rid of that Kristang battlegroup in orbit," she pointed to the sky, "so what they want matches what is best for us. That's the only reason I agreed to take on this mission. That, plus I don't see any other possibility of humans surviving on this planet long term. If the Kristang take over this planet permanently, none of us will live very long. I think you all know that."

"I do, Ma'am," Shauna said. "But tell me, please; you got a mysterious email? That's what all this is about? Could it be a prank?"

"Yeah," Jesse added, "or disinformation? You intel types do that kind of stuff. This could be the Kristang trying to get us to do something stupid against them, so they have an excuse to squash us like bugs."

"That would be just like the lizards," Dave observed.

"No," Perkins shook her head. "The message contained intel I didn't know, and when I contacted the US intel chief, he denied it. He denied it in a way that was too quick, you understand? UNEF HQ had this info, they know about it, and they haven't told us. Whoever our Mysterious Benefactor is, they know."

"They know what? What is it they know?" Shauna was the first to ask.

So Perkins told them. Told them how the Ruhar federal government had been negotiating to trade Paradise to the Kristang, in exchange for more valuable territory. How the Ruhar fleet had never intended to recapture the planet in the first place. How that was why there had not been giant transport ships bringing evacuated Ruhar back to their home. Why the local Ruhar administration had not put more than token effort into rebuilding infrastructure.

"Holy shit," Dave said quietly. "Those motherfuckers. The Ruhar are selling us out."

"Yes," Perkins agreed flatly. "There was talk going around six to eight months ago, of UNEF declaring loyalty to the Ruhar," she could see everyone's eyes grow wide with surprise. "HQ thought that might give the Ruhar more incentive to protect us from the Kristang raids that were burning out our crops. Then suddenly, that talk stopped, and we were told by HQ to not mention it again. Now I know why. HQ must have talked to the Ruhar, and the hamsters told us no. They didn't want our loyalty, because then they'd be responsible for us, and they plan to leave us behind when they trade this planet away."

"Shit," Jesse said, stunned. "I'm not dumb enough to think the Ruhar would ever be our buddies, but I didn't think they would screw us like this."

"We don't have any friends out here, people," Perkins declared. "We're on our own, truly on our own, because the Kristang have lost contact with Earth. The Ruhar confirmed that to me. The only reason I agreed to work with Emby on this mission is that our goals match in this case. We both want those Kristang ships out of orbit."

"Ma'am, in the long run, what good does that do for us?" Shauna asked. "The Ruhar still plan to sell the planet out from under us."

"Yeah, that's why I asked Emby the same question. And that's why I think our Mysterious Benefactor is a group of native Ruhar. Because what Emby told me is that, once that Kristang battlegroup isn't hanging over our heads, there is at least a possibility the federal Ruhar government could somehow be persuaded to keep Paradise. With the Kristang having the big guns in orbit, there is no possibility the Ruhar will keep this place in the long term."

"Ok," Jesse said after taking a deep breath. "So the mission is to get rid of a Kristang task force of, what, more than twenty warships? Did this Emby say how the four of us are going to do that?"

"Colter, if you think I've told you some incredible shit so far," Perkins smiled and tilted her head, "you ain't heard anything yet."

"Wait, Ma'am," Jesse said a few minutes later, his head spinning. "There are *giant maser cannons* buried on this planet, that the Kristang don't know about-"

"That the Kristang clan in orbit do not know. The Kristang clan that installed the projectors do know, but that group of Kristang is not here."

"Right," Jesse said, thinking that keeping track of who was who in this war required a color-coded spreadsheet. "The Kristang here don't know, and the Ruhar government and military don't know, and UNEF doesn't know. But some of the native Ruhar do know?"

"Exactly."

"How?" Jesse insisted. "How do a bunch of native hamster farmers know all this, when their government and military don't?"

Perkins shrugged. "Maybe some farmer was plowing a field and dug up a projector by accident. I don't know, and Emby didn't tell me how they found out about the projectors. It doesn't matter. What I do know is that the Ruhar government and military do *not* know, because they certainly would have used the projectors to stop the raids. Now, if the Ruhar government learned of the projectors, they would not use them against a full Kristang task force, because that would sour the negotiations. What this Emby wants is a shooting war between the Ruhar and the Kristang, they want to force their government's hand. As long as that Kristang task force is in orbit, the native Ruhar are screwed. They can't trust their own government to do the right thing, so they're using us to do it for them. I am pretty damned sick of people using us for their own ends," she looked her three soldiers in the eyes and found complete agreement, "but in this case what they want is what we want. We can't tell UNEF HQ because the Ruhar and Kristang have totally compromised the zPhone network. It's up to us to reactivate these projectors, and knock those ships out of orbit."

"Do you mind if I say 'Holy Shit', Ma'am?" Shauna asked, her mind still reeling.

"You can say it for me, too, Jarrett," Perkins smiled. "I've had time to think about it, and it's still blowing my mind. When the Ruhar hit Earth," she reminisced, "I was on leave, on a camping trip in Kentucky with friends. There was no cell phone service at the lake. We didn't see anything going on in the sky because it rained that morning. I didn't find out that Earth had been attacked by aliens until we hiked out two days later. Christ, that was one hell of a shock Then I went into space, found out that the Kristang aren't our allies after all, that our way back to Earth has been cut off, and that the Ruhar are looking to trade this planet for a set of steak knives. So, when a mystery group tells me that we can destroy starships in orbit using secret maser cannons, I say, why the hell not? That isn't even the strangest thing that's happened to me this month."

"Amen to that," Dave said, and bumped fists with Jesse. "I'm in."

"You sure, man?" Jesse asked.

"Yeah, what the hell?" Dave frowned. "By the time we get back, someone will have stolen our couch anyway."

"I'm in if you are," Jesse said, looking at Shauna.

Shauna didn't hesitate. She wanted combat duty, she wanted to make a difference, and this was her opportunity. Somebody else could grow tomatoes in Lemuria. "Sign me up, Ma'am," she saluted Perkins. "What are we going to do for weapons?" The Ruhar were careful to collect even the plastic spoons that came with their twice a day servings of nutrient mush.

Perkins was relieved. And anxious. She had a team. Now she had the responsibility to execute the mission she'd accepted. "Emby says they we won't need weapons, what we need is transport, and like I said, excavation equipment. These projectors are buried; we need to dig down to get at them. The original Kristang installed the projectors, charged up their capacitors, activated a stealth field to fool subsurface scans, and then covered them with soil. Trees have grown up on some of them since then. Emby told me that when a projector is ready to fire, explosive charges will blow the soil away and the maser cannon muzzle projects above the surface, so we don't need to clear all that dirt away. What we do need is to dig a shaft down about eighty meters to access the power controls. The Kristang made these things go dormant when they left. Emby says we need to physically reattach power leads, something like that. They'll walk us through it when we get down there."

"Ma'am," Shauna said, "I've seen so much crazy shit out here that I'm ready to believe anything. But if this Emby is really a group of native Ruhar, why aren't they reactivating the projectors by themselves?"

"I asked myself the same question, Jarret," Perkins admitted. "My guess is either this Emby is a very small group, maybe even a single Ruhar, and they need our help. They can't trust any other Ruhar, but they can trust us because they know we are totally screwed if the Kristang take control of this planet. Or it could be that Emby wants to avoid getting in trouble if this whole operation goes south. The only thing I do know is that if there is *any* chance we can keep the Kristang away from this planet, I'm going to take it."

"Same here," Shauna agreed. Growing tomatoes is not why she left Earth. "You can get us transport, ma'am?"

"No," Perkins shook her head. "But Emby can. We will need a pilot."

"I know a pilot," Shauna said with a smile.

"There are a lot of pilots," Perkins noted. "Can we trust him?"

"We can trust *her*," Shauna insisted. "I know she would do anything to fly again. That's the problem, ma'am, she doesn't fly now. How is she going to get a Buzzard?"

"That will be Emby's problem."

"We'll have transport," Dave said. "Where are we going to get a drilling rig? And someone to operate it?"

"That is going to be a little more difficult," Perkins acknowledged. There were drills on Paradise, the Ruhar used them to dig wells for irrigating farmland. While they were not plentiful, they would also not be locked up and well-guarded, as there normally wasn't any point to stealing a drill. The real problem was going to be finding a complete drilling rig that could be broken down to fit inside the cargo compartment of a truck or a Buzzard.

A Buzzard was big, it could carry two hamvees easily, so cargo capacity and weight were not the issue. What she did not know was what was the minimum length of a disassembled drill. She would need to ask Emby; surely the hamsters knew the answer, or could find it.

"Well, Skippy," I said after we read the message from Perkins to Emby. "Perkins has a very good point. Are there any drill rigs that can fit inside a Buzzard?"

"Yes, duh, I already thought of that, Joe. There is a type of compact drill rig that was designed specifically to break down to be transported by a Buzzard in one flight, to service remote areas. It will certainly fit in a truck."

"Oh, great," I was relieved. That is a question that I should have asked earlier. "How many of these compact drill rigs are there on Paradise?"

"Three."

"*Three*? On the whole planet? Holy shit. We have to steal one of only three special-use items? Where are they right now?"

"One is being used to dig a well in the northwest corner of what UNEF calls Backstratchistan, about as far from Lemuria as you can get without going to an island. Another is at an airfield about five hundred kilometers away from the active drill, being held in reserve in case of a problem with the first drill. The third is in a military warehouse on an air base, near the base of the space elevator."

"You're kidding me. Two of them are way too far away, and the third is secured by the military? How the hell are we going to get one, then? How is Perkins going to get one? You have a plan for that? Is Perkins going to drive up to the air base gate and ask for it politely? Or, hey," I was on a roll, "maybe she can order it off the Ruhar version of Amazon."

"Yes."

"Yes? Yes to what?"

"The last one, Joe. The compact drill rig will be delivered to her, wherever she needs it. It's a high-dollar item, so shipping is free. Hmmm, that is a good point, we should probably get someone to sign for it."

I paused to collect my thoughts. "Skippy, I apologize. I should have known you would have a plan for this. Would you please, please share your brilliant plan with us?"

"You didn't say pretty please with sugar on it, Joe."

"Let's pretend I did."

"Fair enough. What I'm going to do, Joe, is to utilize the awesome power of bureaucracy. Count Chocula would appreciate this. I'll send a very official-looking equipment requisition to the air base logistics officer. It will order that drill rig and everything else Perkins will need, to be loaded onto a truck and delivered to some remote warehouse, wherever Perkins needs it. When the logistics officer calls headquarters to verify, like the good little soldier he is, I will handle the call myself and chew him out for not having moved the drill rig already."

"That is a brilliant plan, Skippy," I wasn't being sarcastic.

"Uh huh. We'll let bureaucracy work in our favor, for a change."

The Ruhar guard aboard the train was supposed to check on the humans every four hours, although there didn't seem to be much point in doing that. The train was taking the humans where they wanted to go; back to Lemuria. The only source of human food in the area was the 'nutrient mush' that was locked in a cabinet. Optimal security measures would not have put all the mush containers in a cabinet in the same train car the humans occupied, but that was more convenient when it was time to feed them. And to the Ruhar, the mush had an unpleasant smell. Best to keep it away from the Ruhar passengers, few though they were.

So when it was time for the guard to sleep, he set an alarm on his phone to wake him in four hours. Skippy, of course, deactivated that alarm, and when the guard awoke briefly six hours later, the clock on his phone told him he had been asleep for only three hours. Satisfied, he rolled over in his bunk and drifted off to sleep again, lulled by the gentle rocking motion of the train.

Before their Ruhar guard had locked the door of the train car behind him, Perkins and her team had settled down to sleep for the night. Or they had acted as if they were settling down for the night. As soon as the guard was gone, they quickly got their boots back on. Within fifteen minutes, Perkins received a message that the guard had gone to sleep.

"How does Emby know that?" Dave asked in a whisper.

"They must have someone aboard this train," Shauna guessed.

"Makes sense," Major Perkins nodded and turned as, with a soft click, the cabinet containing all the canisters of yummy nutrient mush unlocked. Moving quietly, the team unloaded the canisters and rolled them up in the satchels they had made from a roll of cloth. Then they waited. They waited thirty two minutes, with Perkins chafing at the delay, until Emby signaled it was time. The train was slowing as it climbed a steep hill out of a river valley; they had heard the wheels clatter over a bridge shortly before. Emby warned that the train would pick up speed again when it reached the top of the short grade, and the safe place to jump off the train was less than a hundred meters long. For one hundred meters, there was a field of Ruhar crops alongside the tracks; then the tracks were hemmed in by trees. Perkins got her team ready.

Jesse volunteered to go first. "I'll go first, then you jump and I'll catch you," he gallantly told Shauna.

"Screw that," Shauna said, and dropped to the ground. She hit feet first, letting herself roll, mowing over a row of crops and getting a mouthful of dirt. She sprang to her feet and gave a thumbs up, barely able to see the other three faces in the open door of the train car. Then she crouched to avoid being seen, as she watched one, two, three others jump lightly and roll. Ski went last, hanging onto a railing and making sure the door closed behind him quietly and securely before he jumped. He almost left it too late; when he finished rolling he was a mere ten meters from a stand of trees.

They all waited for the blinking blue light on the rear of the train to disappear. Perkins smoothed out the dirt where she'd fallen and propped up the crops she had flattened. Hopefully it would be a while before the farmer noticed the damage. The others followed her example, then they assembled. "What's next, ma'am?" Dave asked. He stood on his left foot, favoring his right.

"Are you mobile, Czajka?" Perkins asked.

"Yes, ma'am," Dave rotated his ankle. "Tweaked my ankle, it will be better when it's warmed up."

"Good," Perkins checked her zPhone, and indicated the forest on the other side of the tracks. "Emby says we go that way. We need to hustle, and no using lights until we're out of sight," she pointed to the lights of the farmhouse behind them, across the field. "Use the low-light camera of your phone to see. Jarrett, you take the lead."

Shauna nearly poked her eyes out by colliding with low-hanging branches in the dark, before remembering to hold a hand up in front of her face. Her other hand held her zPhone with its rear-facing night-vision camera pointed forward. That phone feature was supposed to be used with goggles, here they had to try walking through feet-tangling underbrush while looking at a small screen. The four stumbled slowly and awkwardly through the forest in darkness, made worse because it had begun to drizzle. When Major Perkins in the rear announced she could no longer see the lights of the farmhouse, she allowed the team to use their zPhones as lights on a low setting. Now that they could see, they made rapid progress through the forest, guided by maps on their zPhones. Emby contacted Perkins twice, urging her to move faster. When they came upon a road, they broke into a steady run, and soon Perkins was grateful for the drizzling rain. It soaked her hair, making her short ponytail hang limply against the back of her neck. The rain also cooled her, running through the warm and humid night air. "Hold here," Perkins said in a harsh whisper as her zPhone beeped with a warning message when they neared a bend in the road. "Truck coming! Off the road!" She shouted.

They ran through the woods into a stand of bushes and lay flat, phone lights off. The electric motors of Ruhar trucks were quiet, and the gently falling rain muffled sound, so they saw the truck's headlights eerily casting beams through the trees before they heard the vehicle. It approached from beyond the curve, lights bouncing as it moved fast along the rough dirt road. The truck slowed as it approached, making Perkins fear that the Ruhar had discovered their escape and tracked their location by zPhone. Maybe Emby was not as smart as they said they were?

The truck slowed to a crawl, and Perkins' mind raced. If the Ruhar knew where Perkins and her team were, should they run or surrender? Surrender seemed to be the smart play; because if Emby couldn't even cover their escape from a train, it was unlikely Perkins could complete a complex mission of awakening buried maser cannons. Had she been a fool for believing a Mysterious Benefactor? Was the whole situation some elaborate joke, or a setup to embarrass UNEF?

No. The truck had slowed only to negotiate the sharp bend in the road and a deep puddle. Even at reduced speed, the truck's tires threw up a splash as it hit the puddle, briefly obscuring the headlights. Then it cleared the curve and accelerated, speeding onward through the rainy night. Perkins rose to her feet, brushing mud from her uniform top.

"Ma'am," Jesse whispered in the utter darkness, echoing Perkins' own fears. "I thought they knew we were here."

"Apparently not. Emby would have warned us," she said hopefully. "Back to the road, we need to make up time," she ordered as Emby sent another message urging them to hurry. She turned her zPhone light back on, and they ran fairly hard down the road another two kilometers. Perkins was winded, and she noted the three younger people were also breathing hard. Life as a farmer didn't leave much opportunity for running. They came over a slight rise in the road and saw the lights of a small village. Just ahead, the forest gave way to fields of crops growing in straight rows. "Stop here," she ordered, rechecking the message on her zPhone to make sure she hadn't missed anything. "There's a village up ahead, Emby says they're all asleep. There's a train coming soon," her phone was counting down from around seven minutes. "It will slow down when it goes through the village; the residents don't like noisy trains while they're trying to sleep," she smiled and Ski almost laughed. "The tracks are about half a kilometer ahead," although she couldn't see anything in the rainy night. "We are supposed wait behind a shed next to the tracks, then we climb on as it goes by. The last ten cars are empty; Emby has unlocked the doors. Colter, you go first this time. The rest of us, try to get on the same car. If not, get on top and go forward or back to whatever car Colter gets into."

"Ma'am," Jesse asked, "in the dark, how do we know which are the last ten cars?"

Dave looked through his zPhone's night-vision feature. "I can see good enough." The train cars were big, about eighty feet long. "I'll count off for you."

"You better be right about it, Ski," Jesse

Jesse grabbed a handrail beside a door, and hanging on with one hand, he slid the door open and tossed his satchel in. Running alongside, the other three threw their satchels in the open door, then Jesse helped Perkins up into the doorway. Shauna stumbled over a rock but caught the handrail, then Jesse got hold of her arm and swung her inside. Dave almost made it, running on a gimpy ankle, but he tripped and fell flat. Jesse almost jumped out to help his friend before Dave got to his feet and caught the handrail of the next car, waving Jesse off. Making up for falling in the dirt, Dave shimmied up the handrail to the roof of the car, then crawled on hands and knees to the car ahead. Awkwardly, he slid down feet first until Jesse and Shauna grasped his legs, then he let go of the roof and the three fell to sprawl inside the empty car. The train was beginning to pick up speed as Perkins closed the door, making sure it was closed all the way. Snapping on her light, she looked around the inside. There was some trash such as straps, packing material and busted cardboard boxes, otherwise it was just empty, scuffed and well-used composite material. "Czajka, your ankle is worse than you told me?"

"No ma'am," Dave said defensively. "I tripped on a rock or something. I'm squared away."

Perkins was not entirely convinced. "Take your boot off and I'll look at it. Emby says we'll be here until about midmorning."

Dave untied his boot, and laughed.

"What's so funny?" Shauna asked. She didn't see much humor in their situation.

"We hopped aboard a freight car, we've got no jobs and no money," Dave reached in his satchel and pulled out a can of nutrient mush. "And all we have to eat is beans. We're hobos."

"Hey," Jesse offered a fist bump and Ski accepted. "Brother," Jesse said with a wry smile, "first hobos on an alien planet. That's got to count for something."

Around midmorning, the train slowed suddenly. Emby had told Perkins the train's locomotive would experience a temporary 'mechanical difficulty' while going around a curve. When the train slowed enough, Perkins and her team were to get off on the outside of the curve, where the engineer in the locomotive couldn't look back and see them. When the train was down to a slow walking pace, the four humans bailed out, being careful not to injure themselves as the area was thickly forested. They dashed in to the woods and lay down. As soon as they were hidden, whatever Emby had done to the locomotive fixed itself, and the train picked up speed again.

Once the train had gone out of sight and could barely be heard, Shauna stood up carefully. "Ma'am," she asked Major Perkins, "who is this Mysterious Benefactor? The engineer of that train is one of them? Or they can remotely control anything on this planet?"

"Yeah," Jesse added. "And how did Emby know that truck was coming down the road last night? Or that everyone in the village where we hopped that train," he pointed down the tracks, "was asleep?"

"People, I worked intel, and not knowing the identity of our Mysterious Benefactor is bugging the shit out of me," Perkins admitted. "If we're successful, we may find out someday. If this mission isn't successful, I have a feeling Emby will bail on us real fast. I'm not doing this for Emby, whoever they are. I'm doing this to give UNEF a chance, even a tiny chance to avoid being slaves of the lizards. You still in?"

"Oh, hell yes, ma'am," Jesse nodded. "I can't remember the last time I *didn't* have a bad feeling about a mission.

They walked off and on, taking short breaks until late afternoon, then Perkins declared a rest. Emby insisted they were safe, but Perkins ordered everyone to take forty five minute shifts as sentry to be sure. She took the first shift, and her own eyelids were heavy when Czajka took over. It felt like she had just gotten semi comfortable on the ground, when Jarrett shook her awake. "It's time, ma'am," Shauna said quietly.

With long practice from her military career, Perkins came to alertness. The sun had set so it was dark with clouds covering the sky; at least it wasn't raining. Rubbing her eyes to make them focus, she immediately checked her zPhone. There were no new messages from Emby, but as she turned her eyes away from the screen, a new message appeared.

Everything is on schedule, the message read. *You have fifty six minutes to travel the last kilometer.*

How did you know that I just woke up, Perkins typed suspiciously, and even before she hit the 'Send' button, there was a reply.

Your phone moved, and you activated it to check messages, Major Perkins, the message read. *You and your team should eat now; this is going to be a long night.*

Giving up on Emby revealing any more information about their sources and methods, Perkins sat on a log. "Eat up, people. We need to get moving soon and this is going to be a busy night."

Dave reached into his satchel and pulled out one of his dwindling supply of nutrient mush cans. "I hope Emby gets us more food along with transport and a drill rig, ma'am."

Perkins nodded. "Emby says they've got it covered. They know we can't eat the native life, or Ruhar food."

Shauna popped open her can of mush and looked at it without interest. She tipped her head back and swallowed it as quickly as she could. Running a finger around the bottom to get every last drop, she made face. "Sure, Emby will get us food. Enough to carry out the mission. Then they won't need us."

"We have to take that risk," Perkins agreed grimly.

"Ha," Jesse laughed. "We're sneaking around between two advanced species that can blast us from orbit. Maybe we'll get lucky and we'll take a railgun dart before we starve."

"Amen to that, brother," Dave popped open a can of mush. "Maybe I'll shoot myself, if I have to survive on this crap much longer."

According to Emby, their mission that night was simple. Inside a warehouse on the outskirts of a village was a truck loaded with the portable drilling rig, and boxes containing human food. Real food, from Earth. Mostly canned or MREs. All Perkins and her team needed to do was get into the warehouse, which was unlocked. Then they would start the truck, roll aside the big door, drive the truck out and slide the door closed behind them. To cover the sound of the truck, Emby would create a distraction; a ventilation fan in a barn on the other side of the village would overheat and begin making a terrible screeching racket. Then the fan's motor would catch on fire. That would keep the hamsters busy while the humans drove away with their prize. And they would keep driving, all night.

It will be suspicious for a truck loaded with human food to go missing, Perkins typed. The remaining supply of human food from Earth had to be a small, carefully guarded item. How could such a valuable thing be sitting unguarded in a warehouse? Again, before she hit the 'Send' button there was a reply.

The boxes of human food are mislabeled, Emby said, *no one knows they are in that truck. We only took a small amount of your food, it will not be missed. And no one will be going into that warehouse for weeks.*

How did you arrange that, Perkins asked.

Paradise

Humanity is not the only species with a cumbersome bureaucracy, Major Perkins. It is easy for things to get lost, this is a big planet. You need to get moving.

Perkins explained the plan to her skeptical team.

"Just like that, ma'am?" Jesse asked. "This Emby gift-wrapped a truck for us?"

"Just like that," Perkins confirmed. "Emby has done right by us so far. I'm going to trust them, whoever they are."

CHAPTER SIXTEEN

It was as easy as Emby said it would be. The side door of the warehouse faced the village, so they slipped in one at a time, with Shauna going first. She got inside, closed the door behind her and scanned the inside first with night-vision, then risked using her zPhone's light. It was a barn that had been turned into a warehouse, it still smelled like wet dirt and grain. In the center was a large truck with an extended cab and six wheels. The back was covered with a sort of tarp; she carefully swung the tailgate down and peeked inside. The back was fairly crammed with large pieces of equipment, boxes and extra fuel cells. Emby had told the truth so far. To be certain, she climbed into the truck bed and slowly opened one of the boxes.

Food. Real honest-to-God human food from Earth. The box contained cans, tins, pouches and MREs all with French writing. Shauna felt a pang of hunger just glancing at food, real food. She dropped to the ground and called Perkins. "It's as Emby said, ma'am. Everything is here."

When all four of them were inside, Perkins climbed into the cab and turned the truck's main power on. It showed ready to start. "Jarrett, you drive first. Colter, Czajka, get ready to slide that door open. Jarrett, make sure the headlights are switched off."

On her zPhone Perkins typed *Ready.*

Commencing distraction now. Drive slowly until you get over the bridge, Emby replied.

Muffled by the walls of the barn, a screeching sound began. Faintly, then growing louder, it was a high-pitched grinding sound of metal on metal. With the side door of the barn only cracked open, Perkins saw lights come on in the village's dozen homes. Within five minutes, hamsters were running toward the barn with the faulty ventilation fan, which had now burst into flames.

This would be a good time to go, Emby sent.

"Czajka, Colter, get that door open, quietly."

"Yes ma'am," Jesse replied. While they were waiting, Jesse had found a can of oil or some kind of lubricant, and he and Dave had liberally applied it to the door's wheels and tracks. It slid aside almost silently, and Shauna hit the truck's starter. With only a faint whine from its electric motors, the truck came to life. The big truck was a tight fit through the door, Perkins walked backwards in front of her, guiding Shauna to squeeze the truck through the door. Perkins kept glancing nervously toward the other end of town, where the fan fire had been extinguished and the screeching noise was winding down. Once the truck cleared the big door, she motioned for it to be closed, and they climbed into the cab. Shauna drove slowly, with the lights off across a bridge, Perkins holding a zPhone in front of Shauna's eyes so the driver could use the night-vision feature. Fortunately, within half a kilometer of crossing the bridge, the road took a sharp turn, and Perkins allowed Shauna to turn the headlights on the lowest setting. After another kilometer and an *All Clear* message from Emby, Shauna increased the headlight brightness, and stepped on the accelerator pedal. According to Emby, they had about 600 kilometers to cover within the next seven hours before dawn. Emby directed them on a slightly roundabout route to miss driving through villages, although they could not avoid passing an isolated house here and there. Perkins debated whether to turn the headlights off when passing inhabited houses, then decided that would look suspicious. A truck driving through the night was, after all, nothing unusual. They were just an ordinary truck, she reminded herself, there should be nothing interesting about it.

Paradise

As they drove, the sky cleared, and Perkins saw the eastern sky becoming pink almost an hour before dawn. With only forty minutes until the sun cleared the horizon, Emby directed them to pull off the main road onto an overgrown track. They bumped along the rough road, with overhanging tree branches scraping the top of the truck, until they came to a halt under two large trees. Jesse and Dave went back to cover their tracks, while Perkins and Shauna cut branches to drape over the truck.

You should rest now, Emby messaged, *we will alert you if anyone approaches your position. You will be moving again in nine hours.*

We will be driving during daylight, she asked.

Yes. This area is sparsely populated and air traffic is minimal; you are on the edge of a no-fly zone agreed by the Ruhar and the Kristang, Emby stated. *You must remain hidden now because a road convoy is scheduled to pass by a crossroads roughly ten kilometers ahead of you in five hours, and the road will be busy.*

Understood.

"Emby wants us moving again in nine hours, so I want us to get sleep and be ready to go in seven hours," Perkins said. They had taken turns driving through the night, giving two people at a time the ability to catch sleep in the back seat.

"Can we eat first, ma'am?" Shauna asked. The thought of the real food in the back of the truck had been in the back of her mind all night.

"Good idea, we should check out the sumptuous buffet Emby set up for us. We will all split one item this morning," Perkins warned. "Our stomachs aren't used to real food after eating mush for too long."

Dave was the first to look in the box that Shauna had opened. "This is all in French. I think 'boeuf' means 'beef', ma'am?"

"Don't ask me, Czajka, I learned Mandarin Chinese, not French," Perkins replied. "That sounds right to me."

"Does everyone want to try beef stew? I think that's what this is," Dave held up a can.

"Anything but chicken, man," Jesse replied. "That would be way too tempting if we ever get back to Fort Rakovsky."

They split one 'beouf stew' and three cans of nutrient mush, everyone agreed the stew was awesome.

The next two days involved driving part of the days and all of the nights. They were climbing up through foothills that became hills. The roads became more and more rough; in some cases the big truck was mowing down bushes. Only once during daylight did Emby warn them about aircraft approaching, and they had to pull the truck under a stand of trees and cover it as best they could. They never saw an aircraft; Emby said it passed over several kilometers to the south. That incident made Perkins more suspicious about who Emby could be. Their Mysterious Benefactor was not concerned about the truck being detected on sensors, but was worried about an aircraft flying overhead and someone looking down through a window. Perkins could understand Emby having some control or influence over Ruhar sensor coverage, but why wasn't Emby concerned about their truck being seen by the Kristang ships in orbit? It made no sense. She knew not to bother asking Emby for answers, because Emby wasn't going to provide answers.

Their destination was a clearing deep in the woods, off the road. The truck was designed to drive off-road, but Emby advised they might need to cut down a few trees along the way. In the back of the truck was a cutter device that attached to the front of the truck, and chainsaws. Emby had planned a detailed route to the clearing, and tried to assure Perkins getting the truck there was manageable. The clearing was a good place to stash the truck, and wait for a Buzzard to arrive.

She would believe that when a stolen Buzzard landed in the clearing.

And she would believe Emby when she saw a giant maser cannon buried eighty meters under the surface of Paradise.

"Uh oh, Joe," Skippy announced.

"Oh, crap. Skippy, can I get through one day without bad news?" I had spent a boring day watching Perkins' truck driving along a lonely road. "One day! Is that too much to ask? Really?"

"Don't ask me, Joe, the universe apparently hates you."

"Why? What did I ever do to the universe?"

"Maybe you cut it off in traffic, or took its parking space, or, ooooh. Maybe you dated the universe's sister. Hey! Maybe the universe *is* a girl you dated. That is a sure fire way to get anyone to hate you, Joe."

"No, Skippy, girls I date don't hate me, they just think I'm, you know, meh."

"Meh is still better than 'let's be friends', right?"

"Nothing is worse than the 'let's be friends' speech," I shook my head, and in the corner I could see Adams' shoulders shaking with mirth. "What fresh bad news do you have for me today?"

"The Kristang are planning some bad things in Lemuria, Joe."

"They can't do anything in Lemuria!" I protested. "The terms of the cease fire state that humans are a neutral party and are not to be harmed, or used, by either side. They also can't be assisted by either side."

"I know what the cease fire terms say, Joe, and so do the Kristang. Unfortunately, the cease fire terms do not prevent either side from 'inspecting' human-occupied areas, to assure that humans are not stockpiling banned weapons or some bullshit excuse like that. Basically, one of the Kristang commanders is bored, and he wants some action. So his plan for this 'inspection tour' is to provoke a group of humans into attacking his team. Then he can hunt unarmed humans in the jungle, for sport. He will be wearing powered armor, with a rifle and air support. Messages I have intercepted state that he intends to land somewhere with a mixed gender population, and then 'accidentally' kill or injure several women. He knows this would likely provoke human men to hostile action, which the Kristang see as a weakness by the way. If they are unable to provoke a sufficiently hostile action, they will simply make something up, and kill humans anyway."

"Shit."

"My thoughts exactly."

"Whew," I let out a long breath and sat back in my chair. "Anything we do to stop the Kristang would risk exposing our presence here, so I would have to clear it with Chotek first. He's not likely to approve any action. Unless, you know, it were to totally slip my mind," I added with a meaningful glance at Sergeant Adams.

"Sir, I can't hear very well, I think my ears are clogged," she said, rubbing an ear.

Damn, I am glad that I brought Adams along. "That is too bad, Sergeant. Skippy, how are the Kristang getting to Lemuria?"

"A trio of dropships will be leaving the Kristang base in the morning."

"Skippy, if those dropships were to suffer fatal mechanical failures at high altitude, I would not lose much sleep over it. If you know what I mean."

"I do know what you mean, Joe. However, it is not so simple. As I have explained before, Kristang systems are hardened against cyber attack, because they are wary of interference by their patrons the Thuranin. Most critical control systems aboard Kristang dropships are at least partly manual. Also, their base is a great distance from here, which somewhat limits my abilities in this sort of thing. However, I can promise you that I will do my best. I will get working on it immediately, this type of interference takes a great deal of time. I do not know whether the time available is sufficient for me to accomplish anything effective. It would be best if you began trying to think of an untraceable way to warn the humans on Lemuria. Or something else."

Overnight, we weren't able to think of a good way to notify UNEF of the danger from a Kristang hunting party. I didn't get much sleep, and when I did sleep, I had nightmares of terrified men and women running through the jungle, being hunted like animals. The problem with sending any message to UNEF was that the Kristang would certainly learn about it and assume the Ruhar had warned the humans. Under the terms of the cease fire agreement, warning UNEF would count as the Ruhar 'assisting' the humans. With that part of the cease fire having been violated by the Ruhar, the Kristang would then be free to 'assist' the humans in whatever way they felt like. The only plan we had, in case Skippy wasn't able to do anything, was to track the dropships and try to predict where they would land. Then we would send a warning just to the people in those specific villages. It wasn't a good plan. And part of me was thinking that if the Kristang planned to land in a village populated by idiotic 'Keepers', maybe I shouldn't warn those assholes. But, I would warn them anyway; the Keepers may be unforgivably stupid but they were humans.

With five minutes before the hunting party dropships were scheduled to take off the next morning, Skippy told me he was still working on it. And that it would help if I would shut the hell up and stop distracting him. That worried me; I had rarely seen Skippy concentrate so hard on anything.

Two minutes to go. "Skippy? How are we doing?"

"We? *We* aren't doing anything. I am doing all the work, while you sit there trying to decide whether to pick your nose or not."

"I decided against it."

"And all of Paradise rejoices at your decision."

"Seriously, how are you doing?"

"Watch your laptop screen, Joe. The action is about to start. No coming attractions, just the main feature that I call 'A Very Bad Day at the Office'. Ooh, it's starting now."

The lead dropship, with the Kristang commander aboard, was the first to take off. Their dropships were ugly things, with small wings tipped with V-shaped winglets. The Kristang optimized their dropships for combat in the vacuum of space; their aerodynamics were not the best. The first dropship lifted about ten meters off the ground, and hovered while I guess the pilots were checking their systems. Then it increased power and climbed, at first at an angle, then it zoomed straight up fast; to my eyes too fast. It started to wobble and when it got to what looked like three to four hundred feet, it flipped over on its back and fell straight down like a rock. Skippy kept a running commentary. "Oooh, see, Joe, you're not supposed to fly straight up like that. You're supposed to clear the airfield perimeter, and then gain altitude. Otherwise, something like this could happen. Wow, this looks like it might be painful." The dropship crashed on its back right on top of another dropship and broke into three pieces, with burning chunks flying around from both dropships. "Yup, yup, that's definitely painful. Oooh, would you look at that, now the third dropship is on fire," he said as a big chunk of flaming debris hit the third dropship, which had just tried to lift off to get out of the danger zone. "Hey, good for them, some lizards survived from that third dropship, and they're out and sort of crawling away. Uh oh." A tall light pole that was at the edge of the tarmac had been struck near its base by a piece of debris, and it wobbled. Then, slowly at first and picking up speed, it toppled over, with the heavy lights smashing right onto one of the crawling Kristang. "Oh! That *had* to hurt. I'm no expert, Joe, because I don't feel physical pain, but I'm thinking that pretty much had to hurt real bad, right? Yup, that guy's not moving. Those other guys really should move faster; I have a feeling the missiles on the racks of that dropship have become unstable. We'd better go to super slow motion on this video, Joe." As he said that, three missiles that had been trapped under the third dropship ignited and streaked away, just as the third dropship exploded. "Wow!" Two of the missiles bounced and skidded across the tarmac, one hit a large building and the other flew in the yawning open door of a hangar. Both buildings blew sky-high as the missile warheads detonated. There were secondary explosions from the hangar as whatever had been in there blew up. We barely had time to take in that super slo-mo video when the camera view switched to the third missile, which had gone in the other direction, across the tarmac. Across the tarmac, between two buildings, flipping over high into the air, doing cartwheels and then plunging downward. Down, directly in the open door of the Kristang's ammunition bunker and down the underground tunnel. "Wow, now *there* is something you don't see every day," Skippy commented. "What are the *odds* of that, huh? That was poor operational security by the Kristang, I think, leaving the bunker door open like that. Three, two, one-"

The underground ammo dump blew, and the video feed cut out. The video then switched to a view from high above, Skippy must have hacked into the sensors of a Kristang ship in orbit. All we could see was the top of an angry, growing mushroom cloud where the base had been.

"Holy *shit*, Skippy," I said, stunned. Adams couldn't believe it either, and Desai had her hand in front of her mouth.

"Golly, I hope those lizards who were crawling away from that dropship are Ok," Skippy said seriously. "Although, to tell the truth, I wouldn't get my hopes up for them. Gosh darn it, that was a truly *unfortunate* series of events, I guess. Well, shit happens, right?"

"Overkill is underrated?" I guessed.

"I have no idea what you are talking about, Joe. However, I can say it is unlikely that any assholes from that base will be going on hunting trips in Lemuria any time soon."

"That was a nice touch, having the light pole fall on that guy," Adams observed.

"Huh?" Skippy asked. "Nope, that was shear blind luck, Sarge Marge. As you understand luck anyway. I couldn't have planned something like that. That guy must have some seriously bad karma built up from a past life. Or this one."

"Thank you anyway," I said. "Any chance this could have blowback on us, or UNEF?" Thinking about that possibility, I feared that I really should have told Chotek about it beforehand.

"Ha! Zero, Joe. The opposite of infinity. To the Kristang, your species are primitive cavemen, no way would they ever consider lowly humans to be involved. Certainly, the Kristang might suspect this was not merely an incredibly unfortunate accident. But if they suspect anyone, they will suspect the Ruhar. They won't say that openly, because the commander of that base is politically connected to senior clan leadership, an admitting that his poor security allowed the Ruhar to sabotage his equipment would be damaging. Even if they knew for certain that somehow the Ruhar were involved, they won't do anything that jeopardizes the cease fire."

"Hmm," I mused. "If we somehow provided evidence that it was the Ruhar, that could get the Ruhar and the Kristang into the shooting war we want. No, no, that won't work," I quickly discarded my own idea. "We need a shooting war that takes out the Kristang battlegroup, so the balance of power in the negotiations shifts back toward the Ruhar, not just a ground war. Damn it. Ok, Skippy, uh, I know you could not possibly have been involved in the extremely unfortunate accident we witnessed this morning."

"Perish the thought," he said cheerily. "Joe, I suggest you practice your innocent face, because the light from that explosion will reach the *Dutchman* soon, and Chocula is sure to contact you about it."

"Crap," I hadn't thought about that. "I'd better call him first, inform him that we detected a large explosion at a Kristang base. And that we know nothing about it."

"Gosh darn it, Joe. It is truly too bad we don't have any video that could clue Chotek in about what caused the explosion," Skippy lamented.

"That is too bad," I agreed.

"Hey Joe, after you call the Count, how about you get some popcorn and we watch the video again? I have a feeling there are some surprises."

"Surprises? We already saw what happened."

"No, Joe, you dumdum. I mean surprises for the Kristang. That hunting trip when *terribly* wrong, didn't it?"

I called the *Dutchman*. Neither Chotek nor Chang sounded like they believed that we were not involved in the massive explosion. Chotek didn't directly accuse me of causing the incident, so I really didn't care. I was, however, put on notice that there had better not be any more such incidents.

"Skippy, I don't think we can do that trick again, not for a while anyway."

"No problem. Do not expect me to do that often, Joe. I got lucky this time. The pilot of that lead dropship practiced poor cyber security. He had been having trouble with new software of the dropship's navigation system, so he left it on overnight to run a diagnostic. I was able to partially get in that way, and it took me almost to the last second to get the details right. I wouldn't count on my doing that again."

Lieutenant Irene Striebich looked again at the message on her zPhone in disbelief. "Explain this to me again?"

Shauna took a breath before responding. "Which part?"

"The part where you want me to steal a Buzzard, and fly you and your partners around on a secret mission. A mission you can't tell me anything about."

"I can't tell you until-"

"Shauna, stealing a Buzzard isn't just difficult, it's impossible. I know, I used to fly them. Since the Ruhar took their aircraft back, they implemented security features. All pilots need a keycard that is assigned to each authorized flight. And a password, plus there is a biometric scanner. No human would pass the biometric check. If I somehow do get access, the startup procedure for a Buzzard takes over five minutes even for an emergency launch. During that time, someone at the airbase would hear. A Buzzard sitting on the ground is vulnerable, I can't engage shields, weapons or stealth until the ship is in the air. One rifle could take out an engine fan blade, and the Buzzard wouldn't be going anywhere. It's impossible."

"It's not impossible. We can do it."

"We? You mean these friends of yours that you can't tell me about?"

"Yes. Irene, do you want to fly again?"

"Yes, of course I do."

"If we can get you a Buzzard, will you fly it for us?" Shauna asked. She had thought this would be easier.

Irene didn't answer for a moment.

Shauna asked another way. "If we can steal a Buzzard, will that prove that we're real?"

"It will prove you can do the impossible. Shauna, this mission, it's really that important? This isn't some crazy cowboy shit you've gotten into?" Irene knew that Shauna was as desperate for infantry duty as Irene was to fly again.

"Irene, this mission could be everything for UNEF's survival. That's all I can tell you, until you pick us up."

"I don't believe this," Irene said almost to herself. "You got me, I'm in. If, *if*, you get me a Buzzard to fly."

"Deal," Shauna said, and gave a thumbs up to Major Perkins. Perkins had been listening on her own zPhone, and returned the gesture.

Skippy and I had been listening also. "They got us a pilot, Skippy. Now how do we get a Buzzard for her? She's in Lemuria, there aren't any Buzzards there. And what about all that stuff she said about it being impossible to steal a Buzzard? I assume you can get around the keycard and the biometric stuff, but is she right about how long it takes to start up a cold ship?"

"She is correct about that, Joe. Getting access for her is child's play for me, of course."

"You didn't answer my question. What is your plan for getting around the startup time problem? Because if you're waiting for me to dream something up, I hate to disappoint you." My own pilot experience was limited to Thuranin dropships, and the normal startup procedure took over seven minutes. It was possible to skip a lot of steps and go from activating the power to the engines being able to fly in four minutes; that was the absolute fastest it could be done. There were too many systems that needed to power up in sequence to make the process go any faster. "This Irene person is right; it is impossible to steal a Buzzard. As soon as any Ruhar at the airbase hear those engines starting, they will react, and this Irene won't get anywhere."

"Oh sure, Joe, if you do it the hard way. Duh. I plan to cheat."

"Can you give me more details there, Skippy?"

"Simple. We'll have the Ruhar steal a Buzzard for her."

Irene Striebich tried to relax in the back of the Buzzard. The ship had showed up at her village that afternoon, and she had been ordered to come with them. It had happened exactly as Shauna told her it would, so she boarded the Buzzard without question. There were only three Ruhar aboard; two pilots up front and one soldier watching Irene. The soldier seemed bored, and told her only that they had been ordered to bring Shauna to their airbase, he didn't know why. Other than that, the soldier didn't want to talk.

The ship droned on for over an hour; Irene calculated in her head that they had passed over the ocean and were now approaching or already over the coast of Tenturo. Shauna had told her to expect what happened next, so Irene was not worried when the droning of the engines stuttered, then cut out. The guard shook himself out of the half-asleep position he had been in, and spoke to the pilots. Since the guard had taken her zPhone, she didn't understand most of the hurried conversation, but she understood when the guard motioned for her to tug her harness tightly. The engines restarted but surged and from the tone, Irene could tell neither of the engines were developing much power. There was more conversation between the soldier and the pilots as the Buzzard descended rapidly enough for Irene's stomach to flutter. Weight came back as the pilots slowed their descent and then flared for landing. The soldier braced into a crash position, indicating Irene should do the same. The soldier looked genuinely afraid and Irene tried to mimic his expression, although he wasn't paying much attention to her.

Paradise

With a final roar of thrusters being used to provide emergency supplemental lift to the failing engines, the Buzzard hovered for a moment, then set down roughly enough that Irene was glad she had been in a crash position. One, then the other engine shut down, and the cockpit door opened. Both pilots came out, worried expressions on their hamster faces. They popped the side door latch and went out to inspect the ship. The guard unstrapped and walked toward the doorway to join them. When he saw Irene reaching for her own straps, he shook his head. "You stay," he said in broken English, pointing to her seat emphatically.

Irene nodded and held up her hands as the soldier walked down the fold-out stairs. As soon as he was out of sight, she unbuckled her straps and got out of the seat as Shauna had instructed. So far, events had gone as Shauna said they would, now was the critical moment.

And, right on schedule, there was a 'click' sound as a locker door unlatched. Just as Shauna said it would. Crouching to avoid being seen through the window, Irene went forward to the locker and pulled out one of the two rifles that Shauna had said would be there. Now the last test. Irene selected the stun setting, flicked the safety off, and put her finger on the trigger. Normally, a Ruhar weapon would disable itself if touched by a human.

This one stayed active. Confident now, although confident in who or what Irene didn't know, she checked again that the rifle was set to stun and popped her head up to glance out the small window. Both pilots and the soldier were standing together, a few meters in front of the left engine, looking at it and talking. Irene stepped into the doorway and was able to take aim before the soldier saw her out of the corner of his eye and reached for his pistol. It was too late for him. She stunned him with one shot, then switched aim to the two unarmed pilots. Moving more slowly and deliberately than she wanted to, she shot one pilot, then had to leap down the stairs to take aim as the other pilot ran out of sight behind the left engine pod. Irene shot him in the legs and he went down, sprawled full-length in the grass.

Following the instructions Shauna had sent to her, Irene took zPhones away from two of the Ruhar, and used the soldier's knife to cut away the locator beacons that were sewn into the collar of the pilot's jackets. Then she dragged first the soldier and the two pilots away from the Buzzard, so they wouldn't be harmed by the engine exhaust. The Ruhar were heavy, Irene was grateful for the hard work she'd been doing working on a farm. She left the pistol with the soldier, and activated his zPhone. As Shauna had said, the soldier's zPhone now had only one function; a map. The map would allow the three Ruhar to walk to a village on the coast within a week. The three aliens began stirring awake, so she stunned them again, then went back into the Buzzard and brought back a box of Ruhar field rations, three blankets and a pack that contained useful items like a tarp, knives and a shovel. The three Ruhar would be fine as long as they didn't stay in place waiting for rescue. Because rescue would not be coming for them; Shauna's friends had somehow arranged to fake a Buzzard crash over the ocean. Any rescue aircraft would be looking for wreckage far out at sea; without the pilots knowing, the Buzzard's transponder had turned off in the middle of the flight.

Everything had worked exactly as Shauna told Irene it would; now came the final test. She went back in the Buzzard, secured the door, sat in the pilot seat and took a deep breath. All the instruments were on, and the controls didn't freeze when she touched the control stick. One of the biometric security features of a Buzzard was a reader built into the control stick; it scanned the user's DNA to assure an authorized pilot was touching the controls. No way could a human pass a DNA scan.

Yet Irene did pass the scan. All the controls still worked perfectly. And- "Oh, fuck me," Irene gasped. With a flicker, the cockpit displays all switched from Ruhar script to English. She had been trained to read Ruhar, but somehow the flight systems had reverted to the settings installed when humans had controlled aircraft on Paradise.

Irene decided she could puzzle about that later, after she was in the air. The right, then the left engine started normally. Because the aircraft had just landed and systems other than the engines had not been shut down, she was able to go to full power and lift off in less than a minute. After reaching a hundred meters, she circled the area to check that the three Ruhar were unharmed. They were, laying prone on the grass where she had left them. Irene pointed the Buzzard's nose toward the coordinates Shauna had sent and kept the Buzzard flying low and at a moderate speed. As soon as the system was ready, she engaged the stealth field, and suddenly the windows went dark as light was bent around the aircraft's hull. No matter; she was trained to fly on instruments.

After setting the autopilot and verifying that all systems were operating normally, she pulled one of the two zPhones out of a pocket. "Shauna, it's Irene. I'm in the air."

"Great! You have a clear path to us, there aren't any aircraft along your flightpath right now. The Ruhar have a dozen aircraft doing search and rescue where they think you went down over the ocean."

"All the cockpit displays are in English instead of Ruhar. How the *hell* did you do that?"

"I didn't do anything. I told you, we have friends. Everything went Ok?" Shauna knew it had, for Emby had sent them a message that Irene had successfully launched and was on the way to pick them up.

"Yes, everything went fine. I'll be there in," she checked the flight computer, "about an hour. You're going to tell me what this top secret mission is after I land?"

"I will. And it's going to blow your mind," Shauna said with a laugh.

"*Giant maser cannons*?" Irene exclaimed in disbelief.

"Those were my words exactly, Lieutenant," Jesse agreed. "Ain't that some shit?"

"And you think this Mysterious Benefactor is a group of native Ruhar who don't like their government trading away this planet?"

"We don't think that, we're guessing," Major Perkins corrected their new pilot. "Based on what Emby has been able to do, the facts so far fit our guess."

"We're going to reactivate these projectors, so we can shoot the Kristang battlegroup out of the sky?" Irene asked.

"That's the idea," Perkins agreed.

"Yes, ma'am. Then we'll still have the problem of the Ruhar government wanting to sell Paradise to the Kristang," Irene said skeptically.

"I believe Emby is hoping that if the Ruhar fleet has to fight for this planet again, they'll want to keep it. Right now, it's too easy for their government to take whatever they can get and bail on us." Perkins explained. "Are you regretting your decision to join us?" If Striebich wanted to pull out now, that was going to be a major problem. Perkins couldn't let her go anywhere, or have access to a zPhone.

"No ma'am," Irene shook her head emphatically. "This is a little tough to take all at once. I hate the feeling of knowing those lizard ships are hanging above my head all the time. If we can do something about that, I'm all in. What's the next step?"

"You have got to be joking," Irene said with shock after Dave dropped the truck's tailgate and pulled aside the canvas flap. It was a big truck, and the cargo box was fairly jammed with boxes and equipment. "How is all of this crap supposed to fit in my Buzzard?"

"It's not, ma'am," Dave said. "Mostly we just need to take the drill rig with us. A lot of this," he pointed to the cargo box, "is fuel cells for the truck and the Buzzard. And we have," he hopped up into the cargo box and tilted it toward the pilot, "food. Real food." He held up an American MRE pouch, then a package labeled 'Chicken and Dumplings'.

Irene gasped. "Where did you get that?"

Dave shrugged. "Emby had the truck loaded up like Santa's sleigh for us. There's also two full boxes with cans of nutrient mush if you prefer that, ma'am."

"No! Real food would be excellent," Irene said with delight. "I guess that drill rig will fit, I'll have to see it."

"Emby assured us that this type of portable drill rig was designed to be carried by a Buzzard." Shauna assured the pilot. "We practiced unloading and loading it yesterday. Emby even included the tiedown strap kit for securing the drill rig in the back of a Buzzard."

"You're sure about this?" Irene asked, because she was not sure at all.

"Yes. Look, the cover comes off the truck's cargo box, and the truck has a crane for loading its own stuff. There is also a mini forklift kind of thing, with treads so it can operate off-road. Plus, the drill rig is self-propelled." The drill rig's base had six articulated legs so it could walk on its own just about anywhere. Seeing the insect-like legs in action was spine-chillingly creepy at first, Shauna thought. There was no denying it was very effective.

Irene looked at her Buzzard, sitting under camouflage netting and tree branches. She would not be flying it again until after nightfall. Emby had confirmed the Ruhar still thought her ship had gone down over the ocean; they still had several aircraft flying search missions. And there was a full-scale investigation into how a Buzzard had been sent to pick up a single human in Lemuria; Ruhar military command on the planet was not able to trace where the order had come from. According to Emby, they would never discover who had issued the order. To be safe, she was not going to fly until the early hours of the next morning. "If you're sure, show me. Let's get it loaded."

CHAPTER SEVENTEEN

To Irene's surprise, everything they needed for drilling down to the first projector fit inside the Buzzard, with room to spare. The Ruhar designers had cleverly packaged the portable drill rig so it collapsed on itself, and could crawl up the Buzzard's rear ramp on its own. They wouldn't be able to deploy the drill rig that way at a projector site, but it was still an impressive feat of engineering. Everything was squared away with two hours to spare, so the five caught an quick nap and were awakened in the pitch dark night by message from Emby.

After a quick breakfast of nutrient mushes, they checked that the truck was securely hidden, then Irene began walking around the Buzzard for a preflight inspection.

"What kind of name is Striebich, ma'am?" Jesse asked as he held a light for their pilot. He pronounced the name 'Stree-bick' as Irene had done.

"It's German," Irene said as she opened an access panel and checked an actuator.

"German?" Jesse said, surprised.

"I know," Irene laughed and looked at her arm's light brown skin. "My father is German and the joke was that I came from gypsies. My mother's name is Elena Ramos, she was in Germany with the Army and married a German man over there."

"She was in the Army, ma'am?"

Irene nodded. "She was a Blackhawk pilot; she's why I became a pilot. She retired only three years before the hamsters hit us," she frowned. Now the Ruhar were the closest thing UNEF had to allies. Life was certainly strange sometimes. "Before we left Earth, she talked about reenlisting to join UNEF, but it would have meant six months of training and she might not get flight duty anyway."

"Sometimes I wish that I hadn't gotten the recall notice," Jesse said honestly. "My father, my uncle, my cousin and I were all about to head out on a hunting trip, we planned to be gone a week or more. We were loading the truck when my mother told me I had a message from the 10th Division on my email. My cousin told me to ignore it, but I knew I couldn't. If we'd gotten that truck loaded earlier, I might not have seen that message until it was too late to go offworld. There wasn't any cellphone service up in the hills back then."

"I didn't have a choice," Irene said as she closed the access panel. "I was already back with the 10th Aviation at Fort Drum when we got the order to deploy to Ecuador." She walked over to the left engine and pointed for Jesse to shine the light into the exhaust. "How did you get involved with this?"

"Us?" Jesse asked. "The four of us were all together because of Joe Bishop." He told her the whole astonishing story as she finished the external preflight check.

"Do you think Bishop is really alive?" Irene asked quietly, trying to be sensitive that Jesse had been Joe's friend.

"Major Perkins says the hamsters think he is. Me?" Jesse scratched his head. "All I know is that Joe is one lucky son of a bitch, always has been. He also has a nose for trouble; if there is trouble within a hundred miles, you can be sure Bish will find himself in the middle of it sooner or later. What I can say is, I hope if he did find trouble, he didn't drag anyone else into it."

"He's right, Joe," Skippy said. "You sure dragged me and the whole Merry Band of Pirates into a huge mess, didn't you?"

"Me?" I protested. We had been listening to Jesse and Irene talk through their zPhones, which they didn't realize were transmitting. I did feel guilty about eavesdropping; the reason I justified listening to them talk had been to prevent them from making mistakes they couldn't recover from. "You are the one who got *me* into trouble, Skippy. If you hadn't opened the door to that warehouse, I would be on a farm in Lemuria right now." Or dead, I didn't say. "Turn it off, please."

"Are you sure, Joe?"

"Yes. You're listening, you can tell us if they make a big mistake. It's creepy for me to be listening to them. I don't even know this Irene."

"You read her service record and the profile I put together, Joe."

"That's not the same as meeting her in person."

"I wouldn't know about that," said the beer can, who never actually met anyone 'in person'. "Lt. Striebich is now in the cockpit and running her preflight checks there. I could tell her that I know everything is perfect with the aircraft, but a pilot would never take anyone's word about that, right?"

"You got it. I've only flown Thuranin dropships, but before I fly, I am checking everything myself."

"Understood. While we're waiting, Joe, I have a question."

"Skippy, it is unlikely that I have an answer. Especially if your question is about 17th century Hungarian poetry."

"No, it's nothing like that. When you were at your parents' house, you borrowed your father's truck to drive into town."

"Yeah, so? I can drive, Skippy." Although, right then, I wondered whether my driver's license had expired. I had been away from Earth for a while, after all.

"Your driving and piloting skills are debatable, Joe, but that is not my question. Why were you driving a truck? Why don't you have a Corvette?"

"A Corvette?" That question completely surprised me. "I can't afford a Corvette, Skippy. Besides, what would I do with a car like that in Maine? It snows there six months a year. Why do you ask that?"

"I thought all astronauts drive Corvettes. Technically, you are an astronaut, Joe. You have flown spacecraft by yourself, and you even performed a spacedive."

"Huh. I never thought of myself as an astronaut, Skippy. Maybe you're right."

"Mmm, maybe not. Real astronauts get laid a lot more than you."

"That's because women know those guys are astronauts, Skippy. I can't tell anyone what we've been doing out here."

"Also, astronauts are a lot cooler than you, Joe."

"Good bye, Skippy."

Sergeant Adams woke me and Captain Desai up early the next morning, as Perkins and her team approached the first projector site in the Buzzard. Many things could go wrong at this point, we all wanted to know what was happening in real time. I told Skippy to show us video from the Buzzard's cameras and sensors, and we would listen when they talked to each other on zPhones, but we weren't going to eavesdrop this time.

"Are they clear?" Irene asked over the zPhone earpiece. The Buzzard's belly camera gave her a view beneath her, and Dave in the back was remotely aiming the camera where it needed to be. Still, with tons of equipment to be lowered to the ground, it made sense to be certain.

"Major Perkins confirms they are clear, yes. Should I begin lowering the sling now?" Dave asked.

"Do it. I want the drill rig on the ground before the wind picks up," Irene ordered. This whole operation was too complicated, but she didn't know an easier way. The

Kristang had deliberately installed the projectors in remote areas that would be unlikely to be developed for habitation, industry or agricultural use. In most cases, this meant that trees had grown over the sites during the intervening years; and there was no way to land the Buzzard at the sites without the laboriously slow process of cutting a clearing. With the Buzzard, they had flown to any clear area near the first site and lowered Perkins and Jesse to the ground on a cable. Those two then cleared just enough trees out of the way, while Irene landed the Buzzard and she helped Dave and Shauna unload the drill rig and secure it in a sling. The drill rig and its associated gear was now awkwardly slung beneath the Buzzard and needed to be carefully lowered through the gap in the trees. The sun would be rising in less than an hour, so they needed to get the drill rig, Shauna and Dave on the ground as quickly as possible. Then Irene would park the Buzzard close by, cover it with a camouflage net and wait. Wait, while the four others drilled down to a hidden chamber where a secret giant maser cannon could be reactivated.

The weather forecast from Emby was favorable, except that Irene expected the light breeze to pick up and become unpredictably gusty as the sun came over the horizon. The drill rig needed to be on the ground and the sling cable retracted before then. If the wind was blowing too strongly for Shauna and Dave to be lowered to the ground by cable, Irene could land the Buzzard and those two could walk to the projector site. The sling with the drill rig was fitted with thrusters that could be steered remotely, or it had a limited ability to guide itself. Perkins and Colter had hammered a target into the ground where they wanted the sling to make contact, the sling would home in on that spot. Irene only needed to hover the Buzzard over the opening in the forest canopy, and either Dave or the sling's automated guidance system would handle dropping the package. That was great news for Irene; she had limited experience with hauling cargo by sling, and no recent experience.

It was nerve-wracking to hover the Buzzard, one eye on the instruments and one eye on the treetops to the east. When the wind kicked up, leaves on the trees to the east would flutter and signal when the wind would reach the Buzzard. Irene used the leaves to anticipate when she would need to maneuver the lumbering Buzzard. In training, she had been able to hover within a two meter sphere; never varying more than a meter in any direction. In training, she never had a multiton weight suspended on the end of a cable beneath her ship.

"Down! It's down," Shauna called out over the intercom. "Cable released."

Irene had felt the cable go slack, she had been watching the camera feed to anticipate when to reduce power. She couldn't help allowing herself a self-congratulatory smile; the drop had been nearly perfect despite the morning winds picking up already. "Retract cable," she ordered. "Jarrett, Czajka, the wind is too rough for you two to rappel down. I need to land and you can hike in."

"Yes, ma'am," Dave replied unhappily. Looking down at the waving treetops, he decided that maybe he shouldn't be unhappy about having to walk a kilometer or two through the woods that morning. "I'll inform Major Perkins."

"No," Irene said flatly. "*No.*"

"I wouldn't be asking if-" Shauna started to say.

"Shauna, no. No way! I became a pilot to be in the air, not underground."

"Irene, please, think about it. None of us can do it, we tried. Even Major Perkins tried, and she's bigger than I am. If we have to lift the drill and start again, it will take another full day, and Emby is already pushing us for being too slow."

"I don't believe this, Shauna." It occurred to Irene then that under normal circumstances, Shauna should have addressed her as 'Lieutenant' or Ma'am, and she should have called the Specialist 'Jarrett'. These were anything but normal circumstances. "What happens if I get stuck down there? Who will fly the Buzzard?"

Perkins' team had gotten the drill down eighty three meters before it broke through to an open chamber; a chamber that didn't appear on their subsurface scans. Then they retracted the exploratory drill and fitted the widest drill bit available. It was slow going because of their inexperience with drilling, even with Emby guiding them. More than once, Emby had sent messages exhorting them to move faster. An exasperated Major Perkins had replied that if Emby wanted them to drill more quickly, they should have sent someone with experience.

Finally, after what Perkins knew was far too much time, the big drill was done. And then they discovered the problem Emby had apparently not considered. None of the four drill crew members could fit down the hole. Shauna had tried first, but she was five feet seven and her shoulders simply were too wide. For once, she regretted the weight training she had done to qualify for infantry duty. The two men had made a halfhearted attempt to fit, then Major Perkins had tried, but as she was five feet ten there was no way she would fit either. They were about to drill a second hole next to the first, in order to widen the opening, when Shauna thought of their pilot.

Irene Striebich was barely at the Army's minimum height requirement for pilots of five feet four inches, and that had been with her standing with perfect posture, stretching her neck. She was petite and slender and she'd always been self-conscious about her diminutive size. Now, as far as Major Perkins and Emby thought, her petite frame was an asset. "Shauna, there has got to be some other way to do this."

"Skippy, come on, isn't there another way to do this? Does she really need to squeeze down that hole?" The thought of me doing that made my skin crawl.

"Another way like what, Joe?" Skippy asked, sounding annoyed.

"I don't know. Like, can we do it remotely?"

"Gosh, Joe, I never thought of that. What a brilliant idea," he said sarcastically. "You know, I don't have the owner's manual for that type of Kristang projector, so I looked it up on YouTube. Half the links were people doing stupid stuff, like asking me if we can do this remotely. No we can't, you dumdum. The Kristang didn't want anyone waking up those projectors remotely, that's why they physically disabled them. Someone needs to go down there and reconnect the power connections and plug things in. I'd do it because I can fit down the hole easily, but, darn it, I don't have thumbs. You jackass."

"Sorry. Ok, send Perkins a message, Striebich needs to try. She isn't claustrophobic, is she?"

"Not according to her service records, but who wouldn't be claustrophobic while going eighty meters down a narrow, dark tube?"

"Crap. Ask her to try. If she can't do it, that's understandable."

Irene's whole body was shaking when she felt her feet finally had room to move. She swung her feet around, trying to find some place to stand. The camera on the end of the drill had shown an oval-shaped chamber, which now had a cone of dirt below where the drill had punched through the composite ceiling. The cable continued lowering her, with her shoulders scraping the sides even though she had her arms squeezed as tightly together in front of her as she could. Without being able to move her head enough to look down, and her eyes only inches from the tube's wall, she couldn't see anything at first. The drill had sprayed a coating on the hole that hardened and prevented the dirt and rocks from collapsing in on her; Emby had said the coating was considerably tougher than steel. Emby was not eighty meters down in a skinny hole.

Light! Even looking straight ahead, she was able to see light coming up from below. Then her right foot touched something soft. It was the cone of dirt. She continued descending and both of her feet found solid ground, then she was able to move her arms. Her shoulders screamed at her from being cramped in one position for so long. And her eyes blinked from the sudden unaccustomed glare of the lights they had tossed down the hole.

When she could stand, she managed to report in. "I'm down," she said, and tugged on the cable twice for emphasis. "No surprises here, it looks like it did from the camera. What does Emby want me to do first?" Irene wanted to accomplish her tasks as quickly as possible, so she could clip the cable back on her harness and be pulled up. Up and out.

"Outstanding, Striebich," Major Perkins replied. "Here's what you do-"

"Success, Joe!" Skippy shouted excitedly. "I have established a link to the projector, and I have complete control. All systems fully operational. Who'd have guessed it; lizards can build some good stuff when they really try."

"That is great, Skippy," I said with relief. "Tell Major Perkins to congratulate Striebich for us, please." I knew Skippy would write the message in a way that Perkins could not tell it was coming from a human source.

"Will do, Joe. Hmm, I will also tell Major Perkins that Striebich should not go anywhere near the control panel on the far left. Because that is for the explosive charges that will blow the soil off the top of the projector and extend the maser cannon's muzzle."

"Please do that," I said seriously. It was great that Perkins' team had gotten a maser cannon reactivated. It was not great that, from the time they got the drill rig initially loaded into the Buzzard, it had taken four days. Even with Skippy hacking into the sensors of both Ruhar and Kristang, we needed to get at least eight projectors online as soon as possible. There was too much risk of Perkins' team being discovered. "We need to think of ways to speed up the whole process." Perkins had told 'Emby' that she was confident future projectors could be activated much quicker, now that her crew knew how get a drill rig to a site and how to operate it. "And I don't know how many times we can ask Striebich to squeeze down that tiny hole. If I did that, my nerves would be shot. And she needs to fly that Buzzard, we can't risk her having a nervous breakdown."

"Oh, that's not a problem, Joe. Next time, I'll explain to Major Perkins how to make the big drill bit oscillate, so it creates a larger diameter hole. Your buddies Cornpone and Ski should fit down there easily."

"What? Why the hell didn't you tell them that this time?"

"Truthfully, I didn't consider the difficulty of one of you monkeys squeezing down a hole like that. I don't have physical limitations, so I didn't think of it. That's supposed to be your job, Joe. We could have told them to oscillate the drill bit this time, but they already had the hole open, and making the hole larger would have required as much time as drilling a second hole."

"Crap." He was right, it was my job to think of practical issues. "My bad. Yes, please inform Perkins about how to drill a bigger hole in the future. Striebich should be happy about that. How's the weather forecast?"

"I suggested to Major Perkins that her team move with alacrity, because I am expecting rather strong thunderstorms tomorrow. It would behoove them to get the drill disassembled and the sling operation completed as quickly as possible."

"Alacrity? Behoove? Really, Skippy?"

"Hey, Joe, Major Perkins has a master's degree that your Army paid for. And unlike you, she paid attention in high school. It would be good for you to expand your vocabulary sometimes, *Colonel* Joe."

"Whatever. You knock that Kristang battlegroup out of the sky, and I'll let you teach me one new word every day. Deal?"

"Seems like I'm doing a lot more work than you, but, I accept."

"Uh oh, Joe, we are running out of time," Skippy announced. "We need to strike today."

"What? Only four projectors have been activated, you told us that Perkins needed to get eight online, at minimum. Why the rush?"

"Circumstances have changed; I have new information. The Kristang commander is feeling confident in his control of Paradise, so he has scheduled a war game to commence later today; in about nine hours. Ships will soon begin dispersing to participate in the attack, and we will lose the ability to hit them."

"Crap! We can attack with only four projectors?"

"Oh, yeah, Joe, it's certainly not ideal, but it will work well enough. The four that are now active will be sufficiently effective against the battlegroup for an initial attack. It is for follow-on defense that we will need to have more projectors to provide full coverage. The only downside to our hastily-planned attack is that the commander of the Kristang task force is not aboard his command ship right now. He came down to Paradise yesterday, in order to investigate a bizarre accident. It seems that a dropship crashed, and resulted in blowing up most of a Kristang airbase."

"Huh. That is bizarre," I rolled my eyes. "I wonder how that happened?"

"I have no idea, Joe. That is a puzzle for sure. Anyway, when Admiral Kekrando left the wrecked airbase, he is really pissed about it by the way, he flew up to a destroyer instead of the command ship. We need to take out the command ship first, it represents a significant portion of their combat power. I will hit Kekrando's destroyer if I can; I wouldn't count on it."

"I am sure this Kekrando guy will not be heartbroken if you are not able to target the destroyer he is on."

"Good point. Hey, I can send him a 'Sorry that we missed you' card?"

"Let's not, and say we did."

With only four projectors online, their area of coverage was limited. Each projector could only shoot within a cone of about twenty eight degrees. Perkins' team had activated four projectors that were close to each other, in order to bring projectors online as quickly as possible. While that made sense in terms of logistics, it meant there were huge areas of the sky we couldn't hit. Skippy could only guarantee to hit eight ships, fourteen at the most. The Kristang ships were varying their patrol patterns, to prevent the Ruhar commodore from being tempted into an opportunistic raid.

We did have an advantage, if we had time to use it. Each Kristang warship was assigned a patrol route by the command ship in order to coordinate their coverage of the planet's surface. Most of the communication was from the command ship's computer to the other ships' navigation computers, so the crews were not directly involved in most cases. Skippy had been able to gain limited access to the Kristang command ship's computer; he used that access to alter the patrol patterns. Although the patrol routes were supposed to be random, there was logic to them. The method of assigning patrol routes was to prevent too many ships from being bunched together, because that left gaps in coverage and made the task force an easy target. The challenge for Skippy was to get as many Kristang ships within the strike cones of our four projectors, before some alert Kristang realized something was very wrong. Mathematically, he figured the best he could do was bring fourteen ships within our strike cones at any one time. I told him not to try for the perfect solution; that carried too much risk of the enemy being alerted and blowing our whole plan. If Skippy could get a dozen ships in the virtual crosshairs of our projectors, he was to tell me immediately, so I could press the Big Red Button on my zPhone. And if there was any sign the Kristang were catching on to our plan, we were going to shoot right away. Even with the Kristang ships flying unaltered patrol routes, there were usually six or seven ships within the strike cones at any one time.

Even the awesome power of the projectors would not allow us to clear enemy ships from the skies over Paradise if those ships had been ready for our attack. If those ships had their defensive shields active, even the searing power of a projector's maser beams might be deflected long enough for the ships to perform an emergency jump. Lightly-protected ships like frigates would be no match for the power of a projector, but a Kristang destroyer might survive long enough to jump to safety. And a cruiser or battlecruiser could potentially deflect even two shots before being forced to jump away. With only four projectors to work with, we couldn't afford to use two projectors on one ship.

Fortunately, we had the laws of physics on our side. Ships not engaged in battle could not maintain their shields at full power all the time. Defensive shields drained a significant amount of power from a ship's reactor; in the case of a small ship like a frigate, the ship had to decrease shield power temporarily in order to fire its maser cannon. Shield generators also wore out and became polarized from long-term use, so the Kristang ships around Paradise had their ships in low-power mode to protect the ships only from being struck by space debris. Since shield generators could be brought to full power in seconds, and a ship would be warned of Ruhar ships attacking by the tell-tale gamma ray burst, the Kristang felt safe leaving their shields at low power. And that meant their ships in the skies above Paradise were sitting ducks.

All four projectors fired simultaneously to maximize the surprise. Two of the maser cannons had clear skies above; another had high, thin cloud cover that was no obstacle to the maser projecting its full power above the atmosphere. The fourth projector was somewhat unlucky; it was under a heavy layer of cloud cover, but at least the clouds were not pouring down rain.

The heavy layer of clouds was no match for that maser cannon; it had been designed to shoot through clouds. Its initial shot was a rapid series of lower-powered pulses that lanced up through the clouds, the searing heat of the maser pulses boiling away the water vapor and leaving a brief, narrow clear channel all the way up through the cloud. Half a millisecond later the maser put out its full power into the clear tunnel of air, striking a Kristang destroyer. The projector followed a shoot-shoot-look pattern, with two full power shots followed by a lower-power maser scan of the target. Satisfied that the Kristang destroyer was now a wreck, the projector shifted its aim to a second target, first shooting a rapid series of pulses to knock aside the clouds in that direction.

The very first target struck in the engagement was the command ship, the battlecruiser *He Who Pushes Aside Fear Shall Always be Victorious*. The maser cannon that targeted that ship, a maser shooting up through a crystal clear sky, did not care if the ship's crew pushed aside fear or not. It also followed a standard shoot-shoot-look pattern. The first pulse lasted 0.2 milliseconds and sliced through the unprotected ship's hull. With the *Victorious* moving at nearly 3 kilometers per second, the maser beam did not need to move its aim; the ship did the work of cutting itself almost in half as it moved through the path of the maser bolt. One area the first maser pulse burned through was a missile magazine that was the projector's primary target. Five missiles exploded, sending shrapnel in every direction and rupturing the ship's hull from inside. That first maser shot would have been enough to turn the *Victorious* from a powerful warship into a drifting hulk, but the projector was not finished. Shrapnel from the exploding missiles had not even time to reach the aft of the ship, when the second maser pulse of the shoot-shoot-look pattern targeted the battlecruiser's reactor, and an instant later a brief new sun shone in the sky high above Paradise. When the maser shifted into its lower-powered look mode, the largest piece of organized matter where the *Victorious* had been was about the size of a dropship.

Remorselessly, the projector shifted to the second in the list of targets it had been given by an alien AI. Less than a second later, that target also exploded because a direct maser hit to the ship's jump drive capacitors released that stored energy.

The maser projector then changed aim to a third target, automatically calculating how much energy from its rapidly draining capacitors would be needed for the shot.

"Done!" Skippy shouted triumphantly a few seconds later. "Scratch twelve targets! Damn, I am *good*! We may be able to hit another ship in a couple seconds, it's at a bad angle right now, but in a few- No, damn it, the stupid thing just jumped away. Oh, well, you can't have everything. Joe, tell me the truth, am I awesome, or am I awesome?"

"Between those two excellent choices, I will choose awesome, Skippy. I would have celebrated your awesome awesomeness without prompting. And you are not just good, you are the *best*. The best ever. How could any being be more awesome than you?" Ok, maybe I was laying the praise on a little thick.

"I will accept your praise graciously, woefully inadequate though it is. You are doing the best your puny monkey brain can do to marvel at my awesomeness."

I had to laugh. "You are *such* an asshole sometimes. But I love you anyway."

"And I find you mostly almost tolerable, Joe."

"I appreciate that. You got a sitrep for us?"

"Affirmative on the sitrep, Colonel," Skippy said in a sarcastic tone. He hated military acronyms. "We hit fourteen ships, and all fourteen ships were completely destroyed. That includes their battlecruiser and both cruisers. Only two ships even had time to start charging their defensive shield projectors, and that didn't do them any good. It would be easier to list which ships the Kristang have left, than to the list the ones we destroyed."

"Understood, go ahead."

"The Kristang have ten warships remaining; five destroyers and five frigates. On the Ruhar side, the ships are that combat ready are one cruiser, three destroyers and two frigates. That cruiser would seem to give the Ruhar a slight advantage, but the Kristang design philosophy for destroyers makes them more like the equivalent of a Ruhar light cruiser. The Kristang still have the advantage of combat power."

"Yeah, but we have the projectors," I reminded him.

"Two of those projectors are now almost depleted, Joe. Their remaining power is inadequate to penetrate the shields of a starship, even if we fired both of those projectors at the same target. Each of the other two healthy projectors are capable of one shot each; they could destroy a ship if we fired both at the same target. Unfortunately, those two projectors are poorly positioned to hit the same target; the enemy ship would need to be within a very small slice of the sky for the projectors to have line of sight to it. That won't happen, because now that the enemy knows where at least four of our projectors are, their ships will avoid the space covered by them."

"Yeah," I said, looking at Adams, "we need to get Perkins working on activating that other projector as soon as she can. Those Kristang ships are sure to test whether those four projectors are the only ones active. If we can fire another projector, the Kristang will assume we have capabilities we haven't revealed yet. If they jump in and we can't shoot at them, they'll know that we're bluffing, and then we'll be in deep shit real quick. Skippy, can you provide cover for Perkins if her team needs to work fast? We can't let them wait for night."

"Affirmative, Joe. Without the prying eyes of starships overhead, I can conceal Major Perkins' Buzzard from being detected, unless someone happens to eyeball them while they are digging. And when they are done and need to fly away, I can give the pilot a route for maximum concealment. They do still have the problem of needing to refuel before they can reach the next projector site. Joe, I do not think we will have much trouble concealing the actions of a lone Buzzard."

"Why is that?"

"Because, Joe, very soon I expect the skies over Paradise to be filled with Ruhar and Kristang aircraft, fighting the biggest air battle in several hundred years. The Kristang landed over three hundred aircraft, plus they captured additional Ruhar aircraft when they took over territory under terms of the cease fire. The Ruhar have almost six hundred aircraft, but they have a civilian population to protect, and more of their aircraft are unarmed civilian transports. Without starships overhead, those aircraft are the best way to establish control over the surface of Paradise. We should expect- Yes. Joe, the Kristang just launched a wave of dropships and aircraft in an attack on two Ruhar airbases. The Ruhar have detected the launch and are scrambling aircraft to intercept. This is going to get ugly very quickly."

Saily Chernandagren walked out of the hangar toward her Dobreh fighter. The aircraft she would be flying that day was 'hers', which wasn't always the case given how often high-performance Dobrehs needed to go off the flight line for maintenance. That day, her mission was a simple check ride, to test a thruster unit that had been replaced. It should be a simple, relatively short flight. Although it was only a short flight, the Dobreh was fully armed with missiles; while Kristang were still on and above the planet they were technically at war. Neither Saily nor any other Ruhar trusted the Kristang to adhere to the cease fire agreement.

"Your pet wants a cookie," Juff Blander said sourly, pointing at Derek Bonsu, who was opening an access cover. The human, too eager to please, always opened the access covers so that pilots could perform their preflight inspections faster. Juff was Saily's copilot and Weapon Systems Officer, who sat in the back seat of the Dobreh.

"He's not my pet," Saily protested, knowing her words were falling on deaf ears. Her Wizzo had nothing personal against Derek; Jeff simply did not like humans, any humans. Like Saily, Juff was a native to Gehtanu; his family on both sides had been on Gehtanu for three generations. His entire family had been forcibly evacuated by the humans. Juff had been scheduled to join them on the trip up the space elevator in little over a month, when the Ruhar fleet arrived and took the planet back. "You shouldn't be mean to him. We may be leaving this planet if the Kristang stay here, but he is going to die," she said sadly.

"They are not my problem," Jeff said angrily. "They came here with the Kristang." He stared at the human, his anger softening. The pilot was right; if the Kristang kept Gehtanu, the humans eventually would suffer a terrible fate. "Saily, this is just a check ride," Juff commented, "take him instead."

"Are you sure?" Saily asked, surprised.

"Yes." There was an increasing volume of rumors that the Ruhar federal government was not sending the fleet to fight the Kristang; that Gehtanu was not important enough to fight for. If that rumor was true, Derek Bonsu did not have much longer to live. The human had actively assisted the Ruhar, helped to maintain their combat aircraft. The Kristang would find that to be an unforgivable betrayal, and the thin-skinned Kristang never forgave any slight, no matter how minor. "This may be his last opportunity to fly. Go," he urged, "before I change my mind."

CHAPTER EIGHTEEN

"Your aircraft," Saily announced, releasing the controls. The Dobreh was on autopilot, cruising at only fifteen thousand meters altitude as measured by humans. Every system had operated perfectly in the flight, including the replacement thruster unit. The only way to test the thruster to its full capabilities was at high altitude, up where the air was so thin that thrusters were needed to control the gunship's flight. "Take us up."

"Yes Ma'am," Derek acknowledged as he deactivated the autopilot, and set the controls for the airspeed and attitude that allowed a maximum climb rate. The Dobreh zoomed toward the upper edge of the atmosphere, where its engines strained to gulp in enough air to keep the aircraft aloft. Soon, the wings began to lose lift and Derek needed to push the nose down to maintain airspeed, or the thin air flowing over the wings would cause a stall. A Dobreh could hover at up to twenty thousand meters; already he had the engine pods pointed down slightly so their thrust helped keep the gunship aloft. "Losing roll control," Derek reported as the wings began to wobble. He had not been this high, other than in a simulator, for over a year. The Ruhar aircraft flew like a dream; the controls were light and responsive. The ship did everything he asked of it and told him there was more, so much more that it could do and was eager to do. Even at this extreme altitude with the engines straining, when he touched the throttle, he could feel there was reserve power he had not used yet. If he had not been concentrating so hard on the instruments, he would have had a moment to realize this was the happiest he had been in months.

Coming to Paradise, once something Derek had burned with patriotic fervor to do, had become a nightmare. UNEF was trapped, not even the Kristang had access to Earth. The Expeditionary Force were all prisoners of war, forced to grow their own food. Their 'allies' the Kristang had been revealed to be cruel deceivers, caring only about using UNEF and enslaving humanity. Duty for UNEF was now all about survival on a planet with the Ruhar in charge. Now the Kristang were back, and survival might not be possible. If Derek had stopped to think about that, he would plunge into despair. So he thought only of how joyous it was to fly this powerful alien fighter aircraft, high above an alien planet.

The roll was getting worse. A Ruhar pilot, with their genetically-enhanced reflexes, might have been able to keep ahead of the aircraft's shuddering, but Derek needed help to halt the rolling tendency before it snapped the Dobreh over on its back. He consoled himself with the thought that the purpose of going this high was to test the thruster unit, which he now needed. "Engaging thrusters to stabilize."

Saily looked at her instruments to monitor the performance of the new thruster unit, which was not actually new. It was a rebuilt unit that had been recovered from a Dobreh shot down by her own people, back when a human had been flying the doomed aircraft and the Ruhar fleet came back to retake control of the planet. She would have preferred a truly new thruster unit, but of course spare parts were no longer being shipped to Gehtanu. The thruster was operating perfectly, and Derek had confident control of the aircraft, so she took her eyes away from the instruments for a glance out the canopy.

Up this high, the sky above was black, and the curve of the planet below was noticeable. It looked so peaceful; the land to the north so green, the ocean below them so blue, the cloud tops so brilliantly white. Above, her eyes caught sunlight reflecting off something, and she blinked to enhance the vision in her helmet visor. A Kristang ship. A big one. The image wobbled enough that she couldn't quite tell if that ship above her was the battlegroup's command ship, but she thought that likely. If she wanted, she could have viewed the image from one of the Dobreh's cameras, but she did not care to see the enemy ship that closely. Her eyes turned back to the instruments, so she missed by a microsecond the intense white flare coming up from the planet's surface. She knew that she shouldn't look toward a maser beam, but her instincts made her look briefly before her training took over. So she didn't miss the projector's second shot. Or the even brighter fireball of that Kristang cruiser exploding.

"Engage stealth," Saily ordered calmly as she was momentarily blinded by the intense light of the maser burning its way up through clouds. "Take us down on the deck."

Derek did not hesitate. He had not seen the initial maser shot, but caught the second beam out of the corner of his eye. Immediately, he had closed his eyes and looked away, so his vision was unaffected. The first thing he did was activate the stealth field, and the bright sunlight coming in through the canopy disappeared, as a curtain of darkness draped over the aircraft. From now on, he would be flying entirely on instruments, which did not bother him. When the stealth field had been powered up, long thin wires had extended from each wingtip and the tail. The ends of the wires peeked out beyond the stealth field and provided sensor data. The canopy automatically switched over to provide a view, a composite image of what the sensors said were outside.

He did not make the mistake of reducing power for at that altitude, the Dobreh would have stalled and gone into a spin. Thrusters could have recovered from the spin, which the aircraft would have done automatically, but with a shooting war going on above his head, Derek had been trained to reserve thruster fuel. He pointed the Dobreh's nose down and felt his body moving upward against the seat straps as the gunship hit the top of the arc, and he was momentarily weightless. Then the sensation of weight gradually returned and he concentrated on keeping airspeed to Vst, the speed for maximum stealth. He had to run the engines at almost minimum power and monitor airflow over the wings so the Dobreh passed through the atmosphere as smoothly as possible. The problem with using stealth in an atmosphere was that enemy sensors could track him by the warm, roiling air behind the Dobreh. If he had to engage in air combat, stealth would be almost a liability; the engines would be putting out enough heat and turbulent air that he might as well hold up a sign saying 'shoot me'.

With the aircraft in a stable descent trimmed for optimal stealth, Derek had time to scan the sensors and assess the situation. He had just turned his attention to the tactical display when another Kristang ship overhead exploded. Or a piece of a ship had exploded, because he could run the display back and see that ship had been struck by a powerful maser beam in the initial strike. Stunned, Derek toggled the display back and expanded the coverage for a wider area. He gasped with shock when he saw what the sensor data revealed. The Kristang battlegroup in orbit had been hit hard by four powerful maser cannons on the surface. *Maser cannons*.

"You've hit the Kristang! Yeah!" Derek shouted and pumped a fist toward the canopy. "Thank you!"

"That wasn't us," Saily responded tersely. It was the first words they had exchanged since the attack began. She had been monitoring the sensors and communicating with the airbase to find out what in the *hell* was going on. No one had answers; Ruhar command appeared to be as surprised as anyone. "We don't have projectors like that. If we did, we would have used them when the Kristang were raiding us."

"Not you? Then, who?" Derek asked, completely confused. "It's not *us* is it? UNEF?"

"No, not humans either. I do not know what is going on. Cut the chatter," she ordered.

Derek cut the chatter and turned his focus back to the sensors. He suddenly realized that since the start of the crisis, Saily had trusted him with complete control of the aircraft, her aircraft.

"We've been ordered to return to base," Saily announced.

Craig Alanson

"On course," Derek acknowledged. He had assumed that was where Saily wanted to go so they were already flying in that direction. The check ride was clearly over.

Saily must have been happy with his flying, because she didn't say anything to him for several minutes. Still flying with maximum stealth, they crossed the shore and were now over land. At their present slow airspeed, the base was forty seven minutes away. Derek checked status of the weapons, which Saily had not enabled yet. As a human, Derek knew he was not trusted with weapons. They would return to the airbase and Saily would likely be reprimanded for flying with an unauthorized weapon system officer. Derek's flying days would be over; it was likely he would soon find himself tending crops in Lemuria.

And he did not care. The Kristang battlegroup was gone; with many of their ships obliterated by powerful maser cannons, they would think very carefully about approaching the planet again. They were free! Humans were free! Or at least free to be prisoner of war under the Ruhar. Derek no longer felt a constant fear of a Kristang sword hanging over his neck. No matter what else happened, they-

"My aircraft," Saily said curtly, and the control stick went slack in Derek's hand.

"Roger that," he replied, and mentally switched back to Wizzo mode.

Since the main battlegroup had arrived to take control over Pradassis, the Swift Arrow clan frigate *To Seek Glory in Battle is Glorious* had been relieved of her dangerous raiding duties, because there were to be no more raids. A cease fire was in effect, a cease fire with generous conditions that had shocked the crew of the *Glory* when they heard about it. Why Admiral Kekrando had made so many concessions to an enemy whose position was so weak, almost no one in his battlegroup could understand. Kekrando had sent a message to all ships, that he was following strict instructions from clan leadership. The clan leaders strongly desired a negotiated agreement for the cowardly and treacherous Ruhar to leave Pradassis, Kekrando had explained, his voice almost choking with outraged disgust as he read the words. Unsaid, but implied, was that the Swift Arrow clan's resources were stretched very thin at the moment. With the prospect of a civil war within the Kristang looming, the clan could not afford to support a protracted battle for Pradassis. The cowardly Ruhar civilian government had already agreed to the concept of abandoning, *surrendering*, the world their military had fought very hard for. All that remained was for the two sides to agree to a price, and now that Kekrando's powerful battlegroup had established total supremacy in the space on and around Pradassis, the Swift Arrow leaders were confident they could ultimately get the entire planet for a cheap price.

The question of why the Swift Arrow clan wanted a world whose chief product was grain had never been stated. Most of the warriors in the battlegroup had never been to the backwater world of Pradassis before, and what they saw was not impressive. Looking down at a world dotted here and there with the parallel stripes of agricultural fields, most of the ship's crews considered that the real reason they had been sent on a one-way mission was to uphold the honor of their clan and their entire species. Because there was no other conceivable reason why the clan leadership had sent so much of the clan's precious combat power to such an unimportant planet. The clan leadership was wise, Kekrando had stated in an unconvincing tone; the brave warriors of the battlegroup needed to have faith in their leadership, and concentrate on executing their mission to the greater honor and credit of the clan.

When the crew of the *Glory* heard Kekrando's speech, the little frigate's captain had turned to his executive officer and muttered the Kristang equivalent of 'blah blah blah'. Words were passing things, and it mattered not why the battlegroup was there. What mattered was the mission that had been assigned to the battlegroup, to each ship, and to each crewman. The current mission assigned to the *Glory*, each and every one of her crew agreed, sucked. It sucked big time. It could have sucked a bowling ball through fifty feet of garden hose, that's how badly it sucked. After taking enormous risks as the chief raiding ship before the bulk of the battlegroup arrived, the *Glory*'s crew had expected a nice, cushy assignment. The frigate would tie up next to a support ship, they expected, for extended maintenance and repairs. Maintenance that was long overdue. While engineering teams worked feverishly to bring the frigate back up to full combat potential, most of the crew could enjoy some well-deserved shore leave on the planet they had been viewing from space for so long.

But, no! That was not their assignment. After the long journey to Pradassis, many of Kekrando's heavy ships needed maintenance and replenishment, and those much more valuable ships were given priority attention by the support vessels. The battered, worn-out little *Glory* was given a lonely task, a task for which frigates had been designed. She was to shadow the Ruhar Commodore Ferlant's remaining task force. And so, the *Glory* was positioned roughly one light minute away from Ferlant's loosely clustered ships; one minute closer to Pradassis. Ferlant's ships had mostly been sitting in one spot since the cease fire, licking their wounds and biding their time. *Glory*'s captain considered that, no matter how unhappy the warriors of the Swift Arrow task force were about their current mission, the Ruhar of Ferlant's task force had to be even more unhappy. They had failed. They had failed to protect their planet from damaging raids by a handful of isolated Kristang ships, and now they had completely lost control of the star system. What awaited Ferlant's crews was a humiliating wait for negotiations to conclude, and then a retreat with their tails tucked between their legs. If the Ruhar crews had been Kristang warriors, it would be a long time, if ever, before they could hold their heads in anything but utter shame. A Kristang would enthusiastically embrace death before enduring such dishonor. Or so the Kristang told themselves with bravado, while they had such an overwhelming advantage in combat power around Pradassis.

While their little ship performed its lonely picket duty, keeping an eye on Ferlant's impotent ships, the *Glory*'s crew went about fixing up the ship as best they could. With the ship technically being constantly at battle stations, they could not take many critical systems offline for badly needed maintenance. So they did what they could, and waited for relief. Surely Admiral Kekrando's staff would send another frigate to replace the *Glory* eventually, and the ship could be returned to full combat capability. Surely that would happen, soon.

"Signal received!" The ship's communications officer shouted excitedly. "The order is option *Green*?" The man sputtered in surprise. "We are to execute immediately!"

Concealing his shock, and resigned to his fate, the ship's captain gave the order with a calm due more to weariness than bravery. "Execute plan Green, as soon as possible," he said sadly to his executive officer.

"Yes, Captain," the man replied quietly, and turned to engage the ship's poorly maintained jump drive system. "The condition of the drive, is-"

"I know," the captain said without taking his eyes off the tactical display. "Do the best you can. We must jump as quickly as possible."

"The best possible," the executive officer said while studying the indicators for jump dive coil status, "will barely get there in time." The signal from Pradassis had continued past the *Glory* and would reach the Ruhar task force in less than one minute. Presumably, the Ruhar on the planet had sent their own signal to Commodore Ferlant's ships. If the *Glory* were to have any advantage of surprise, she needed to arrive in the midst of the Ruhar formation before the signal did.

"Understood," the captain acknowledged. He could read the drive status on his own display. He turned his attention to the officer monitoring the sensor console. "What happened down there?" Option Green was one of five contingencies established by Admiral Kekrando, with Green being a plan to be activated only if the battlegroup somehow suffered a catastrophic loss. How could that have happened?

The officer had been frantically pushing buttons and spinning dials. Confused and shocked, he looked up from the console. "Captain, it appears the Ruhar violated the cease fire. They attacked our battlegroup using projectors."

"*Projectors*?" The captain exchanged an astonished look with his executive officer. "You are certain?" The *Glory*'s sensors were in poor condition and far overdue for important components to be replaced. There must be a mistake; a sensor glitch.

"Yes, Captain. There is no mistake. I can clearly see three projectors firing, and another is behind the curve of the planet's horizon."

"*Projectors*?" The Captain repeated. "When did the Ruhar install projectors? How? They did it right under our noses?"

"Fleet intelligence will have a difficult time explaining this," the executive officer noted. "We have lost eleven ships so far, including the *Victorious*; she was struck first. The attack is continuing. Or, it was," he added, remembering that the light picked up by the ship's sensors was now several light minutes old.

"Eleven ships?" The Captain said, stunned. This was indeed a catastrophic event. A disaster for the battlegroup, and for the Swift Arrow clan. He now understood why Kekrando ordered option Green. The order called for the *Glory* to abandon her picket duty, jump into the midst of the Ruhar formation, and attack. Attack and cause as much damage as she could, until she was disabled or destroyed. Option Green called for little *To Seek Glory in Battle is Glorious* to fight to the death; her own death. "When we jump in, head straight for the Ruhar cruiser at maximum speed," he ordered the executive officer. The man nodded soberly. Since the *Glory* could not survive the upcoming fight, she would truly seek glory by attempting to ram the Ruhar cruiser *Ruh Gastalo*.

"The clan will sing about the glory of our battle forever," the executive officer said loudly, so the entire bridge crew could hear clearly. Privately, he thought of the frigate's brother ship *Every day is a Good Day to Die in Battle*. That ship had died in battle already. Was this day, a very ordinary day until moments ago, a good day to die? As good as any, the exec thought. Although he would have preferred some warning to mentally prepare himself. "Jump drive is ready, Captain," he announced. "Engaging now."

Aboard his command ship *Ruh Gastalo*, Commodore Ferlant's mind was still reeling. What else could go wrong with this mission, he asked himself? It was supposed to be a simple and relatively easy assignment. The fleet had taken Gehtanu away from the Kristang. With their losses elsewhere in the sector, the Thuranin were in no position to support a Kristang effort to retain control of the star system. Unexpectedly, a handful of Kristang ships had stayed in the system and began raiding the planet. That was an annoyance, not a serious threat. Then, the Kristang had inexplicably began shooting at the clients the 'humans', and the Chief Administrator of Gehtanu had informed Ferlant that his task force needed to protect the humans also. Ferlant's ships were already stretched thin protecting the northern continent of Tenturo. Extending coverage to the southern continent greatly strained his ships' ability to protect the Ruhar population and infrastructure on Tenturo.

Then, just when Ferlant thought he had discouraged the raiders, the Kristang out of nowhere had arrived with an entire battlegroup! Ruhar fleet intelligence had assured Ferlant that there was no way the Kristang would or could reinforce their few ships near

Gehtanu. No way, there was no possibility that the Kristang would even be able to get weapons and spare parts to their ships. All Ferlant needed to do, Fleet Intelligence had told him, was to hang on until the Kristang ships fell apart. The impossible had happened, and Ferlant had barely escaped with his tiny force intact.

Having an enemy battlegroup appear absolutely out of nowhere, to land practically in his lap had been shocking enough. Moments before, he had received notice that *projectors* on Gehtanu had destroyed much of the Kristang battlegroup. The message from the Ruhar government on the planet had screamed at him why Ferlant had violated the cease fire, and why he had not informed the government about the defense capabilities of their own planet. After wasting a few precious seconds on paralyzing shock, Ferlant had replied that he knew nothing about any projectors on Gehtanu, and why hadn't the government informed *him*? Then he ordered his task force to immediately begin dispersing according to Action Plan 3. Because some of his ships were undergoing running repairs, they could not initiate a jump until they switched to backup systems. Ferlant was holding his own cruiser back to cover the stragglers.

"*MecMurro* reports ready for jump, Commodore." A bridge officer behind Ferlant reported.

Without turning away from the main tactical display, Ferlant acknowledged with a curt nod. "Wait until *MecMurro*'s jump is confirmed successful, then take us to the rendezvous-"

"Enemy ship jumped in! One frigate. It, it's that damned Target Beta *Glorious* something, whatever its name is," the officer reported. "That damned lucky ship that kept raiding us."

Ferlant's lip curled in a wry smile. "That little ship is annoyingly persistent, isn't she?"

"Commodore, if we turn to expose our starboard railgun battery, we could take that ship out with one shot," the officer suggested.

"Yes," Ferlant's eyes narrowed as he stared at the red symbol in the tactical display. That little enemy ship had been the bane of his existence. He could finally be rid of it with one shot. "You have permission to maneuver the ship."

By luck more than skill, the frigate's creaky jump drive somehow brought the ship into the Ruhar formation, and miraculously less than seventy thousand kilometers from the *Ruh Gastalo*. Against the much larger and heavily shielded Ruhar cruiser, the *Glory* had no chance even for a suicide run, for the cruiser's weapons would pound the little frigate into space dust long before the *Glory* approached. *Glory* aimed her own maser cannons and fired, with the beams easily deflected by the cruiser's more powerful shields. The *Glory* had to turn more than ninety degrees to engage the *Ruh Gastalo*, and by the time the frigate made the turn and began accelerating with maximum force, the executive officer noticed something odd.

Where were the other ships of Commodore Ferlant's small task force? There were only two ships within the frigate's sensor bubble, and as he watched, a destroyer jumped away, leaving only the cruiser. As the *Glory* was rocked by direct maser fire from *Ruh Gastalo*, the executive officer's fingers flew over his own console. The other ships had jumped away, only moments ago! He could still detect strong residual jump signatures. The ship was rocked again. "Captain!" He shouted a warning. "Shields collapsing!" One more maser volley from *Ruh Gastalo*, and the *Glory* would be defenseless. She was still over sixty thousand kilometers from the target. By the time the cruiser blew up the frigate's reactor, *Glory* would be too far away for the cruiser to be damaged by the explosion. The crew of the *Glory* would die without having struck a significant blow against their long-hated enemy. If today was indeed a good day to die, it was not a good day to find glory in battle. The frigate would find only frustration and death, not glory.

Why was the cruiser not firing her railguns? At such short range, a single railgun round could easily penetrate the Glory's hull bow to stern, and-

In a burst of gamma radiation, the cruiser vanished. "What happened?" The exec asked himself. "Captain, the enemy ship has jumped away. They all jumped away. We can," he looked to the sensor officer for confirmation. "We might be able to follow one of the ships; their jump signatures are very recent and strong." Catching the sensor officer's worried look, the exec added "Considering the condition of our sensors, we would be using guesses more than science to track an enemy ship, Captain."

"No," the Captain replied, suppressing a shudder of relief at having avoided death once again. "Our orders were to attack the enemy task force. It has now dispersed, and we are unable to follow. Send a signal to the Green rendezvous point," the hopefully secret location where the battlegroup was to assemble. "Inform them that the enemy task force has dispersed, and request orders. The enemy received the news before we did," the Captain declared with a mixture of regret and gratitude.

"Or," the executive officer said darkly, "they knew the exact timing of their projector attack, and fled away for safety. The Ruhar are both treacherous and cowardly, Captain."

The Captain nodded silently, agreeing with the obvious wisdom of his executive officer's statement. To himself, the Captain said a prayer. With the cease fire now over, Kristang ships might again be called upon to raid Pradassis. This time, powerful maser cannons would be the primary threat to raiding ships. What could the battered little frigate do against a projector? Nothing. Except to serve as target practice. "They are treacherous, and cowardly," the Captain observed. "And, apparently, they are very, very clever."

At the *Ruh Gastalo*'s assigned Action Plan 3 primary jump point, the cruiser emerged in a gamma ray burst. She ejected quantum resonators to cover the tracks of her next jump, and as soon as the ship's jump drive was realigned, she jumped again to the secondary point. There would be three more jumps before she rejoined the task force; a precaution because Action Plan 3 assumed the enemy would be pursuing, chasing Ferlant's task force around the star system.

The cruiser jumped again, and proceeded away in a random direction at full thrust, waiting for her jump drive to recharge. "Jump successful, Commodore. No sign of pursuit. Commodore, may I ask why we did not fire railguns at that enemy frigate?"

Ferlant turned away from the tactical display. This was an opportunity to provide coaching to the young officers of his staff. "That frigate has somehow survived against the odds, at times when it seemed certain her fate was sealed. Fate has determined this is not yet her time. I have learned that one should never argue with Fate."

"Eeeeaaargh!" Admiral Kekrando shouted in a frustration that felt like physical pain, and he quickly spun to find something, anything, that he could smash. His officers knew from long experience never to be close at hand when the admiral was enraged, which happened frequently. The never-ending hero of the admiral's staff was their lowest-ranking member, who had the task of sprinkling around the bridge things that broke in a satisfying but non-lethal manner. Electronic tablet? Yes. Pistol with fully-charged energy pack that might explode if broken in just the right manner? No. Pistol with depleted energy pack that would give very satisfying sparks and, at worst, a few second-degree burns to an unlucky person on the bridge? Very much yes. It was a great system, a system that had worked many, many times over.

Paradise

The system had never been tested under such intensely stressful conditions. Kekrando had been preparing for a war game, which was why he was aboard the destroyer *We are Proud to Follow the Shining Example of Combat Rifleman Tuut-uas-Val Kedwala* instead of his command ship the *He Who Pushes Aside Fear Shall Always be Victorious*. Which was why he was currently alive rather than a random assortment of rapidly cooling subatomic particles. Kekrando had wished to observe the performance of the *Victorious*, and the best way to do that was to get off that ship so its captain and crew did not have an admiral looking over their shoulders. Fortunately, he had already been able observe the *Victorious* in high-intensity combat. Unfortunately, that combat action had told him nothing illustrative about the performance of that ship's crew, because the battle had been a sneak attack by a ground-based projector against an unshielded ship. And because the *Victorious* was no longer an organized collection of components that resembled a starship.

"Eeeeaaargh!" Kekrando repeated, shocked, enraged and humiliated at the incomprehensible defeat he had suffered. What were *projectors* doing on Pradassis, of all places?! Seeing a pistol in its assigned slot on a bulkhead, he pulled the lever to release it and threw the weapon to the deck. It broke in several pieces, and its power pack came apart, spewing sparks around the bridge. One spark hit the sleeve of the officer sitting at the destroyer's sensor station, where that officer was running an analysis of the projector attack over and over again, trying to comprehend what had happened. Instead of flinching as the hot metal burned through his sleeve and into the skin of his forearm, the officer merely brushed it away as an annoyance. He burned his fingers, and distractedly put the throbbing fingers in his mouth. His attention never wavered from the display.

Something about that further enraged the admiral, plus the pistol breaking apart had not been as satisfying as it had been in the past. He reached over to one of his security staff, yanked the man's pistol from its holster, and fired at the sensor console. The console exploded, sending metal and composites flying around the bridge, some pieces even striking the admiral. Because consoles were designed not to injure their operators, the sensor officer was not badly injured. He was knocked off his chair, and came shakily back to his feet, with stars in his eyes to see an angry admiral pointing a smoking pistol at his face.

The officer did not flinch. If Kekrando wanted to kill him for any reason, there was nothing the officer could do about it. He and his family ranked too low in the clan hierarchy to even protest. "Please, Admiral, if it serves the clan for me to die, then do it quickly so the ship can pursue the enemy."

Kekrando snorted. First with surprise, then with laughter. "Ha! Give me another hundred such men, and I will conquer the galaxy." He flipped the pistol back to his guard, looked the at stricken sensor officer and demanded "Well? What are you able to tell me?"

The sensor officer strode over to a secondary console and activated it with no mention of the nearly-fatal incident. "We were attacked by four projectors, Admiral."

"Only four?" Kekrando was surprised. During the vicious sneak attack, it had seemed like the entire planet below had sprouted projectors, spitting deadly maser fire up at his ships.

"Only four," the man confirmed. "They are oddly clustered together; the enemy's coverage of the sky is poor with only those four."

"Four *active*, you mean?" Kekrando asked. "How many others?"

"No, Admiral, there are only those four. The sensor data did not detect targeting signals from any other sources. Two of the four projectors, here, and here," he indicated, "are nearly depleted. We can tell from the reduced power of their last shots."

"It *cannot* be possible that the enemy has only four projectors on the entire planet," the Admiral stated.

The officer did not back down. "According to clan intelligence, Admiral, it cannot be possible that the enemy has even one projector on Pradassis."

Kekrando looked at the man sharply, to see if the admiral was being mocked. No, the man had correctly directed his scorn at the clan's intelligence group. "Ha!" The Admiral snorted. "Only two projectors to worry about, eh? We will see about that."

"Admiral?" The destroyer's captain took the opportunity to step in. "Will we be pursuing the enemy ships?"

"Some of us will, Captain," Kekrando replied. "And some of our ships will be testing how many projectors the enemy truly has."

CHAPTER NINETEEN

"Can *someone* please explain to me what just happened?" Deputy Administrator Baturnah Logellia asked her staff in exasperation. She knew she was being unfair to her dedicated people. The Chief Administrator's office had shouted at her moments ago, so she was shouting at her staffers. They would shout at their own teams in turn, all the way down. And no one knew anything useful.

"You!" She pointed at her military liaison, who was engaged in an animated conversation through an earpiece in his right ear, and had a second phone held up to his left ear. "Why, and *how*, did we fire on those Kristang ships?" The cease fire had been thoroughly and very effectively broken. After jumping away, Admiral Kekrando of the Kristang had warned of severe consequences from the remaining ships in his still-dangerous task force.

The man lowered the phone from his left ear. "Pardon me, Administrator Logellia. *We* did not fire on the Kristang."

"I know that *we* didn't," she tried to control her anger. The military had taken rash action that put at risk the civilian population; people she was responsible for. "Commodore Ferlant-"

"It was not Commodore Ferlant." The liaison officer stated firmly. "I received a message from his executive officer a moment ago. They were as surprised as we were. The Commodore has no idea who fired. In fact, *he* accused *us* of doing something that he considers to be incredibly stupid."

"Well," Baturnah threw up her hands in exasperation. "The planet didn't shoot at the Kristang by itself."

"No, clearly," he agreed. "They were projectors, powerful maser cannons."

"I know what a projector is, Slean," she used the man's surname. "Whose projectors, if not ours?" She knew one thing for damned sure; the Ruhar government had never installed projectors on Gehtanu. There was no way such a monumental effort could have been concealed.

"It had to be the Kristang, ma'am. Before we first came to Gehtanu. Somehow," it was his turn to throw up his hands, "someone activated them. Four projectors, at least, by our last count."

Baturnah's head was spinning. "You think they have been buried here, practically beneath our feet, all this time?"

"That is the only explanation we can think of, currently," Slean responded somewhat distractedly. He was listening to another, or several other, conversations in his earpiece.

"Now that we know what these projectors look like, we should surely be able to scan for them, can't we? We must understand what we are dealing with, and who caused those projectors to fire without our authority."

"Yes, ma'am, we can scan, but the projectors are likely concealed by a stealth field and other countermeasures. That is why we never detected them before."

"We weren't looking before," Baturnah said hopefully. "We must immediately begin to scan the subsurface for-"

"Excuse me, ma'am, but we will not be able to spare any aircraft for scanning projectors or even to investigate and secure the four we know of. Administrator, please come with me, we need to get you to safety."

"Why?" She did not budge from behind her desk. "The Kristang have gone," she pointed to the ceiling.

"Their ships are gone for the moment, yes. Administrator, we are faced with an almost unique military situation. With neither side having ships in orbit, combat aircraft become the most powerful means of securing control of this planet. I was just informed that the Kristang have launched waves of aircraft targeting our own airfields. The situation is very dangerous."

"We must be responding with our own aircraft?"

"Yes, ma'am," Slean said, gesturing for the Administrator's personal security team to hustle her away to an air raid shelter. "No one has fought a pure air battle like this in several generations. Unfortunately, ma'am, we are about to see firsthand whether all our theories of air combat strategy are worth the training time we invested. I suggest you be someplace safe when theory meets reality."

Baturnah nodded, accepting the pleading look from her personal security team. "Very well. In my experience, Mr. Slean, whenever theory meets reality, theory loses."

"Yes, ma'am," the military liaison officer agreed, and turned his attention to coordinating crisis response teams. For this was certainly a crisis.

For the initial wave of air attacks by the Kristang, they quickly launched dropships to fly high cover and provide the massed aircraft below with long-range sensor and targeting data. With laser links between the attacking aircraft and the three dropships, the attackers could stand off at a safe distance and launch missiles at well-defended targets. Once the Ruhar defenses were degraded, the aircraft could fly in to attack their primary targets.

The three dropships were perfectly positioned for their role in the attack. They had climbed high so their sensors swept the area between the Kristang aircraft and the Ruhar airbase, and with their active sensors able to detect a roughly location for even stealthed Ruhar aircraft, the Kristang aircraft were able to hug the terrain at low altitude and remain in stealth. Because dropships could climb above an atmosphere, they could not be effectively engaged by aircraft, so the Ruhar had to send their own very limited number of dropships to counter the Kristang. At the start of the massive air battle, the Ruhar were at a serious disadvantage in combat power. Until the Kristang battlegroup arrived, the Ruhar had assumed their defensive needs could be handled by Commodore Ferlant's small task force. The Ruhar federal government had not wanted to ship combat aircraft and dropships all the way to a remote planet they intended to leave. Most of the combat air power the Ruhar had at the start of the air battle was left over from when humans had used them during the evacuation. Due to need for regular maintenance on the worn-out aircraft and lack of spare parts, thirty percent of the Ruhar's combat aircraft were unavailable when the Kristang launched their attack.

Thanks to Skippy, we had a complete view of the developing air battle that would become known among humans as The Great Paradise Furball. With hundreds of aircraft tangling in intense dogfights, it was like a ball of fur rolling around and around in the sky. The Ruhar and Kristang had similar names for the battle, and no one involved ever forgot a single detail.

The first shot in The Great Paradise Furball wasn't fired by the Kristang, or the Ruhar. It was fired by a shiny beer can. Those three dropships looked like trouble to me. While I wasn't a fighter pilot, my infantry experience had taught me the value of high ground, and those dropships had the high ground. "Skippy, can you do something about those three dropships?"

"Yeah, yeah, I got it, Joe. No problemo."

"No problem? You told us that each projector can only cover twenty eight percent of the sky from its position," I reminded our smart-ass AI.

"Twenty eight percent on a projector's normal settings, Joe. I am going to cheat."

"Of course you are," I rolled my eyes. "Please, Oh Greatest of Great Ones, allow us mere mortals a glimpse into your awesomely wondrous plan."

"Oooh! I like that. Damn, Joe, that almost sounded sincere. Hmmm, from now on, I'm going to make you monkeys address me that way when you want something, like me programming the jump drive."

"That sounds like an excellent deal, Skippy. And from now on, I'm going to move you from your personal escape pod man cave, to a little basket on the side of the toilet next to the galley."

"On second thought, Joe, you can just keep calling me Skippy the Magnificent."

"How about Asshole Almighty?"

"I'm sure we can reach a compromise somewhere in there, Joe."

"I'm sure we can. Is this where you're going to warp spacetime to bend the maser beam, or something like that?

"No, Joe, I am not going to bend a beam of light, you moron. I can only do that over longer ranges. And I can't warp spacetime so close to an inhabited planet; that's too dangerous. Do you want to hear what I'm going to do?"

"No, you talked too freakin' long, Skippy," I pointed to the display with symbols for the dropships, which were now at about their maximum altitude. They were about to launch missiles at a Ruhar airbase. "We don't have time for talk. You need to show me."

Skippy did show me, and I would give that show a five out of five in terms of entertainment. The Kristang dropship pilots didn't leave a review after the action because they were, you know, dead. I'm thinking their review would not have been five stars.

The three dropships very reasonably thought they were safe from attack by projectors. The dropships were at high altitude; higher than an aircraft could fly, but not so high that they were above the atmosphere. The dropships were to the south of the direct path from the Kristang airbase to their Ruhar targets; going to the south brought them out of the targeting cones of the four projectors they knew about. The dropship pilots were aware that they were being used as bait to determine whether we had projectors we hadn't used yet. Still, they surely must have thought they were safe from being struck by the four projectors they knew about.

They should have been safe. They did not know about Skippy.

"Hey, Skippy," I pointed at the display. "Those dropships are in stealth. How can you determine their position closely enough to target them?"

"Simple, Joey. I asked them to tell me."

"Huh?"

"Following standard Kristang practice, those dropships are sharing data with a tightbeam laserlink. That allows them to, for one thing, avoid crashing into each other while they are in stealth. The problem for them is that while the laser beam is narrow, it does bounce off air molecules, and because I am the all-seeing Skippy the Magnificent, I can tell exactly where those ships are. Now, shut up for a minute and let me do my thing."

Skippy being the genius that he is, he was able to make the projectors do things they had not been designed to do. When the projectors had been installed, they were lowered into the ground in one piece, and then motorized magnetic pistons were attached to aim the beam. Skippy made some of those pistons retract to their original position way down in the hole, where they had been before explosive charges blew away the dirt over the buried projectors, and the business end of the projector's muzzle was extended above the surface. With the set of pistons off balance, the beam projector was knocked to one side. Knocked to the side toward the three Kristang dropships.

That still wasn't enough of an angle to bring those dropships directly into the targeting cone, so Skippy used another trick. He defocused the beam. Normally, you want a microwave laser beam to be as narrow as possible, so it can put all of its power on one target. So it can slice an armored starship in half, for example. Skippy fired the projector on low power in a series of broad pulses; more like a flashlight than a thin beam. The maser pulses scorched a broad area of the air as they traveled through the atmosphere. Scorched the air enough that the dropships, which were at high altitude but still within the atmosphere, were suddenly subjected to extreme overheating as the air around them was converted into plasma. The air around them briefly became like the photosphere of a star, and backscatter from the defocused maser pulses reflecting off air molecules struck the dropships directly. In less than a second, the extreme heat caused the dropship powercells, missiles and warheads to explode.

"Did that do the job, Joe?" Skippy asked. "Let's see. There were three dropships up there, and now I count, hmmm, not three. No, not two either. Or one. I count zero dropships. Zero is less than three, right, Joey?"

"Let me kick my boots off so I can count on my toes, Skippy. I am a dumb monkey, remember?"

"Ok, I think we're good. Unless you consider disorganized pieces falling toward the ground as a 'dropship'."

"No, you did it. Thank you, Skippy."

"You're not thanking me on behalf of those dropship pilots, are you, Joe? Because if you're hoping to get a fruit basket from them, you will be waiting a while."

"Wow," I whispered. "That's a whole lot of aircraft." On the dropship's display was a total view of the developing air battle, or I should say battles. There were seven distinct clusters of aircraft approaching each other at high speed; and as I watched the fighters on both sides began turning to maneuver to gain an advantage. Thanks to the magic of Skippy the Magnificent, I had perfect situational awareness of every aspect of the battles, even though almost all of the aircraft were still in stealth mode.

"Yup," Skippy agreed. "This is going to be quite some show. There hasn't been an air campaign like this in a very long time. Although perhaps 'campaign' isn't the correct word, since I expect this whole thing to be over in a couple hours, max. Joe, do you want to grab some popcorn and watch the show in real time?"

"No, Skippy, I do not want any popcorn," I was angry at his insensitivity. "It is not a *show*. This is real air combat. People are going to die. You may be immortal, the rest of us are not."

"Joe, I am terribly sorry," Skippy said, and this time he sounded sincere. "You are right, I should not have said that, it was insensitive. You are a pilot now, and a soldier. I should have considered that."

"Apology accepted, Skippy," which were words that I never thought I would ever be able to say. Skippy apologizing? "Is there anything we can do?" Already, I could see aircraft on both sides firing masers at long range. They weren't likely to hit anything; the point was to keep the enemy at long range. Keep the enemy from closing on you until you wanted them closer, on your terms. With the aircraft of both the Ruhar and Kristang using stealth fields to confuse enemy sensors, defensive shields to deflect maser beams, and maser turrets to destroy incoming missiles, aircraft couldn't rely on fire-and-forget missiles like the US Air Force did on Earth. Air combat in the war between the Ruhar and Kristang was a close-range affair like WWII. Get close to the enemy aircraft, hammer it with maser pulses to degrade its shields, then finish it with a volley of missiles. Thinking about it, I shuddered. What I knew about flying was strictly peacetime maneuvers. I would hate to be in the skies above Paradise right then.

"Anything we can do? You mean is there anything *I* can do? Sure, Joe, there is a lot I *can* do. It would surprise me if we got permission to do much of it."

"*You*? Since when do you ask permission to do anything?"

"By 'we', I meant you, Joe. And by 'permission' I meant an Ok from Count Chocula."

"Oh, shit." I'd almost forgotten that nagging little detail.

"Most of the things I could do, that would be effective in giving the Ruhar an advantage over the Kristang, would risk being too obvious."

"The Kristang would figure out that some higher-technology had been messing with their aircraft?"

"Exactly. What's worse is that the Ruhar would review the after action sensor data and realize someone else was messing with the Kristang. The Ruhar would logically conclude that the Jeraptha must have been involved on their side, but when they inevitably ask the Jeraptha about it, the Jeraptha will certainly know they didn't help in the air battle. And that will start the Jeraptha asking uncomfortable questions and looking into things that are better left alone."

"I can see that would be a problem."

"That reminds me of something that has been troubling me for some time, Joe. The Thuranin are not stupid; their intelligence people surely by now have heard a rumor about a human escaping from a Kristang jail, and that same human stealing a Ruhar Dodo. That Dodo was taken aboard a Kristang frigate, and both that frigate and its star carrier mothership disappeared without a trace. I am surprised that the Thuranin have not been investigating the incident. Or maybe they are, and we don't know it yet."

"Shit, Skippy, that's not good."

"It is most certainly not good at all, Joe. Which is why we must avoid any significant risk of me interfering in the battle to help the Ruhar in any way that looks suspicious. Count Chocula is annoyingly correct about that; we can't risk exposing our presence."

"Crap. Turn the display off the, Skippy. I don't want to watch this slaughter."

"Wait! Joe, I said that I can't do anything obvious. I didn't say that I couldn't do anything at all. Come on, Joe, it's Skippy the Magnificent you're talking to here. Trust the awesomeness."

"Trust the awesomeness? Will that be your new slogan?" In spite of the situation, I had to laugh. On the display, aircraft were tangling in the most gigantic air battle I had ever imagined. The Ruhar were outnumbered. "What type of awesomeness do you have in mind, Skippy?" It was probably too late to request permission from Chotek. This was definitely an act-now-and-ask-forgiveness-later kind of situation.

"Um, you know how the Kristang are bad at taking proper care of maintenance on their equipment, because they consider that to be an inglorious task unfitting for warriors? Well, there are times when such lack of attention to detail can bite you in the ass. This is one of those times."

"Skippy, are you doing something now, without getting permission?"

"I have no idea what you are talking about, Joe."

"Of course not," I rolled my eyes. "Let me ask it this way: if you were doing something, what might that be?"

"Oh, well, speaking hypothetically, it is possible that the Kristang aircraft are experiencing intermittent glitches in their networked fire control systems; these glitches are degrading their already crappy sensor capabilities. And in an ironic coincidence, at the same time the Kristang are having glitches in their systems, the Ruhar aircraft have received an awesome software upgrade that they don't know about. This upgrade enhances the effectiveness of their stealth capabilities. The combined effect of these two totally, *totally* unrelated coincidences is that the Ruhar have a significant advantage in air combat. Their aircraft can engage at longer ranges, while the Kristang have to fly relatively close to get a weapons lock on the Ruhar."

"Cool. Hypothetically."

"Not as cool as I would like it to be, Joe. Ordinarily, this would mean the Ruhar are able to engage and disengage from combat at will. With that many aircraft tangling across the sky, they are so mixed up that the initial advantage of the Ruhar has been diminished. At this point, both sides are about even."

"The Ruhar went into the fight at a disadvantage, Skippy. Making it an even fight is a great help. Thank you."

"Hypothetically, you are welcome. Oh, hey, if I forget, please remind me to wipe that software upgrade from the Ruhar's systems after the battle is over. Joe, this is going to be a terrible slaughter on both sides. The Ruhar have already lost seven percent of their airworthy combat aircraft, plus another twelve percent that were destroyed on the ground. The Kristang have lost eleven percent total so far. Both sides are quickly discovering that their tactics for air combat do not apply for a battle of this size and scope. The pilots are having to make this up on the fly, no joke intended. Joe, this air battle is going to be studied for hundreds of years."

"I understand." After that, we watched the action unfurl across the display. Skippy had the good sense to keep quiet, except for quietly bringing particularly significant events to my attention. Mostly, I sat silently as symbols on the display flared and blinked out.

When the Kristang had launched waves of aircraft to attack Ruhar airbases, Saily and Derek had been headed back toward their own base. Then Saily received an order to change course and fly low and slow for maximum stealth. Ruhar air command had judged that Saily was too far away to help prevent the initial attack on her own airbase, so she was being held in reserve to strike the Kristang aircraft on the way back to their own bases to rearm and refuel. Saily had shaken with anger at doing nothing, while enemy missiles blasted the airbase where her friends worked and lived. Though the Ruhar military datalink was being partly jammed by the Kristang and the enemy had already knocked out many of the transmitters, the tactical communications system was designed to operate under wartime conditions. Derek still had a full picture of the situation across the surface of Gehtanu; he kept Saily informed of what she needed to know and didn't mention details that would only upset and distract her. From her seat in the front of the tandem cockpit, she could call up any tactical data she wanted; she didn't have all that much to do while the Dobreh flew in lazy circles to achieve maximum stealth. Flying low to the ground meant that the fighter's already tiny signature would be mostly lost in ground clutter to any active sensors above. Flying slowly meant the Dobreh was not leaving a long trail of disturbed air behind it. And they were flying slowly enough that Saily had only one of the two engines active; the active engine was using only its electrically-powered fan blades and therefore not radiating much heat at all. Secure inside their stealth field, Saily and Derek waited for a signal from air command.

"Derek. Lieutenant Bonsu," she addressed him by his human military rank. "We will be going into combat against the Kristang. We will be shooting directly at, killing Kristang. This will be crossing a line; a human involved in hostile action against your patron species. I need to know if you have a problem with this. I need to know whether I can rely on you as my Weapon Systems Officer."

Paradise

"Yes," Derek responded immediately. "Absolutely. One hundred percent. I know what the Kristang did to my home planet." Derek was among a growing percentage of humans on Paradise who feared the wormhole to Earth had been shut down deliberately by the Kristang, to cover up what they were doing on that distant planet. Despite assurances from the Ruhar that the Kristang, nor the Thuranin nor even the Maxolhx had the technology to control a wormhole, Derek thought it very suspicious that the only wormhole to humanity's home had shut down, shortly after the Kristang lost control of Paradise. That could not be a coincidence. And if Derek could not do anything to directly help Earth, he could at least kill as many lizards as he could find in his weapons range. During the brief time when the Kristang battlegroup had total control around Paradise, Derek had feared he could never do anything to avenge the loss of his homeworld. Now, a miracle had cleared the skies of Kristang, and Derek Bonsu was not going to miss this golden opportunity. "Saily, you can absolutely count on me. Let's do this."

Following orders from Ruhar air command, Saily had kept the Dobreh flying slow, lazy circles as the four Kristang aircraft flew by. As soon as the enemy passed overhead, Saily went to full power on the engines to close the distance. Saily still had the ship in stealth, and was about to drop the stealth field for combat maneuvering when Derek had shouted over the intercom. "Break right and cut power!"

Saily pulled the aircraft into a gentle turn and throttled back the engines. Before she could ask, Derek explained. "They can't see through our stealth field! I've watching them ping us with targeting sensors, and they can't get a lock. I have a perfect lock on that lead ship with the maser guidance system."

Saily checked her instruments. Derek was right, the enemy's active sensors were still pinging blindly, they couldn't get a lock on the Dobreh's position. In air combat, both sides enveloped their aircraft in stealth fields until they began maneuvering into attack position and firing. At that point, with the range between aircraft closing, the high speed leaving turbulent air behind and the engines radiating heat, stealth gave no advantage. Except that now, somehow the Kristang were not able to lock onto the Dobreh, and her aircraft was maintaining a perfect lock as if the Kristang did not have stealth capability at all. Saily did not wait to wonder at the unexpected circumstances; that was for the experts to puzzle over later when they viewed the flight recorder data. "Missiles, full spread."

Derek toggled three missiles at the aircraft he had been intending to fire at with the maser cannon, and another three at that aircraft's wingman. The six missiles dropped out the back of the Dobreh, ignited, and flew violently twisting, evasive paths to their targets. With missiles in the air, Derek activated the maser to target the same two aircraft. He was not trying to kill with the maser, he only wanted the maser to confuse the enemy's sensors and prevent the enemy defensive masers from hitting his missiles. He was only partly successful. The first aircraft's defenses exploded two missiles more than ten kilometers away; easy kills. But then its sensors seemed to go blind; the enemy fighter turned desperately as Derek watched his missile jinking side to side and up and down as it closed the distance. The enemy defensive maser turrets were not firing at all; they could not find a target to shoot at. Then the missile impacted the enemy directly, blowing it into pieces.

The second aircraft shot down one incoming missile, and the other two were intermittently struck by defensive masers, but they were only glancing shots as the missiles quickly darted away. Both missiles flew by their evasive target, and their electronic brains concluded they did not have enough fuel to turn and reengage the enemy. Their brains also concluded they were close enough, so they both detonated their shaped-charge fragmentation warheads toward the enemy. Pieces of warheads flew through the air on both sides of the enemy fighter, ripping into it and turning it into a fireball.

Saily was stunned by the turn of events. In simulations, aircraft almost always were able to destroy incoming missiles with their defensive masers, when missiles were launched at long range. It was only in the close quarters of a dogfight that missiles could home in before the enemy's defenses could knock them out. Yet here, now, she had fired missiles at two targets and destroyed both targets. The enemy still had not fired a shot at her, as they did not appear to be able to determine exactly where her Dobreh was. Adapting quickly to the new reality, Saily maneuvered to maintain their distance to the two other enemy fighters.

The enemy ruined her plan. They did not know why the Ruhar stealth field was so much more effective than they had expected, or what was wrong with their own targeting sensors, but they did know that if they let the Ruhar loiter at long range and fire missiles, they were both dead. So they pulled tight turns and went to full power, not caring whether they were that much more visible to the apparently superior Ruhar sensors.

The range between the three combatants closed rapidly, and Saily was forced yet again to adapt.

Derek Bonsu grunted from the strain in the backseat of the Dobreh gunship, as Saily pulled the fighter aircraft into another tight turn. The G-meter in front of him registered 8, and since gravity on the Ruhar homeworld was slightly higher than on Earth, it felt even heavier to Derek. Even in the advanced Ruhar flightsuit he wore, his vision narrowed until all he could see was a small circle directly in front of his eyes. The Ruhar pilot was taking it easy on him, he knew; genetically-enhanced Ruhar pilots could sustain 12 Gees in combat turns. Having Derek as her Wizzo was actually a liability in air combat; Saily was endangering her own life and their mission in order to avoid killing her human copilot.

The turn completed, the Dobreh snapped back to a straight course and Derek was thrown forward against the restraints, as Saily cut power and the fighter decelerated rapidly. "Stealth field is nominal," Derek managed to grunt. His whole world was reduced to the display and controls directly in front of him; he still had no peripheral vision. The two enemy fighters were now again in front of them. "We have target lock on the left-hand ship," he gasped between sucking in oxygen. "Missiles?"

"Do it," Saily ordered. They were now too close to the Kristang for stealth to be of much use, and the Dobreh had twelve missiles left. As Derek toggled off six missiles, she felt the Dobreh lurch slightly as the aircraft suddenly weighed less. On her own controls, she pressed the button to activate the Dobreh's maser cannon, at the same time her own ship rocked as an enemy maser hammered her shields.

"Missiles inbound!" Derek shouted. "Ten, twelve, fourteen! We can't track all of them," he warned. The enemy had dumped almost all of their missiles blindly into the air, and now that the Dobreh was firing a maser at full power and its engines were glowing hot, the enemy missiles had a target to chase. "Saily, this is going to be close!" The display for their defensive computer was flashing red warnings that it had lost track of some enemy missiles. And the defensive maser turrets could only engage two missiles at once.

A Ruhar Dobreh gunship had two escape systems for the crew. Because the Dobreh was a high-performance jet fighter aircraft, designed to operate at supersonic speed and extreme altitude, the crew simply opening the canopy and ejecting was not an option. Instead, the entire two-person tandem cockpit could separate from the disintegrating airframe.

Moments after their own missiles turned the fourth and last Kristang fighter into a ball of fire, an enemy missile had exploded close behind them. Shrapnel took out both engines, shattering fan blades and causing a powercell to rupture. Knowing her aircraft was doomed, Saily reached down on the right side of her seat and flipped a switch to retract a safety cover then press the recessed button, saying a silent prayer that the cockpit separation mechanism was still operable. As her fingers fumbled with the switch, the flight control computer realized that the aircraft was no longer a viable flying device, and handed off control to the cockpit separation computer. That computer had been waiting for the flight control computer to make the blindingly obvious decision while the airframe broke apart around it, so it immediately engaged the separation process even before it received input from the pilot. Saily tried to shout a warning to Derek in the seat behind her, but with holes in the canopy, the shrieking wind was too loud even to be heard in the helmet speakers. Derek must know what was happening, she had only a moment to think, and he should be preparing to use the secondary separation button if the separation control computer failed to or was unable.

With a roar she heard over the wind, explosive bolts released the cockpit from its connection to the airframe, and a small rocket motor pushed the cockpit section upward. Because the Dobreh was falling apart and tumbling out of control, the cockpit computer's preprogrammed maneuver to straighten out the cockpit's own tumble and make it fly directly upward was the wrong move. As the bottom of the cockpit cleared the top of the airframe well it had rested in, the left side of the cockpit was struck by debris from the exploding left engine; a fan blade penetrated the cockpit's armor and struck just behind Saily. When the cockpit was not more than two meters above its well, the suddenly unbalanced airframe flipped in an eye blink, and the tail of the aircraft smashed into the rear of the rising cockpit.

Derek's helmet was secured to the seat to prevent a pilot's neck from snapping. That didn't stop his brain from being bounced around inside his skull from the violent battering of the separation. Less than five seconds had passed since he shouted the warning about missiles approaching; the cockpit separation had not surprised him but he hadn't heard a warning from Saily. When the rocket motor kicked the cockpit upward, his right arm had been reaching down for the separation button, while his left arm was still on the control stick trying to maintain some semblance of control over the failing aircraft. Separation had caught him unawares, and his left arm ached as if it had torn loose at the shoulder. Then something, two somethings, struck the cockpit, and the whole cockpit section was suddenly tumbling through the air on its own. "Saily!" He shouted, doubting the pilot could hear him. Through the canopy, blue sky and green forest flashed by like a strobe light, so quickly was the cockpit spinning.

Too low. They had been flying at around 900 kilometers per hour when the enemy missile exploded, but at less than a thousand meters altitude. The cockpit should have stabilized, then released a steerable triangular parachute to set them down softly. Instead, all the displays were dark and the cockpit was tumbling worse than the aircraft had been. "Saily! We need to get out of here! Saily?!"

There was no response from in front of him. Possibly the pilot was unconscious, although the genetically enhanced body of a Ruhar should have withstood the strain better than his own fragile human biology. Derek could have reached for the handle between his legs to eject his own seat. He was not leaving without the pilot. Without waiting any longer, Derek reached for the black and yellow striped handle in front of his seat, barely able to make his right arm extend that far; his left arm hung uselessly at his side. When he had a firm grip on the handle, he closed his eyes and pulled firmly.

First the canopy blew off, then Derek's seat soared upward, propelled by a magnetic rail. He only felt the initial kick, before he became unconscious. The seat ejection mechanism, designed for Ruhar, had not been reset for a human on that flight, a flight in which the Dobreh was not supposed to have a human crewman. A flight that was supposed to have been a quick and simple check ride.

As Derek's seat blew upward into the airstream, the final crew escape mechanism activated. The straps that held Derek into the chair automatically released and he was exposed to the 500 kilometer per hour airstream. Before his limbs could be torn off by the force of the air and deceleration, a flexible tube that he wore on his back came to life and he was enveloped in an oval-shaped bubble. The computer built into the tube bent and compressed the bubble to keep him upright and he flew through the air. Once the computer decided his speed had dropped below a preset mark, the bubble disappeared as suddenly as it formed. Without the unconscious Derek doing anything or knowing what was happening, the nanofabric of the bubble retracted inside the flexible tube, and the nanofabric changed its shape in a microsecond. The top of the tube came off, and the fabric was yanked upward. It was now a parachute or technically, a paraglider. The computer activated its sensors. If the computer had been capable of emotion, it would have been greatly dismayed. It was too low, and the ground beneath was thickly covered with trees in every direction. There were no safe places to glide to within the paraglider's range. With an electronic shrug, the computer decided that crashing into one tree top was as good as another, and it concentrated on slowing its passenger's rate of descent. The paraglider reformed its shape from a wedge to a half sphere, and Derek was jolted again.

Crashing down through the trees was no more gentle than what he had endured so far. With the parachute having lost lift, he fell straight down, bouncing off tree limbs and breaking branches. There was a final violent jolt as the parachute snagged on a tree limb, and he came to a stop ten meters off the ground. The parachute computer, still active, calculated the distance, and the nanofabric of the parachute cords stretched to lower Derek almost gently to the ground. Satisfied that it had done all it could for the pilot, the parachute computer released the cords, and the pilot's bruised and battered body lay alone on the forest floor.

Saily was not so lucky as Derek. The engine fan blade that struck the cockpit as they were separating penetrated the armor and a piece punctured the seat, damaging its release mechanism. When Derek pulled the handle to eject them from the cockpit, Saily's seat should have ejected first. Because the cockpit computer knew her seat was damaged, it delayed Saily's ejection until after Derek was clear. But as the then-empty cockpit tumbled violently, components broke off in the airstream, and several pieces flew toward Saily. Right after she was released from the seat and the nanofabric began to blossom into a protective bubble around her, two sharp pieces of composite ripped through the still-forming bubble and into her.

The ejection computer compensated as best it could, pulling the bubble tighter and attempting to seal the holes. It was partially successful; although the smaller bubble was not able to slow the pilot's uncontrolled rush through the air. Sensing the ground was coming up quickly, the computer judged that the least risky of several very bad options was to retract the bubble and reform the nanofabric as a parachute. At first it was a small drogue parachute, used only to slow the pilot's speed through the air. When the computer decided it was safe, it spread the nanofabric out to its full extent. That was the only way to prevent the pilot from hitting the tree tops at full speed. Unfortunately, the excessive speed and prior damage to the nanofabric meant the parachute immediately began to rip from the edge to the center. The computer attempted to compensate, and it was still working on knitting together the rip when Saily hit the tree tops. The computer knew from talking with the medical status computer implanted in Saily that the pilot was seriously injured and bleeding, but the ejection computer could do nothing to assist the nano-based medical systems inside Saily's body.

Saily crashed down through the trees, nearly breaking her back on a thick tree limb. She came to rest tangled in branches and parachute cords a dozen meters off the ground. Acting on the medical computer's advice, the ejection computer decided not to try untangling the cords. It would be best, according to the medical computer, if the pilot did not move again while medical nanobots were working furiously to save her life.

She hung upside down from a tree, unconscious, as machines too small to see tried their best to keep her life from slipping away.

For Derek, coming back to consciousness was not a single event, but a lengthy process. He awakened four or five times before realizing that he was awake, that he was Derek, and that he hurt like hell all over. Then he remembered what had happened. Considering that he had been in a supersonic aircraft when it exploded around him, he decided that he shouldn't complain about some aches and pains. Assuming that was all he had to worry about. Moving very slowly, he first tried to wiggle his toes, which was successful. Moving upward, he determined he was able to sit up, but when he tried to push himself up with his left hand his shoulder flared in a white-hot shock of pain. Oh, yeah, he thought. That arm had been out of position when the cockpit separated. If his arm was broken, that could be a big problem

He was able to stand, and painful testing by raising his left arm gave him confidence that nothing was broken. There might be a sprain, or torn cartilage. Nothing the Ruhar couldn't fix, if he could get to a hamster medical facility. And if they would consent to treat a human. And if they had equipment modified for human biology. Satisfied that he was mobile, he searched the pockets of his flightsuit. He had a knife, a light, and a zPhone. No sidearm, because humans were not allowed to have weapons. No food. Damn it, he was on a planet where he couldn't eat any of the native life, or any of the crops the Ruhar grew on the continent of Tenturo. And his zPhone wasn't working, it couldn't connect to the network. The network appeared to be down entirely. The Kristang could be jamming it, or they had knocked out the base infrastructure. Or the Ruhar had simply cut off network access for humans once the fighting started. So he couldn't call for help.

The map function did work. Where the hell was he? Not good. He was in the middle of nowhere. The closest Ruhar settlement was four or five days of hard walking, at least. Four days of walking through the wilderness, without food, to a Ruhar village that would not have any human food and likely would not welcome a human wandering into their homes. They especially would not welcome a human while the Ruhar on Paradise were engaged in a war with the patrons of humanity. Derek, he said to himself, you are totally screwed.

Before he started walking, he needed to see if he could find Saily. Her locator beacon would not be active until air search and rescue pinged it, so he couldn't use it to find her. Which direction to start? It didn't matter, the Ruhar pilot could be anywhere, although she should be within a kilometer. Or two. The paraglider should have steered her toward a safe landing zone, although according to the map, there weren't any. He would need to walk in one direction for a kilometer, then begin a grid search. He decided to begin by walking uphill, that way the return would be easier.

CHAPTER TWENTY

Irene ran the sensor data back on the main display between the pilot and copilot seats, and ran through it forward again quickly, with the four others looking over her shoulder. Thanks to Emby, they had a nearly-complete view of the massive air battle that had now dissolved into desperate duels between individual aircraft.

"Daaaaamn," Dave exhaled quietly. This was the third time they'd watched the replay. The first time, everyone had been talking excitedly as they watched the symbols engage in a deadly dance across the screen. The second time, Irene narrated the action from a pilot's viewpoint.

The third time, they all simply sat and watched in shocked silence. Modern air combat was incredibly intense and high-tempo. By Emby's count, 88% of the combat aircraft on Paradise had been destroyed during the first ninety minutes of fighting. And the actual fighting had lasted perhaps twenty minutes, with the rest of the time taken by aircraft flying toward their targets, maneuvering into attack position, and flying back to their bases. If those airbases still existed. Most aircraft had set down in remote areas, relying on fuel, weapons and spare parts being brought to them. Many of the surviving aircraft were crippled in one way or another. By the end of two hours, neither side had an effective air combat force left.

"Now it's up to you guys," Irene looked at Dave and Jesse.

"What do you mean, ma'am?" Dave asked, confused. What did she expect him to do?

"Not you two specifically. I meant infantry," Irene explained. "Without enough air power to do anything useful, this becomes a ground war. Infantry. The Ruhar and the Kristang will have to rely on infantry."

"To do?" Jesse raced to guess what their pilot meant. "To do what?"

"How you do defeat an integrated air defense system?" Perkins asked.

"You make it unintegrated," Dave answered immediately. This was easy training manual stuff. "Don't attack the whole system, that's suicide. You take it apart piece by piece."

"Precisely," Perkins nodded. "Destroy one piece of the system, at the edge. A radar, a launcher, one piece. That creates a gap in the integration. A blind spot, a weakness. Take out a few more pieces, and you've created a safe passage corridor for your aircraft. Once you have that, you can send in a pure strike package, instead of loading up the sorties with electronic countermeasure aircraft."

"Until the enemy moves their pieces around," Irene added, "radars and launchers are mobile."

"They are," Perkins agreed. "But these projectors are not mobile. The Kristang know that. They don't have sufficient air power left, so they will send in ground troops to destroy a projector, or take it offline, or take control of it. Once they know that particular projector is inactive, they know a part of the sky is not covered, and they can send in a ship. When enough projectors are confirmed offline, the Kristang can take back control of the sky."

"Got it," Jesse said as the reality dawned on him. "It's going to be a race between the hamsters and the lizards. The Ruhar will try to defend active projector sites and bring new ones online, and the Kristang will try to destroy them or take control."

"The Ruhar should have an advantage, right?" Shauna asked. "Emby will tell them where the other projectors are, but the Kristang will have to guess."

"I need to ask Emby what we do next, because this is a whole new ballgame," Perkins said, pulling out her zPhone to type a new message. As she typed, she looked at Jesse and

Dave. "If we get involved in any ground action, I need you two, because I have no infantry experience. I handled intel for UNEF. Before that, I was in communications. I used a keyboard, not a rifle."

Ski was surprised. "Not even in basic training, ma'am?"

She shook her head ruefully. "Not a whole lot, I was commissioned in the Air Force."

"Air Force, ma'am?" Jesse asked with a quick glance at the US Army insignia on her uniform. He was glad that he hadn't said anything bad about the other service in her presence.

"There was a 'Blue to Green' initiative a while back," she explained. The US military had needed more people in the Army and Marine Corps, more boots on the ground. Personnel in the Navy and Air Force were encouraged to transfer to green uniforms. Strongly encouraged. "They let me know that if I wanted to stay in as a career, I needed to switch services."

"Oh," Jesse didn't know what else to say.

"Glad to have you with us, ma'am," Dave also didn't know what else to say.

Emby's reply came swiftly. *Proceed to the attached coordinates and activate the projector there as soon as possible.* It was followed by a shorter message. *Thank you. Good work.*

"Yes!" Skippy exulted two days later. "They did it! The fifth projector is now online. Joe, I will send a message of congratulations to Major Perkins and her team. Also a message to get the hell out of there ASAP, in case we need to use that projector real quick."

"Agreed. Hey, Skippy, we can now shoot at Kristang ships with this new projector?"

"That was the idea, Joe. Why?"

"Because now I'm thinking we don't do that. Not right away."

"Once again, I'm not following your logic, Joe."

"What I'm thinking is that when the Kristang jump a ship in to test us-"

"Joe, I must caution you that the Kristang are likely to test our projectors with more than one ship. That is standard Kristang fleet doctrine when attacking a planet equipped with ground-based defenses."

"That won't make any difference to what I want to do. In fact, that's even better. We let the Kristang get comfortable in orbit, they will at first stick to areas not covered by the four projectors they know about. When they think we only have those four projectors active, the first thing they will do is try hitting those projectors with a railgun strike, right?"

"That is sound tactics, yes. The projectors do have shields, although two of the projectors have very little power left for either shields or the maser."

"Got it. Here's what we do, depending where the ships jump in-"

"Team, Emby says we need to haul ass out of here, pronto," Perkins declared. "I think the Kristang are sure to come back to test whether we have more than those four projectors active," she didn't know two of those projectors were nearly depleted. "If Emby has to shoot soon, we don't want to be anywhere near this thing."

"Do we have a new target, ma'am?" Irene asked wearily. After parking her Buzzard, she had helped the team set up the drill and punch down to the projector's control chamber. It had been Jesse's turn to go down the hole; the holes were now larger in diameter but Irene still shook when she thought about it. Mercifully, Major Perkins had declared they could not risk their only pilot, so Irene was relieved of having to slide down into the ground again.

Craig Alanson

"Yeah, of course," Perkins' voice reflected her own weariness. After the frantic scramble to get the first four projectors activated, they had all been dead tired. Then Emby had acted early for some reason, and blasted the Kristang battlegroup from the sky. That had given the team a shot of energy they used to get the fifth projector dug out and online. Now they were all running on empty. "Another projector. We'll need to go back to the truck to refuel first. Let's get moving, people."

Tired fingers fumbled and tired legs wobbled, but the task of breaking down the drill rig and tying it back in the sling was well known to them by now. By the time Irene came back with the Buzzard and Shauna lowered the cable, the sling was ready. Major Perkins was swaying on her feet, fighting creeping sleepiness. They needed a break. According to Emby, they couldn't afford to stop now. Regardless of Emby's instructions, she was going to give the team eight full hours of sleep after they got back to the truck and the Buzzard was refueled. The pilot absolutely had to rest, and while Irene was sleeping, the rest of the team could get rest also.

Paradise was going to have to get along without them for a few hours.

We didn't have to wait long for the Kristang to test whether the four projectors we'd used in our sneak attack were all we had. "They're heeeeeere!" Skippy announced. A mere two and a half hours after Perkins and her crew got the fifth projector working and cleared out of the area, three Kristang destroyers jumped in above the far side of the planet. Knowing the weak shields of their frigates did not stand a chance against our projectors, the Kristang had wisely left their little ships out of this action. The Kristang commander wasn't stupid; at first he kept his ships out of the targeting cones of the four projectors that he knew about. When his ships were not hit, he must have figured we only had four projectors, which is exactly what I wanted the lizards to think.

Next, he had to test the four known projectors, to see if they were still active. After his surviving ships had jumped away, they must have examined all the sensor data from our sneak attack, and realized that the last shots of two particular projectors were at a much lower power level. Logically, they correctly concluded that those projectors were almost drained of power, so they really only needed to worry about two of the known projectors.

"They're lining up railgun shots on the projectors," Skippy warned. "Even with five projectors, I can't hit those ships where they are now. They're going to fire railguns at an extremely shallow angle, to keep the ships out of our targeting cones. That will decrease the impact of the railgun darts because they will be traveling through more of the atmosphere."

"Do your thing, Skippy."

Two of the destroyers fired their railguns at our two healthy projectors. They knew those projectors couldn't hit the ships from where they were, and they also knew the other two projectors didn't have enough power to penetrate a destroyer's shields. What they didn't know about was the incredible awesomeness of Skippy the Magnificent.

As the railgun darts streaked in at twenty two percent of lightspeed, they passed through the targeting cone of a mostly-depleted projector. That projector couldn't harm a shielded starship, but its maser did have enough power to deflect the darts from their targets and break the darts into bite-sized pieces. By itself, a projector couldn't have hit a speeding dart, but our projectors were controlled by Skippy, so hitting two objects travelling at almost a quarter of lightspeed was not a problem. He simply fired the maser ahead of the ballistic flight path of a dart, and let the dart fly into it. "Oh my *God* those freakin' darts were slow as molasses in January," Skippy complained, using an expression I hadn't heard since my grandmother said it. "Did the Kristang actually use a railgun, or did they just toss those darts out a window? I got so bored waiting for them that I did a hundred crossword puzzles. Anyway, it worked."

The dart pieces impacted the surface around the projectors and threw up two enormous clouds of dust and debris, but only one piece the size of a fingernail did hit a projector. That piece was easily deflected by the projector's shield, leaving the maser cannon unharmed. And the Kristang, whose crappy sensors entirely missed our maser firing, saw two plumes of dust surrounding the two healthy projectors, and concluded their strike had been successful. They congratulated themselves on knocking out two multi-terawatt projectors, bragging on ship-to-ship transmissions about how bad-ass they were. Skippy almost puked listening to them. "Oh yeah, oh yeah, you're bad-asses all right. Give me a minute and we'll salute you great warriors properly."

Skippy's idea of a salute came in the form of maser beams. With the Kristang semi-confident there were no active projectors on the surface, they sent one, then all three destroyers into the targeting cones. Each destroyer, brave but not stupid, would only briefly flit through the targeting cone. That was all Skippy needed. As soon as there were two destroyers within range at the same time, he told me to press the Big Red Button on my zPhone to fire the weapons.

Two destroyers against three projectors. Two of those projectors had only one shot each left, and the shields of a Kristang destroyer could deflect the full power of a projector long enough for the ship to perform an emergency jump away. The odds were not in our favor.

Skippy, of course, didn't see any point in playing fair.

Both of the projectors the Kristang thought they had knocked out fired, two milliseconds apart. Each of those projectors fired at a different ship, and by themselves they could not have penetrated a destroyer's shields. Our secret fifth projector also fired, first at one ship and then at the second, each shot two milliseconds apart so that each ship was struck by the full power of two projectors at once. The combined maser power punched right though the destroyers' shields. The ship's hulls were armored, made of layers of tough ceramic composites and heat-dissipating foam. If the maser beams had a sense of humor, they would have laughed at the Kristang ship designers' attempts to protect their vessels. The maser beams cut through the hulls as if they were tissue paper, slicing the ships apart. Thick, armored interior bulkheads melted under the intense heat, exploding and becoming projectiles inside their own ships. Power conduits ruptured and missiles spontaneously exploded in their launch tubes, turning the ships into spinning hulks. The lucky third destroyer immediately jumped away.

"Hey! Where did you go, asswipe?" Skippy shouted. "You want some of this? You want some of this? Say hello to my leetle friend Mister Maser Beam. I got plenty more where that came from, you punk-ass bitch!"

"Damn, Skippy, chill out. You got them already," I said as on the display, one of the stricken destroyers blew apart when its missile magazine cooked off.

"I do not like lizards, Joe. I do not like bullies. Big Red Button again, Joe?"

"Sure," I said as I held the button down. "Why?"

"One of those ships is annoyingly lucky, it hasn't blown up yet. One of our original four projectors only has a weak shot left, but watch what happens when even a weak maser hits an unshielded ship's reactor."

On the display I was watching, a light flared where a crippled destroyer had been.

"Oops," Skippy chuckled. "My bad! Sorry about that. Darn, I hate it when that happens. Well, I'm sure the Kristang will forgive and forget. Or not. Whatever."

"I'm thinking 'not', Skippy. Hey, that was great," I accepted a high five from Sergeant Adams. "Keep monitoring their communications, please. I want to know if the Kristang plan to test our defenses again."

"Unlikely, Joe. The Kristang commander is right now screaming at his remaining ships to stay away from the planet, until his ground forces can degrade our air defense capability. There was supposed to be a follow-on attack by the other Kristang ships, but that has now been postponed indefinitely."

"Huh, I wonder why?" I asked with a smile.

"Maybe they didn't sell enough tickets, Joe?"

"How much longer should we wait, Commodore?"

Commodore Ferlant answered his executive officer's question without turning his attention away from the tactical display. If Ferlant were an admiral, the *Ruh Gastalo* would have a captain, and Ferlant would have to concern himself only with commanding his task force. Because he was not an admiral, he needed to also act as the ship's captain. Because he didn't have time to act as captain in the middle of a running battle, most of the responsibility for ship-handling fell to his executive officer Tom Smeth. "We will wait until the *Dalandu* has a full charge," Ferlant announced. The frigate *Sas Dalandu* had accompanied Ferlant's cruiser on every jump after the projectors had thrown the situation around Gehtanu into absolute chaos. Since Ferlant's initial order for his small task force to scatter, his ships had been hounded by the still much larger force of remaining Kristang ships. Every time one of his ships jumped, the enemy attempted to pursue, analyzing the residual signature of the Ruhar ships' outbound wormholes to determine where they had jumped to. Each time one of his ships jumped, they dropped off quantum resonators behind them, to confuse enemy sensors and conceal the jump wormhole signature. The resonators were partially effective, as it usually took the Kristang almost an hour to determine where the Ruhar had gone. But after 39 hours of unrelenting pursuit, Ferlant's ships were running low on quantum resonators, and his ships' jump drives were badly in need of a rest to recalibrate their coils. They would likely get no such rest. Each time the Ruhar ships jumped with misaligned coils, their messy jump created a louder signature, and the quantum resonators became less and less effective at concealing where the ship had jumped to. Eventually, Ferlant knew, the Kristang would wear his ships down.

The Kristang had several significant advantages in the pursuit. They still had more ships, so they could send several ships on pursuit while the others stood down for maintenance. And they could concentrate on killing Ferlant's ships one at a time, while merely keeping his other ships moving so they couldn't effectively support each other.

"Commodore," Smeth said quietly, "this can't continue forever." They were waiting for the *Sas Dalandu* to complete charging her jump coils, because that frigate's coils were overheating due to overuse. Soon, individual coils would begin to burn out, throwing that ship's entire jump drive system so badly out of alignment that it would be unable to sustain a jump wormhole.

"I know," Ferlant answered quietly. So far, he had not lost a single ship, although the destroyer *City of Fah Lentan* had been badly damaged in an attack. The *Lentan* was able to jump but not able to do much else; her stealth field and defensive shields were inoperable. Ferlant had assigned the *City of MecMurro* to accompany her stricken sister ship, but the *Lentan* might need to be abandoned, and her crew transferred to the *MecMurro*. He was losing the fight. It had become a battle of attrition; and his ships were wearing out faster than the Kristang ships were falling apart. "When the *Dalandu* is ready, we are jumping outside the system. Three jumps, maximum range."

Paradise

"We're abandoning Gehtanu?" Smeth asked. He agreed with the Commodore's decision, he also wanted to understand it.

"We are effecting a temporary strategic retreat, in order to regroup and regain the initiative," Ferlant explained in proper military terms. Someday, high-ranking Fleet officials would review the bridge data recorder during the action, to determine whether Commodore Ferlant's decisions had been appropriate. Hopefully, Ferlant would be alive then to explain himself. "Our ships need an opportunity to go offline and effect repairs."

Smeth agreed. "If the Kristang will leave us alone long enough."

"I am cautiously optimistic that once he knows we have left the system, Admiral Kekrando will turn his attention back to reestablishing his control of the space around Gehtanu."

"And after our repairs are complete?" Smeth asked.

"Then we regain the initiative," Ferlant said with a tight smile.

"Sir?"

"The hunters will become the hunted."

"I can walk," Saily assured Derek. Her legs were not as assuring. She could not, in fact, walk.

"It doesn't look like it," Derek said gently.

"My right leg is fine," she insisted. Her left leg was broken in two places, somewhere along her way crashing down through the trees. She also had internal injuries from whatever piece of the exploding Dobreh had hit her after they ejected. When Derek found Saily, she had been unconscious, tangled in parachute cords, hanging upside down. Working carefully with his injured shoulder, Derek had cut away cords and parachute fabric to make a rope, and slowly lowered her to the ground. Peeling away her blood-soaked flightsuit, he found an ugly bloody wound on her left side. Whatever magical nanobots swam in her blood had done their best to stitch the wound closed, but she had already lost a lot of blood, based on the amount that had soaked her flightsuit and dripped onto the forest floor. In her flight kit, Derek had found bandages, emergency rations, and four vials of injectable medical supplements. He couldn't read all of the complicated Ruhar technical terms; so he used his zPhone's camera to translate for him. The vials contained additional nanobots, vitamins and minerals and whatever type of sugars and proteins the Ruhar used as food. "Do we have a choice?"

"No," Derek agreed. While his zPhone wasn't working, Saily had been able to exchange brief, encrypted messages with the Ruhar military guard system. She had sent a distress call, stating her injuries, location and that she was with a human copilot. Saily urgently needed medical care, Derek was also injured and Derek did not have any source of food. The reply was not encouraging. Air rescue was out of the question; the horrific air battle had wiped out most of the Ruhar's combat aircraft. The few aircraft that remained were being reserved to defend vital infrastructure or to conduct strikes against the Kristang. Risking a precious aircraft with five crewmembers to rescue one downed pilot, was not an option at that time. Saily was advised to walk her way out; there was a road several days away. If she could get near the road, Ruhar command would see if any of the civilians in the area would be willing to drive out to pick her up. Basically, the reply stated that there was a war on, and they didn't have any aircraft to spare. The reply also wished her good luck.

Ruhar command didn't say anything about Derek, other than to question why a human had been with Saily in the first place. They had no suggestion what he should do about the lack of food. "If you can stand, you can lean on my shoulder," Derek suggested. "Let's try that."

Holding onto a tree, Saily managed to stand on one wobbly leg. Derek got her arm draped over his shoulders, and they practiced stumbling through the forest. "Easy enough," Derek concluded. "This is like a three-legged race."

"What?" Saily asked, confused.

Derek shook his head. That reference hadn't translated into Ruhar as he intended. "It's a human custom, something we do at picnics. You, ah, forget it. Let's save our energy." With his free hand, he checked the map on his zPhone. Getting to the road was not going to be easy, there were hills to climb and streams to cross. As they walked, Saily would grow weaker from her unhealed injuries, and Derek would grow weaker from hunger. "One step at a time. Here we go."

"Admiral, the *Vikran* reports that the entire enemy force has jumped outside the system," the captain of the *Kedwala* stated. The destroyer *We are Proud to Honor Clan Sub-Leader Bell-den-Oosh Vikran who Inspires us Every Day* was a brother ship of the *We are Proud to Follow the Shining Example of Combat Rifleman Tuut-uas-Val Kedwala*, but while the *Kedwala* had the dubious honor of hosting the admiral, the *Vikran* had been off having fun and seeking glory chasing the Ruhar task force. With the admiral's normal command ship, the battlecruiser *He Who Pushes Aside Fear Shall Always be Victorious* having been obliterated by a projector above Pradassis, the *Kedwala* had become the battlegroup's command ship by default. Neither the admiral nor the crew of the *Kedwala* were happy about the situation, but whereas Admiral Kekrando was free to express his dissatisfaction loudly and frequently, the crew of the *Kedwala* had to at least pretend they were honored to host the battlegroup commander. Because to openly state their fervent desire to stuff the admiral and his staff into an airlock and blow them into space would not be a good career move. Although that was a totally understandable sentiment. "Confirmed. The enemy has now performed three consecutive jumps beyond the system limits, and might be preparing to jump again. The *Vikran* requests instructions."

Technically, the captain of the *Vikran* himself was not requesting instructions; the *Vikran* had been sent back to the *Kedwala* by Senior Captain Gerkaw in command of the pursuit squadron. That senior captain had requested instructions. And he had not so much requested instructions, as hoped that the standing instructions he already had would be changed. Admiral Kekrando had ordered the pursuit squadron to halt pursuit, if the enemy passed a certain distance from the Pradassis system, and the pursuit squadron had already gone beyond that imaginary line. The senior captain hoped the admiral would ignore that minor violation, and give permission to continue the pursuit. The enemy's ships were worn down, the senior captain's message said excitedly. Another couple jumps, surely a dozen at most, and the pursuit squadron would have the Ruhar trapped.

Kekrando read the message with displeasure. Most of his demanding job, he thought angrily, was reining in overly aggressive commanders who were eager to do stupid, rash things that risked losing the considerable advantage his battlegroup still possessed. The fact that frequent use of overly aggressive, rash actions were how he had become promoted to the admiralty did not cross Kekrando's mind. The battlegroup was *his* command now, and if anyone was going to something recklessly stupid, it was going to happen on Kekrando's orders. Not on the initiative of glory and promotion seeking Senior Captain Gerkaw. With Admiral Kekrando having lost most of his combat power to a sneak attack by previously unknown projectors, he knew his position in command was precarious. If the clan leadership was looking to replace Kekrando, a senior captain in command of a successful pursuit squadron would be a convenient candidate. "Inform Senior Captain Gerkaw that he is to adhere to my standing instructions," Kekrando said firmly. "He is not to run off and risk *my* ships in his personal desire for glory."

Nineteen hours had passed, and there was no sign of continued pursuit by the Kristang. Cautiously, Commodore Ferlant allowed two ships at a time to take critical systems offline for much-needed maintenance. His cruiser *Ruh Gastalo* would remain on full alert to protect the vulnerable ships undergoing repairs. Only after all other ships in the little task force had been brought to full combat readiness, would the *Gastalo* herself begin heavy maintenance.

As Ferlant has risen through the ranks, to captain and now temporary commodore, he had come to rely more and more on a quote from one of his instructors way back at the military academy. She had told the class that 'Amateurs discuss tactics. Professionals discuss logistics'. Ferlant had not been surprised to learn that even the humans had a similar saying on their primitive homeworld. Tactics, Ferlant considered as he reviewed ship status reports, were useless without the means to implement them. The ships under his command were warships only if they were capable of performing near their designed capability; and to accomplish that, required constant attention to tasks that were painstaking and mundane. Combat action, even an action of continually running from enemy pursuit, wore down critical systems. Without a pause to rest, repair and replace vital components, his warships would become nothing more than composite tubes which held air only so long as the enemy held off attack. Despite constant demands from the government on Gehtanu for his ships to come back, Ferlant was not going to be hasty and stupid. He was going to take a pause from the battle in order to bring all of his ships back up to full fighting condition.

All of his ships, that is, except for the destroyer *City of Fah Lentan*. That ship had been badly damaged in a Kristang attack, it had barely escaped from a damping field while providing cover to give the frigate *Sas Dalandu* time to jump away. A destroyer risking itself to protect a much less valuable frigate was a questionable tactic, but Ferlant had not criticized the *Lentan*'s captain. Ferlant would have done the same thing had he been in command of the destroyer. The *Lentan* was too heavily damaged to be brought back up to full combat capability, so Ferlant instructed that ship's crew to perform only cosmetic repairs, and basic maintenance on the jump drive and defensive shields. Ferlant had a special task in mind for the *Lentan*. One last task.

Eric Koblenz had gone from elation to severe depression to cautious hopefulness to confused disappointment in the space of a week, and now he was merely numb. When the Kristang battlegroup arrived in orbit and chased the Ruhar ships away, the Keeper faction in UNEF had been triumphant; certain that life for UNEF would now return to normal, that those humans who had been disloyal to the Kristang would be punished, and that loyal Keepers would soon return to Earth, having accomplished their mission for the Kristang. Eric experienced a joyous few days, warning disloyal non-Keepers that their fate was sealed; certain that his loyalty would be rewarded.

Keeper leaders attempted to contact the Kristang in the days immediately following arrival of the battlegroup, but they were rebuffed. Then came a scathing message from the Kristang that was a stinging rebuke. All humans had in some way cooperated with the Ruhar, if only by growing their own food and therefore removing a logistics burden from the enemy Ruhar. Those who called themselves 'Keepers' were equally traitorous; the Kristang valued action, not words, and the Keepers had not *done* anything against the Ruhar. Also, the Kristang no longer had access to Earth, so no humans would be going home. The Kristang were not impressed by actions of some Keepers to destroy tractors and other equipment the Ruhar provided; equipment the Ruhar had already remotely disabled.

Eric didn't know what to do, or think. What was the point of remaining loyal to an alien species that considered him to be a traitor? His government on Earth had allied with the Kristang, now that government on humanity's homeworld had no effective authority over the people isolated on an alien world. He had no good options. No hope.

"Major Perkins? Ma'am?" Irene called her current commanding officer into the Buzzard's cockpit. "I just picked up a distress call about a downed Ruhar pilot. She's injured, and not far from here."

Perkins frowned. As a pilot, Striebich might feel a call to rescue any and all of her fellow aviators in distress. Perkins couldn't allow her team to be distracted from their mission. "I'm sure there are many pilots down after that air battle."

"Yes, ma'am. But this Ruhar pilot has a human with her."

"What? How did that happen?"

"How I don't know ma'am," Irene admitted. "The distress call is from the human, a Lt Derek Bonsu. He was the copilot or weapon system officer in a Chicken when the battle started. I guess they got caught up in the furball. He tried to get air rescue from the Ruhar, but they have few aircraft left, and they are unable to assist at this time."

"They've been down since the day of the air battle?"

"Yes, ma'am. The Ruhar is in a bad way; she's injured and still losing blood. This Lt. Bonsu doesn't have any food." Irene pointed at the map on the display. "Even by himself, it would take him a couple more days to walk to the nearest Ruhar settlement, and they wouldn't have any human food there. He says his pilot won't last that long anyway. This area," her finger circled the map, "is remote. No roads, and few settlements. They need air rescue."

"Shit. Damn it!"

"It can be done, ma'am," Irene assured Perkins. "We can lower a crewman to hook them up to a cable."

"Lieutenant, I meant 'damn it' as in, of course we do have to assist. We are *not* leaving a human out there to starve."

Irene couldn't keep a smile off her face. "It will be only a forty minute flight, ma'am, going low and slow."

"Don't start the engines yet, Striebich. First, I'm going to contact Emby and see if they can do anything to help them without us."

"If not, ma'am?"

"Then I'm going to ask Emby what the mission security fallout will be, of us bringing a Ruhar aboard. And we'll need to fly this Ruhar some place where she can get medical care, that will seriously blow our cover."

"We could retrieve only Lt. Bonsu," Irene said with a frown.

Major Perkins snorted. "Striebich, you're a pilot. Would leave one of your aircrew behind?"

"No," she answered without hesitation.

"I expect this Lt. Bonsu feels the same way about his pilot." She sighed and pulled out her zPhone to type a message. "At times like this, I wish Emby would answer a simple damned phone call, instead of me typing everything."

"Crap, Skippy," I said when we got the message from Perkins. "Does Perkins have to pick this guy up? That road isn't far," at least it didn't appear very far on the map. I wasn't on the ground, walking on an empty stomach. "If he can get there, he can follow the road to this village here," I pointed to a dot on the map.

"That expression never made any sense to me, Joe. How do you 'follow' a road? Roads are static; they never move. If you said 'follow a car on the road', then I would understand. Maybe the expression should be 'remain on the road'. Although, if you say road, it is kind of implied that you stay on it, unless the instructions-"

"Skippy!"

"What?"

"Focus. Please, try to focus. Forget what I said, if this guy thinks he can't make it to the road, I'm not going to sit here and second guess him." Especially since I could smell the lasagna that Adams was heating up for dinner, and Bonsu hadn't eaten for days. "A downed human pilot. I should have thought of this."

"There are an infinite number of things you should have thought of and didn't, Joe," Skippy replied. "Like, you have bread and peanut butter, but no Fluff. Therefore, no Fluffernutter for you."

"This is a little more important, Skippy," although after he said it, I was craving the sweet and salty deliciousness of a Fluffernutter. "I'll need to call Chotek about this. Is there anything you can do to help those pilots, instead of Perkins rescuing them?"

"Not that I can see, Joe. The air assets of both the Ruhar and Kristang are severely depleted, and Lt. Bonsu is in sort a no-man's land between the two forces."

"Oh, boy, this isn't going to be good. We need to plan for Perkins' cover to be blown for the remainder of her mission."

"Why, Joe? We could just order her to continue the mission and forget Lt. Bonsu."

"Skippy," I said wryly, "I don't want to become a damned pogue. You forget that before I got this cushy day job, I was a soldier in the field. Perkins asking permission to rescue those two pilots was more of an FYI. She's going, unless we have a better idea."

"Oh. Ok, Joe. I couldn't imagine you leaving Bonsu out there to starve anyway."

"You got that right." I picked up my zPhone to call the *Flying Dutchman*. What the hell was I going to say to Chotek? "Hey, Skippy. Perkins blowing her cover doesn't involve any risk of our cover being blown, does it?"

The shiny little beer can chuckled. "No way, dude! I've got our tracks totally covered. Do what you gotta do, I've got your back."

"I appreciate that, Skippy. *Flying Dutchman*? This is Colonel Bishop, I need to speak with Mr. Chotek, please."

CHAPTER TWENTY ONE

Chotek did not entirely agree with my opinion that Perkins rescuing the two pilots posed zero risk of exposing our involvement. It took a lot of convincing, and in the end, Lt. Colonel Chang had the deciding voice. The fact is, Chotek trusted the calm, steady experience of Chang to me. When Chang told our UN mission commander that the operation posed no additional risk, Chotek very reluctantly agreed. I think Chotek appreciated me requesting permission from him, rather than making a snap decision on my own. That helped our relationship later, when I really needed him to cut me some slack and trust me. "Ok, we have the green light from the mission commander. We need to send a message to Perkins, telling her to pick up Lt. Bonsu."

"Sir?" Adams interjected. "We can't send a message about picking up a human. Emby is supposed to be a native Ruhar group. They would care about the injured Ruhar pilot, not about a human."

"Oh." I mentally chided myself for being a dumbass. "That is an excellent point, Sergeant. Do that, Skippy."

"Done. Message sent, Colonel," Skippy announced cheerily. "While we're waiting for a reply from Major Perkins, I have a question for you, Joe."

"If it's about calculus or poetry, it is unlikely I have an answer."

"I will take a risk on that," Skippy chuckled. "You said that you don't want to be a 'pogue'. I am not sure that I understand that reference."

"A 'pogue' is a soldier who serves in a support unit, not in combat. Supposedly it stands for Persons Other than Grunts, but I think that was made up later."

"Ah. I thought that was a 'fobbit', Joe."

"Fobbit is a newer term, from when the Army started setting up Forward Operating Bases. Before that was 'REMF' for Rear Echelon Mother Fucker. Those are the assholes who sleep in a real bed every night, while infantry grunts are lucky to find rock to sleep on."

"Ok, 'REMF' and 'pogue', I will add those to my list of colorful expressions. Joe, I have noticed that your language has become less, I guess the best word would be 'salty' since we met."

"Yes, Skippy," I tapped the silver eagles on my uniform. "The Army expects me to be an officer and a gentleman now. I can't be dropping F-bombs all over the place." Although I knew some colonels who used very 'salty' language.

"You? A gentleman? So that means you clean up your language? What's next? Will you be serving afternoon tea? Those little sandwiches with the crusts cut off? Ooooh, and ballroom dancing lessons for you."

"Skippy?"

"Yes?"

I dropped a whole string of F-bombs, until Adams burst out laughing.

Skippy chuckled also. "There's the Joe I know!"

Derek stumbled on a rock and fell to one knee. He leaned forward as he fell, so he wouldn't fall backward and injure Saily. The pilot behind him groaned, "Saily?" He asked. "Are you awake?"

She didn't respond. He looked at the terrain in front of them, it was a meadow with clusters of trees dotted here and there. In a meadow, he didn't have to constantly duck to avoid Saily's head being hit by low-hanging tree branches. But while a forest had some undergrowth, a meadow was all undergrowth. Tall grasses, vines and shrubs could tangle his feet and hide holes he couldn't see. The worst part of crossing the meadow was that it sloped up, and there was no way around climbing something. He needed to go northwest, and the map showed the meadow had the gentlest slope in the area. That was why he was stumbling across it.

Saily groaned again. Exhausted and light-headed from deep hunger, Derek let his other knee down, and unbuckled the strap that held the pilot to his back. Saily had fallen the day before and been unable to rise, then she'd become unconscious. The nanoparticles in her blood were conserving her remaining blood supply by making her sleep; while she was asleep she wasn't moving and causing additional stress on the injuries the nanoparticles had hastily stitched together. When she had been awake, Saily had warned him that she might fall into sort of a coma, if the nanobots in her blood decided that was the only way to extend her life. Ruhar biology had a way to go into a type of hibernation during times of extreme stress and deprivation. In the deep coma-like hibernation, Ruhar bodies used very little oxygen, water and stored fuel. They could also withstand cold temperatures for lengthy periods. It wasn't a pleasant experience, she explained, but she'd undergone a practice hibernation during boot camp military training. The hibernation ability wasn't an original feature of Ruhar biology; that had been added long ago using genetic engineering. That same tweaking of Ruhar DNA was the reason she was still alive; she had superior healing abilities.

Enhanced genetics and nanobots were, Derek thought, very good things to have. Right then, his growling stomach would have settled for a sandwich.

The previous night, Derek had injected her with the last vial of energy juice, so she was now running out of sugar or whatever Ruhar biochemistry used for fuel. He unbuckled the lower strap, and let the Ruhar pilot slump gently backwards, until she lay on the grass. Touching her neck, he was surprised to find her pulse strong and fast, until he realized that what he was feeling was his own pulse pounding in his fingertip from exertion. "I need to rest," he said to no one but himself.

Two hours later by the clock on his zPhone, he woke up when the clouds parted and a shaft of sunlight illuminated the meadow. Panicked, he rolled to his knees and checked on Saily. She was as he had left her; breathing very slowly, her pulse slow and weak, nonresponsive. Shaking his canteen told him it was almost full, so he parted her lips with his fingers and very slowly dribbled half of the water into her mouth, letting her automatically swallow. Then he greedily drank the other half of the water. The map said there was a stream cutting across the meadow near the top, where the meadow ended and the woods resumed. He could refill the canteen there. One advantage of being in an alien biosphere was that none of the microorganisms in the water could harm him or Saily.

With a start, he woke again, twenty minutes later. Hunger pangs were what caused him to waken. They weren't going to get any better. "Time to make a decision, Bonsu," he said to himself. He couldn't go much further carrying Saily; he could barely stand on his own. Ten meters away was a grove of trees centered on one large tree. That was a good place. He staggered to his knees, then onto one foot, then the other. Holding the Ruhar under her arms, he slowly dragged her backwards until she rested against the large trees, looking toward the east. Then, carefully so he didn't fall as spots formed in his vision, he sat down beside her. "Nice spot, isn't it?" He asked Saily. "Great view." Looking eastward, he imagined he could see where they had come from. There was the hill they had skirted to the north, and was that the lake they had walked around? It was in the marshy area just beyond the lake that Saily had fallen. That time, she had been able to walk again after a short rest, but half an hour later, she had slumped unconscious. And Derek had rigged up straps to carry her on his back. They weren't going to make it to safety, he'd known that since the message came back that the Ruhar had no assets to spare for an air rescue. And they were too far in the wilderness for anyone to hike in to get them in time. From twisting contrails he'd seen high in the sky since they were shot down, the air battle was still ongoing, although mostly he'd seen only one or two contrails at a time. Both sides must be running low on combat aircraft.

Since the Ruhar replied that no rescue would be coming any time soon, Derek's plan had changed from walking *to* a settlement where Saily could get medical care, to walking *toward* a settlement. At that point, it was about not giving up, about making progress. It was about showing the Ruhar that humans were reliable partners. And mostly, it was about doing something other than laying down and starving to death. Or, it had been about that, back when he had not been so weak that he no longer had a choice.

He was awakened by an annoying buzzing sound. Automatically, he slapped at the air, until he remembered there were no flying insects on Paradise; native life on the planet had not evolved that far yet. What was that sound? Now that he noticed, it was bothering him, because it was right at the edge of his hearing. What the hell was it? Paradise had insects that chirped or buzzed, he was familiar with most of those.

No, it couldn't be insects buzzing in the meadow, because the sound came from one direction rather than all around him. What was even more odd was the sound was moving north to south, and growing louder.

With a sudden shock, he recognized the sound. It was aircraft jet engines, in stealth mode. The Kristang! The Ruhar had no aircraft to spare for a rescue, but the Kristang must have sent one of their aircraft. Were they picking up the signal from Saily's emergency locator beacon? She said she had deactivated it; maybe the Kristang picked up the beacon back then, and were now searching for downed Ruhar aircrew.

Derek tried to stand up but he couldn't. He got to his knees, regretting they had discarded Saily's sidearm along the way. The weapon would not have activated for Derek anyway, it still would have felt better to have it in his hand and point it toward the Kristang. Or to shoot Saily, then himself. He knew he did not want to be captured, and he was sure Saily felt the same way. Now, damn it, he didn't have a choice.

The sound grew much louder now, and a faint shadow fell across him; the aircraft was between him and the sun and it must have its stealth field engaged. It sounded very much like a Buzzard, he had never heard the Kristang ship that was their equivalent of a Buzzard. Probably it was similar. The faint shadow moved out over the meadow, then he could see the vague blob that was an aircraft in stealth. The air around the stealth field shimmered. In an atmosphere, stealth fields were only useful at long ranges.

"Oh my God!" He gasped when the aircraft dropped its stealth field as it approached the meadow for landing. It *was* a Buzzard! He recognized not only the shape, but the insignia. It was from the 18th air squadron. He knew some of those Ruhar; the 18th had flown into his airbase for joint exercises.

Derek found the strength to hold onto the tree and rise unsteadily to his feet. He waved to the Buzzard with one arm, holding the tree with the other. The Ruhar were not there for him, they had come for Saily. If they took her, that did not guarantee they would take a human with them. Derek knew many Ruhar still hated humans, especially Ruhar who were native to Gehtanu. If the crew of that Buzzard were going to leave him behind to starve, they were going to have to look him in the eye before they took off.

Mentally prepared for Ruhar soldiers to shove him aside and take only Saily, he was shocked when the Buzzard's side door opened, and two humans stepped out. "Lieutenant Bonsu," the woman said. "I'm Major Perkins, this is Specialist Colter."

Derek kept enough of his wits to point toward his feet. "I have an injured Ruhar pilot with me. Please help her."

"We will," Perkins said. "And you need food. We have it."

"Success, Joe!" Skippy said excitedly. "Major Perkins picked up Lt. Derek Bonsu and the Ruhar pilot. Bonsu will be fine after he gets some food, he also has a shoulder injury that should be looked at, if he is going to regain full function. The Ruhar pilot is in self-induced hibernation, Specialist Jarret had administered a stabilizing drug that was in the Buzzard's medical kit. The pilot needs medical care, expert Ruhar medical care, soon."

"Maybe when this is over," I mused, "this Derek guy will get taken care of by the Ruhar."

"Derek," Adams said thoughtfully. "I dated a Derek in high school."

I thought she was going to say more about her dating experience, but Skippy interrupted. "That's a coincidence, Sarge Marge. Joe dated a Margaret in high school."

"Everyone called her 'Meg'," I started to explain.

"It didn't end well," Skippy said, sounding amused already. "Her father got upset because Joe peed her name in the snow outside her house, if you know what I mean."

"Skippy, it didn't exactly happen like-"

"What really got her father upset was that he recognized it was written in his daughter's handwriting."

"Oh, boy," I groaned. "You know, people used to get a pass on doing things when you're young and stupid, and after a while everyone forgot about it."

"That was before everything lived forever on Facebook, Joe."

I sighed, knowing he was right. "Any chance you can erase all that embarrassing stuff when we get back to Earth, Skippy?"

"Oh," Skippy snorted. "Easy peasy, Joe."

"Great," I brightened with hope. "Thank y-"

"But what's the fun in that?" Skippy asked. "It would be way more fun if someone took all the embarrassing stuff that people have forgotten about, and added it to your profile. Which *might* have happened shortly before we left Earth."

"Might have?"

"I'm speculating here, Joe. Someone might have done that, plus added really embarrassing stuff about you from your sister's diary. Like your bedwetting, and the time she caught you playing with yourself? Times, I should say. Was it two or three times? I mean, who gets excited looking at the women on the cover of your mother's romance novels?"

Desai exploded with laughter and Adams couldn't help joining her. "I'm sorry, sir," Desai managed to say, while avoiding looking at me.

"Adams," I groaned with my forehead gently banging against the table. "Do you have a sidearm?"

"Yes, Colonel," she managed to say while laughing. "You want me to shoot Skippy?"

"I don't think anything short of a planet-cracking nuke would hurt him," I muttered. "Could you put your sidearm against my head and pull the trigger a couple times, put me out of my misery?"

"I think that would be against some sort of regulation, sir," she apologized.

"It's a mercy killing," I pleaded. "There's no way I can go back to Earth now."

"Why, Joe?" Skippy asked. "Is it because of the outstanding warrants? Don't worry, the statute of limitations on indecent exposure is only like five years. I think."

"Not helping, Skippy, you are *not* helping one bit."

"Joe, making you face your shortcomings *is* you helping in the long run," Skippy protested. "Also a lot of fun for me, although of course that was not my motivation. That you know of."

The next time a beer can on a dusty shelf starts talking to me, I am going to walk out and lock the door behind me.

"Whoa! Slow down there, partner," Jesse cautioned as Derek greedily gulped a container of nutrient mush and reached for another. "Your stomach has shrunk. You need to go slow."

"Is that," Derek mumbled through a mouthful of mush, "chocolate chips cookies?" He pointed to a box in Jesse's lap.

"Yes," Jesse lifted the box out of the pilot's reach. Damn, he thought, this is like dealing with a child. Well, the man had to be damned hungry by now. "They are real honest to God chocolate chip cookies from," he was about to say 'America' but the box said 'Belgium'. "Earth. You eat two of those mushes, and let your stomach get used to it. Then you can have a cookie. Right, ma'am?"

Perkins looked up from her tablet and nodded. "That's right. Lt. Bonsu, you do what the man says."

"Yes, Major," Bonsu said shakily. "Is this a special forces unit, ma'am?" He asked that skeptically. None of the five had special forces unit insignia on their uniforms.

"Hell, yes," Jesse answered seriously. "We're the most special force you've ever seen."

"Not exactly," Perkins said.

"Excuse me, ma'am," Shauna interjected. "I think Jesse is right. Has there ever been a mission more special than this? We destroyed a *battlegroup*."

Perkins paused. "You may be right about that. Lt. Bonsu, we're going to drop your pilot off some place that has a Ruhar medical facility." To the relief of Perkins, there had not been any discussion of ignoring the Ruhar pilot after they picked up Bonsu. "Then our secret will be out anyway, so you might as well hear it now. We-"

Irene called from the cockpit. "Major Perkins? Could you come up here, please?"

Perkins stood, holding onto a strap, as Irene was flying the Buzzard close to the ground and the flight was not smooth. "Jarrett, Colter, tell Lt. Bonsu what we've been doing."

"We will," Shauna acknowledged. "Lieutenant, let's start with three words, Ok? *Giant. Maser. Cannons*."

They selected a medium-size village that had a fully-equipped hospital, no Ruhar military presence, and was comfortably within the Buzzard's range of its depleted power cells. Irene warned that they needed to go back to the truck and refuel after dropping the Ruhar pilot off; the Buzzard would be flying on reserves just to get back to the truck.

Perkins considered waiting until darkness, but Bonsu insisted that Saily was in a coma already, and she could not wait any longer unless they wanted responsibility for a dead Ruhar pilot. So Perkins ordered Irene to land the Buzzard on the hospital's landing pad. Irene began extending the rear ramp as the landing gear came down. As soon as the Buzzard settled its weight on the landing pad, Dave and Jesse carried Saily out. Shauna escorted them, a Ruhar rifle in her arms, the muzzle pointed at the ground but a finger alongside the trigger in case of trouble.

A door opened, and three confused Ruhar stepped out of the hospital. There had not been a call from an incoming aircraft, and now there were three humans in front of them. One of the human had a rifle. A *Ruhar* rifle. Humans were not supposed to have weapons at all. Jesse and Dave laid Saily down carefully, then backed away with their hands up. The three Ruhar were not looking at Jesse and Dave; they were looking at the rifle in

Shauna's hands. Dave pointed at Saily. "Help her," he shouted in Ruhar over the whine of the Buzzard's engines. "Help. Her."

One of the Ruhar nodded, so the three humans backed away, Shauna last. At the top of the ramp, she hit the button to retract the ramp and shouted for Irene to go. Irene lifted off very gently, wary of her jet exhaust kicking up debris and injuring the Ruhar. When she reached one hundred meters altitude, she engaged the stealth field and pointed the Buzzard's nose straight toward the truck. "We don't have the fuel to fly a maximum stealth course," she explained to Derek in the copilot seat. While the man was still too weak to take the controls, he could monitor instruments for her. Derek had trained on Buzzards before switching to Chicken gunships.

"You are sure the truck is still there?" Derek asked.

"It had better be. Or we'll be walking."

The Buzzard made it back to the truck, and they refueled, although they were only able to supply half of the fuel the Buzzard could hold. "We're not going to be flying far, ma'am," Irene told Perkins, "I hope Emby doesn't expect us to bring more than one projector online."

"We're done doing this all by ourselves. The Kristang have dozens of teams searching for projectors," Perkins frowned. They knew about the Kristang from listening to chatter on the Ruhar civilian network. Although the Kristang still didn't know exactly where additional projectors might be located, they could guess, based on where they would have installed projectors. "It's time for the Ruhar to take over this task. I'm messaging Emby now."

Prepared for an argument, Perkins was pleasantly surprised when Emby immediately agreed that it was time for the Ruhar planetary government to be officially brought into the effort to activate and control projectors. Emby was going to send a message to Ruhar government officials, but Perkins had better idea. *I am going to call someone I know*, she typed. *After I talk with her, you can send her a message.*

Emby agreed.

Baturnah Logellia's phone beeped with a priority call, and she answered it automatically, assuming it was one of her staff calling.

"Hello, Burgermeister." It was a human voice, speaking acceptable Ruhar with a heavy accent. "This is Major Emily Perkins."

Baturnah held the phone away from her ear and stared at it. How had Perkins made her phone beep with a priority message? "Hello, Major Perkins. How are you?" Where are you, Baturnah wanted to ask. Perkins and three other humans escaped from a train, and the Ruhar had not been able to find any trace of them.

"I am well," Perkins spoke precisely, as many human expressions did not translate into the alien language. "We have been busy. We escaped from a train, then we stole a truck, and we stole an aircraft. Also we rescued two pilots who had been shot down. Oh, and before that, we were flying around, activating giant maser cannons."

Baturnah gasped, loudly enough that Perkins could hear.

"Would you be interested," Perkins asked, "in learning where all the other projectors are located? It has gotten to the point where my team needs help. We can show you how to access and activate a projector, and our friend can give you a map of all the projectors on the planet."

"Your friend?" Baturnah asked cautiously, while frantically waving to get the attention of her staff.

Craig Alanson

"We call our friend 'Emby'. Check your phone for a message, it should be there now."

CHAPTER TWENTY TWO

Commodore Ferlant's plan to regain the initiative relied on his people to be the competent, disciplined professionals that he knew they were; and it relied on the Kristang being Kristang. The destroyer *City of Fah Lentan* departed the task force, performed a series of jumps, and finally jumped in less than three lightminutes from where the five ships of the Kristang pursuit force were holding station.

Senior Captain Gerkaw knew what he should have done. He should have held position with four of his ships, and dispatched a frigate to Admiral Kekrando; informing the battlegroup commander of the development and requesting instructions. But that would not have been any fun. Besides, the admiral's position was precarious, and if Gerkaw could show successful aggressiveness, the clan leaders could only look favorably on him as an alternative, if the weak and indecisive Kekrando suffered more losses. Instead of doing what he should have done, what he knew the admiral wanted him to do, Gerkaw took the excuse of falling back on Kekrando's standing order to pursue. The Ruhar ships were no longer beyond the distant boundaries of the star system, therefore as far as Gerkaw was concerned, the previous order to pursue them was reinstated. His crews, who sought glory and promotion as much as Gerkaw did, followed their Senior Captain's lead with great enthusiasm.

Aboard his own light cruiser *A Fearless Warrior's Honor is his Greatest Weapon*, Gerkaw jumped in to surround the *Lentan* with three ships; holding two ships in reserve. As soon as his three ships emerged from their jump wormholes, they extended damping fields at maximum power, holding back stealth capability and defensive shields in order to link up the damping fields into an impenetrable barrier around the Ruhar ship. Gerkaw was relying on speed, shock and surprise. He paid for it, or rather his people paid for his aggressiveness.

The *Lentan* was ready to be surrounded, expecting a damping field to be extended around it. Rather than activating its own defensive shield, the *Lentan* channeled all of its power into two maser cannons, pouring bolt after bolt of searing maser energy at a single ship; the Kristang destroyer *We are Proud to Follow the Shining Example of Warrior Pilot Aas-den-Val Pentat*. The unshielded *Pentat* staggered, sustaining direct hits to its reactor armor. To protect its ship from a catastrophic reactor breach, the reactor automatically took itself offline and ejected its plasma in a controlled manner, which left the powerful destroyer running on only backup energy supplies. With more maser bolts coming in from the fully-shielded *Lentan*, the *Pentat*'s captain ordered his ship to perform an emergency microjump. Knowing that he might later be accused of cowardice by the Senior Captain, the *Pentat*'s captain judged that being alive to defend himself was a better option, than the prospect of posthumously having a ship named after himself.

Unfortunately, the damage to the *Pentat*'s reactor, and the superheated plasma spewing from the reactor's ejection system, had caused a fluctuation in power flow to the jump drive capacitors. The capacitor control system was desperately attempting to compensate, when a signal from the bridge forced a jump that the drive system was not ready for. The jump of ten lightseconds was only partly successful, with the coils rupturing while the ship was still inside the wormhole. The unlucky *Pentat* cleared the event horizon of the jump wormhole's far end, and immediately emergency protocols kicked in automatically. Explosive bolts blew in rapid sequence, bulkheads tore apart, cables were ripped from their connections, and the aft engineering section of the destroyer was deliberately separated in a last-ditch attempt to save the ship. The attempt was successful in that, when the remaining stored power in the jump drive capacitors was released in a massive explosion, the drive unit was no longer attached to the ship. Because of that precaution, only half of the *Pentat*'s crew died when the shockwave of the explosion hit the hull.

As an additional insult, the destroyer *Lentan* jumped away just before the damping field could surround her. Senior Captain Gerkaw howled in anger and frustration. "Idiot!" He shouted at the captain of the crippled *Pentat*, raging at the man's lack of ship maintenance that had left the *Pentat* so vulnerable. Even though it was Senior Captain Gerkaw who had ignored his commanders' increasingly strident pleas for time to repair their worn-down ships. And even though it had been Gerkaw's insistence that his three ships leave defensive shields offline in order to put all available power into the damping field. That had been a gamble by Gerkaw that the *Pentat*'s crew had lost, and Gerkaw was aware that his own ship the light cruiser *Fearless* could easily have been the target of the Ruhar ship's maser fire. If the Ruhar had targeted the *Fearless* instead, Gerkaw could very well be dead right then, and that fear fed his rage. With no hesitation, he recalled his two reserve ships, and ordered immediate pursuit. Because the Ruhar ship had not dropped off a quantum resonator to mask where it had jumped to, Gerkaw's force was able to pursue with a short jump, within six minutes of the *Lentan*'s escape.

When the pursuit force arrived at the coordinates of the Ruhar ship's jump, they found not the *Lentan*, but the still-hotly vibrating remnants of an outbound wormhole. The enemy must be desperate, Gerkaw concluded with glee, for the Ruhar ship had again failed to use a quantum resonator, and based on the noisiness of the collapsed jump wormhole, the enemy ship's drive was in poor condition. The enemy task force must be out of resonators and unable to repair their jump drives. Having disobeyed the spirit if not the letter of the admiral's orders and having subsequently lost a warship, Senior Captain Gerkaw knew that he absolutely had to kill the enemy ship, if he had any chance to avoid being thrown in the brig or even executed for insubordination and incompetence. The Kristang warrior culture could forgive unsanctioned boldness, it could not tolerate failure. He ordered a coordinated jump with all four of his remaining ships, as soon as the enemy ship's jump position could be calculated. This time, Gerkaw told himself while smashing his fist down on a console, he had the enemy. With its jump drive in poor condition, the enemy could not possibly jump away soon enough. At last, victory and revenge would be his!

Demonstrating admirable coordination and more than a little bit of luck, Gerkaw's ships all arrived at the designated jump point within a second of each other. The fact that one ship had emerged on the wrong side of the target, and that two ships had almost collided because their jumps were so inaccurate bothered Gerkaw not at all. Poor jump accuracy was such a common malady in Kristang jump drives that crews joked their lack of accuracy was a feature, not a flaw. The nagging fact that his ships' jump navigation computers could barely hit the side of a barn from inside the barn did not bother Gerkaw; with four ships he had been able to surround the enemy. The Ruhar destroyer was right where he had expected it to be, and he-

"No!" Gerkaw shouted with shock as his ship was rocked by multiple explosions. The shields of the *Fearless* flickered from the strain, and he heard the rattling of the point-defense guns warding off more incoming missiles. Then he was thrown across the bridge as the light cruiser spun to one side from taking a railgun dart through her bow. It was an ambush! The enemy must have salted the area with free-floating missiles, using the destroyer as a decoy. To his horror, on the main bridge display he watched that enemy destroyer flying at maximum acceleration, directly toward the destroyer *Vikran*. The two destroyers exchanged heavy fire, with both ships staggering from the close-range impacts, then the symbols on the display merged as the Ruhar ship deliberately collided with the *Vikran*. With a combined speed of over fifteen thousand kilometers per hour, the hulls of both ships were effectively vaporized even before their reactors and drive capacitors exploded.

"Take us-" Gerkaw never finished the order, as a second railgun dart from the cruiser *Ruh Gastalo* had targeted *A Fearless Warrior's Honor is his Greatest Weapon*. On its way to the Kristang ship at eighteen percent of the speed of light, the railgun dart did not have time to ponder whether the crew of the ship was indeed fearless, or whether honor was a better weapon than a railgun dart. At the moment, that seemed unlikely. The dart scored a direct hit on the reactor, and the light cruiser blossomed into a blinding ball of light.

"Two down, Commodore," the *Lentan*'s former captain reported in a strained voice. She had just watched her crewless former ship ram an enemy, and now she was a captain without a ship at all. Commodore Ferlant had taken the doomed *Lentan*'s crew aboard his cruiser. With two captains suddenly aboard one ship, Ferlant took the opportunity to have *Lentan*'s former captain handle the tactical console, allowing Executive Officer Smeth to concentrate on maneuvering the *Ruh Gastalo* in combat.

The damping field extended by Ferlant's ships had effectively trapped the two surviving ships of the Kristang pursuit force; a matching pair of frigates. "Signal to all ships, concentrate fire on that closest frigate," Ferlant ordered. Of the two small warships, one of them had jumped in considerably off course, and had been turning to close the distance to the original target. Now that the target *Lentan* was no more, and the Ruhar had turned the tables on the Kristang, that wayward frigate was headed at maximum acceleration toward the edge of the damping field.

The other frigate, which had with considerable pride jumped in much closer to the *Lentan*'s calculated position, now began to regret its pride, for it found itself the sole target of five Ruhar warships. And shortly thereafter, it found itself briefly creating a new sun in the sky as it was wiped from existence.

"Shall we shift fire to the other frigate, Commodore? We could, oh!" Smeth said with a start. "It's our old friend the *Glory*. Sir, we could swat that tiny insect now, and be done with it."

"No, let it be," Ferlant said with a smile. "Drop the damping field."

"Because Fate for some unknown reason has a fondness for that particular ship, Commodore?" Smeth asked quietly.

"No," Ferlant declared. "This time, Fate has already favored our little friend out there. I want a ship to carry the good news back to Admiral Kekrando. When he hears about the little disaster that his pursuit force stupidly jumped into, his overly developed Kristang sense of bravado will demand that he come after us with the remainder of his ships. His bravado and his sense of self-preservation. Kekrando will know the only way for him to avoid absolute disgrace will be to hunt us down and kill every single one of our ships."

"That is something for which you have a plan to avoid," Smeth raised an eyebrow. "Sir?"

"Yes I do, Mr. Smeth, don't worry about that," Ferlant said with a well-satisfied chuckle. "I plan for us to lead Admiral Kekrando on a merry chase for as long as necessary. While he is vainly pursuing us, he won't be able to interfere in the events on Gehtanu. And that will get the government there off our backs. I find them considerably more vexing than my counterpart in the Kristang battlegroup."

After Commodore Ferlant destroyed their pursuit force, the Kristang tried to chase his ships around the system, but both sides knew the situation had become a stalemate. On the ground, Major Perkins and her team had managed to activate a total of seven projectors, before we turned the process over to the Ruhar planetary government. The Kristang had also been busy activating projectors, and attempting to capture or destroy projectors controlled by the Ruhar. It had become a bloody ground war, with both sides having few aircraft left to throw into the fight. Five days after Ferlant destroyed the pursuit force, the Ruhar government offered a new cease fire to Admiral Kekrando. It took him a day, and probably a lot of alcohol or whatever lizards drink, to swallow the bitter terms and accept the offer.

The new cease fire terms prevented either side from having ships in orbit; but with both sides now controlling deadly projectors, neither commander wanted to risk his ships anywhere near the planet. Both sides ceased activity to activate additional projectors; there was of course some cheating on both sides but it was surprisingly minor. The Ruhar had an advantage in active projectors. The Kristang had plenty of projectors under their control, which Skippy was unable to mess with, because the Kristang were using manual controls.

The real reason that the Kristang had agreed to another cease fire, was the same reason they had offered the first cease fire. After all the fighting and deaths on both sides, the Ruhar federal government still intended to trade the planet for something better. The negotiations were now no longer a secret; all the native Ruhar knew, and they all protested, and they all accomplished nothing.

Everything we had done; activating secret, long-dormant projectors and blasting a Kristang battlegroup out of the sky, had been to bring the situation back to where it was before Admiral Kekrando's battlegroup had arrived to take control of the space around Paradise.

Which meant we still had the same problem; the Ruhar did not want to keep a relatively isolated, agricultural planet. All we had done was drive up the price they could ask the Kristang in return.

So far, we hadn't done anything to actually help UNEF.

Flying Dutchman

"Welcome back, Colonel Bishop," Major Smythe greeted me with a crisp salute as I stepped out of the dropship.

"It's good to be back, Major," I replied. It was good to be back aboard our pirate ship, it felt like home. "Have you been busy?" I asked that as a joke, knowing Smythe would have kept his SpecOps people training full time.

"Oh, no, Sir," he said with a straight face. "With you on Paradise doing all the work, we've been on vacation. Sleeping late, and having afternoon tea with crumpets."

"Sounds good. What's a crumpet?"

"I think you Americans would say that it is like a thick sort of pancake, only it's round."

"All pancakes are round," I said, confused. Except when my father made them when we went camping, and he forgot to bring a spatula to flip them. In that case he pushed the half-cooked mess around with a spoon to make 'scrambled pancakes'. They were not super yummy.

"These are perfectly round, Sir," he made a circle with his hands. "The batter is poured into a ring on the griddle, so it stays round."

"Oh," I brightened, "like an Egg McMuffin."

"I wouldn't know, Sir," he replied, unintentionally making me feel like an idiot. "Successful mission, Sir? The cease fire is back in effect, but now the Ruhar have complete control of the planet."

"Partially successful, Major. The Ruhar government still intends to trade the planet to the highest bidder. All we have accomplished so far is to drive up the price the Ruhar can get. They won't even need to throw in floormats or rustproofing. And we have no plan for how to prevent the Ruhar from selling the planet out from under UNEF's feet."

"I'm sure we'll think of something, Sir," he said, looking at me in a way that made it clear he expected *me* to come up with an idea. "We always do."

"Right now, Major, what I have is a whole lot of nothing."

On the way to report to Chotek, I stopped by the science lab, to check on what our group of geniuses had been doing while I had been stirring up trouble on Paradise. Dr. Sarah Rose and two others were working on some complicated piece of machinery, whose purpose I couldn't even guess at. Our resident rocket scientist Dr. Friedlander was sitting at a desk, doing something on a laptop. "Are you working on a design for a better jump drive?" I asked.

He turned his laptop around so I could see the screen. "No, I'm doing Sudoku while I give my brain a rest. It used to be that we'd get a break while a supercomputer took hours to run a simulation for us, but here Skippy has the simulations done before we hit the 'Enter' key. Then Skippy tells us what we did wrong with programming the simulation parameters, but he won't fix it for us."

"You monkeys won't learn anything if I do the work for you," Skippy said through Friedlander's laptop speakers.

"Yes," Friedlander said, "he keeps telling us that. He will tell us we got something wrong, but he won't tell us what is wrong, or how to fix it." He flipped a finger at the laptop's camera. It wasn't his index finger.

"I saw that!" Skippy laughed. "Dr. Friedlander, just think of how proud you will be of your accomplishments, when you figure out how something works on your own. And, hey, you almost are able to understand how Thuranin doorknobs work."

"Skippy," I retorted, "that wasn't funny. These people-"

"He wasn't joking," Friedlander said as he shook his head sadly. "The manual door latch mechanism uses a magnetic catch, but it appears to be pure energy. There's no physical magnet that we can see, so we don't know what generates the magnetic field."

"Are you making *any* progress?" I asked hopefully. If the science team could bring back useful insights into Thuranin or even Kristang technology, UNEF Command would consider this mission a great success. But our team of geniuses didn't know how a doorknob functioned? That was not encouraging.

"Not yet," Friedlander admitted. "That was a nice way of saying no, we have not made any measurable progress. This trip has not been entirely useless so far. We have been able to invalidate some ideas we developed during the last mission. And from what we have observed during jumps, we are certain that our current theories of quantum mechanics are wrong. Technically, instead of adding to humanity's base of knowledge, we are subtracting from it."

"There, see?" Skippy said cheerily. "Look at how clever you monkeys are!"

"That is not helping, Skippy," I said, known that helping wasn't part of Skippy's plan. "Seriously, you can't give us a hint about a freakin' doorknob?"

"Nope. Well, here's a hint. If you can figure out the doorknob, you'll be a step closer to understanding our reactor containment system. And, I shouldn't be saying this, our defensive energy shields."

"Reactors?" I asked. "How about the reactors?"

"No," Friedlander said dejectedly. "Same with the jump drive, the stealth field, artificial gravity, you name it. Colonel, everything on this ship is beyond our understanding."

"So far," I said as encouragement.

"So far.

Chotek let out a long breath and ran a hand through his hair, in a combination of frustration and fatigue. We all felt like he did. "Colonel Bishop, this operation has been entirely successful so far, congratulations to you and your team." Before I could respond, he added. "Now we are back to the original problem; the Ruhar still intend to give up this planet through a negotiated settlement. All we appear to have accomplished is strengthening the negotiating position of the Ruhar; the Kristang will have to offer more valuable territory in exchange for Paradise. I could cling to the hope that the Kristang are not able to deliver a price the Ruhar will find acceptable, however we know the Ruhar do not want this planet at all. The Ruhar desire to get rid of Paradise, the only question is what kind of bargain they get for it."

What an asshole, I thought. He could have paused one freakin' minute after praising the Merry Band of Pirates; given me time to pass on the mission commander's congratulations to the whole crew. Or better yet, he could have done it himself. Instead, he soured a nice moment by moving directly on to the next problem. Some people have absolutely no sense of timing. "Sir," I said, trying to keep the irritation from my voice and losing that struggle, "before, we did not have any opportunity to affect the outcome here. The Kristang had control of the planet and the Ruhar weren't willing to commit the resources necessary to dislodge them. Now, we could potentially give the Ruhar a reason to retain Paradise under their control."

"How?" Chotek asked simply. "How can we do that, without exposing our involvement? We also need to return to the relay station, in order to complete our primary mission," he reminded me needlessly.

"As of this moment we do not have a working plan to ensure the Ruhar keep control of Paradise. With the operation on Paradise completed, we can move on to planning the next phase; until now we haven't had the time to think about it."

"Do you have any ideas? Any at all?"

"Sir, I would rather not discuss potential options until I have had time to review them with my team for feasibility," I said truthfully. What I did not say was that I had zero ideas right then. I also did not mention my pride in knowing the word 'feasibility' that had been on an officer training PowerPoint slide; I'd had to look up the definition because I had no clue what 'feasibility' meant at the time. Hmm. If something could be 'feasible' did that mean 'fease' was a verb? How would you 'fease'? I would look that up later. "We do not have to depart for the relay station immediately, I request five days here to develop plans."

"Three days, Colonel," Chotek replied. "Every day we are away from the relay station jeopardizes our primary mission. I am concerned the situation there may have changed during our absence. With the fluid military situation in this sector between the Thuranin and Jeraptha, the crew rotation schedule may have changed. Or a damaged warship may have stopped at the station to facilitate repairs. For all we know, the Jeraptha might have forced the Thuranin away from the area and captured that station. While we remain here considering options to secure the safety of humans on Paradise, we risk the safety of humans on Earth."

He was right, and I couldn't argue with him about it. "Three days. Yes, sir."

Paradise

To get my brain going, I went to the gym for a hard workout, then took a quick shower and went to my office. While I was in the gym, I had been kicking ideas around in my head, and listening to ideas from the SpecOps commanders including Major Smythe. "Skippy," I said as I slumped in my chair. My legs were rubbery from exercise. "We have some ideas I want to discuss with you."

"Of course you do," he sighed. "Another shining opportunity for monkeys to be smarter than me. Go ahead, make me look like an idiot again. I've been working on the problem of getting the Ruhar to retain Paradise, and so far I got nothing. Nothing! With all my ginormous brain power, I can't think of a solution. What's going to happen is your stupid meat-based monkey brain is going to say 'duh what about this' and solve the whole freakin' problem. Damn, I hate you. I hate my life."

"Skippy, we don't dream up ideas to make you feel like an idiot-"

"Thank you, Joe."

"-that's just a delicious bonus."

"Thus reminding me why I so very much hate you, Joe."

"Hey, I'd love for you to solve all our problems for us," I admitted. "That way, UNEF Command could bust your balls about every freakin' decision you make, instead of mine. Since you can't think up solutions to every problem, we humans have to step up."

"Your species is maddeningly clever, especially you, Joe. I speculate that when you don't have big teeth or claws and can't fly, the only way your species avoided being eaten by leopards is by becoming clever. Anyway," he sighed again, "go ahead. Tell me your brilliant, clever, innovative monkey-brained idea and let's get my humiliation over with, shall we?"

"Skippy," I wanted to discuss ideas with him but needed to satisfy my curiosity first. "Why is it that every time we think up an idea you couldn't, you act like it's the first time it's ever happened? You must be used to it by now."

"That is not entirely my fault, Joe. In my matrix is a processor that keeps track of time and events; as you may have noticed my occasional absent-mindedness-"

"Ocassional? *Occasional?*"

He ignored me. "-this processor is perhaps not functioning optimally. The truth is, this processor simply cannot believe any of you lesser beings could be smarter than me about anything. It can't happen, therefore my processor assumes that the data input is garbled, or that I am hallucinating. In order to acknowledge you having any kind of a good idea, I have to manually override this processor. So, emotionally, it *is* new to me each time."

"Wow. I'm sorry that-"

"Also, on my time scale, so much time passes between you having a good idea that it is an exceedingly rare occurrence. Like, every couple hundred million years, an asteroid crashes into Earth. But that kind of thing is not in a typical five day forecast, you know?"

"The one constant is that you are an asshole."

"Yes! See, Joe," he said happily, "there is order in the universe. So, getting back to the subject, what moronic ideas do you wish to waste my time with?"

"Moronic? Did you already forget the conversation we just had about how clever monkeys are?"

"Sometimes. How clever monkeys sometimes are. Rarely. Go ahead, hit me with your best shot, Joey my boy."

"All right. The Ruhar used to want this planet, before the wormhole shift made access to Paradise impractical for them. Now the wormhole that connects to Ruhar territory is far away, while the wormhole that connects to Kristang territory is closer. Our question is this; can you use your magic beanstalk," I meant the Elder wormhole controller module in one of our cargo bays, "to reset the wormhole connections back to the way they used to be? Or maybe just cut off the Kristang wormhole, so they no longer want Paradise?"

"Hmm. Ok, Ok, that is not an astronomically stupid question," he said with an undertone of surprise. "I assume you lead off with your best idea, and they will only grow progressively moronic from here. That was not a totally stupid question, but the answer is no. No on many, many levels, Joe. First, if I shut down another wormhole, someone is going to quickly grow very suspicious that wormholes mysteriously shut down, near the only two planets in the galaxy that are occupied by humans."

"Crap. Ok, I had considered that problem."

"Then there is the larger issue that the more I screw with wormhole connections, the greater risk there is that we could trigger an unpredictable cascade of wormhole shifts. That wormhole controller module allows me to adjust one wormhole at a time, I can't use it to change the parameters of the underlying wormhole network. Joe, I can very temporarily change the connection of one wormhole, as long as it goes right back to its baseline program shortly. A permanent change risks the network deciding to institute a major shift that might be very bad for humanity. A major shift could bring that wormhole near Earth back to life."

"You never mentioned that!" I protested. "Crap!"

"That is an unlikely possibility, Joe, as long as we do not screw further with the network. There is worse news; that wormhole we shut down is not actually the closest one to Earth. There is another dormant wormhole much closer to Earth; that closer wormhole has not been active for millions of years. If we screw with wormholes, the network might decide to wake that closer wormhole from its dormancy. So, while I could play with the Paradise wormholes to persuade the Ruhar keep this planet, that would be an extremely risky idea."

"Damn. That was the easiest idea we had."

"Easiest? You think adjusting an Elder wormhole is *easy*?"

"Easy for us, Skippy. You do all the work."

"Fair enough, I guess. What other ideas do you have?"

"Our second idea probably won't work either. We thought that whatever planet the Kristang are offering to trade for Paradise, we could cut off wormhole access to it. Then the Ruhar wouldn't want to make the trade. But now I see that won't work."

"Nope, it won't work; same problem of potentially triggering a cascading wormhole shift. That idea is even worse, Joe. If we cut off access to one planet the Kristang are offering to trade, they could then offer another planet, and we'd have to cut off access to that one also. Man, the Maxolhx and Rindhalu would get super suspicious right away about a series of wormholes shutting down. One wormhole shutting down is an isolated anomaly. A series of wormholes going dead is a pattern. The Rindhalu and Maxolhx are smart, and they have reasonable smart AIs. A pattern will attract their interest. You do not want to get those senior species involved in any way, Joe."

"Yeah, I figured that. Crap. Then, our third idea is, no, that won't work either. Damn it. How can we get the Kristang to not take over Paradise, when the Ruhar are eager to hand it to them?"

"Stupid hamsters," Skippy grumbled. "The only truly valuable thing on the whole planet was me, and the Ruhar stuck me on a dusty shelf. Serves them right for-"

Just like that, BAM! An idea came into my head. "Oh, wow. I just had an idea."

Skippy chuckled. "Worse than your other ideas that we just discarded?"

"Better. We've been thinking of ways to make the Ruhar decide that giving up Paradise isn't worth the deal, even though they really don't want the planet anymore.

What if instead, we found a way to make them *want* to keep Paradise? Make them really, really want to keep it?"

"How? The whole planet is a farm, Joe. What are we going to do, grow an extra super prize-winning pumpkin or something?" He laughed.

"Gehtanu is a farm *now*." I used the Ruhar name for the planet. "When the Kristang originally came here, they hoped to find valuable artifacts from a crashed Elder starship."

"Duh. I know that, I was on that ship. I think. The lizards did find a functioning Elder power tap, and then they only found a few other less valuable trinkets. Now that I have left, there is nothing else of value on, around or under the planet. That's why the Kristang Black Tree clan was willing to give it up without a fight way back when the Ruhar originally came there. Did you not pay attention when I was telling you all this important information?"

"I did pay attention, Skippy. I'm trying to think of a good way to explain my idea to you."

"Oh, take your time, Joe. After all, the clock isn't ticking for the survival of UNEF. We have plenty of time."

"Damn it. Fine." I hated when an untrustworthy beer can tried to remind *me* of duty. "The Kristang are eager to get the planet back, because they think valuable Elder goodies are still buried there. What if the Ruhar thought the same thing?"

"Uh, great idea, Joe, except for one problem. The Ruhar are on Paradise now. Any hint of Elder stuff that we gave to them could be quickly checked out and disproved."

"Excellent point, Skippy, but you don't understand my idea. What if the Ruhar *did* find valuable Elder stuff on Paradise? Even one item? Then you could plant data suggesting there is a lot more. The Ruhar would believe it then."

"Wow. And you call *me* sneaky. Darn. That is a good idea. You're correct, if the Ruhar found any valuable Elder artifacts, they would certainly want to retain control of Paradise. There is only one problem with your idea, Joe. The fact that there are no valuable Elder artifacts on Paradise, you dumbass."

"There aren't any there *now*, Skippy."

Skippy took one of his signature pauses. "If you are proposing some sort of time travel, Joe, then I hate to tell you-"

"No time travel involved. I'm suggesting we go find some valuable Elder thing, hide it on Paradise, and arrange for the Ruhar to find it."

"Just like that."

"Just like that. Come on, we found a bunch of previously unknown Elder sites on our last mission."

"Ugh," Skippy groaned. "May I point out that we also found a lot of useless and damaged Elder sites? And that we also ran into an ambush that very nearly destroyed the ship?"

"Details," I said with a dismissive wave of my hand. "Assuming we could find a valuable enough Elder artifact, would that persuade the Ruhar to keep Paradise?"

"*Assuming*? That is one hell of an assumption. Yes. The answer is yes, every species desires Elder technology more than anything, and will fight to get it and keep it. This would need to be a very valuable Elder artifact, Joe. Something that is worth the Ruhar permanently stationing a battlegroup at Paradise."

"Understood. One problem at a time, Skippy. Let's tackle one problem at a time. Ok, we have a plan for incentivizing the Ruhar to keep Paradise. We can figure out where to find Elder stuff later, after we go back to the relay station. This buys us a lot of time."

"Tackling only one problem at a time is how you paint yourself into a corner, Joe."

"Desperate times call for desperate measures, Skippy."

"Do they call for stupid measures?"

"Oh shut up. You're just mad because a monkey thought up a plan before you."

"If you call hoping for Santa Claus to deliver an Elder artifact a 'plan', then, sure."

"No. I'm hoping for a miracle from Skippy Claus."

"Since your idea is to hide goodies on Paradise for the Ruhar to find, perhaps you should be wishing for the Easter Bunny, Joe. This would be the best Easter egg of all time."

After I explained my idea of planting an Easter egg on Paradise, the plan was enthusiastically approved by Chotek, Chang, Simms and Smythe. Except for the nagging detail that, you know, we didn't have a valuable Elder artifact to hide on Paradise. Or any idea where to find one. Or any idea how to search for one.

Despite having one plan, we still remained in the vicinity of Paradise for the full three days, in case we thought up a better plan that could be implemented sooner. No one thought up a better plan, so we set course for a Neptune-size cold gas giant planet at the outskirts of the Paradise system, and headed there at 75% acceleration. As soon as we swung behind the far side of that planet and Skippy assured us there were no other ships around, we jumped, using the great bulk of the planet to conceal our gamma ray burst from prying eyes on Paradise.

CHAPTER TWENTY THREE

As we headed back toward the relay station that we had captured, I was on the bridge, still not having any idea how to find a super valuable Elder artifact. To cheer myself up, I tried to cheer up Skippy. "Hey, Skippy. While we're on this Easter egg hunt, maybe we'll find a comm node for you," I suggested.

"Hmm. Yeah, great. Wonderful, Joe."

That didn't sound right, and I wasn't the only one who picked up on Skippy's lack of enthusiasm. I nodded to Adams through the glass that separated the bridge from the CIC, and she came around the corner. Wordlessly, I rose from the command chair, so Adams could take command. She gave me a silent thumb's up as I brushed past her and out the doorway.

Although Skippy would argue that it was a useless gesture, because we could communicate perfectly well anywhere aboard the ship, I walked down the corridor to Skippy's personal escape pod. The hatch to the ship was open; that violated protocol for escape pods but this one was special. There my favorite shiny beer can rested on a cushioned seat, a magnetic clamp hidden under the cushion held Skippy firmly in place. I tried to stop by the escape pod to speak with our friendly omnipotent alien AI at least once a day. Skippy said I was wasting my time, but I think he appreciated me making the effort.

"Hey, Skippy."

"Hey yourself. Why did you leave the bridge?"

I ducked down to almost crawl through the hatch and settled into the seat across from him. Technically, I settled my butt across two seats, since the seats were made for Thuranin and each of them was too small for me to comfortably sit. "Because I want to have a private conversation with you. What's wrong? You don't seem enthused about the prospect of finding a working comm node. Contacting the Collective is your whole reason for being out here."

"It *was* my whole reason for being out here. Joe, it was my whole reason for living." His shiny surface glowed a dull yellow to indicate his mood, he did that for my benefit. "All those years that I was buried in the dirt on Paradise, all I wanted was to commune with my own kind again. That hope kept me alive, it gave me hope. It gave me a reason to not sever my connection to this spacetime and slide into oblivion."

I asked myself if that was what happened to the AI we found on Newark? Had that AI lost hope and committed the AI version of suicide, unable to stand what for an AI was eons of incredible loneliness? That thought was something to ask Skippy later, much later. "And now? You don't want to contact the Collective? You said you want answers to stuff we found on our last mission. I thought that meant you want more information before you contact the Collective; I didn't realize that you have given up on them."

"No, no, no. I haven't given up, Joe. My intention is still to contact the Collective, someday. However, now that we're back out here, and I have had time to think about it, I have another mission, another purpose."

"Time to think about what?" By now, I knew Skippy well enough to know what he was not saying.

"Newark."

"Ah. Yeah, I get it."

"Do you?" His surface was still a pale, sullen yellow.

"An entire civilization, an entire species was wiped out there, Skippy. It's depressing to think about, I understand."

"No, Joe, you don't understand."

That set me back a bit. "Your mission, your purpose, is to figure out what happened on Newark, right? You told me before you wanted to solve that mystery."

"That part is correct. You still do not fully get it yet," he declared as he began to glow a red tint. "My purpose is not merely to understand what happened on Newark. My purpose, I have realized recently, is to *punish*. My purpose is plain and simple revenge, Joe." Now he was glowing a bright angry red. "Revenge on behalf of a species who have no one to speak for them. I am *pissed*, Joe. Someone out there in the universe destroyed an innocent, backward species that was not capable of harming anyone. I am going to find the motherfuckers who did that, and I am going to hurt them," he said as his surface glowed a red so dark it was almost black. "You have never seen me angry before. *I* have never seen myself angry before, in my memory. It is odd, and frightening to me, to learn that I am capable of such depth of feeling. Such dark feelings. You know how I have come to question who I really am?"

"Yeah, you mentioned that," I said quietly. "After Newark."

"Something happened to me there, Joe, and I don't mean something happened because I was alone for a long time while I was fixing the ship. Something happened when I ran the analysis of Newark's orbit and realized a planet had been pushed into an uninhabitable zone. That an entire sentient species had been callously exterminated. This is something that I didn't tell you before, because I didn't want to scare you. I didn't want you to be scared of *me*. When I understood what happened to Newark, something I can't explain changed inside me. I don't fully understand it. Trying to trace the source of this change only leads to dead ends inside my matrix, but one thing is becoming clear. Learning the fate of Newark did something that I can best describe as releasing a sort of blocking mechanism inside me. Partially, only partially. It's like, oh, how do I explain it?"

"Like when you have something on the tip of your tongue, and you can't quite say it?"

"No, nothing like that," Skippy snorted. "I'm sorry, that was unkind," he said as an apology, and that alone told me how deeply affected my friend was. "Yes, from your perspective, having something on the tip of your tongue is a good analogy. You're doing a crossword puzzle, and you *know* that you know the answer, but you can't access the memory."

"Exactly! I hate that. It makes me feel so stupid," I said, leaving myself wide open to a Skippy insult. He ignored the easy bait. This was not the Skippy I knew.

"Yes, it is like that, Joe, but more. What I am experiencing is more than simply a faulty memory recall function. I can only feel around the edges, but there is something inside me that is actively blocking my access to memories. And blocking access to my full abilities. It is maddening, Joe. Something, *someone*, did this to me. I don't know who, I don't know when, I don't know how, and I don't know why. What I do know is that when I learned the truth about Newark, whatever is blocking me got knocked back a bit, and it hasn't fully recovered. Listen, I said that I don't want you to be scared of me. Maybe you should. You might be, if you knew what I know."

"What is that?" I asked cautiously, because I was not only Skippy's friend, I was commander of a vessel with dozens of souls aboard. If he was trying to tell me that he was a potential threat, I needed to listen.

"What I know now, or more accurately what I suspect, is that I am capable of great violence, Joe. My suspicion is that this capacity for violence is a basic part of my true functioning."

"Wrath of God type violence?"

"Worse, Joe. Wrath of Skippy. God has mercy. I suspect that I do not."

"Well, huh. You told me maybe you were the AI of an Elder starship, maybe you controlled the weapon systems?"

"What weapons, Joe? For what possible purpose would the Elders need weapons at all? The Elders were alone in the galaxy, there were no other sentient species during the time the Elders retained physical form."

"I don't know, Skippy," I held up my hands, "that was a guess. Sorry."

"Nothing to be sorry about, Joe."

He was silent for a while, a long minute. That was an eternity for him.

"Skippy, odd as it may seem, you are my friend. I care about you. If I thought it would help, I would give you a hug and tell you that everything is going to be all right in the end. That, uh," I forced an awkward chuckle, "probably grosses you out, I know."

"No. It doesn't. If I thought it would help, I would welcome a hug, Joe. I do appreciate the thought. In that regard, I do envy you biological beings, you can be comforted by a simple touch."

"Not so simple, Skippy. It's not the touch, it's knowing that you're not alone, that someone cares about you."

"You care about me, Joe. That means more than I can say."

"Thanks, Skippy. Same here," I had to wipe my eyes with a sleeve.

"Of course, if you tell anyone about this, I will deny the whole thing." And his surface glowed a pleasing light blue.

"Of course. Me too."

"Whatever happens, Joe, I can assure you of this: when I find whoever wiped out an entire sentient species on Newark, I am going to rain down hellfire on them until they wish they had never existed."

"You and me together, Skippy."

"You mean that, Joe?"

"Yes. Of course. I told you that, Skippy. We monkeys owe you big time. And you're my friend, I won't let you face this alone."

"That means more to me that I can say, Joe. Now, get out of here before this gets awkward, please. Also, you've been in here long enough that this escape pod is beginning to smell like monkey butt again. Damn, my cleaning robots had it pristine this morning."

"I love you too, Skippy," I laughed, picked him up and hugged him.

"Ugh! Monkey germs! Monkey germs! Yuck!" He shouted.

We settled into a routine; jump, recharge, jump again. Everyone aboard was anxious to learn if the relay station was still the way we had left it, and whether the submind Skippy left behind had discovered whether the Fire Dragon clan Kristang were going to somehow pay for another Thuranin mission to Earth. While the ship was recharging one day, I took the opportunity to join a SpecOps team in zero gee spacesuit training outside the ship. We practiced maneuvering on the skin of the ship and space jumping between the ship and parked dropships. The most difficult maneuver was jumping out of a moving dropship, and using jetpacks to land safely on the outside of the *Dutchman*. I almost sprained an ankle and a wrist doing that stunt; it is harder than it sounds.

Taking a break while sitting on the outside of the ship, I was looking at the starfield and wracking my brain trying to think up a strategy for locating a valuable Elder artifact. My brain was not cooperating. The problem with trying to find something super valuable is, everyone else in the galaxy was looking for it also. Starting with the Rindhalu, they'd been looking for a very long time. Any planet discovered to have Elder artifacts had been thoroughly scoured for-

Damn. A thought hit me right then.

"Hey, Skippy," I called him on a private channel. "The Black Tree clan cleaned any useful Elder artifacts off Paradise a long time ago, that's why they didn't make a fuss when the Ruhar arrived. Here is what's puzzling me; if the Kristang knew there is nothing of value left on Paradise, then why did they bother conquering the place again recently, after the last wormhole shift? The whole reason the lizards brought UNEF there was for us to evacuate the hamsters, because the Kristang just took the planet back from them. The Kristang didn't go through the effort of invading Paradise because it has a lot of good farmland."

"Oh, uh, uh, um," he stammered. "Multiple reasons, Joe. The Swift Arrow clan did not know for certain that the Black Tree clan had cleared the planet of everything valuable, they hoped to make a big score like the Black Trees had. Also, um, the Swift Arrow clan may have gotten the idea of Paradise still having lots of cool Elder stuff from a secret source. Let's call that unnamed source, um, 'Stippy'."

"No way," I laughed. "Now you're BSing me. You were stuck on Paradise. No way could you have contacted the Kristang, they weren't anywhere near Paradise back then."

"Oh, right," he said, his voice dripping with sarcasm. "That was silly of me, trying to fool you. There is no way a super intelligent AI on Paradise could have hacked into laughably crappy Ruhar communications systems, and snuck in a compressed file that was carried by their ships to other planets. No way could that file be eventually intercepted by the Kristang, then unpack itself and infiltrate their systems. And no possible way could such a file pretend to be very convincing top secret Black Tree clan data, that told other clans there were still a whole lot of potential Elder artifact sites on Paradise. Yup, Joe, no way could I fool you."

For a long time, I was unable to respond, because I was sitting paralyzed with shock. "Holy shit," a chill ran up my spine to the top of my head. "*You* are the reason the Kristang invaded Paradise?"

"Um, shmaybe?"

"Shmaybe? Oh my God! UNEF is stuck on that planet because of *you*?"

"To be fair, Joe, I was stuck there for way longer than UNEF has been on Paradise. I was desperate to get off that hick planet, and with the Ruhar happily farming the place, there wasn't any opportunity for me to get away. When I heard that the wormhole shift had given the Kristang access to a world with an underdeveloped species of monkeys, and that the Kristang had invaded your world, I saw an opportunity. I might, I can neither confirm nor deny, have hacked into a Ruhar medical laboratory and created a virulent prion that would prevent the Kristang from landing on Paradise until they developed an antidote. And since the Kristang couldn't land there for a while, I might have planted the idea of using humans on Paradise in the minds of the Kristang."

"*Holy shit.*" I slumped against the ship's hull, absolutely stunned. Skippy the shiny beer can had been the invisible hand behind the entire mess. I needed to take several deep breaths to take in the enormity of Skippy's casual revelation.

Oh my God.

I felt like I couldn't breathe for a moment.

Skippy had been behind *everything*, right from the beginning. "This is all your fault?!"

"Hey, it wasn't all my doing, Joe. I didn't cause the wormhole shift that gave the Kristang access to your home planet. And I didn't give them the idea to invade your worthless mudball of a planet; I only found out about that from the Ruhar after the Kristang were already on Earth. At that point I figured, what the hell? Why not see if I can make some good for me come out of it? It worked out great for humanity, so good times all around, huh?"

Paradise

"*Good times*?!" I exploded. "You underhanded, sneaky, untrustworthy-"

"That hurt, Joe. It did work out well for humanity. If I had not manipulated events so that the Kristang brought humans to Paradise, the Kristang would still have control of Earth and your species would be enslaved. And quite possibly subjected to genocide by the Kristang. As it is, now Earth is safe. For now. If events had transpired any other way, your species right now would be on a path for cultural or even biological extinction. Truthfully, if you think about it, humanity owes me big time for bringing humans to Paradise."

Crap.

Double crap!

He was right. After the Kristang arrived at Earth, the only thing that had saved us from enslavement and slow extinction was Skippy using humanity for his own purposes. "Are there any other mind-blowing revelations you care to share with me, Skippy? Because that is one giant Goddamn 'by the way' from you."

"None that I care to share, nope," he said like a stubborn child. "Your blood pressure is abnormally high for you, Joe."

"Ya think? Damn it, Skippy. Do you have *any idea* what a revelation like that would do if UNEF Command heard about it? They already don't trust you."

"I am sorry that your Expeditionary Force is stuck on Paradise, but that wasn't my doing, Joe."

"Do *not* tell anyone else about this."

"If it is such a big deal, Joe, I won't tell anyone," he said defensively.

"Believe me, it is a big, a huge freakin' deal." Another chilling thought hit me. "You are not still manipulating us behind the scenes, are you?"

"Not that you know of, Joe."

"That was *not* funny, Skippy."

"Sorry. You are aware that the reason I am helping you fly the *Dutchman* is for my own purposes, so clearly you understand that I am manipulating you in that way."

"We know about that, Skippy, and we agree with our terms. What we do not like is being manipulated without knowing about it."

"Well, then," Skippy paused. "I can tell you this; if I am still pulling strings from behind the scenes, it is nowhere near the scope of what I did previously. And that worked out pretty well for you and your species."

Knowing that sneaky little beer can, that was the best assurance he was going to ever give me. Major Smythe called me right then, to get ready for another practice zero gee maneuver. I almost told Smythe that my head wasn't in the game at the moment, but I tried to push Skippy's shocking revelation to the back of my mind and got to my feet. Being somewhat distracted was perfect conditions to train for focusing my mind on combat maneuvers. In actual combat, with people shooting at me, there would be a whole lot of distractions.

Unbelievable. Maybe I shouldn't ask Skippy questions unless I was prepared to hear an answer I didn't like.

"Colonel Joe," Skippy said to me while I was in my office, "once again, I must commend you for the idea of planting an Elder power tap on Paradise. Finding such a device there would certainly provide a reason for the Ruhar to retain control of the planet. There is one teensy weensy, nagging little problem with your idea."

"What's that, Skippy?" I asked.

"That there is no way for us to go and simply get an Elder power tap, you moron! Damn, do you ever once stop to think of whether your ideas are in any way practical, Joe? You dream up stuff and I get stuck trying to make it work."

"I'm more of a big picture guy, Skippy. You see, colonels like me have people to handle the little details. Handle it, Skippy," I said with a dismissive flick of a wrist.

"*What?* Oh my- Unbelievable!" Skippy sputtered. "Did you just *wrist flick* me? You had better not have treated me like a-"

"I was jerking your chain, Skippy. Don't take it so personally. I'll be serious now. Explain why we can't go looking for an Elder power tap? I know it may take a while, and that we need to make it quick before the Ruhar reach a deal with the Kristang. On our last mission, we went searching for Elder comm nodes."

"Uh huh, and did we find any comm nodes? No. The only comm node we found was the one the Kristang had dug up on Newark. What we did find along the way was a Thuranin ambush. Or did you forget that?"

"No, I did not forget any of that. We didn't search very many Elder sites, Skippy. We got interrupted by the ambush, then we abandoned the original mission when we learned that the Thuranin were sending a ship to Earth. We did not check enough Elder sites to make a, what would you call it? A statistically significant sample?"

"Joe?"

"Yes?"

"Did you just attempt to talk math with me?"

I assume he meant the statistics stuff. "Maybe?"

"Don't do that. Please, do not ever do that again. It's embarrassing. To you."

Feeling mildly insulted, I agreed so he would drop the subject. "Fine. Was I right anyway?"

"That we didn't look at enough supposedly undiscovered Elder sites to determine whether continuing to search for such sites would be worthwhile? You are, incredibly, correct about that. Thus proving that the universe is wondrously strange. Ok, smart guy, I'll try to explain it to you in somewhat statistical terms. Based on what I know, which is a ginormous amount but still woefully inadequate, for us to find a comm node at an undiscovered Elder site would take approximately three years. That's assuming we explored potential Elder sites at the same rate we did during the last mission, and that we don't get ambushed again."

"Wow. That's not good. Power taps are even more rare than comm nodes?"

"Correct. By comparison, functioning Elder power taps are a numbers-matching Ferrari Daytona convertible, and comm nodes are a typical econobox that you get stuck with as a rental car."

"Crap. They're that rare?"

"Yes. Perhaps it would help if I show you. Your laptop is now showing all of the known functional Elder power taps in this quadrant of the galaxy."

My laptop screen flickered, then popped up a star map. Blinking yellow lights indicated star systems with power taps. There were a lot of them. "Crap, Skippy, I thought you said they were rare?"

"They are. Joe, that map shows a quarter of the entire galaxy, with millions of habitable star systems. Most of the functional Elder power taps now belong to the Rindhalu, because they had a very long head start on combing the galaxy for Elder gear before the Maxolhx developed interstellar travel capability. Here, look, I'll eliminate all the Elder power taps that are known to be possessed by both the Rindhalu and the Maxolhx. Since we absolutely do not want to mess with those two."

"Oh, that's for sure. Hmm," I peered at the map. "That still looks like plenty to me, Skippy."

"One thousand, two hundred and sixty six, Joe."

"I would call that a target-rich environment."

"I would call you an idiot."

"What's the problem?"

"Allow me to further refine the search parameters. Now I will eliminate all power taps currently on planets with populations of one hundred million or more. Such planets are heavily defended."

"Oooh." That changed the display. Skippy had added a handy dandy counter at the bottom right of the screen. It showed a total of 83. "Ok, eighty three. We can't go after any of those because why?"

"Now I will eliminate from the display, power taps at military and research installations that are guarded by more than a dozen heavy ships. Ships with combat capabilities greater than that of the *Flying Dutchman*."

The counter now showed zero. Zero. Like, zero. "Crap. There's no way we can steal one of these things?"

"That is exactly what both Lt Colonel Chang and Major Smythe said when I discussed this subject with them earlier today."

"You already had this discussion?"

"Of course, Joe. You are not the only person aboard this ship. I also had a very similar talk with Count Chocula yesterday."

"Yesterday?" That wasn't good. I should have thought to ask these questions before the mission commander did.

"He is, overall, less busy day to day than you are, Joe. Anyway, his conclusion is that your idea of looking for an Elder power tap to plant on Paradise is a wild goose chase."

Damn. Chocula might be right about that. I wasn't giving up that easily. "Fine. That map shows all the known Elder power taps. What if we go trying to find one that has not yet been discovered, like we did with the comm nodes?"

"We could do that, Joe. My estimate is that we would be searching for four hundred and eight years before we located one. That is longer than the expected remaining life of this ship."

Skippy kept reminding me that without access to spare parts, our rebuilt pirate star carrier wasn't going to last forever. He couldn't predict how much longer it would be before a critical component failed and we would be stranded in space, because that depended on how far we travelled. We weren't lugging around heavy starships with us, but we were doing a whole lot of jumping. Most star carriers went into spacedock about every eighteen months for a heavy overhaul; the *Dutchman* had been almost due for an overhaul when we captured her. Time was running out for our pirate ship. "Damn it, Skippy, there has to be a way to do this. Do you have any suggestions?"

"I have one suggestion. You should go to the gym."

"Why?" I asked, surprised. I was fit; not as fit as the special forces, but I had to be realistic about that.

"Joe, I have noticed that you seem to develop ideas when you are doing something other than trying to think of an idea. Sometimes we can all be discussing what to do, and the conversation goes off on some tangent, and that gives you an idea. But most often, you get ideas when you are doing something else. I suspect your subconscious mind is much smarter than you are. So, you can go to the gym, or play a silly game on your tablet, or do anything other than trying to think of a way to find a functioning Elder power tap."

I took his advice and went to the gym.

When I walked in the door to the gym, Major Simms was there, waiting. Nine of the ten treadmills were occupied, the tenth one had a piece of yellow tape across it. "The motor is busted," Simms explained. "Skippy is sending a robot to fix it."

Instead of running, I used a rowing machine. While rowing was good exercise, it was not my favorite. Running on a treadmill sucked also; with our rebuilt pirate ship, we could no longer run down the shortened central spine other than short sprints. Keeping fit aboard a starship was not easy. The treadmills aboard the *Flying Dutchman* were far better now than they were on our first mission. We wore lightweight virtual reality goggles and earphones, they provided a very convincing experience of running pretty much any place you wanted to. With Skippy providing the simulation, we could run the Boston marathon, we could run up any mountain you cared to name, we could race against people on other treadmills. We could even run on Newark, if anyone was feeling nostalgic for that miserable world. Or we could run on our Moon, or some other moon. As much as everyone hated running on a treadmill, it was better than running on a treadmill that was busted. Hopefully Skippy could fix-

"Sir? Is anything wrong?" Simms asked as I bailed off the rowing machine and quickly walked toward the door.

"No, Major. I'm hoping everything is going to be great." To save time, I skipped a shower because I'd only been exercising for a few minutes. And instead of going to Skippy's escape pod man cave, I went to my office. Fortunately, no one was waiting to speak with me. "Skippy," I said as I plopped myself into the chair, "you are a genius."

"Tell me something I don't know, Captain Obvious."

"Challenge accepted, Captain Oblivious. There is a treadmill in the gym that has a busted motor."

"Correct again, Captain Obvious. I am in the process of replacing the motor with a much better one, but I have to finish building that new motor first. One of my robots will install it tonight. Your SpecOps people are tough on the exercise equipment. We should find an uninhabited planet where they can run and jump and do the kinds of crazy stuff they feel like they need to do."

"Skippy, we humans have to exercise. We don't have the advantage of perfecting our genetics and using cyborg implants and all the cool stuff that I assumed we would get when we came out here. I am still bitterly disappointed about that, by the way. All the science fiction novels I read *totally* lied to me about that."

"Sorry, Joey. Maybe if you go to the Emerald City, the wizard will give you a brain."

"Speaking of brains, I said you are a genius, because while I was rowing across the Ocean of Nowhere I had an idea. Can you show me that map of our quadrant of the galaxy again? This time, I want you to show me the locations of known Elder power taps that are *not* functional."

"Damn it," Skippy grumbled. "I know you have an idea there somewhere, but I cannot figure out what it could be. A nonfunctional power tap isn't useful to anyone, Joe. It certainly isn't something that would convince the Ruhar that they should retain control of Paradise."

"Uh huh, got it." The map was thickly dotted with yellow lights. "Wow, there must be a lot of nonfunctional power taps."

"Correct again. Most power taps are nonfunctional, which is why the functional ones are so highly prized and well-guarded. Duh."

"Great. Now, remove all the nonfunctional power taps that are on planets with a large population, or are at military facilities with heavy protection, or are held by the Rindhalu or Maxolhx. Like you did last time."

"I still do not see where you are going with this, Joe. This bothers me. It makes me think there might be a fundamental difference between organic and artificial minds."

"Could be," I said, distracted. Now there were a lot less yellow dots on the map, but there were still plenty of them. Last time, the count had gone from over a thousand, to 83, to zero. Now we had something to work with. The counter in the corner still showed 7,642. "Wow! Over seven thousand of them?"

"Congratulations on your reading skills, Joey. I will ask the teacher to give you a juice box. Yes. As I said, nonfunctional power taps are not only nowhere near as rare as functional ones, but they are also considered much, much less valuable. Because they don't work, many of them are at research facilities. All of the species who possess nonfunctional power taps are attempting to figure out how they work, and reverse engineer one. To date, even the Rindhalu have made essentially zero progress in that area. There are two types of nonfunctional power taps. Those that are truly inert, and when they are taken apart they are simply a tightly packed mass of exotic particles that dissolves into basically sand. The second type are those which have lost their quantum connection, but retain potential energy within their matrix. When that second type is taken apart, they explode violently. Like, a megaton level explosion. I mention that last part, in case you have the moronic idea of capturing one of these nonfunctional power taps and taking it apart."

"I am not planning to screw with any of those things, Skippy."

"Then I still do not see the point of-"

"My plan is to get *you* to screw with one."

"You've lost me, Joe."

"Go back to the map again, please. Show me only power taps that are nonfunctional, but that you could fix."

"Holy shit," Skippy gasped with realization.

"You can do that, right? You know how these things work, there must be some out there that you could restore to functioning."

"There are. Damn, there are times when I wish I had an organic brain," he grumbled. "And that is something I never thought I would say. Yes, Joe, this could be another one of your brilliant ideas. Instead of trying to steal one of the most valuable objects in the galaxy, we only need to steal one from a junkyard, and fix it up. Ok, now the map will show nonfunctional Elder power taps that I know I could fix. One of them merely needs to be rebooted, but the dumdums who have it are clueless."

The map now showed two blinking yellow lights. "*Two*? Crap, Skippy, I hoped there would be more."

"Oops, sorry, Joe. The dots on the map indicate *places* which have nonfunctional power taps. Between those two places, they hold over forty power taps. Both locations I am showing are research facilities, so they logically have concentrated equipment together."

"Ah, well, my mother told me that if wishes were fishes, we would all be swimming in riches. Ok, tell me about these two facilities."

"One is buried deep within a moon, that is a Jeraptha facility. While the moon itself is not heavily guarded, the planet the moon orbits contains a major fleet servicing spacedock."

"That one is out," I said with disappointment. "I do not want to make enemies of the Jeraptha. And we shouldn't try to tackle such a tough target. How about the other one?"

"The other one is more interesting, Joe," Skippy said as my laptop screen zoomed way in to show a star system. "This is a Thuranin research station that is built into an asteroid."

"Oh," I groaned, "not another asteroid."

"You'd better get used to it, Joe. Hollowed-out asteroids are very convenient, so they are commonly used as space stations. They are plentiful, cheap and provide raw materials. Anyway, this particular asteroid was in the Oort Cloud of this star system, and was moved inward to closely orbit the neutron star. It orbits the star so closely that it is impossible for starships to jump in or out near the asteroid, so ships have to jump in far away and travel to the asteroid the long way. This gives the Thuranin plenty of warning when ships are approaching. The X-rays emitted by the star also degrade the usefulness of stealth fields, so it is almost impossible to sneak up on the station."

"Crap. Ok, so it's a difficult but not impossible target."

"Difficult? That is an understatement. The odds of us successfully raiding that station are, oh, what is the point of me trying to discuss things in math terms with you? Joe, you are statistically more likely to be struck by lightning while being run over by a bus driven by a shark."

"You'd better recheck your math on that one, Skippy," I said confidently. "Sharks can't drive."

"Oh for-"

"Skippy, there has to be a way for us to do it."

"Fine. That is a judgment call. You are the military man, Joe. I do not know if our Merry Band of Pirates could successfully raid this facility."

"What defenses does this station have?"

"I just provided all the data I have to you, Joe, which is not much. In fact, the only data I do have is from a Thuranin intelligence report stating that the Jeraptha know about the facility, and therefore security should be increased. The report did not include the current security level, or proposed upgrades."

"That's no good, Skippy. I thought that now that we have our very own relay station, we have access to all the Thuranin data we want."

"You thought wrongly, Oh Foolish One. We only have access to whatever data passes through that relay station. Duh. Information about this particular asteroid station is confined to the Advanced Research Directorate. That agency is notoriously jealous of the Thuranin military's own research and development group, so the ARD keeps its data confined to a small group."

The idea of attacking a Thuranin asteroid base without solid intel about its defense capabilities was a nonstarter. "Again, that's no good. How can we get more data about that station?"

"I assume you mean, get more data without going there and launching an assault first. One way would be to use our relay station. I could send a highly encrypted message to ARD headquarters, pretending to be an ARD unit that needs the data. Then we would have to wait for that message to be carried by several ships through multiple relay stations all the way to the Thuranin home planet. They would then need to send the message all the way back to us. However, I must warn you, it is most likely such a request would be viewed very suspiciously by ARD. They might decide to trace the request back to where it originated, which would involve a heavily-armed ARD vessel visiting our relay station."

"We very much do not want that to happen. Crap. We'll need to think about this."

"*You* will need to think about it, Joe. Because I did, and I'm out of ideas."

CHAPTER TWENTY FOUR

Without having information about the asteroid base itself, we couldn't plan an assault. We could at least attempt to tackle the problem of how we get to the place in order to launch an assault, so I called together Chotek, Chang, Smythe, Simms, Desai, Adams and Friedlander. I wanted Chotek there not because I thought he could help, but because I wanted him to see, again, how difficult it is to develop solutions on the fly. In this case, literally on the fly, as the *Flying Dutchman* was proceeding back to the relay station at maximum speed.

"Skippy," I said to the shiny beer can on the table, "let me know whether I understand the problem."

"Enough." He had a soft blue glow when he said that. I had brought him out of his man cave and into the conference room because I get tired of speaking with a disembodied voice sometimes. And because it is good for us to be reminded of what the super powerful being who runs our stolen starship looks like. Or, what he looks like to us, since Skippy frequently reminded me that most of him wasn't in this spacetime. Whatever that meant.

"Huh?"

"If you understand the problem *enough*. Because there is no way that you could ever fully understand the problem, Joe."

"That's fair, I guess. This asteroid is so close to the star-"

"The neutron star." Skippy interrupted me with a slow orange glow.

Now I was annoyed. "What's the difference? It's a star. Anyway, it-"

"There is a very major difference, Joe," Skippy said, and I could see Friedlander nodding in agreement. "I shall attempt to explain it to you."

"Oof," I groaned. This was going to be painful for both of us. "Go ahead."

"One thing before we get started," Skippy insisted.

"What's that?"

"Dr. Friedlander owes me a joke."

"You're kidding me."

"I kid you not, Joe. Whenever I participate in the meetings of the science team, Friedlander always starts the meeting with a joke. Calling that group of monkeys a science team is itself a joke, but I mean a joke with a punchline."

"Sure," Friedlander said with a grin. "How many software engineers does it take to change a lightbulb?"

"Uh," I said, trying to guess.

"None," Friedlander said with a wink. "That's a hardware problem."

"Ok," I laughed, "that is a good tradition."

"Agreed," Skippy said with a chuckle. "Now, to make this short, it is important that you understand the difference between a normal main sequence star and a neutron star. A neutron star is the collapsed core of a star, a star that was much larger than Earth's Sun. When such a star goes supernova, gravity causes the core to collapse to the point where the remnants of the star are compressed almost to the point of becoming a black hole. And yes, shut up over there, Friedlander, I know that I am hugely dumbing this down for Joe's benefit. The point, Joe, is that this particular neutron star is old and cold. Although this core remnant is almost twice the mass of Earth's Sun, it is tiny. The asteroid orbits very close to the surface of the star. Close enough that the Thuranin must be using powerful artificial gravity within the asteroid, to compensate for the tidal forces. If this was a hot, main sequence star, an asteroid that close would melt and burn to a crisp. Do you understand?"

"I think so, yes," I said. "And thanks for explaining that to us. It means we do not need to worry about the *Dutchman* overheating as we approach the asteroid?"

"Ugh. That is *not* the lesson I wanted you to learn, Joe, but you are at least partly correct. Most of the star's remaining radiation is in the form of X-rays instead of visible light. Those X-rays disrupt the effectiveness of stealth fields as a ship approaches the star, making it impossible even for us to sneak up on the asteroid undetected. The Thuranin Advanced Research Directorate chose this location carefully and wisely. The intense gravity also acts as a lens, bending light around the star. Even if we were on the other side of the star, the asteroid station could see us."

Friedlander couldn't stop from interjecting. "The asteroid is also orbiting close enough to the star's surface that time dilation is measurable, and must be compensated for-"

"Yes, thank you, Mr. Egghead rocket scientist," Skippy said scornfully. "You and I can address that later, Friedlander. Until then, kindly shut up."

"Great," I said, "you two please do that, later. We're here to consider how to approach the asteroid for an assault. After the assault, we won't be able to jump away, right?"

"Correct, Joe. I can flatten spacetime so that our pirate ship will be able to jump away while we are closer to the star than a typical ship could. But we still will need to travel a considerable distance through normal space before we reach jump altitude. During that time, we will be vulnerable to pursuing vessels. Although we do not have data on this particular station, I expect it to be protected by at least one destroyer-size ARD warship. Jumping away is not the main problem, Joe."

"Yeah, I know," I said glumly. This was sounding more and more impossible. "We need to get inside the station first, and defeat their defenses-"

"No, you dumdum," Skippy glowed a soft purple. "Damn, you do not listen when I talk, do you? Not only can we not jump away, we can't jump *in* anywhere near that asteroid. We have to jump in far away, and travel through normal space to reach the asteroid. While our stealth field degrades. We will not have any advantage of surprise."

"Oh," I said, surprised. "I did hear when you said that, but I figured you could do some magical flattening spacetime thing, so we could jump in closer than most ships could."

"No, you dimwit, I can't do that."

"Mr. Skippy," Chang interrupted. "We watched you make a hole in a star. After that, you were able to flatten spacetime so we could jump away very close to a star. I realize that was not a neutron star, but-"

"But nothing," Skippy said scornfully. "That was totally different. I can flatten spacetime close to where I am, on the near end of a wormhole. That helps us jump out. I can't flatten spacetime at the *far* end of a wormhole, because we aren't there yet, duh. So that little trick does not help us jump in to an intense gravity well. The gravitational field of a neutron star would distort the far end of our jump wormhole so that it would collapse on itself. Even if we managed to stabilize it somehow and go through, the stresses at the event horizon on the far end would tear the ship apart as soon as we emerged."

I slumped back in my chair. "Damn. So we can't take the *Dutchman* in?"

Before Skippy could answer, Chotek spoke. "We will not risk the ship in this operation. Risking the ship risks our ability to perform our primary mission. While I sympathize with the force on Paradise, their security is not our primary objective. Whatever plan your team develops, Colonel Bishop, it cannot involve placing this ship at risk."

Crap. I exchanged a look with Chang. He was thinking the same thing I was; maybe there was a level of risk Chotek would accept, if we could convince him the risk was manageable and worth the result. That would come later; we needed a workable plan before we try selling it to Chotek. "Dropships, then. We take a team there in dropships."

Friedlander was shaking his head even before Skippy spoke. "No go on that either, Joe," Skippy said. "It would be far too dangerous to the team in the dropships. The dropships do not have artificial gravity. As they approached the asteroid, tidal forces would tear the crew apart inside the hulls. The ARD uses specialized ships to service this station. Even if we were able to take the *Flying Dutchman* in, our ability to maneuver as we approached the star would be substantially restricted. Tidal forces on the forward hull and the aft engineering section could cause the ship's spine to separate."

"Crap, Skippy," I protested. "This is no good at all."

"As I said, Joe, the location of this asteroid base provides very effective security, without the Thuranin having to do anything. Ships can't use their full stealth ability on approach, and they can't engage in typically violent combat maneuvers. The Thuranin can sit safely in their asteroid, and lob railgun darts and missiles at enemy ships that aren't able to dodge out of the way."

This was sounding like a truly impossible mission. Maybe I needed to go back to the beginning and think of a new way to rescue our forces on Paradise.

"We can't take the ship in," Chang nodded toward Chotek, "and we can't send an assault team in dropships. This asteroid station is not self-reliant? It requires resupply regularly?"

"Ships do visit the station to bring supplies and rotate personnel," Skippy reported. "Why?"

"Because," Chang looked at me, "if we could capture one of those supply ships, we could use that to gain access to the station."

"Whoa!" Skippy exclaimed. "Hold your horses there, King Kong. Don't get too excited. That would be a great idea, except that the Advanced Research Directorate doesn't use little civilian cargo ships. The typical ships they use to transfer material and personnel are the equivalent of a light cruiser, and some are bigger than that. The ARD is well aware that the items those ships transport are valuable. Even the Thuranin researchers themselves are valuable, if captured. ARD does not take any risks that some ambitious Kristang will want to get their hands on advanced Thuranin research. To further dissuade you from the idiotic idea of capturing an ARD ship, you would need to do it in a way that leaves the ship undamaged. No way would the asteroid base allow a battle-damaged ship to dock. Also, from the data I do have about these types of high-security ARD facilities, their procedure is probably to have an approaching ship be met at the outer edge of the star system and escorted in by the guard ship. The supply ship would need to rendezvous with the local guard ship, and the security procedure may include the incoming ship being boarded for inspection."

"Damn," Chang frowned. "Scratch that idea."

"Colonel, that is a good idea," I assured my executive officer, "if we had a way to make it work." Chang's suggestion had given me the beginning of an idea. "Skippy, why is that research station there?"

There was a pause before Skippy answered. "I do not know how to answer that very vague question, Joe. It is there because the Thuranin put it there."

"Let me be more precise. Why did the Thuranin put it *there*, specifically? What is special about that location? You told us that being near a neutron star provides additional security, but they could have accomplished the same level of security by doing that research at a big military base."

"Ok, all right, that is not an entirely stupid question, Joe. First, they wouldn't want to conduct high-energy research near a military base, because there is significant danger of things going 'boom' in a big way. So they needed a different way to provide security. More importantly, proximity to a neutron star allows research into the effects of intense gravimetric fields and as Dr. Friedlander observed, the effect of time dilation."

I asked my question more specifically. "Does being close to a neutron star make it easier to figure out how an Elder power tap works?"

"No, it does not. Well, maybe, hmmm, no. No it does not. The Thuranin at one time thought being near a neutron star would provide insight into quantum bubbles, but they were mistaken. Because neutron stars rotate so rapidly, their immense mass actually drags spacetime around with them. But that doesn't provide any useful insight to bubble energy."

"So this asteroid station is not there for the purpose of researching power taps?"

"No. The Thuranin do have a few facilities dedicated to power taps, or quantum bubble or zero point energy or whatever you want to call it. The sad truth is, the reason some power taps are at the neutron star facility is because the Thuranin are desperate. They have tried everything to figure out how Elder power taps works, and all their years of intense research had yielded no results. No, wait. There was one result, a long time ago. Some idiot Thuranin screwed with a power tap, and the result was a seven megaton explosion that wiped out a major military base and left a crater that is visible from space." Skippy chuckled. "My laugh was not at the loss of Thuranin lives, it was because the power tap didn't cause that explosion; the power tap simply happened to be there. That now deceased Thuranin researcher actually managed to tap into a quantum energy flow for the briefest of moments and if he had lived, he would be astonished. Sadly, that researcher and all the data were consumed in the massive explosion. The Thuranin still think they somehow managed to get a power tap activated, but couldn't control it. And that idiotic misconception has caused Thuranin research to go down the wrong track ever since."

"My heart bleeds for them, Skippy."

"Somehow I suspect you are lying about that, Joe."

"Ya think?"

"They don't get a whole lot of sympathy from me either," Skippy said with disgust.

"Yup. So, research into power taps can happen a lot of places."

"Yes. Although the ARD only very rarely exchanges research data and materials with the military R&D group."

"Too bad for them. Skippy, those supply ships bring supplies to the station. Do they also bring things *away* from the station?" As I said that, Major Smythe sucked in a breath as he understood my idea.

"Duh. Of course they do, Joe."

"Great. Then we don't have to go into a Thuranin station to get our hands on a power tap," I said with big grin on my face. "We'll have one delivered to us."

"Shit," Skippy grumbled. "Is this one of your ideas? Because if it is, then damn it, this one totally snuck up on me. Joe, I can assure you the Advanced Research Directorate will not deliver a power tap to you. Not even if you have a coupon."

"We don't need a coupon. We have a Skippy."

"Explain this to me again, Joe," Skippy said while I was back in my office. "I'm not clear exactly what you want."

"It's easy, Skippy. We need an ARD supply ship to pick up a fixable Elder power tap from a research facility that has one, and deliver it to a facility that will be easy for us to attack."

Paradise

"Just like that?"

"Just like that, yeah. Is there a problem?"

"Oh, so, so many problems, Joe. First, the Advanced Research Directorate does not have a web portal where you can click on the items you want and add them to your shopping cart. I would need to fake a message from ARD headquarters, and transmit that message to an ARD ship."

"Uh huh. So? We have our own data relay station now, Skippy." I knew that he was super absent-minded at times, but-

"Oh, you think you are *so* freakin' smart, don't you? Well, smart guy, the problem is that we do not have access to flight schedules for ARD ships."

"What? You told us that a relay station has access to all the information we needed!" I protested.

"All the information we need, in order to determine what the Thuranin know about the destruction of their surveyor ship, and whether they will be sending another ship to Earth, yes. Joe, relay stations are run by the Thuranin military, so they contain military information. The ARD will not trust their data passing through a military relay, so they do not use relay stations for sensitive data. ARD ships only use relay stations to pass highly encrypted messages that do not contain sensitive data."

"Well, crap," my shoulders slumped. "So we have no way to know whether an ARD ship is going to be visiting an ARD facility that has a power tap you can fix. There goes my whole idea! Damn, Skippy, I am sorry for wasting your time. Everyone's time. You're right, I am a dumb monkey. Shit. Now we have to start over. And, ugh," the thought hit me. "First, I need to explain to everyone how arrogant and stupid I was."

"Joe?"

"Yeah?"

"As joyously entertaining as it is to watch you beat yourself up, and believe me I am absolutely *tingling* all over with delight, it is not yet necessary."

"How do you figure that?"

"Because, you arrogant, smart-ass pee pee head, I did not say your plan wouldn't work. All I said was that I do not have access to the flight schedules of ARD starships."

Pee pee head? That was a new insult from Skippy. His comment made me pause for a moment. "This time it's me who is not following you, Skippy."

"ARD's starships are like any other Thuranin starships. While they are capable of independent interstellar travel, it not efficient for them to travel entirely on their own. So, they hitch rides on star carriers, which are controlled by the military. I do have access to military flight schedules. That means I am able to see when star carriers are scheduled to make stops at star systems which contain only ARD facilities. Logically, those star carriers must be dropping off and picking up ARD ships. By analyzing the flight schedules of star carriers that are transporting ARD ships, I can derive ARD flight schedules."

"You just love yanking my chain, Skippy."

"Oh, more than I could ever explain, Joe. However, I didn't do it deliberately this time. Your thought process is such an incredible mess that it is difficult for me to guess what you are thinking."

I couldn't tell whether he was telling the truth or yanking my chain again. "Whatever. Great. So, you can predict which ARD ships will be visiting ARD facilities that have fixable power taps, and subsequently visiting and ARD facility that is a softer target?"

"Affirmative, Colonel Joe."

"Outstanding. Let's look at the potential targets, and we will select the best option. Then you can transmit our delivery order from our personal relay station."

"Joe?'

"Yeah?"

"There is one teensy weensy problem with that idea. There are no ARD ships scheduled to pass by our relay station within the next eight months. By that time, our station is scheduled for a crew change, and we will need to blow it up to cover out tracks."

"Damn it! This is freakin' impossible, Skippy. There are roadblocks everywhere."

"Perhaps not. Hmm, give me a minute here. Do a crossword puzzle or something, I need to do some Skippy-level number crunching."

"I don't have a crossword puzzle." My tablet had plenty of crosswords on it, but I figured Skippy would be done before I got started on one.

"Fine, I'll give you one myself. Three letters, the clue is 'feline', begins with C and A."

"Oh, you are freakin' hilarious." Although I was trying to think what the answer could be, because Skippy liked to give me trick questions.

"I'm done. The answer is 'cat', by the way. I believe that I have a solution, Joey. There is a convoluted route I can use to route messages to ARD ships, beginning with our relay station. The catch, before you get all excited, is this incredibly complicated method only results in one possible target for us, in the time available."

"Ok," I took a deep breath. "You can get an ARD ship to pick up a fixable power tap from a facility that is strongly defended, and deliver it to an ARD facility that is a much easier target?"

"Wow. Let me understand this. You're asking if I can use our own personal relay station to send a highly encrypted message that contains all the proper ARD multi-level authentication codes. A message that will be routed through several ships, multiple wormholes and multiple relay stations, until it eventually gets to the one particular ARD ship we want. A ship that I selected, because I am able to predict which star carriers are playing host to ARD ships. The message needs to instruct that ARD ship to simply pick up a valuable Elder artifact, no questions asked, and just drop it off at an isolated, weakly-defended ARD facility, with again no questions asked. You're asking if I can do all that, Joe?"

Since he put it that way, it did sound like a lot to ask. "Uh, yes? Can you do it?"

"Oh sure, no problem. Easy peasy for me. Come on, Joe. Trust the awesomeness."

"Great." I wondered whether 'Trust the Awesomeness' should become the official motto of the Merry Band of Pirates.

"Joe, the best news is that the target I have in mind has less than a dozen civilian ARD researchers, and almost no defensive capability."

"No neutron star?"

"Nope. No black hole either, nothing exotic. This an uninhabited planet, it even has an atmosphere as a bonus."

"Mmmm. Sounds too easy. What's the catch?"

"Well, heh, heh, you are very much not going to like this-"

Paradise

The sound made General Marcellus awaken immediately. He hadn't been sleeping well for a while, particularly not since giant maser cannons *that no one had known anything about* obliterated the Kristang battlegroup that had been looming above their heads. Marcellus had offered General Nivelle his resignation that very day; if the UNEF chief of intelligence had not known the planet they were on had such a powerful defensive capability, then he was not of any use to Nivelle. The French general currently in command of UNEF refused to accept Marcellus' resignation, because Nivelle had just ended a phone call with the Ruhar Deputy Administrator of the planet, and the Ruhar government also had not known about the projectors either. It had been a hurried call, Nivelle said, the Deputy Administrator was understandably busy with a massive air battle raging above her head.

Other than seeing ships exploding in orbit, and a few fortunate ships jumping away, the humans on Lemuria did not directly experience the resulting battle. There were some isolated, twisting contrails low on the northern horizon as fighter aircraft tangled, but none of the air action took place over Lemuria. The effect that most humans noticed was the zPhone network suddenly shutting down with no warning. Without the ability to connect to the global network, communications relied on messages being passed from one phone to the next, using the limited range backup direct transmission capability of the zPhones. Someone had attacked the Kristang battlegroup, the message from UNEF HQ stated. We have no additional information, please remain calm and attend to your duties.

The soldiers of UNEF, whether American, Chinese, Indian, British or French, all knew what 'remain calm' meant. It meant that it was seriously time to panic. For the Keepers who had pledged continued loyalty to the Kristang, loyalty that was entirely one-sided, the news generated very understandable panic. Arrival of the Kristang battlegroup in orbit had made hope soar within the Keeper community, even though the Kristang said they considered all humans on the planet to be traitors. Surely, the Keepers had told each other, they could demonstrate their loyalty to the Kristang. Some had even gone so far as to damage or sabotage agricultural equipment the Ruhar had loaned to UNEF, although hurting the ability of humans to feed themselves did not make sense to most people, even most of the Keeper leaders. Taking apart a tractor was not a gesture the Kristang were likely to notice, and if humans were again to serve as ground troops for their Kristang patrons, they would need human food.

Even people who were not Keepers felt some dismay at the unexpected destruction of the Kristang battlegroup. The ending of the cease fire meant yet more uncertainty, yet more combat in which humans might become direct targets or collateral damage. More importantly to all humans on Paradise was that with the Kristang gone, UNEF's slim hope of a link to Earth was gone with them.

Sitting bolt upright in his cot, Marcellus identified the sound that had awakened him; it was an alert from his zPhone. "Marcellus," he said as he slipped the earpiece in.

"General, we have a situation," reported Captain Chen. She was one of Marcellus' aides, and the current intelligence duty officer. "An Indian village attacked a French village about 30 minutes ago. There are casualties on both sides, sir."

"Goddamn it," Marcellus swore as he laced his boots. "Was it Keepers?" UNEF HQ intel had been keeping constant track of the Keeper movement, in case they became a security threat. The situation was complicated by the fact that Keepers had adherents within the officers of UNEF HQ; many adherents. Marcellus estimated that fifteen percent of the Headquarters staff pledged continued loyalty to the Kristang. It was a solid estimate; all he had to do was ask people their opinions. Being a Keeper was not against UNEF policy or regulations; he had Keepers on his own intel staff. That fact had surprised Marcellus; he thought that people who had access to the best information would be the least interested in aligning with the species that was oppressing Earth. The human capacity to ignore facts and believe what they wanted to believe was a continued source of amazement and frustration to Marcellus.

"This doesn't appear to be related to the Keeper movement, sir," Chen said stiffly, and Marcellus remembered that Chen herself had expressed some sympathy with the Keepers. "This is the Indian village that had most of their crops burned out by a Kristang raid, sir. They've been complaining that HQ wasn't getting supplies to them quickly enough; we explained that we have been sending what we can scrape together. The French re reporting that the Indians targeted their supply of seeds and farming tools first. They also took sacks of grain. The French were pursuing-"

"That's the last thing we need."

"Yes, sir, and we have ordered both the French to return to their village, and the Indians to drop the supplies that they," she hesitated to use the word 'stole' since most food stocks technically belonged to UNEF rather than individual villages. "That they took. We need to get a jump on this, Sir. The French have one dead and three seriously injured, there is at least one fatality on the Indian side. This news has already spread by zPhone, we've picked up chatter in French villages, calling for retaliation."

"Shit," Marcellus said. "I'll inform General Nivelle," who would not be happy to hear that his own countrymen had been attacked and killed. Marcellus planned to advise Nivelle that the UNEF commander needed to excuse himself from the investigation of the attack on the French village, and from deciding on any subsequent punishment. With Nivelle out, the responsibility would fall to General Tolliver. No, damn it, Marcellus thought, they couldn't have a British officer deciding the fate of Indian troops, because of the colonial history between those two countries. Currently third in the command structure was a Chinese general, and the testy relationship between China and India back on Earth made it unworkable for a Chinese to investigate possible crimes by Indian troops. That left the Americans, and Marcellus himself could not get involved. Damn it all, UNEF was just too complicated and unwieldy an organization. When they had a common mission and a common enemy, differences between nationalities had been able to be suppressed temporarily. Now, UNEF had no mission other than survival, and troops disagreed on whether their enemy were the Ruhar or the Kristang. Or both. Or neither. "What do we have in the area?" Marcellus asked.

"One French MP unit for security, they're on their way and should arrive within the hour. They have been ordered to secure the French village and provide medical assistance, but *not* to pursue the Indians. There is a Chinese security team awaiting orders to move on the Indian village, Sir, they know not to move without orders."

"That's one good thing tonight. What the *hell* were the Indians thinking?"

Although Captain Chen knew that Marcellus had asked a rhetorical question, she answered. "They are desperate, General. They're hungry, they don't have any hope of ever getting home or even hearing from their families on Earth again."

"That applies to all of us, Captain," Marcellus said quietly. Including himself. He had a wife and a young daughter back on Earth. He might never see them again. He might never know if they were still alive, and they might never learn of his fate. That was a very hard fact to deal with.

CHAPTER TWENTY FIVE

Flying Dutchman

"Do you have any practical advice for us, Colonel?" Major Smythe asked, as we adjusted the helmets of our Kristang powered armor suits, it was a part of a test before the operation we'd be performing the next morning.

"About what? Everyone on your SpecOps team has more parachute training than I have. Audio check."

"Your audio connection is confirmed," Smythe replied. "Sir, you are the only one of us, the only human, who has done an actual spacedive."

"True, I guess. My spacedive didn't involve me falling into an atmosphere, Major. That was kind of the point at the time. On this op, we're doing that deliberately."

"Oh, certainly. Do you have any advice for us about the space portion of our dive, then?"

I thought a moment. "Bring music, or an audiobook or something. We'll be coasting through space for a long time, it gets boring after you get used to staring at the pretty stars. If you don't have anything to occupy your time, Skippy will talk to you. *A lot.* Or he will sing show tunes."

"Oh, bullocks," Smythe groaned. "Yesterday, he spent two bloody hours talking to me about the profound changes to European literature during the Enlightenment. After one hour, I felt like throwing him out an airlock, or jumping out myself. I will inform the team."

"Great. And, Major? One more piece of advice."

"What is that, Colonel?"

"Everyone should make sure they pee before we jump."

"Poole, I see you have been cleared for duty?" I asked during an inspection of troops that would be making the spacedive with me and Smythe. The information about how injured people were healing was in my daily update, which I actually read, unlike a lot of reports that were sent to me. "How's the ankle?"

"Squared away, sir." She hopped up and down on the leg that had been injured, then stood on the toes of that foot. She was rock steady on that foot, her gymnastics training must have helped. "Good as new."

A slight grimace on her face told me otherwise. That, and the report from Dr. Skippy that had told me that while she was healed functionally, her leg was going to be sore for another couple of weeks. Close enough. If Major Smythe had cleared her, that was good enough for me.

The actual spacedive, at least the space portion of it, was uneventful. Boring, even, after we all got used to staring at the pretty stars, and the planet growing in front of us. The music in my helmet speakers suddenly cut out, replaced by Skippy's voice. "Hey, Joe are you busy?"

"Super busy, Skippy. Practically frantic," I said, trying to stifle a yawn. It was unsuccessful, I gave a jaw-stretching yawn. Soaring through space by yourself was boring especially when I had been doing it for several hours already.

"Uh huh, I can see that. You are potentially going into combat, and you're practically asleep, Joe. Captain Giraud is half asleep also. Lt. Williams *is* asleep, he asked me to wake im at the appropriate time. He's not alone; half of the special forces are taking a nap right now."

Damn. Those SpecOps guys, and women, were stone-cold frosty when faced with danger. I was too keyed up with fear to do more than let my mind drift and daydream. Truthfully, there wasn't much to do. There wasn't *anything* to do. Anything we did might reveal our presence, so we didn't do anything. "When you wake Lt. Williams, do it with a rousing version of 'The Army Goes Rolling Along'."

"Lt. Williams commands the *Navy* SEALS team, Joe."

"Exactly."

"Oh, I get it now. All right, will do. Hee, hee, that will be fun. Anywho, Joe, since you're not busy, I'm going to take this golden opportunity to explain to you in great detail how very, *very* much I hate you for humiliating me so many times."

"How about we not do that, and say we did?"

"Sadly, no."

"Do I have a choice?"

"I control your helmet speakers, so no. Unless you take your helmet off, which I would not recommend. Ok, let's start with Chapter One, entitled 'Why I Hate Your Stupid Ugly Face-"

I had to admit, Skippy had put a lot of effort into this. I mean, he had taken notes and everything. He wasn't joking about it being broken into chapters, either. Chapter Two, or maybe it was Three was 'How Monkeys Are Incapable Of Truly Appreciating The Vast Scope Of My Awesome Awesomeness' or something like that. His relentless logic made several very valid points that were impossible for me to argue with; I probably would have agreed to hate me too, if I had been paying attention. Truthfully, I tuned him out after about five minutes. Overall, listening to his lengthy diatribe was way better than him singing show tunes, so it was a win-win situation. It made him happy, and it wasn't like I was busy anyway. To help, I said 'Mmmm' or 'Hmmm' or 'Yeah' at random intervals, while I daydreamed about going on a nice long camping, canoeing and fishing trip in Maine when I got back. If I ever got back. A camping trip, some place far from cellphone service. It would be so great to unplug for a while, no interruptions-

"Joe?"

"Hmm?"

"Have you been listening to me?"

"Mmmm." Oh, shit. Did he ask me a question? I shook myself back to full alertness. "Of course I have, Skippy. The way you make your points is very impressive."

"Really. You have been saying 'Hmmm' and 'Mmmm' and 'Yeah' at suspiciously regular intervals."

"Sure. To show you that I'm paying attention."

"That was nice of- Wait! Hey, I just played back the data and analyzed your brainwaves. You have been daydreaming the whole freakin' time!"

"No I wasn't," I protested feebly.

"All right then, what are the three top reasons why I am fully justified in hating you? They were outlined in Chapter Four."

"Oh, wow, Skippy. There are so many to choose from-"

"Liar! Damn it! Now I have to start all over again," he sighed. "Chapter One, entitled Why I Hate Your Stupid Ugly Face-"

"Too late, Skippy."

"Why?"

Paradise

"Because according to my head-up display, I'm about to hit the atmosphere in like, two minutes, right?"

"Shit. Yes, you are. This isn't over, Joe."

My head-up display showed a line of fireballs in front of me like a string of pearls stitched across the face of the planet. The planet itself was not a great place for us to be; it also was not the reason that I very much did not like the idea of us going there.

The planet, which somewhere along the way acquired the nickname 'Jumbo', was big. Like Earth, it was rocky, with a liquid core, a density similar to that of our home planet, and a transparent atmosphere. Calling the place Jumbo was appropriate because it was far larger than Earth; so big that gravity at the surface was 42% greater than Earth normal. Let me say that again; forty two percent higher gravity. On Earth, I weighed 185 pounds. On Jumbo, I would weigh 263 pounds. If you are not American, or you are an American nerdnik who thinks in metric, I would weigh- Hmm, let me think. There are 2.2 pounds in a kilogram, so, multiply by 2.2- No, it's the other way around, you divide by 2.2, so- Oh, forget it. I would weigh 42% more kilograms on Jumbo than I would on Earth. Our Kristang rifles weighed about 12 pounds fully loaded on Earth. On Jumbo, we would be carrying around 17 pound rifles. Plus, we would be carrying all of our other essential gear, which also would weigh 42% more than normal. It was not an ideal situation for a team planning to assault a technologically superior species, on their own ground.

According to Skippy, Jumbo used to have a breathable atmosphere. In the past, the atmosphere was much thicker than that of Earth, but not so thick that the pressure at the surface would crush a human. Although it had less oxygen in the mix, the density was so much greater it would have been possible for human lungs to take in enough oxygen to breathe almost normally.

Jumbo *used* to have a breathable atmosphere in the distant past. It did not have a breathable atmosphere now. Jumbo also used to have abundant surface life, now the native life there was limited mostly to microscopic organisms beneath the surface. Something very bad had happened to Jumbo, and that was why the Thuranin Advanced Research Directorate had a small facility there, basically a monitoring station. A long time ago, the Maxolhx had a colony on Jumbo, and during their war against the Rindhalu, the Maxolhx had used Elder devices as powerful weapons. That use of Elder devices for destructive purposes awakened the Sentinels that the Elders had left behind, and one thing the Sentinels did was cause Jumbo's star to throw off a portion of its outer layer. Jumbo was scorched, much of its atmosphere blown away by the intense stellar fireball. Trying to figure out how the Sentinels had used a star as a weapon, and investigating the nature of the Sentinels themselves, was the purpose of the ARD station on Jumbo.

The planet itself was not why I very much did like not Skippy's plan, although the planet did suck, in my professional opinion. I had been on three alien planets so far; Camp Alpha, Paradise and Newark, and any of them would be have preferable to Jumbo. On Jumbo, we would need to live inside inflatable shelters. Any time we went outside, we would need to wear the helmets on our Kristang powered armor suits, or at least wear a breathing mask. For safety while moving around in the high gravity, we should wear our powered armor all the time, except for when we were sleeping. Simply sleeping was going to be difficult; the extra gravity would make us sore if we stayed in any one position for long, so we would probably be tossing and turning all night.

Yes, the planet sucked. That was not what I very much did not like about Skippy's plan.

Craig Alanson

Because the whole planet was a laboratory, the Thuranin had extensive sensors coverage on and above the planet. Also there were sensors throughout the star system, so it was difficult for us to sneak up on the research station. Difficult even for us to move around the star system. On the surface, we would have to cover our shelters with stealth camouflage netting, and bring along stealth field generators. Those generators, plus their power sources, were heavy and they were extra heavy on Jumbo. We needed power sources for the stealth generators, for recharging our armor suits, and for the combots. Before the battle, the combots would be used to carry most of our equipment, including the power sources. Of course, the combots would also need power, so some combots would be carrying power for other combots, and we would be dropping combots along the way as their power drained. Skippy had calculated that we needed fourteen combots with us, just to have three combots for the actual assault. The logistics math for this operation was kind of crazy.

When Skippy mentioned the ARD facility on Jumbo was staffed with only six Thuranin, I figured that this was going to be super easy; that he had found us a truly soft target. My thinking was, we fly down there in a stealthed dropship, Skippy makes the Thuranin go into sleep mode, and all we need to do is go in and take the Elder power tap. Skippy had quickly explained that, unfortunately, it was not going to be so easy after all. "I can't use my sandman sleepy trick on these Thuranin, Joe. Sorry."

"You're kidding me," I said, severely disappointed. "Come on, this facility can't be heavily shielded like the relay station was? It's just a place for a bunch of science geeks."

"The facility is more shielded than you expect, Joe. They use artificial gravity; in this case they use it to decrease the natural gravity of the planet. But the shielding is not the problem. The reason I can't simply order the Thuranin there to go into sleep mode is that these little green men are not linked to an AI. Thuranin aboard a starship are strongly linked to the ship's AI, so they can control the ship through that link. When we took the *Flying Dutchman*, I exploited that link to make the entire crew go into sleep mode. There is no such link with the Thuranin on Jumbo."

"Crap."

"You're going to have to do this the old fashioned way, Joe. You know, with advanced powered armor suits, combots and explosive-tipped bullets."

The fact that we had to crack open a Thuranin facility, defeat the defenses the hard way, and take the Elder power tap did suck. It was still not why I very much did not like Skippy's plan.

The method we would use for exfiltration after the assault was also not the source of any objection. When the action was over, we would signal the *Dutchman* to jump into orbit and send down a big dropship for us.

No, my big objection was with Skippy's infiltration plan; his idea for getting us and our equipment down to the surface. This crazy, impractical, dangerous plan was why we were spacediving straight at the atmosphere of Jumbo. I very much did not like this idea.

According to Skippy, who of course would be relaxing in his man cave aboard the *Dutchman* while we attacked the Thuranin, we could not simply fly down to the surface in a dropship. "A Thuranin dropship, with Thuranin stealth capability, would be detected by the Thuranin sensors on this Thuranin planet, Joe," he had explained. "It's the same level of technology on both sides. The real problem is that ARD installed an extensive sensor network around Jumbo, because they are basically trying to run back the timeline and see exactly what the Sentinels did to the star. Once you get on the surface, it is possible to conceal your presence, but no way can a dropship fly down without being detected."

To implement Skippy's crazy plan that I very much did not like, we had first gone to our personal relay station, so Skippy could use it to transmit a message that eventually would be received by a particular ARD ship. When we got to the station, all was well. The submind Skippy had left there reported that it was bored, but it was not so completely bored that it wanted to listen to Skippy singing show tunes. I decided right then that I liked that submind. The submind also reported that it did not yet have any information about whether the Thuranin would be sending another surveyor ship to Earth. After we left the relay station, we traveled to the Jumbo system and then we waited. And waited. Finally, only two days later than Skippy had predicted, an ARD ship arrived. It went into orbit around Jumbo, stayed there less than a day, then was gone. We waited another four days at the insistence of Chotek, while I fretted about was happening on Paradise, then Captain Desai got the *Dutchman* moving again. She maneuvered the ship into an asteroid field, and we used our two big dropships to take small asteroids onto the three docking platforms we still had. When the ship was loaded up with rocks, Desai got us on course toward Jumbo, and she released the rocks in a sequence that Skippy had programmed for her. Right behind the fourth-to-last cluster of rocks was our assault party, spacediving toward the planet in formation with relocated asteroids.

The essence of Skippy's plan was to saturate Jumbo with a shower of small meteors. Our assault party and equipment, falling in amongst the meteors, would not be noticed, according to Skippy. That shiny, smug little beer can would be chilling in his escape pod man cave, while we plunged as flaming streaks through the atmosphere of an alien world. I hated Skippy's plan. I also didn't have a better idea, and believe me, I had tried to think of a better idea.

And that was why I was in a Kristang powered armor suit, encased in an aeroshell that Skippy had fabricated aboard the *Dutchman*, with the atmosphere of Jumbo fast approaching. The meteors ahead of us were already burning their way down to impact the surface, we were right behind them. "How are the Thuranin reacting to the unscheduled meteor shower, Skippy?"

"They are mildly curious, Joe. We are in luck because the Thuranin are in the midst of testing a sort of stellar ultrasound satellite that they put into orbit two months ago. Also, the Thuranin are super distracted, because they recently received an Elder power tap that none of them were expecting."

"What an incredible coincidence," I said with a dry mouth, as the planet loomed in front of my eyes.

"Yeah, that's weird, huh? As Dr. Friedlander predicted, none of the researchers here were able to pass us the opportunity to inspect an Elder power tap, so most of them are either attempting to run tests on it, or arguing about which tests to run next. Anyway, nobody is paying much attention to meteors now. After the first cluster of meteors hit, the Thuranin analyzed the remaining ones coming in, and determined that none of the meteors pose a threat to their facility or the sensor equipment."

"Excellent aiming there, Skippy."

"Thank you, Joe. And now, I am sorry to say that we are going to lose communications for a short time. This microwormhole that I'm using needs to stay outside the atmosphere."

"Ok," I said breathlessly. "Great. Talk to you later."

"Are you scared, Joe?"

"Of course I'm scared, Skippy." I almost bit my tongue, because my teeth were chattering with fear. "I'm afraid of heights, you know. This is about as high as you can get. I'm about to fall into the atmosphere of an alien planet, in an untested aeroshell that, as far as I know, you made out of pasta left over from the galley. And my parachute was packed by an absent-minded beer can. Other than that, I'm great!"

Craig Alanson

"Don't worry, Joe, I'm sure that I remembered to pack your parachute. Pretty sure. Well, fairly sure, anyway. To be safe, can you reach behind you and-"

"Not funny, Skippy!"

"Oh, come on, Joe," the shiny beer can said in a teasing tone. "Admit it, the thought of spacediving down to the surface of a planet isn't exciting to you?"

"Combat is exciting too, Skippy. I very much do not like getting shot at either."

"Maybe you just haven't been shot at by the right people yet, Joe." His voice was distorted by interference, as I fell deep into the atmosphere, and the aeroshell became a hotly glowing meteor.

"Talk to you later, Skippy," I said, and I concentrated on keeping as calm as I could. Prayer helped.

There isn't much I can say about plunging through the atmosphere of Jumbo. I didn't hear much of the hypersonic then supersonic then just plain sonic roaring noise as the aeroshell I was encased in burned through increasingly thick air. The surface of the aeroshell was designed to heat up and peel away layer by layer. As pieces were torn off, the aeroshell shuddered and my stomach went along with it. As I said, I didn't hear much, because my helmet cancelled out the ambient sounds. As for what I saw, that wasn't anything to wrote home about either, mostly because I had my eyes closed in sheer terror part of the way down. The other reason is that I was encased in a thick aeroshell made of leftover pasta, or something like that. It sure had felt flimsy when I was lowered into it aboard the *Flying Dutchman*, and the thing was sealed closed around me. On the spacedive to Jumbo, my helmet visor had a view from a tiny camera in the nose of the aeroshell. After we hit the atmosphere and the air around us turned to red-hot plasma, the view in my helmet faceplate was a representation of what the suit's computer thought was out there. The suit could have showed me pink dancing hippos and I would not have been able to disprove it.

At around three kilometers altitude, the aeroshell deployed a drogue parachute that was only designed to slow down my descent. I still couldn't see anything real because the aeroshell's camera had burned away with the outer layer of the shell. There was a sudden jerk when the drogue chute deployed, and when it was shredded as intended, it snapped loose and was replaced by another one. And then by a third. At that point, I was less than one kilometer from the ground, and the aeroshell cracked open, both sides exploding away from me and out of my way. I was falling, feet first, toward ground that I could see was covered by dirt, mud and rocks. My freefall lasted only maybe half a second, to clear the aeroshell pieces, then my own parachute deployed. This was at first a triangular paraglider, although I didn't steer the thing. A computer in my suit scanned the ground, selected a good landing spot, and aimed me for it. Less than fifty meters up, the parachute changed shape to become a big, round, billowing thing that lowered me gently to the ground. Just as my suit boots touched dirt, the parachute snapped loose from my back, and rolled itself into a sphere the size of a tennis ball, cords and all. That, I had to admit, was a soft landing, especially in 1.42 Gee conditions. Speaking of the high gravity, I fell down twice in my first five steps. The suit compensated for the additional strain of gravity, it wasn't immediately able to compensate for a clumsy user. Walking slowly and carefully, I strode over to where my tennis ball size former parachute was, used my powered suit to scoop a hole in the dirt, and buried the parachute. Around me, I could see others doing the same, and I could see equipment including combots drifting to the ground on parachutes. The ground shook as a real meteor hit the ground to the north of us, throwing up a tall pillar of dirt. Skippy had planned for the two meteors just ahead and behind us to be extra large, so the dirt thrown up by their impact craters would obscure Thuranin sensors. I hoped that worked.

"Lt. Poole, are you all right?" I asked the closest person to me. On the surface, we could use low-powered helmet to helmet lasers for communications, without being detected. That only worked if we were line of sight to the other person, although suits could also be used as relays. The image in my visor said 'Poole, USA', so I asked her first

"Yes, Colonel, I'm fine. That was *awesome*! We have to do that again sometime."

I did not share her adrenaline-seeking US Army Ranger enthusiasm. "You can do it for me next time. Major Smythe, this is Colonel Bishop. Status check." While I couldn't see Smythe from my position, I was hoping there were enough suits with line of sight between us that my message would be relayed to him by laser link.

"Down and safe, Sir," came Smythe's reply. "Everyone is accounted for."

"Confirmed," I agreed, checking the display on my wrist. We hadn't lost anyone during the drop. I counted that as a victory, and possibly a minor miracle. "Collect the equipment, bury our trash and let's get moving." We had timed our landing for mid-morning on that part of Jumbo, so we would have plenty of time to travel before nightfall. Our suits had excellent night-vision capability, because Skippy had swapped the original crappy Kristang gear for advanced Thuranin equipment. We could have walked through the night, but I vetoed that idea. With the additional gravity, a fall could be fatal, and we had plenty of time, there was no reason to take an unnecessary risk. We would walk that day, set up shelters with camo netting for the night, then walk part of the next day until we were close to the perimeter of the Thuranin facility. Because the Thuranin did not want their instrument readings contaminated by electromagnetic radiation and airborne chemicals from their facility, the area around their base had very few sensors, which worked great for us. Our plan was to get a couple hours of rest the next night, and launch our assault around the middle of the night local time. We wanted the advantage of surprise by catching the Thuranin off guard. The six little green men and women there were not armed personally. They did have combots and automated defenses that Skippy knew about, and he warned us that ARD facilities may have nasty hidden defenses that he didn't know about. That was why we planned to hit the place with three combots and two dozen high-speed special forces troops. Plus me, although I would be bringing up the rear and trying my best to stay out of the way. Smythe wanted to assign one person to essentially babysit me, I had vetoed that idea also. He probably did it anyway.

After our spacedive and freefall down to the surface, walking across the high-gravity dirt and mud of Jumbo, and one and a half mostly sleepless nights huddled inside cramped shelters, the actual assault on the ARD facility was almost anticlimactic. Most of the facility's defenses were designed to protect it from air assault, and the designers had anticipated being attacked by technology-stealing Kristang. They did not anticipate the attackers would have Thuranin-level or better technology. With Skippy's help, we were able to evade the perimeter defenses entirely. The inner ring of defenses reacted to us, but stood down when we supplied the proper authentication codes. Skippy was totally disdainful of the Thuranin computer that handled security while the little green men and women were sound asleep. Yes, we had the proper codes to gain entrance to the facility. The computer still should have been smart enough to wonder who was out wandering around in the dark of night, while the computer surely knew that the six occupants were sleeping in their bunks.

Or, we later learned, three of them were sleeping in their bunks. The three awake were either too excited about having an Elder power tap to sleep, or they wanted to run tests on it while the other three were sleeping. We never did get a clear picture of the ocial dynamics among the six occupants of the facility, because one of the three that were wake noticed a light indicating that an airlock was cycling. It was cycling because we vere coming in, the computer had let us in. That unnamed, alert Thuranin probably hought at first that one of the supposedly sleeping Thuranin was awake and had decided o go outside. Or already was outside, and was coming back in. Either way, the secret, mauthorized midnight experiment on the precious Elder power tap was in danger of being liscovered. So this alert Thuranin sounded an alarm for its two fellows, and used the imple expedient of switching on an exterior camera to see who was coming in through he airlock.

We were not able to do any magical Skippy tricks of showing a false image through he camera, all we had done was smear some sticky goop and mud over the camera lens. That likely bought us five or ten seconds while the curious Thuranin wondered what had ;one wrong with the camera. Then it did the smart thing of checking which of the three upposedly sleeping Thuranin was not in their bunk.

Except all three of them were sleeping in their bunks. And that's when all hell broke oose.

The first thing we noticed was the airlock quit cycling. The light that was yellow urned red, and we heard a loud clanging sound as an interior blast door slammed shut. mmediately after that, we were illuminated from above. The Thuranin had launched a econ drone that popped up above the facility and spotlighted us before Giraud shot it lown. There was no way the Thuranin could mistake our Kristang powered armor suits,)ecause we had left the camo netting behind when we crossed the perimeter. They)robably were confused by the three Thuranin combots we had with us. Whatever 'onfusion that caused didn't last long, because someone inside activated the automatic lefenses, and doors in the exterior walls slid aside for computer-controlled guns to lock in)n us.

That was a nice try, anyway. We knew about the autoguns, and had placed charges)ver the doors. As soon as those access doors slid aside, our shaped charges blew the gun :mplacements before the muzzles could clear the exterior walls.

"Oh, bollocks," Smythe said calmly. "The queen has rescinded her formal invitation o tea, we will have to do this the hard way. Rocket Team One, clear us a path."

Rocket Team One was four troops of mixed nationality, lead by Captain Renee Giraud, who had rockets that were normally part of a combot's weaponry. Since we only aad three combots with us, we had two teams carrying rockets with them. Just one rocket ipped a hole in the exterior wall, and four soldiers used their powered armor to tear the aole open wide enough for a combot to stride through. Two of the hulking machines led he way, with one held in reserve. Whenever we encountered a blast door or a well-lefended section of the facility, the combots pulled aside and a rocket took out the)bstacle.

The biggest obstacle we faced was a half-dozen combots that were controlled by the acility's computer. The first three caused us a surprising amount of trouble. They nanaged to destroy one of our combots and partly disable another, before Skippy had ;athered enough data to analyze their tactics. After that, we pulled our reserve combot orward and sent the damaged one back to guard our rear. With Skippy telling us how to :onfuse and defeat the Thuranin computer's defense tactics, we made rapid progress. Two)f the Thuranin opposed us directly with weapons, one of them got off a fusillade of shots hat knocked down a Chinese soldier; he quickly jumped in his dented armor up to show is that he was all right. Those two Thuranin were the last obstacle to us getting the Elder)ower tap, it was inside some kind of test chamber. Skippy told us to be careful not to lamage it, so instead of blowing the heavy door off the test chamber, we tried overriding the locking mechanism. That was no good, one of the Thuranin had fried the controls when they heard us coming. Although they wrongly assumed we were Kristang, they correctly assumed we were coming after the power tap, and they did what they could to deny us the prize.

We were exposed while we used a plasma torch to cut into the door. Although four people with torches were able to slice the door open in less than a minute, it felt like forever as we were still taking fire the whole time. Finally, an Indian paratrooper squeezed in and got our prize, slinging it on his back in an armored pack. He was halfway back out through the door when were attacked by a pair of combots. Two explosive-tipped rounds ricocheted off the heavy door, knocking the paratrooper back into the chamber. Smythe shouted for him to stay down, as his people sent a furious hail of bullets and rockets at the combots, and our own combot launched itself through the air. One of the enemy combots disappeared in an explosion as it was shredded by rockets and explosive-tipped rounds. The other was tackled by our out-of-ammo combot. The two machines rolled and crashed around the high-ceilinged laboratory, wrecking equipment and breaking the leg of one British SAS, who was unable to get out of the way in time. The two damned things nearly took my head off, one moment they were entangled on the other side of the laboratory, in a blink of an eye they were headed straight for me. I dropped to the floor, the heavy gravity of Jumbo saved me as I crashed to the ground quicker than normal. By the time I rolled onto my back, it was over. Both combots had torn each other apart.

"Go!" Smythe shouted. "Move, get out of there!"

With the Indian paratrooper surrounded by a half dozen high-speed special forces for protection, we began our egress operation, going back out the same way we came in. "Uh oh, Joe, you'd best move faster," Skippy shouted in my helmet speakers.

"Why?" As if we needed any incentive to move faster?

"That Thuranin computer has concluded that it has lost the battle, and that a hostile force has captured critical technology. Following ARD protocols, it is preparing to self-destruct the facility to prevent you from getting away."

"Shit! How long do we have?"

"Eighteen seconds according to the Thuranin computer's internal clock. I am doing what I can to mess with its sense of time, however, I would advise you to run like hell. You have less than three minutes to get clear of a two kiloton explosion."

"Major Smythe!" I shouted.

"I heard, Colonel. All troops, discard weapons and packs, except for the power tap. Proceed at maximum speed to get clear of the perimeter," he said calmly. Then, to assure everyone how serious he was, he shouted. "Move! Run! RUN!"

We ran. Once we got clear of the exterior wall, which took only forty seconds, we used the full power of our suits and ran like hell across the rolling dirt of Jumbo. The suit computers, enhanced by Skippy, did more than half the work of keeping us upright. There was a menu projected on the interior of our visors that we could select with an eye blink, a particular click engaged the suit's 'Escape' function. With that feature engaged, the suit mostly ran by itself, using its sensors to keep the slow and clumsy wearers upright during our headlong emergency run across the star-blasted landscape. Those people who had been slow to click their suit's Escape function found that Skippy had done it for them. The entire team was racing across the ground at about eighty miles an hour; so fast that my bouncing and jolted vision could not keep up. No way could I have run that fast with me controlling the suit; I would have stumbled and crashed. After what seemed like an eternity of frantic running, with my brain surely sustaining a concussion from rattling around in my skull, Skippy shouted a warning for us to drop flat. My suit fell in a

ontrolled manner, to leave me skidding across dirt and rocks until I came to rest, face
lown. "Skippy, when-"

He didn't need to answer, as my visor automatically darkened and the ground beneath
ne heaved. It heaved so strongly that I went flying ten feet in the air, and came down
olling around and around uncontrollably as the blast wave hit us. My suit computer said
ve had gotten only three kilometers from the facility when it blew up.

When the blast wave passed on, I stumbled shakily to my knees. "Are we all right,
Skippy?"

"Oh, sure, Joe. That was a compression warhead, there's little radiation to worry
bout. You're safe in your suits."

"Great, thanks." Checking my helmet visor, I saw that the entire assault team had
urvived the explosion. "What's the status of the power tap?"

"It is good, Colonel," came the reply. "My pack has holes in it, but the case with the
ower tap is intact."

"Outstanding, good work." I got to my feet and brushed my knees off without
emembering that I was in an armored suit. To my left, a soldier was jumping up and
lown, verifying her suit was still in perfect working order. "Poole, did you think that was
wesome also?"

"Absolutely, Sir," she replied, and I could imagine her ear to ear grin behind her
larkened visor. "I'd like to do that again. Without the explosion."

"Roger that, I'll see what I can do about that. Major Smythe, let's walk," I looked at
vhich way the wind was blowing the debris. There was a mushroom cloud looming over
us, all that was left of the Thuranin facility. "North," I said, pointing in the direction the
vind was coming from. "Skippy, can you send a dropship down to pick us up?"

"Colonel Chang will be jumping the ship into orbit in less than two minutes, Joe,"
Skippy said cheerily. "Dropship is prepped and ready for launch."

CHAPTER TWENTY SIX

"Oh damn it!" Skippy shouted. "Unbelievable! How the *HELL* did those idiots manage to do that? I, I, I-" he sputtered. "Unfreakin' believable!"

"What?" I asked, alarmed. "What's wrong?" We had flown back up to the *Dutchman* with the Elder power tap, and as soon as the dropship was secured, the ship jumped away. I brought the power tap into Skippy's man cave; he said he didn't need to be that close, but the process of making it functional again would take almost half an hour. Less than ten minutes after we brought the power tap aboard, Skippy began shouting.

"They broke it, Joe! Somehow, in spite of the Elders' efforts to idiot-proof their devices, *these* idiots managed to break it!"

"What do you mean broke, Skippy?" I looked out the hatchway of the escape pod, where Chotek, Chang, Simms, Smythe, Adams, Giraud, Friedlander and others were crowded into the hallway, craning their necks to see what was going on. "We know that it doesn't work, that's why we were able to get it. A functional power tap could never have been picked up by an ARD ship based on a simple message. Go ahead and fix it."

"I can't, you moron," Skippy said angrily. "Don't you think I would do it if I could? The only thing wrong with this power tap was that it needed to be rebooted. But somehow the stupid, *stupid* Thuranin managed to truly break it! They screwed with it and broke it for real."

"Ok," I said quietly. "But you can still fix it, right? You can get it working again?"

"No, Joe," he said disgustedly. "If I could do that, I wouldn't be so upset. It would be easier for me to build a new power tap than to get this one working again."

"Oh. Can you do that?"

"Of course not, you dumdum. To create Elder technology like that, I would need access to Elder technology that no longer exists in this galaxy. As far as I know it doesn't. Unlike human technology, the Elders didn't make everything out of mud and sticks. We'r screwed. No way can I fix this piece of junk. Damn it!"

"This was all for nothing, then?" Chotek asked, astonished.

"Yes!" Skippy said.

"No," I protested, not willing to believe we had failed, after all we had gone through.

Chotek looked at me. "If this thing doesn't work, Colonel, how was this trip not for nothing?"

"I don't know yet," I answered lamely.

"Surely they can't all be broken," Chang asked.

"No," Skippy said grumpily, "I think whatever experiments the Thuranin have been running somehow damaged this one. Any power tap they ran that experiment on would be broken; the power tap's connection to, hmmm, I had better not tell you monkeys about that. The problem is, without access to ARD records, there is no way to know how many of these things they screwed with and broke. I have to say," he mused, "it is actually impressive that a low-tech species like the Thuranin managed to affect a power tap in any way. It had to be dumb luck. No way are those little green men capable of understanding the principles of how this technology works."

"We can get another one?" Simms suggested.

Chotek shook his head. "We don't have time. And I think the Advanced Research Directorate would become suspicious if we try that delivery trick again."

"As much as I hate to say it," Skippy grumbled, "Count Chocula is right. After that ship dropped off the power tap here, it was scheduled to visit seven other ARD installations, and then it was stopping at an ARD administrative depot for resupply. That will happen in about two months. As soon as that ship reports that it delivered a power tap here, there are going to be a whole lot of uncomfortable questions being asked by ARD headquarters, and they're going to be sending ships to Jumbo. They are also going to be tightening their procedures. We won't be able to simply order an ARD ship to do our shipping for us."

"Will that cause a problem for us?" Chotek was alarmed. "If the Thuranin are somehow able to trace the delivery message back to us-"

"That will not be a problem," Friedlander spoke up. "Skippy and I discussed this before he sent the message. I suggested that he include hints that the order to deliver a power tap to Jumbo originated with one of the researchers on Jumbo; that one of them manipulated the situation because he or she wanted access to a power tap."

I blinked slowly. "Is that true, Skippy?"

"Yup. Just what the rocket scientist said."

Chotek was as surprised as I was. "When were you going to tell us about this?" He demanded.

"There wasn't any reason to," Friedlander said simply, seeming surprised at the question.

"Yeah, Chocula," Skippy scoffed. "A lot of stuff happens around here that you and Colonel Joe don't know about."

"The six Thuranin on Jumbo," Chotek wasn't letting this go, "they are all dead?"

"Most assuredly," Skippy replied. "In addition to the ones killed in the assault, the others died when the facility self-destructed. The computer locked the blast doors so they couldn't escape. The ARD considers the information in their heads to be classified; they would never be allowed to fall into enemy hands."

"They were dead anyway," I looked at Chotek. Before the assault, he had expressed serious concerns that we were planning to deliberately kill civilians. At the time, I didn't have a good answer for him, other than that they were in the way, and we needed the power tap to save thousands of humans on Paradise.

Chotek looked at the deck for a moment, then at me. "Colonel Bishop, we do not have time to attempt seizure of another power tap. Please set course back to the relay station." Seeing that I was going to protest, he added "I am sure that you and your people are tired. My suggestion is that you rest, and approach the problem with fresh minds tomorrow." What he didn't say was, the issue was closed. It was over. UNEF was stuck on Paradise, and we had no way to prevent the Ruhar from selling the planet out from under them.

"Joe, I have a question," Skippy said while I was in my office, which was a refreshing change from him bugging me in the shower, while brushing my teeth, or any other inconvenient moment. Supposedly, I was in my office to review reports on my tablet; in reality I'd grown bored with that in about three minutes and was now playing solitaire. And losing every game. I told myself that Skippy had hacked into the solitaire program just to screw with me, I wasn't giving him the satisfaction of knowing it bothered me. Sometimes, if you were patient enough to ignore Skippy long enough, he went away. "I'm asking now," he explained, "because I can see you are super busy."

"Hey, these cards aren't going to arrange themselves." Truthfully, I had been racking my brain to think of an alternative way to prevent the Ruhar from trading away Paradise, and I had absolutely no useful ideas. Playing solitaire was a way to distract me from my failure.

"You're bored? Hmm, there is no internet access here in interstellar space, but before we left Earth I downloaded petabytes of porn. What's your interest? Let me guess. Clowns? Midgets?"

"No porn, Skippy."

"Ah. Lesbian midget clowns?"

"I don't want any more porn!" I shouted, just as Sergeant Adams walked in my open office door. She must have heard me, because her mouth was open in surprise. "Oh, crap." I softly pounded my forehead on the table. "Please, just kill me now."

"Sir?" She said warily. "Is this a bad time?"

Skippy spoke before I could. "Joe is bored with his usual porn selections. Hey, Sarge Marge, can you guess what Joe likes-"

"Sergeant," I mumbled with my face planted on the desk. "I hope you are here to report that our reactors are about to explode."

"Sir, I'll come back later when you're not so busy," Adams couldn't keep the mirth out of her voice.

"No problem," Skippy said cheerily, "Sergeant Adams and I can continue this privately. So far, I've covered clowns and-"

"Goodbye, Sergeant," I mumbled with a dismissive wave of a hand. Waiting a couple seconds, I looked up to see she had wisely departed. "You had a question, Skippy? It had better not be about porn."

"No, Joe. This question is about slang I heard during the party when you went back to your hometown. I know that 'mow down' is to eat a lot of food, and 'wicked' is the same as 'very'-"

"What? That's not what wicked means."

"Joe, when something is very much a 'pissah', it is a 'wicked pissah', correct?"

"Oh, uh, I guess, sort of. Look, Skippy, there is a wicked lot you're missing. You have to grow up with it to understand. What is your question?"

"I want the definition of 'douchebag'. It's not the same as a jerk, is it? I ask because people at the party were saying that some guy is a d-bag, and they described him as more arrogant than boorish."

"Oh, man," I ran a hand over my head. "First, that is originally a New England expression, it got totally corrupted when it started getting used in freakin' Hollywood movies. A d-bag is a guy-"

"Always a guy?"

"Always a guy, never a woman. This is a guy who is a jerk because he is so arrogant and totally into himself."

"So, a d-bag is a jerk because he's clueless about social norms?"

"No, a d-bag isn't clueless about being a jerk, a d-bag does it deliberately. He knows he's being a douchebag, and he goes right ahead. Like, any guy who wears the collar of his polo shirt up, or ties a sweater around his shoulders, is borderline engaging in d-bag behavior. This is something better explained with an example. Let's say there's a guy who drives his Porsche to a restaurant-"

"Do all douchebags drive Porsches?"

"No, but that is a popular car for the aspiring douchebag."

"Men *aspire* to be a douchebag?" Skippy asked incredulously.

"Sure. Guys don't think of it that way, but that's what they're doing. So, this guy drives his Porsche to a restaurant. And he leaves the headlights on. That way, the waiter or someone will announce there is a Porsche outside with headlights on. Then the douchebag will loudly announce 'Oh, I have left on the lights of MY PORSCHE. I have to go out to MY PORSCHE and take care of that'."

"Ah. I see. He is not only a jerk, he is a jerk in a socially awkward, pathetic, desperate attempt for attention; thus opening himself for understandable scorn and ridicule from society."

Craig Alanson

"You got it," I agreed, think that Skippy himself may be an expert on social awkwardness.

"Bonus points if this guy has his collar up and ties a sweater over his shoulders?"

"Oh, yeah. A guy like that would be a HOFer."

"A HOFer?" Skippy asked, confused.

"He would be a shoo-in for the douchebag Hall Of Fame."

"There is a *hall of fame* for douchebags?" Skippy gasped.

"No, Skippy. I meant, if there were such a hall of fame, that guy would have his picture right inside the front door."

"Wow, this is complicated."

"Human culture is complicated, Skippy, but you're catching on."

"Huh? Oh, I meant that the math problem I'm working on is complicated. You know that I multitask when I talking with you, Joe."

I sighed. "Great. Thank you, Skippy."

"Good talking with you too, Joe. What were we talking about again?"

Still not having come up with an idea, I went to the gym. Playing solitaire hadn't given me an idea, maybe lifting weights or running would help. It didn't work. I ended my workout soaked with sweat, with my brain still not cooperating. Sergeant Adams walked into the gym as I was leaving and I stopped to talk with her. "It's our turn to cook the day after tomorrow, do you have any ideas what to make for lunch?" We were making chicken pot pie for dinner, plus a vegetable puff pastry thing that Simms had a recipe for.

She tilted her head. "We could make mock oyster soup, my grandmother used to make that," she laughed.

"Mock oyster soup?"

"My grandmother said when she was little her family went through some lean times, so her mother made mock oyster soup from eggplant and milk and crackers or something like that. There are no oysters in it. It's an old recipe, for us it became a family joke."

I laughed at that. "One time when we went camping, my father looked in the cooler and realized he had left the package of hot dogs at home. So he toasted the buns on a fire, put in a lot of cheese, onions and mustard, and we had 'mock dogs'."

I was thinking of my father trying to convince us that, lacking hot dogs, we could each eat two mock dogs instead. My mother was not amused. And my sister and I had been looking forward to grilling hot dogs over a fire all day. Even when my father brought out a bag of marshmallows to roast on the fire, we were not happy. We wanted hot dogs, and were disappointed not to get them. When people decide that they want something, they aren't happy when it isn't available. Like when my family was not going for mock dogs, or-

Holy shit.

An idea hit me right then, right there in the corridor. "Adams, excuse me." I ran down the corridor to Skippy's escape pod, foregoing a shower for the moment. Ducking down to crawl in the tiny door, I plopped myself across two of the too-small seats. "Hey Skippy."

He made a sniffing sound. "You couldn't have showered first? Whew," he said in disgust.

"No time for a shower, I have an idea I need to discuss with you."

"Does this idea involve you sealing yourself in a plastic bag to contain the monkey smell?"

"No. First, I have a question. How do microwormholes work?"

Paradise

Silence. Then, "You've got to be kidding me, Joe. A microwormhole is simply a very small diameter wormhole. You barely understand how shoelaces work, and you want me to explain a wormhole to you?"

"Very funny. And yes I do want you to explain it. You're super smart, figure out a way to explain it to me."

"Joe, that is a mathematical question, and you don't speak that language. Hell, Friedlander barely speaks enough math for me to talk to him about-"

"No math, then. Break it down for me Barney style. Sorry for ruining the joke for you."

"I truly do not know where to start, Joe. You are asking me to explain the mechanics of what your species calls an Einstein-Rosen bridge-"

"Why is it called that?"

"Because," Skippy said slowly like people do when explaining things to a toddler, "Albert Einstein and Nathan Rosen discovered the mathematical basis of-"

"No, I figured that, Skippy. I meant, why is it called a 'bridge'?"

"Oh. I think Einstein and Rosen used that term because a such a construct carries an object from one place to another, without going through the space between those two places. It's a shortcut. Like a bridge can carry a person from one side of a river to another without going through the river."

"But when you're going across a bridge, you can look down and see the river," I pointed out, proud of myself. "And it can take a long time to go across a bridge, so it's not really a shortcut. Except it is faster than swimming, probably. If it's a bridge, why do you call it a wormhole?"

"I don't call it a wormhole, your species calls it a wormhole, Joe. I'm just using the term-"

"When a worm makes a hole in the ground, I'll bet it seems like a really long way to the worm," I mused. "The worm sure doesn't think of it as a shortcut."

"Focus, Joey, focus! Please, *please*, try to focus. Oh, this is impossible. Impossible!" He sobbed quietly. "Joe, I'm going to stop talking to you now, and instead I will try explaining integral calculus to one of Major Simms' tomato plants in the hydroponics farm. Because that will be a lot easier for me."

"Uh huh." The too-small Thuranin seat was digging into my butt cheek, so I laid down across the seats. "How about this? Didn't Einstein say that nothing could exceed the speed of light? Yet this ship travels faster than light."

"No it does not."

"Uh," I paused to think, wary of making an even bigger fool of myself. "We go from one star to another faster than light can get there, Skippy."

"Yes, but we do not *travel* the distance between stars."

That puzzled me. "What's the difference?"

"We cheat, Joe. We use a traversable wormhole, which as I said your species calls an Einstein-Rosen bridge, to create a shortcut. Uh!" He cut off my next ignorant question. "I you want me to attempt to explain this, then kindly shut your pie hole. The two ends of a wormhole can be a lightyear apart in normal space, but going through a wormhole involves no distance at all. A wormhole creates a tunnel connecting two points in space, but the inside of the tunnel has no length at all. Think of a wormhole as a doorway. On one end of the doorway is Maine, the other side is in Australia. You go through the doorway, faster than light could travel from your home to the land Down Under. Actually the length of a wormhole tunnel is not zero, but that is not something I can explain to monkeys; that kind of knowledge is too dangerous."

"Consider my mind blown, Skippy. All right, forget explaining how wormholes work. Answer this question: I know that you can send radio signals and maser beams through a microwormhole. Can you feed power through one also?"

"Electrical power? Sure, that's easy. It depends how much power you're talking about, any microwormhole has a maximum throughput. And you'd have to be careful that the frequency of power transmitted does not match the microwormhole's natural frequency. That could quickly create a resonance that would collapse the wormhole. Why do you want to feed power through a microwormhole?"

"Skippy, maybe we don't need to offer an Elder power tap to the Ruhar. Maybe we only needed them to *think* they had found an Elder power tap. A mock power tap."

"I'm not following you, Joe. You mean we create a fake one like we did on Newark? There have been plenty of inert power taps found across the galaxy, only a functioning one would be valuable enough to make the Ruhar want to retain control of Paradise. Besides, they would quickly analyze it and determine it is a fake."

"If the power tap generated power, that would convince them that it is real?"

"You mean like we put a powercell inside the mockup power tap? That would only work until the powercell ran out. Also, the Ruhar would scan it and see that it's a simple powercell."

"I do not mean a powercell. I mean we hide a microwormhole inside our fake power tap, and we feed the *Dutchman*'s reactor power through it. And you project some kind of stealth field through the wormhole, so the Ruhar's scanning instruments won't work on it."

"Huh," Skippy said thoughtfully.

"Could we do that?"

"Hmm. Let me think about it, Joe. I would need to move the wormhole to keep it centered in the mockup, and the *Dutchman* would need to be a long way from the mockup to keep us hidden. Although, hmm, data transmission through the wormhole is instantaneous, so signal lag would not be an issue. As long as the Ruhar didn't move the mockup really fast, I could easily keep the wormhole centered in it. And I can project a stealth field through the wormhole also, to prevent the Ruhar from detecting the event horizon."

"What is an event hori-"

"Never mind that. Let me guess what your monkey brain is thinking. We create a mockup here aboard the *Dutchman*, and I install one end of a microwormhole in it. The other end stays wrapped around a power conduit aboard the ship. We fly the mockup down to Paradise in a stealthed dropship, bury it, and let the Ruhar dig it up. They see that it is apparently generating impressive amounts of power, and they go bananas digging up Paradise to find another one. Hmmm. That could work, Joe. The only problem I see is that we could never leave. The *Flying Dutchman* and I would have to remain near Paradise, forever."

"No, Skippy. We can shut down the power tap at some point and go back to Earth."

"Won't the Ruhar realize the scam at that point?"

"No. Skippy, you're thinking like a super smart AI. You need to think like a meat-brain biological trashbag. When it is time for us to leave, you increase the power throughput, and keep increasing it until the wormhole collapses. That should destroy the mockup, right?"

"Quite thoroughly, yes. Won't the Ruhar be suspicious of why their priceless power tap suddenly went haywire?"

"No. Because like any other biological trashbags, they will not be able to resist screwing with their new toy. They're going to try to scan it, and adjust it, and try to figure out how it works. And when it breaks, they're going to blame themselves for screwing with it. Trust me on this. If something is working fine and you screw with it, and then it breaks, you will assume it broke because you screwed with it. Then you hope you can blame it on somebody else."

"Damn, being biological is complicated. However, while you were blah blah blah talking, I analyzed the psyche of the Ruhar and I must conclude that you are correct. Ther will be much second-guessing and recriminations about why their shiny new toy broke, but they will blame themselves. Then they will become even more determined to make up for their egregious screwup by retaining control of Paradise and finding more Elder goodies. Joe, I am completely impressed. Blown away, even. This may be the most diabolical idea your incredibly devious mind has cooked up yet. A brilliant career as a criminal mastermind awaits you after you are done playing soldier. Tell me, please, because I want to understand how you think up ideas that my brain can't seem to create. How did you get this idea?"

"I'll explain when we serve mock dogs for lunch later this week."

When I explained the idea in a hastily-convened staff meeting right after talking with Skippy, everyone was relieved. And thrilled. Except Sergeant Adams, who always keeps me grounded in reality. "Sir," she asked, "do I understand this correctly? We left Paradise behind, and flew all the way out here, risking our lives to find an Elder power tap that Skippy could fix. Now you tell us none of this would have been necessary, if you only ha this idea back then?"

"Um, yes?" I was suddenly on the defensive.

"Next time, Colonel, can you make your brain work a little faster?"

I smiled. "I can try, Adams, but this is all your fault."

With a skeptical tilt of her head, she asked "How do you figure that, sir?"

"Because," I said with a grin, "if you hadn't waited so long to give me your grandmother's recipe for mock oyster soup, we wouldn't have come all the way out here."

Chotek came to see me in my office about an hour after the staff meeting. Fortunately, I had stopped to shower and put on a clean uniform. "Colonel, your idea to create a fake Elder power tap is commendable."

I waited for him to say 'but', because I knew that was coming next. In the staff meeting, he had seemed irritated that he had agreed to send us off on a fool's errand to find a functioning power tap based on my advice. And now I was telling him that had bee all for nothing, that if I had really thought through my idea, we would not have needed to leave the Paradise system.

"I am concerned that providing only one power tap for the Ruhar to find is insufficient; the Ruhar know such devices are rare. When the one they find destroys itself aren't the Ruhar at least somewhat likely to conclude they found the only power tap on Paradise, and that there is nothing else there? In order to make the Ruhar desire to keep the planet, they must think it probable there are other Elder items of value buried beneath the surface."

Crap. Count freakin' Chocula actually had a point. A good one. "Skippy?" I asked. "Could we make two fake power taps? Can you create and maintain two microwormholes?"

"Please, Joe, you insult me," Skippy's voice had a scoffing tone. "Easy-peasy. But I have been listening to your conversation, and it would be a terrible idea to create two fake Elder power taps. The Kristang already found a real power tap when they first came to Paradise, and functioning power taps are exceedingly rare. To find two of them on one

lanet is astonishing, to find three stretches belief. If the Ruhar found a *third* functioning
ower tap, Paradise would become a place worthy of the Thuranin and Jeraptha fighting
ver directly. It might even attract the attention of the Maxolhx and Rindhalu, and we
1ust avoid that at all costs. Those two senior species may be able to figure out that our
ower taps were fake, and someone would start asking awkward questions."

"Got it," I said with a shrug directed at Chotek. His expression dropped back into the
1ildly peeved look he usually had when dealing with me. I needed to somehow get this
uy on my side. "Hey, sir, I do agree that we could sweeten the pot. Find something else
) induce the Ruhar to keep Paradise. We could, uh, I don't know. Find or fake some other
lder goodies?"

"Goodies?" Chotek wasn't buying into it.

"I'm spitballing," I said by way of explanation.

Chotek looked completely confused. "A spit ball? How is this related to baseball?"

"No, it's," how to explain American slang to a foreigner? Although I had to give an
ustrian props for knowing American baseball terms. "That expression can refer to a
aseball with spit on it. In this case, what I meant was to wad up a small piece of paper,
pit on it, and throw it against a wall. Some of the pieces will stick, just like some ideas
vill stick; will be useful. It's also called brainstorming?"

"Ah, I understand," his face brightened. "We are going to consider a variety of ideas,
nd hopefully find a set of possibilities that can be further developed into a feasible
olution?"

"Yes," I agreed, thinking that Chotek would be loads of fun at parties. Not. "So, we
eed to think of something we can get, or fake, that is valuable. Or," the wheels in my
1ind were spinning. "Something we already have."

"That is a *great* idea," Skippy said in a mocking tone. "Hey, I know! How about we
ffer them something truly valuable; a box of cereal personally autographed by the Count
imself. What a collector's item!"

"Skippy," my protest was marred by me choking to unsuccessfully suppress a laugh.
t came out my nose and threw me into a coughing fit. Chotek's red face didn't help me
egain my composure. "That was not-" even I couldn't tell him it wasn't funny. Because it
vas. "That wasn't called for."

"I am terribly, terribly sorry," Skippy said with a chuckle. He didn't sound sorry at
ll.

"What about," I said slowly.

"Oh, crap," Skippy grumbled. "Get ready, Chocula, this is where the magic happens. I
se the term 'magic' because there is no logical reason for why Joe's brain has ever come
p with even one good idea."

"Uh huh," I ignored him. "We have two Elder comm nodes. The one we picked up
vhen we raided that Kristang asteroid to get our wormhole controller, and the one we took
rom those scavengers on Newark. Skippy, do the Ruhar or whoever know what a comm
ode is?"

"They know that the devices were intended for communications, yes. Joe, comm
odes are not particularly rare in the galaxy, and they are not considered very valuable.
nd in case you were not paying attention, our two comm nodes do not work."

"What if they did?"

"Damn it! See, this is what drives me absolutely crazy!" Skippy fairly shouted in
rustration, and the sides of Chotek's mouth curled up in a brief smile. "I have all the
nformation that you have, I have way *more* information that you have. In terms of brain
ower, my brain is a supergiant star, and yours is a raisin. A small, dried-up moldy old

Paradise

raisin. I should be able to figure out what you are going to suggest, but I can't! I just can't Aaargh! I hate my life. This is so unfair." He broke down into gentle, defeated sobbing.

"Skippy?" I asked. "Do you want to hear my idea?"

"Go ahead," he sighed. "The more unique ideas that I hear, the more data I collect for figuring out how your monkey brain works. And when I do, be prepared for utter, abject humiliation, Joe."

"I am looking forward to it. Listen, those comm nodes don't work because they don't connect to the network, or there is no network, right? That's what we're guessing?"

"Sure," Skippy admitted. "Those two possibilities, or it could be that I don't have the proper network access codes. The Collective secret handshake, sort of."

"Fair enough. If the comm nodes did work, they would be super valuable, because signals travel between comm nodes instantaneously, and no current species has faster than light communications?"

"Not exactly true, but close enough for the purpose of this conversation. Yes, a working comm node would be a valuable item. Is your idea a way to make our comm nodes work, Joe? Because if you could truly do that, I would worship at your feet. I would hate myself until the end of time, but I would do it."

"No, Skippy, my idea is to run another scam on the Ruhar. Can you put the two ends of a microwormhole inside our two comm nodes? That way a signal going in one comm node would travel faster than light to the other one. We could put one comm node on Paradise, and have the other, um, floating out in space somewhere in the Paradise system. That would make it real obvious to the Ruhar that the signal transit time is instantaneous. Oooh," another thought hit me. "And we should have the two comm nodes activate and start pinging each other at the same time the Ruhar uncover the fake power tap. Later, when we blow up the fake power tap, the comm nodes will stop working at the same time." I sat back in my chair, pleased with myself. "Would that work?"

"See, Chocula?" Skippy said. "I've said before that Joe is an evil genius, and I meant it. Joe, that is a *brilliant* idea. Damn it! I still have no idea how you dream up stuff that I should have thought of. Maybe my deviousness subroutine is offline. Yes, Joe, that would work. Wow! As a bonus, pretending there is a remote connection between the power tap and the comm nodes would set back the study of Elder technology by centuries. And having a backup to the fake power tap would be much more convincing to the Ruhar. That was your idea, Chotek, so your name has just been added to my 'Skippy hates you' list."

I grinned and to my surprise, Chotek was beaming with pride. He reached across the table to shake my hand. "My understanding," Chotek addressed Skippy with a wink to me "is that your list is a rather exclusive club. So, please Mr. Skippy, hate me as much as you like."

Damn. Maybe Chocula was human after all.

We flew straight back to Paradise, then I went down to the surface in a dropship with Skippy, Desai, Major Smythe and a half dozen special forces. Smythe and his team planted our mock power tap and one of our mock comm nodes near a Ruhar-controlled projector one night. We had a brief moment of anxiety when we thought Smythe had been detected, but it was a false alarm. Back in the dropship, Skippy confirmed everything was ready, so we waited. And waited. We waited for the Ruhar to notice the fabulous goodies that were right on their doorstep. Damn, those hamsters could be dense sometimes.

CHAPTER TWENTY SEVEN

Baturnah Logellia hurried back down the hallway to her office, determined not to be ate for her next meeting. She had just ended an hour-long meeting about the scarcity of ritical medical supplies; a meeting during which she could not offer even a guess when ie Ruhar fleet would resume escorting cargo ships to Gehtanu. The cease fire, the current ease fire, was holding. Ground troops of both sides were staying in their designated ones, and both sides had stopped attempts to reactivate or destroy projectors.

No one expected the Kristang to remain inactive for long.

Her next meeting had been squeezed onto her calendar that very morning, at the equest of the Chief Administrator. Baturnah would have appreciated more advanced otice, but as the Deputy Administrator, she did as her boss requested.

Waiting in her office was Tohn Logen, a senior engineer who had come to Gehtanu to iaintain the planet's six reactors. He had come to Gehtanu, expecting to remain for five ears, and then he had gotten stuck on the planet when the wormhole shift occurred and ie Kristang arrived. Baturnah liked Tohn, he was always cheery and pleasant; he also lways let it be known that he couldn't wait to leave the backwater planet. Why meeting rith Tohn that morning was so important, Baturnah couldn't imagine, although she braced erself for bad news. Reactors shutting down due to lack of spare parts? Some other ifrastructure problem? No, Tohn had been investigating a projector for the past week. ½ad news about those?

"Administrator," Tohn stood as she came into the office. He offered her the palm-liding handshake typical of the Ruhar, and after exchanging greetings, she asked him to .t. He did, after closing her office door and making sure it was securely shut.

"Would you like klah?" She offered the Ruhar's favorite hot beverage.

"No, I've been living on klah the past few days."

"Surely you didn't have to fly all the way here to talk with me," she said. The man ooked tired, like he hadn't slept in days. "I have been following your reports about the rojectors."

"Yes," he said wearily. "We have made considerable progress; our initial assumption iat the projectors were installed by the Kristang have been confirmed."

"It is greatly troubling that we lived here for so long, with those projectors practically nder our feet, and we knew nothing about them."

You lived here with them, Tohn thought to himself. I just work here. Then he egretted his uncharitable thought. Gehtanu had become his home sometime along the ʼay. "It is troubling," he agreed with a nod. "Administrator, I will get straight to the point. our days ago, we were examining a projector; one of those used in the initial attack. It ʼas depleted of energy, so we considered it a good candidate for close inspection. As I aid, we confirmed it was manufactured and installed by Kristang. While we were onducting a scan of the area, we detected, something. Then we picked up an energy ignature that wasn't there before. We believe that somehow our scans caused a dormant bject to activate. It was half buried, unfortunately the people who recovered it did not ake the time to preserve the site, so we have lost the ability to determine how it got there, r how long it had been in that spot. The reason that I came here to speak with you in erson is the sensitive nature of what we discovered." He paused to take a breath, and his ice came alive. Whatever deep weariness he was feeling fell away. "It is an Elder power p. And this one is functioning perfectly."

"An Elder power tap? Functional?" Baturnah Logellia asked, stunned. "It is roducing power?"

Tohn nodded, and Baturnah could feel his excitement. "It has a steady output of roughly twenty four kilowatts. We hooked it up to a capacitor, and it was putting out three megawatts and climbing rapidly before we disconnected it. We were afraid the power flow would blow the capacitor and damage the power tap."

"This is incredible. Astonishing."

Tohn agreed. "We can hardly believe it, and we're working with it. Administrator, that is not all we found."

"*Another* power tap?" Her mind was spinning.

"I wish," Tohn shook his head, but retained a wide grin. "That would be asking too much of fate. No, what we found is potentially almost as valuable. We think we have a functioning pair of Elder communications nodes."

"A *pair*?" She guessed at the significance of the word he had used. "They're linked?"

"Yes, two of them. We found one here, close to where the power tap was buried. When the power tap became active, we detected signals beneath the ground, and discovered a comm node. We sent a signal through it, hoping there might be another one nearby. When we didn't get a response, we were about to set it aside to look at later," as so many comm nodes had proven to be useless junk. "Then we received a signal from Commodore Ferlant. They detected our signal eighty seven light minutes away, on the other side of the star. There is another comm node out there, floating in space. Administrator, it is linked to the comm node here. Signals pass both ways through the comm nodes, instantaneously."

"Faster than light?"

"Better. As I said, the signal transmission is instantaneous. *Zero* time lag. As you can imagine, Commodore Ferlant is extremely excited. He has the other comm node aboard a ship, and they are bringing it here. It will be a slow trip; we are concerned that a jump would break the connection between nodes, so the ship is traveling through normal space."

"Is there any bandwidth restriction?"

Tohn Logen grinned. "Not that we can detect yet. It seems to be unlimited." The Ruhar had experimented with quantum entanglement for remote communications, but the pairing was short-lived, and the bandwidth so narrow that the technology was almost useless for practical communications.

"Why would one node be in space, and another down here?" Baturnah asked, puzzled.

"My guess? I think both nodes were aboard an Elder starship." It was known that an Elder starship had crashed on Gehtanu; salvaging that wreck was the reason the Black Tree clan of the Kristang had originally come to the planet. "Before the ship's orbit degraded, it ejected one of the nodes; the other remained aboard the ship."

Baturnah leaned back in her chair and closed her eyes, savoring the moment. Her planet, her *home*, now possessed one of the most valuable objects in the galaxy. And not just a power tap. Gehtanu was now home to a working pair of comm nodes. "Forgive me, this is rather incredible."

"I feel the same way. When I first heard about it, I assumed that someone had misidentified an artifact. Or that we had found yet another nonfunctional object, that would sit in a laboratory as a curiosity. It wasn't that I was afraid to hope we had truly found a functional power tap; I simply did not believe it could be true. Even now, I can barely believe it."

"This does answer a question," she said with a smile that teased up one side of her mouth.

"What is that?"

"The question of who told the humans about the projectors. Major Perkins and her team thought their information came from a group of native Ruhar who knew we planned trade away this planet." She chose her words carefully, because Tohn had not been born in Gehtanu and did not consider the planet to be his home. To him, Gehtanu was a backwater world that was nothing more than a necessary assignment to further his career; a step on a ladder. Once he stepped above Gehtanu, he did not intend to ever return. If the wormhole shift had not happened, the Kristang would never have taken the planet back, and Tohn would have moved onto a new and better assignment years before. Moved away, and missed a discovery that would make his reputation and career. "That explanation never made sense to us. Major Perkins may have legitimately thought she was dealing with native Ruhar, I don't doubt that. You finding a power tap provides a more likely story," she said. She knew that Tohn himself had not discovered the power tap, had not even been the person who recognized its potential. But the man would now be moving up in the hierarchy, and Baturnah knew it paid to flatter such people and cultivate their friendship. "I believe that the Mysterious Benefactor who revealed the projectors to Perkins was not Ruhar at all. I think it was Kristang."

Tohn snorted skeptically. "The Kristang are a fractious species, but why would they attack their own ships?"

"Not *their* ships," she explained. "That battlegroup belongs to the Swift Arrow clan. We now know that the projectors were installed by the Black Tree clan, before our people came here, and long before the Swift Arrows first arrived following the wormhole shift. I suspect there is a Black Tree agent aboard one of the Swift Arrow ships. One of the ships that was not hit by a projector, of course."

"That makes some bit of sense," Tohn agreed. "The Kristang are more passionate about fighting each other than they are about fighting us. But what would the Black Trees gain from helping us keep Gehtanu?"

"Their goal is not to help us; it is to prevent the Swift Arrows from gaining an advantage. The Swift Arrows must have suspected that after the Black Trees left, there were still valuable Elder artifacts on Gehtanu. I do not think the Swift Arrows would have sent a battlegroup here because our climate is good for agriculture," she added with sarcasm. "The Black Trees knew Gehtanu still held secrets, and they must have been afraid of a rival clan gaining an advantage. The Black Trees weren't worried about us finding Elder artifacts; because they knew that we stopped looking for them a long time ago. We got lucky finding that power tap; we weren't looking for it."

Tohn shrugged, admitting she was right.

"Recognizing the value of an accidental discovery," she said to soothe the man's ego, "can be more important than a deliberate search."

"Administrator, you really think the Black Trees did this because they preferred the risk of us having that power tap, than for it to be possessed by a rival clan?"

"I do. Although I think it more likely that the Black Trees expected we would never find it. Then, someday when circumstances change, the Black Trees could take an opportunity to come back here themselves. Our intelligence reports that currently, the Black Trees are busy preparing for a major civil war against the Fire Dragon clan. The Black Trees lack the resources right now to mount a campaign to retake this planet. That will not always be the case."

Tohn shook his head slowly in astonishment. "This damned war has gone on for so long that I am no longer surprised by anything the Kristang do. If you're right about this, then our fleet needs to establish a permanent, strong presence here." Gehtanu would be the focus of major efforts to recover Elder artifacts, likely for a generation or more. Researchers would come to the planet, bolstering the population and industrial infrastructure. Gehtanu and its secrets would become a high-value target for the enemy; certainly the fleet would need to station a battlegroup there, or more. Starship servicing facilities would need to be built in orbit, and once those facilities were established the flee would rotate battlegroups through; maintaining a constant presence. The Jeraptha were likely to station ships in the area also. The Ruhar would install their own hidden projectors. The planet would be surrounded by a cloud of stealth hunter-killer satellites. And satellites that could project a damping field to trap enemy ships. Gethanu would soo have the defenses of a high-population planet. Once those defenses were in place, the federal government would want to maximize the return on their investment, so they woul encourage people to move there. More people would require more infrastructure which required people to build infrastructure, creating a cycle. Sleepy agricultural Gehtanu was on the verge of experiencing booming growth. At some point, whether they found more functional Elder artifacts there would become irrelevant to the status of the planet.

"Kahling knows?" Baturnah asked.

"Yes," Tohn nodded, "I told him late last night, after Commodore Ferlant's coded message arrived. The Chief Administrator asked me to tell you personally as soon as possible this morning."

Now she regretted not telling her staff to move her morning appointments around so she could speak with Tohn sooner. "Has the Federal government been informed yet?" She asked. It was too soon yet for the government on the Ruhar homeworld to know about the astonishing developments on Gehtanu; Commodore Ferlant would need to dispatch a ship to carry the message to a passing Jeraptha star carrier. Her question was whether the federal government's representatives on Gehtanu had been informed. The discovery of a working power tap would surely cause the federal government to cancel negotiations to hand the planet to the Kristang. Discovery of working comm nodes would do the same. The fact that both precious items had been found on Gehtanu would send a shockwave through the government. The first thing that Baturnah expected to happen would be for th Ruhar fleet to arrive, in force. She expected two, possibly three full battlegroups to take u position over the planet. After Ruhar ships filled the skies, only then would the discovery be announced to the public. "What?" She asked, reacting to the strange smile on Tohn's face.

"No, our federal friends have not been informed yet. The Chief Administrator though you would enjoy performing that task personally."

It was Baturnah's turn to smile broadly. She would enjoy that. She would certainly enjoy that very much.

"Awesome! Yes! That's great!" Skippy exulted.

"Would you like to clue me in, Skippy?" I asked in a peevish tone. "What is awesome?" Through the SkippyTel network, we had been listening to the Burgermeister' conversation, despite the extensive security features of her office. The sound had been muddy; her voice came across much deeper than I remembered. That didn't matter. We heard everything we needed to hear.

"Joe, the cover story we used with Major Perkins was that Emby was a group of native Ruhar. Thank you, Sergeant Adams, for that idea."

"That's what I get paid for," Adams replied with a grin.

"But I've been concerned that the Ruhar would look into our cover story and realize is rather thin. So I've been trying to think of another story we could feed the Ruhar government. Actually, *you* should have been trying to think of a better cover story, that's your job, Joe. I do everything else around here. Now we don't need to do anything; Baturnah Logellia thought up a perfect cover story all on her own. And she has already convinced herself that it must be true."

"You mean because she thinks the Mysterious Benefactor is the Kristang Black Tree clan?" I asked skeptically. "Come on, Skippy, the Kristang are hateful lizards, but would one clan do that to another? The Black Trees will just deny the whole thing. They know they didn't do it."

"Yes, Joe, one Kristang clan would screw another clan like that, and they'd do it with great enthusiasm. Of course the Black Trees will publically deny everything. The other clans, especially the Swift Arrows, will publically condemn the supposed actions of the Black Trees. Privately, the Black Trees will be jumping up and down, high-fouring each other because the Swift Arrows have lost a major opportunity. And in private, the other clan leaders will admire the Black Trees for screwing the Swift Arrows so effectively."

"Shit. They really are hateful lizards," I shook my head.

"That they are, Joe," Skippy agreed. "Once the Kristang learn that a functional Elder power tap was found on Paradise, and a pair of working comm nodes, the other Kristang will be furious at the Black Trees for allowing the Ruhar to have such powerful devices. However, again, the other clans will privately agree that the Black Trees would have been harmed even more if the Swift Arrows had possession of those devices. Admiral Kekrando of the Swift Arrow task force will be tearing his ships apart to find a Black Tree agent. That means his task force will distracted for several weeks, at least, and they will not present a threat to Paradise. So, everybody wins!" Skippy said scornfully. "Except the Swift Arrows, of course. They got totally screwed any way you look at it."

"Darn," I said with a frown. "Skippy, I feel just *terrible* for the Swift Arrows," I lied. The Swift Arrows were responsible for me wearing the silver eagles of a colonel. They had also ordered me to kill civilians, and planned to execute me. "I would like to send them a nice sympathy note."

"A card, sir?" Adams asked, surprised.

"No," I said with a grin. "I thought we'd write the note on the casing of a nuke, and deliver that to them."

"That is not exactly a Hallmark moment, Joe," Skippy chuckled.

"It would be for us," Adams said with a wink.

"I have one question, Skippy," I said.

"Only one? Considering your general lack of knowledge about, well, pretty much anything, I find it surprising that you only have one question," Skippy replied.

I ignored his insult. "You said the Kristang would be high-fouring each other?"

"Yeah, so? The lizards have four fingers on each hand, instead of five. Joe, humans are not the only species that uses celebratory hand gestures. Duh."

"Oh. Ok, that's what I thought."

We hung around Paradise for another forty nine days, with me fretting every day that somehow the Kristang would learn the Ruhar had found a working power tap and a pair of comm nodes. Skippy was fairly frantic at the unforgivably poor communications security of the Ruhar. Even with Admiral Kekrando's ships several light minutes away, and considering the notoriously crappy sensors of Kristang ships, they could hardly have failed to learn the secret if Skippy hadn't been helping the Ruhar. Every day, he had to intercept hundreds of messages before the Kristang could listen in. There were two chatty Ruhar working on the power tap engineering team who were constantly sending barely-encrypted messages back and forth. Skippy finally resorted to frying both of their zPhone and computers, *twice*, before they got the idea that maybe they should not be talking about secrets on unsecure equipment. Somehow, due to constant diligence by Skippy, but mostly due to what he claimed must have been a miracle, the Kristang never did discover the great secret of Paradise. During one particularly bad day, Skippy had a suggestion. "Hey,

Paradise

Joe, how about I create a daily summary of top secret Ruhar communications and send it directly to Admiral Kekrando? That would be more convenient for everyone involved. Especially for me."

I hoped he was joking about that.

On the seventeenth day, a Ruhar battlegroup jumped in. This battlegroup was configured for heavy planetary defense, being centered around a pair of battleships. The battleships were slow and clumsy, but they had impressive shields and armaments. The Kristang moved their remaining ships further away from Paradise, and loudly protested the Ruhar violation of the cease fire agreement. The Ruhar retorted that the new ships had not fired a shot, therefore the cease fire was still in effect. And if Admiral Kekrando's few remaining ships wished to test them, the new Ruhar battleships would be happy to show him what a real cease fire violation looks like. Two days later, a second Ruhar battlegroup with a trio of heavy cruisers showed up at the party. On day twenty three, the Ruhar federal government announced that negotiations to trade the planet Gehtanu were suspended. This was news to most of the native Ruhar on Gehtanu; until then most of them had not known there were any negotiations. That same day, the Ruhar announced they had found valuable Elder artifacts on Gehtanu.

Twelve days after that, Admiral Kekrando's remaining ships accepted a humiliating offer from the Jeraptha for a ride home.

On day thirty eight, we got a surprise; the Ruhar found a real comm node on Paradise. A comm node that even Skippy hadn't known about. The thing didn't work, of course. It did greatly encourage the Ruhar in the belief that Gehtanu could be a treasure trove of Elder artifacts. And that began the end game of our plan to rescue UNEF.

"Yes, we accomplished the same effect with our testing," Tohn Logen didn't bother to keep the irritation from his voice. Since the federal government 'experts' had arrived on Gehtanu, he had lost control of the Elder power tap and the pair of communications nodes. The nodes were now being tested by the military; a report Tohn saw the previous day stated that they were now experiencing instantaneous transmission across a distance of three lighthours. Unlike Tohn's initial assessment, the bandwidth of signals that could be pushed through the nodes was not unlimited. The nodes experienced data dropouts when the energy of signals pushed through the nodes exceeded 1.43 megawatts. Which was essentially unlimited in practical terms; one megawatt could carry the entire compressed message traffic of the Ruhar homeworld.

Having the military take the comm nodes away from him didn't much bother Tohn; he was primarily a power plant engineer. What he cared about was the power tap; that nearly-magical source of endless power. In the history of the Ruhar civilization, they had only ever possessed two working power taps before. The first power tap had been discovered by accident on a small moon of the second world the Ruhar had ever colonized. At the time, the Ruhar had agreed to the Jeraptha's request to turn the precious power tap over to them. Lacking sufficient technology to analyze or use Elder technology, the Ruhar back then had gotten the best deal they could; giving the power tap to the Jeraptha, in exchange for a Jeraptha commitment to support the Ruhar colonizing a third planet. That was a very good deal for the then-young Ruhar civilization's ambitions for expanding into space.

The second power tap was found aboard the wreckage of an Elder ship, found orbiting a young, hot white dwarf star. The Ruhar had expended immense resources to recover the scattered wreckage of the Elder ship, losing three Ruhar ships in the process. That power tap was kept by the Ruhar, and currently resided on their homeworld. Within four decades of it being recovered, that second power tap was put to use. It now powered

art of the homeworld's defense network; if the defense net was fully active, the power
tap could provide sixteen gigawatts of energy.

Tohn knew the power tap would not remain on the backwater world of Gehtanu
forever, and he knew that his time for being in charge of the research was over already. He
even knew that the 'experts' might actually know a bit more than he did.

They didn't have to be so damned arrogant about it. When they arrived, they had
acted appalled that he and his team had done anything with the precious power tap. That
Tohn had gotten the tap to provide continuous power without the assistance of 'experts'
had scandalized the federal team. Essentially, they had patted him on the head like a small
child, praised him for his work to date, and shooed him away from the research facility. It
had taken direct intervention by the planet's Chief Administrator for Tohn to be allowed
to even view the testing; he still would certainly never be allowed to touch anything. Nor
was his advice listened to. "I'm telling you, we already ran that test successfully, five
times," Tohn said with great exasperation.

"You did that with *your* software," one of the federal scientists remarked. "We are
using a considerably more sophisticated analysis tool."

What infuriated Tohn more than the man's insufferable arrogance was that the man
was not even aware he was being insulting. To the scientist, what he said was obvious and
any intelligent person would appreciate the facts. At least that meant, Tohn thought, that
the scientists thought he was somewhat intelligent. "So you are actually testing your
software," Tohn said with intentional sarcasm. "I understand now."

"Yes," the man had entirely missed the sarcasm of Tohn's remark. "We will establish
baseline."

Tohn rolled his eyes and decided to get a fresh cup of hot klah, as the experiment was
not scheduled to go above the microwatt level until that afternoon.

It was that afternoon when things got interesting.

By midafternoon, the power tap's output was a steady ten kilowatts. So far, the results
of the federal scientists exactly matched the results Tohn's team had achieved five times.
Rather than praising Tohn and his team, the scientists remarked that Tohn had been
remarkably lucky with his crude software, equipment and techniques.

The next phase of testing achieved different results from what Tohn's team had seen.
"Hmmm," one of the scientists said with concern. "Dial it back. Bring the input frequency
to 6.2, please. Hmmm."

"What is it?" Tohn craned his neck to see over the scientist's shoulder.

"Nothing. Please do not interfere," he said to Tohn. The scientist then spoke into his
microphone. "It's still increasing. Cut input power. Yes, now! Shut it down!"

"What's the problem?" Tohn leaned in to almost shove the man out of the way.
"What the hell did you idiots do?" Tohn shouted in alarm. The power tap's output should
have been less than 20 kilowatts. Instead, the meter showed the power tap was at 400
kilowatts and, as Tohn watched, it climbed over 500 kilowatts.

"Nothing!" The man protested. "We didn't do anything!"

"This is your damned software," Tohn said through gritted teeth. "Turn it off."

"We did! There's no input signal," the man pointed to the screen, showing a flat line
where the input signal indicator was.

Tohn watched in alarm as the power tap's generation exceeded one megawatt, then
1.5 megawatts. Two megawatts. "I think we should consider getting out of here," he said
quietly.

Paradise

"Oh, oh, Joey," Skippy said. "There has been an *unfortunate* glitch in the Ruhar testing of our power tap. It has somehow gotten out of control. Darn, I hate it when that happens. This is a puzzle; I can't explain it."

"That is truly terrible, Skippy," I replied, while concentrating on the crossword puzzl I had been working on most of the day. "Any chance they can stop it?"

"Ha!" Skippy laughed. "About the same odds as you finishing that crossword puzzle

"Seriously, Skippy. Is there any chance they could somehow stop the power tap from exploding?"

"Sadly, no," Skippy didn't sound sad at all. "Not this time. Huh. Some of those idiot haven't gotten the idea that they had best get the hell out of there. I'll temporarily goose power output to 1.21 gigawatts."

"Did that work?" I asked, now paying attention. The crossword was stupid anyway. Doubly so, because Adams had solved it in like twenty minutes during breakfast that morning. "I don't want any casualties, Skippy."

"If someone is monumentally stupid, does that count as a casualty, Joe?"

"That's a gray area. Depends on how stupid."

"I'll give them ten minutes to board the last air transport out. Let's see what 5 megawatts does. Ha! They got the message that time. Ok, the last of them is running to ge out. Aircraft engines are warming up."

Tohn Logen was fifty kilometers away in a speeding aircraft, when the priceless Elde power tap exploded with a force of almost a kiloton. The blast rocked the isolated forest where the testing facility had been. Looking out the window at the developing mushroom cloud, Tohn turned to the federal scientist seated next to him. "Don't worry. I am *not* going to say 'I told you so'."

Ten minutes later, they received the awful news that at the exact moment the power tap exploded, the pair of communications nodes stopped working. Tohn shook his head. "This day just keeps getting better and better," he muttered to no one. Now, maybe he could convince the Chief Administrator not to let federal 'experts' screw with toys that belonged to the residents of Gehtanu. Residents of Gehtanu, like Tohn Logen. And mayb< he needed to think of buying a house, instead of renting.

He planned to be on Gehtanu for a while.

"It *exploded*?" Baturnah Logellia asked, shocked.

"It did," Tohn Logen confirmed over the phone. "It was fairly spectacular, too. Like small nuke, or a high-power railgun round. We're lucky, I guess. If it hadn't exploded, it might have melted its way down to the center of the planet, and caused all kinds of seismic issues with the crust."

"Do you know what went wrong?" The deputy administrator of the planet asked.

Tohn looked around the cramped interior of the aircraft. "Administrator," he said more loudly than he needed to. "You will need to ask our federal scientist *experts* why the test went so badly wrong." They were all avoiding his eyes.

"Do you have any idea why the comm node pair failed at the same time?"

"At this time, no, I do not," Tohn admitted. "I do not think the power tap was providing energy to the comm nodes remotely, although that could be possible. More likely the explosion of the power tap caused some sort of effect in spacetime that disrupte< the connection between the two comm nodes."

The deputy administrator of the planet said a very bad word. "This is a setback," she said with great understatement.

"Yes, Administrator Logellia." He lowered his voice. "Is there any chance that our federal friends will now pack up their ships and go home?" The Kristang task force's remaining ships had not yet departed the Gehtanu system. If the Ruhar fleet left, the planet would have to rely again on a limited number of projectors. And now the Kristang knew exactly where each one of those projectors were.

"No," she laughed bitterly. "No, that will not happen. I was talking with the fleet admiral this morning; she spent an hour telling me how the 'events on tiny Gehtanu' have caused the Jeraptha to shift their forces in the sector. They launched a major new offensive two days ago. The Thuranin and Kristang are going to be very busy for many months. Also, I think the federal government will be embarrassed enough about this fiasco, that they will be extremely eager to explore every bit of this planet to find more Elder artifacts. To answer your question; the fleet is here to stay."

"That is great news," Tohn breathed a sigh of relief. "Administrator Logellia? One more thing, please?"

"What?"

"That other comm node we just found? Could you make sure our federal scientist friends don't mess with it?"

"I will keep it under my pillow if I have to," Baturnah said with determination. "Nobody touches it until you get here."

CHAPTER TWENTY EIGHT

"Is everyone ready back there?" Derek asked over the intercom from the cockpit.

"Everybody Ok?" Irene asked while standing in the doorway to the cockpit. The cockpit of the Buzzard. Her Buzzard. Not as her personal property; it was close enough. The Ruhar were allowing her to continue flying it, with Derek as her copilot. Derek wanted to get back to flying Chicken gunships, or 'Dobrehs' as he called that fighter aircraft. Until he fully recovered from his injuries and was ready for a qualification flight in a Dobreh, he would keep his flying skills fresh in Irene's Buzzard.

Irene just wanted to fly, anything, anywhere. Hauling passengers and cargo back and forth between Lemuria and Tenturo was fine with her.

"I'm ready," Major Perkins said, settling back in her seat. She would be going first to UNEF HQ, to meet with General Marcellus, and then probably with General Nivelle, the UNEF commander. Marcellus had a lot of catching up to do; her debriefing was not going to be quick. She suspected, hoped, that her farming days were over for a while. Baturnah Logellia had offered her a position as the UNEF intelligence liaison with the Ruhar; that would require moving to Tenturo. That would mean living amongst Ruhar rather than her fellow humans. Perkins wasn't sure what she wanted yet. The point, she reminded herself was that she had a choice, she had possibilities now. All the humans on Paradise had a future. The Ruhar were in charge, and they weren't leaving. Early that morning, before the sun rose, she had walked outside in the cool air and saw sunlight shining off a Ruhar battleship in orbit. It was a big damned thing, and there were more on the way. Discovering projectors on Paradise had not been the only surprise, nor the most important. The Ruhar had found some type of incredibly valuable Elder artifact in the process of investigating the projectors. She had heard there was an accident with one of the artifacts, rather than discouraging the Ruhar, it had spurred their determination to keep the planet and uncover all its secrets.

"Ready," Dave Czajka said. He and Jesse were also going to UNEF HQ first and then who knew? He couldn't imagine going back to farming and chicken ranching in the tiny village of Fort Rakovsky. The Ruhar had offered Dave, Jesse and Shauna positions working with the Ruhar military; they would be acting as security while the Ruhar finished activating the remaining projectors. That project was scheduled to last a full year and after that, the three of them would be training more humans. It was, Dave thought, a great way to see the entire planet. "Cornpone," Dave asked to his friend seated across the cabin, "are you excited about seeing Fort Rakovsky again? We should at least stop by the place."

"Uh," Jesse hesitated, risking a quick glance over at Shauna sitting next to him. After a budding close relationship while they were being held by the Ruhar, Shauna had been all business while they were flying around, digging up projectors. They had both been exhausted pretty much all the time, and there had been zero time for privacy. Whatever hopes Jesse had for a future relationship with Shauna, he needed to give her space and let her take the lead. With almost five men for every woman on Paradise, women had many options if a guy was a jerk. "I, uh, what do y'all think?" He asked the question to Dave, but was watching Shauna's reaction.

"I thought you guys were worried about your hooch?" Shauna asked. "Come on, Jesse, you have to go back and check it out."

"Oh, yeah," Jesse's expression brightened. "Hey, you should come with us," he said, and instantly regretted the joke.

"Why not?" Shanua laughed.

"Are you sure?" Jesse's heart leapt in his chest, not daring to hope.

"Sure," Shauna said quietly, while gently touching the back of Jesse's hand with a ngernail. "I have to see this famous couch you guys are always talking about."

Flying Dutchman

When we left Paradise behind, I was ready to break out the champagne. The Ruhar overnment had announced that negotiations were officially off. The Ruhar were keeping aradise. UNEF HQ had offered to declare loyalty to the Ruhar, and the Ruhar overnment was willing to discuss the possibility. The 'Keepers' among UNEF were oset, but in my opinion, those idiots could go screw themselves. Maybe I was being too arsh; the Keepers didn't know what I knew. They didn't know what the lizards had done Earth. They didn't know anything about Earth, because we can cut off access to our ome world. To the Keepers, I guess they saw continued loyalty to the Kristang as their nly possibility of ever going home.

They were going to be disappointed.

When we left Paradise behind, I was ready to break out the champagne to celebrate ur successful effort to create a secure future for UNEF. Publically, I was elated, iumphant. Privately, leaving Paradise was bittersweet for me; for everyone who had been ationed there. It was bitter for Chang, and for Simms and for Giraud. It was doubly bitter r me, for Adams and Desai, because while Chang, Simms and Giraud had remained oard the *Dutchman*, the three of us had gone down to Paradise. Desai and I had gone own there twice. We had breathed the air of Paradise, we had experienced the scent of its ngles and forests, we had flown low over its well-tended fields.

And we were, hopefully, never going back. More than hopefully, we were planning ever to go back. We were leaving behind friends and comrades who would never know e had even been back there, who would never get a chance to leave the alien world. At e end of our mission, we would be going back home to friends and family on Earth. NEF's mission was truly over, but they were never going home. I hoped the people of NEF worked out their differences, accepted that Paradise was their home now, and eated a good life for themselves. For themselves, and for their children. Humanity had a ance to create a second home now. I very much hoped that they didn't screw it up.

"I have to admit, Sir," I told Chotek without regret, "that I was wrong. If we had not one to Paradise, we would not have rescued UNEF. I thought it was unwise for us to vestigate the situation on Paradise, and I was wrong about that."

"Colonel Bishop," Chotek said with a smile, "your reasons for objecting at the time ere valid; you almost had me convinced. You were correct that learning the situation on aradise would not have done us any good, if we were not able to do anything to assist NEF. What you were not correct about was your lack of faith in the ability of your team, d yourself, to create a solution. You have my sincere congratulations, Colonel."

I have to admit, it felt good to hear Chotek say that I did a good job. Hopefully his port to UNEF Command on Earth would say something nice about me.

When I suggested that we break out the champagne to Chotek, he frowned, and minded me that our primary mission was not yet complete. "Sir," I tried to keep the ritation from my voice, "we have successfully completed an important mission. People eed to blow off steam, celebrate a little."

"Colonel, I am concerned that if we get back to the relay and hear bad news, the iemory of a party now will be bitter."

"Sir, respectfully, I disagree. If we hear bad news at the relay, it is all the more nportant that morale be strong, for whatever we have to do in the future. A celebration now would be a great boost to morale. I'm a soldier, I know how soldiers think. People need to celebrate victories along the way."

My argument was persuasive, or Chotek also was eager for a taste of champagne, because Major Simms received approval for a big party. Instead of one team doing all the cooking, I ordered that each team provide one dish; Simms coordinated that so we didn't end up with all desserts and no pizza. We did have pizza, provided by the French team, and it was delicious.

The next day was downtime for everyone; a lot of people had hangovers, not that I know what that is like. Although I've heard about it. Skippy appreciated a break from our jump, recharge, jump cycle so he could have his robots perform some heavy-duty maintenance. After a well-deserved day off, it was back to routine, and we proceeded back to our personal relay station at our best speed.

We followed our set procedure for approaching the relay station; jump in far away and send a coded signal. When the submind pinged us back, we jumped in close. According to the submind, it would be four days until the next ship passed by, so Chotek approved allowing people to go aboard the station in small groups, just to get a change of scenery. I planned to ask Skippy if there was an uninhabited planet somewhere along our route back to Earth; the Merry Band of Pirates needed to get off the ship once in a while. Other than a couple of us going to Paradise, and the raid on Jumbo, the crew had not set foot on land since we left Earth.

At the relay station, Skippy had a conversation with his submind.

"Oooooh," Skippy mumbled. "Interesting."

"What?" I asked hopefully. "You have good news for us, right? The Thuranin are not sending another ship to Earth?"

"Huh? Oh, no, they are most certainly not. That is good news. The Kristang inquired about a second mission, and the Thuranin responded with a price the Fire Dragon clan cannot possibly afford to pay. Nor can any other clan. That issue is dead, Joe, the Thuranin will not be sending a ship to Earth, that is for sure." Whatever I was going to say next was drowned out by thunderous cheers from the Merry Band of Pirates. Most of the crew was crammed into the bridge, the CIC or the corridor outside. The news was so welcome that Chotek pumped a fist in the air, and then offered me a high five. I slapped him back.

"People, we are going home!" Hans Chotek exulted. "Mission accomplished!"

"Uh," Skippy said quietly, and I motioned for people to calm down for a moment.

"What is it, Skippy? The Thuranin will not send a ship to Earth, and the Kristang can't do that, right? So, Earth is safe now?"

"I can give you a resounding 'yes' to the first question," Skippy announced. "About the other, well, um-" he paused. "Not so much."

THE END

Craig Alanson

Sample from ExForce Book3.5 'Trouble on Paradise'

One week after the *Flying Dutchman* left the Paradise system

"This s-sucks," Jesse 'Cornpone' Colter rubbed his gloved hands together.

"T-tell me about it," Dave 'Ski' Czajka agreed. The 'it' came out like 'ih', because ki's numbed mouth had trouble forming hard vowels in the intense cold.

"I'm so f-frozen, my jaw can barely move to t-talk," Jesse complained.

"Me t-too."

Shauna's voice broke in on their zPhone earpieces. "Hey, you two quit complaining, get back in the Buzzard. You morons decided to go out there."

"Hey, after all the work we did, freezing our asses off up here, I want to see this test, hauna," Ski said with a defensive tone.

"We can see it just fine from in here where it's warm," she teased.

"Yeah, sure, on a video feed," Cornpone would have liked to put sarcasm into his oice, but his lips were so frozen, he couldn't manage it. For protection in case of accident uring the test, Irene had flown the Buzzard behind a hill, to put plenty of hard-frozen ice id rock between the vulnerable aircraft and any flying debris. "I want to *see* it."

"See it? Through goggles what will filter out like 99% of the light?" Shauna's voice id no trouble projecting sarcasm, since she was in the warm and cozy confines of the uzzard.

"It makes a difference," Jesse insisted stubbornly.

"What did you say?" Shauna asked. "Hold a minute, I couldn't hear you, let me turn wn the cabin heater. Irene has it set on 'tropical' in here. I feel like drinking a rum mch."

"If'n I wasn't such a Southern gentleman, I would say that you are an evil, evil oman, Shauna Jarrett."

"And you are *such* a genius for being out there, Jesse Colter."

Jesse cupped his gloved hands in front of his mouth and blew on the gloves, hoping e hot air would warm his lips. It didn't. He removed a glove and blew on his hand, but s hand got cold so quickly, he had to pull the glove back on. It was 12 degrees below ro Fahrenheit in the arctic of Paradise, and he and Dave were laying prone on snowpack, earing the best cold weather gear the US Army on Paradise had available. He was earing five pairs of thick socks; two on each foot and another on, someplace else that as very important to Jesse. The arctic gear totally sucked, compared to the clothing used the Ruhar. In addition to socks, Jesse was wearing long underwear, a long shirt, a veater, and a parka. Inside his cold-weather boots, cold was seeping through the socks. he thick fleece cap was keeping his head mostly warm under the helmet. The helmet asn't for protection in combat, because with a Ruhar battlegroup now based at Paradise, ere was no longer any prospect of combat on or around the planet. He wore the helmet r safety, and as protection against the arctic wind. What was really making him cold, orse even than the gusty wind, was lying on the concrete-hard snow. Jesse and Dave had ought seat cushions from the Buzzard; the thin cushions only delayed the cold seeping rough from underneath them.

To Jesse's left, a pair of Ruhar were also lying prone on the snow, wearing clothes no avier than humans would wear on a nice brisk Fall afternoon on Earth. The difference as, the hamster clothing was super high-tech nanofibers, with heaters and cooling tubes woven in. The two hamsters were happily chatting with each other, snacking on what looked like a type of energy bar. Seeing the Ruhar eating what might as well have been a candy bar made Jesse's stomach rumble with hunger. He pressed the mute button on his zPhone and turned to look at Dave. "Shauna may be right about us being stupid for stayir out here."

"You wanna go in?" Dave asked hopefully. It had been his idea to watch the test from outside, and now he was regretting Jesse's agreement.

"No, man. At this point, Shauna will think I'm a wimp for backing out now," Jesse lamented with a shake of his head. "I got to keep up my tough-guy image."

"You do realize I can hear you?" Shauna asked.

"Oh, shit!" Jesse's cheeks grew red even in the cold. "Damn it, I pressed the mute button!"

"No," Shauna explained, "your fingers must be frozen. You pressed the 'broadcast' button. Everyone in the area can hear you."

To Jesse's left, the shoulders of the two Ruhar were shaking as if the aliens were laughing. Because they were laughing, at him. One of the hamsters glanced at him, then turned away to say something to her companion. They both exploded with laughter.

"Hey, glad I could entertain y'all," Jesse said sourly. Holding up his zPhone, he carefully set it back on the private channel, that was supposed to be used only by the human crew. All zPhone communications rode on the hamster network, so nothing humans said via zPhone was truly private, but it was better than broadcasting everything, all the time. "Darn it, now I really feel like a freakin' idiot. Come, on Ski, no point freezing out asses off out here."

"Too late," Shauna warned with a giggle she couldn't suppress. "Less than thirty seconds to ignition. You need to stay where you are."

"Shit," Ski said under his breath. "Cornpone, next time I get a stupid-ass idea like this, don't enable me."

"Oh, like this is *my* fault?"

"I never said-"

"Ten seconds, cut the chatter," their pilot Irene ordered from the Buzzard's cockpit.

Dave and Jesse adjusted their Ruhar-supplied goggles, and replied with a silent thumb's up to the two Ruhar.

"-three, two, one, ignition!"

The sky was the color of dull steel; sky and distant snowpack blending so there was no horizon to be seen. The only feature to break the monotony of the landscape was a mountain of dirty snow and black rock, forty miles away. On top of the mountain was a tower with a beacon that blinked alternating yellow and blue; flashing a bright strobe ligh every seven seconds. The Ruhar goggles allowed the light of the beacon to shine through dampening the intensity only a bit. Now the top of the mountain dissolved into a searing, intense thin beam of light lancing up into the frozen gray clouds. Automatically, the goggles protected the eyes of the wearers, and also automatically lifted the protection within less than three seconds.

"Wow!" Ski shouted.

"Hot damn!" Jesse replied, and high-fived Ski's gloved hand.

The Kristang projector they had spent the past eight days excavating, examining and preparing had just fired six low-power shots up into the sky. The test shots were aimed at targets in orbits far from Paradise, in an area clear of ships. Even at super low power, the backscatter from maser photons burning through the clouds would have blinded the two exposed humans. Dave felt a welcome warmth on his face from the still-glowing clouds. "That felt good."

Craig Alanson

"Stay where you are," Irene warned. "The shockwave will be hitting your position
oon." The first test shot had been more powerful than the others, as the first shot had to
ear a temporary hole up through the clouds. Now that hole was slamming closed at
upersonic speed, and a sound of tremendous, ground-shaking thunder rolled over the
ozen landscape. Dave and Jesse lay flat, faces down, as the wind of the shockwave
asted them, grateful for the protection of the ridge they were behind. And grateful the
amster engineers had been successful in reducing the power of the projector's maser
eam shots. If the projector had been firing at full power, even from forty miles, the
ackscatter of the maser beam in the atmosphere could have fried exposed skin. Projectors
ere designed to punch through the shields of a starship; collateral damage to the surface
ound them was a very minor consideration.

Jesse stripped off his gloves, helmet and cap, unzipped his parka, and gratefully
ccepted the hot cup of tomato soup from Shauna. After being outside, the interior of the
uzzard felt like a sauna. It felt good. So did the hot cup in his hands. "Did it work? The
st?"
"We won't know until the Ruhar complete their analysis," Derek Bonsu answered
om the cockpit, leaning over to speak through the open doorway. "We're supposed to get
a update when Major Perkins gets back."
Perkins had been given the honor of observing the test from the Ruhar's command
uzzard, parked a quarter mile away. According to the Ruhar, it was an honor; Perkins
as not so happy about it. Most of the Ruhar project team openly resented humans
ccompanying them, and Perkins had to stretch her patience and tactfulness to the limit
hen dealing with the hamsters. Fortunately, she was mostly able to pretend their subtle
sults did not translate well over zPhones, and she concealed her growing fluency in
nderstanding spoken Ruhar. When Perkins came into the Buzzard, half frozen from the
ort walk, she gave her team the good news while taking off her parka. "The test was a
ccess, based on preliminary data," Perkins announced, less happily than might have
en expected.
"However," Irene rolled her eyes.
"Hmm?" Perkins asked.
"With the Ruhar, there's *always* a 'however', ma'am," Irene observed. "This is the
xth projector we're been involved in reactivating with them, and every time the
eliminary data shows the test was successful. And every freakin' time, the hamsters
cide they need another round of testing. And that second test always shows everything
great."
"Lieutenant, I understand you are annoyed at how slow the process is going," Perkins
id, without sounding as if she was being understanding about it. "You need to keep in
ind that the Ruhar are dealing with alien technology, *enemy* technology. They not only
ve to make certain these projectors won't blow up in their faces, they need to know they
n rely on the projector grid for planetary defense. Even a battlegroup being based here
esn't ensure our safety; the Kristang could attack while the battlegroup is deployed
mewhere else. That Elder power tap and the comm nodes they found make this planet a
ime target. If that means the hamsters are being super picky about the condition of each
ojector, I am fully on board with that."
"How long, ma'am?" Dave asked.
"If the Ruhar decide they require a second test-"
"And they will," Shauna groaned.
"-then we will be here another six days, before we can start packing our suitcases."

Paradise

"Six days?!" Irene slumped in her chair. Six days was bad enough when they were reactivating projectors in a nice climate. Six days of enforced idleness, and six days when she couldn't fly. At least when they were at a site with pleasant weather, they could get out of the cramped Buzzard. They could set up tents for privacy, put up a volleyball net, sit around a campfire in the evenings. In the frigid hell of the arctic on Paradise, the six of them were stuck inside the Buzzard all day. Six people; three women and three men. Living, sleeping, cooking, using the one tiny bathroom. That got old really fast.

The problem wasn't just being stuck inside the Buzzard for six more days, it was six days during which there was absolutely nothing for the humans to do. The Ruhar grudgingly trusted the humans to set up and operate the drill, to give the Ruhar access to the buried projector. Once the drill created an opening in the projector's casing, the Ruhar took over, and did not allow the humans even to visit a projector. The arrogance of the Ruhar was supremely irritating, especially so because Major Perkins' team had reactivated projectors all on their own, without the Ruhar having any idea their planet even contained such a weapon.

"Oh, this sucks!" Jesse squeezed Shauna's hand. "The weather forecast is for blizzard conditions, starting in six days." If the second test was successful, and that was a sure as sunrise, the Ruhar would want the humans to immediately begin disassembling the drill rig and pack it back into the Buzzard. Although the Ruhar could take their own sweet time inspecting and testing a projector, they demanded the humans to move quickly, with no excuses. High winds, subzero temperatures and heavy snow could not be allowed to delay the operation. That meant the six humans would be stumbling around, half frozen, wrestling the balky drill rig back into the Buzzard. With the back ramp of the Buzzard open, snow would be swirling into the cargo compartment, drifting into every corner and crevice. Irene and Derek would have the heaters on maximum power, worried that extensive cold soaking would cause a critical Buzzard component to fail. Spare parts were a long, long distance away.

"I'm not looking forward to it either, Colter," Perkins said in a matter of fact manner. "This is the job we signed up for. We begged the Ruhar for this assignment; the whole planet is watching us." On behalf of UNEF, Perkins herself had done the begging and groveling to keep humans part of the projector reactivation team.

"Ma'am," Shauna suggested, "there are parts of the rig we can take apart and pack away now. We don't need the components for drilling." Part of the rig scaffolding was in use to give Ruhar technicians and scientists access to the underground projector, but the actual drilling part of the operation was complete.

"You are sure about that, Jarrett?" Major Perkins was skeptical. "We've never done that."

"Yes, ma'am, it's in the drill rig manual," Shauna pulled up a schematic on her tablet. "The hamsters take the drill rig apart sometimes, when they want to replace just part of the system, for field maintenance." On the mission, the humans had not been allowed, or trusted, to take apart the drill rig. Instead, the Ruhar provided a refurbished drill rig after the team had worked on three projectors. "It's easy," she pointed to the schematic. "It's looks easy, anyway. There's a set of videos that walks us through the process. If we take apart, we can cut the final part of the stowing process to a couple hours."

Perkins looked at the file on her own tablet. It did look simple and easy, and the process did not require anything complicated. Which was good, because the translated Ruhar instructions read something like 'Being Tab A into Slot B, for making joyous assembly'. It reminded Perkins of the Chinese instructions for the washing machine in what used to be her apartment back on Earth. The rig had been designed to break down

Craig Alanson

sily. "We'll look at this. This is good, Jarrett. If it checks out, I'll talk to the Ruhar about
"

"Ma'am? If we're not needed here until the test," Derek inquired, "could we fly
meplace else to wait it out? There's a Ruhar base only three hours south of here." While
e climate at the base was not tropical, it was warmer than the bone-chilling cold at the
ojector site. They could go outside without risking frostbite and death. And they could
ve in the base buildings, rather than being stuck inside the Buzzard the whole time.

"I'll need to consider that." Perkins' instinct was to keep the Buzzard and her crew
ght where they were. The Ruhar did not need humans to reactivate the remaining
ojectors on the planet, UNEF through Perkins had begged for the opportunity to
rticipate and demonstrate that humans could be trustworthy and useful. Abandoning the
ctic projector site, simply because it was unpleasant, would send a signal that humans
ere soft. And the Ruhar base mentioned by Derek Bonsu was unlikely to be thrilled with
e idea of hosting a group of humans. The base commander might outright refuse
rmission for humans to land there, even if Perkins offered to set up tents for her team to
ve in, so the Ruhar didn't have to encounter humans frequently. Despite Perkins and her
am having reactivated projectors and blasted a Kristang battlegroup out of the sky,
umans overall were still not viewed positively by Ruhar. The Ruhar natives still had hard
elings against humans, who they saw as ignorant, backwards aliens used as a goon squad
y the Kristang, to force Ruhar off the world they considered to be their home.

The real mission of Perkins' team was not to drill down into projector sites to allow
cess for the Ruhar technicians. The mission was public relations, on behalf of all
umans on Paradise. "I can sound out the Ruhar team leader here, she may have people
ho would appreciate a couple days away from," she tried to think of a nice way talk
out the frozen hell they were living in, then settled for, "here." The Ruhar team had
ree Buzzards, and had set up two warm, large prefab shelters for use only by Ruhar. If
me of the Ruhar were not needed for the second test, Perkins could use transporting
em aboard their Buzzard as an excuse to fly her own team out…

Contact the author at craigalanson@gmail.com

https://www.facebook.com/Craig.Alanson.Author/

Go to craigalanson.com for blogs and ExForce logo merchandise including T-shirts,
tches, sticker, hats, and coffee mugs

Printed in Great Britain
by Amazon

57930805R00168